STRAY CAT STRUT

STRAY CAT STRUT

BOOK 3

RAVENSDAGGER

Podium

Podium

STRAY CAT STRUT

I refused to sit in the back, out of principle if nothing else.

So, with my legs bunched up, feet digging into the cloth upholstery of the bench, and my arms crossed over my knees, I watched as New Montreal flew by.

The soldier next to me kept his mouth shut, eyes focused on the skies as he diligently obeyed every traffic law. That was probably because of the officer on the bench behind us. The lieutenant was in a bad mood; being seated in the back like a kid didn't suit his sensibilities. He wasn't saying anything, but I knew he'd shared a glare or two with the driver in the rearview.

Maybe it was the large mechanical cat sitting next to him, a helmet carefully held between teeth that could spit plasma.

I watched the neon glow of advertisement-covered buildings scroll by, the signs turned into blurry messes by the constant downpour across the windshield that the car's wipers were only just managing to clear out.

The rain in New Montreal always left things with a rainbow sheen. And it was always raining.

I guess it made it a colorful city, in a way.

We crossed over a section of the city that was little more than slums. You could always tell. The ads there were brighter, if only because everything beneath them was so much darker.

We drove past those soon enough. The traffic always moved a bit faster above the shittier parts of the city, it seemed.

The hotel loomed tall above us some blocks later, and even with the driver keeping to the speed limit, we eventually turned into the large tunnel cutting its way through the entire building.

"Stop here," I said when it became clear the driver intended to get in line and wait. "I'll walk the rest of the way."

The officer said some pleasant-sounding things that I didn't listen to, and then I was out of the car and walking around it, pants flapping about my legs from the hot air pouring out from under the hoverpads. I went around and opened the back door, letting out my mecha-cat, who landed next to me with a click of metallic claws on whatever sort of concrete they were using for the landing zone.

I held back a yawn as I started toward the main entrance, which seemed somewhat calmer than usual. Still plenty of people moving in and out, but not as many as I'd seen before, and the valets looked just as done with everything as I felt.

After Gomorrah left me in Black Bear, I had to threaten the local mining corp, then sit down and pretend to care about some briefing put on by the military brass. Half of them were sitting in offices across the country, calling in their orders over webcams while I was stuck in some tent in the ass-end of nowhere.

I would have complained, but that would have made things take even longer than they did, and they at least tried to placate me with free food and a ride back home, especially after I briefed them on the nasty shit we'd encountered in the mines under the city.

My current goal was to find a nice, hot shower, and a nicer, hotter Lucy to share it with.

The valet by the door took one look at me, in my mud-and-blood-stained coat, frowned, and seemed to want to make trouble.

I fumbled around with my aug, the digital display hovering over my cybernetic eye twitching this way and that with a few stray thoughts until I found the tag I used to open my room door and sent it to him.

He opened the way with a bow. "Welcome back, ma'am," he said. "Um."

"Um?" I repeated, pausing by the door.

"No . . . animals allowed?"

I stared at him, then at the cybernetic tiger standing perfectly still at a pace behind me. "It's a service animal," I said. "The service it renders is killing people that annoy me. Want to see?"

"Uh" was his reply before I moved past him, the mecha-cat close on my heels.

I think a few of the people in the lobby were in a mood to test my patience, but something about my look dissuaded them. Maybe the new full-face helmet, shaped like the face of a growling cat, was giving them pause.

Or maybe it was all the alien blood and sh . . . stuff.

I desperately needed a shower.

My cat and I got in the elevator, and then it was up to the top. I was bouncing on the balls of my feet the entire ride. I was getting eager to arrive, to hug Lucy until she squeaked, and to annoy the kittens to make sure they were all right.

When the doors opened with a ding, I rushed over to the penthouse's door, then knocked twice before barging in.

It was chaos.

Two of the kittens were rolling on the floor, screaming. Another was watching television at a volume that would render most deaf within the week.

Catkiller, the dog, was rubbing his ass across the carpet, and Junior was eating cereal with Katerine, both girls eating out of the same bowl with two spoons, a rifle partially disassembled on the table next to them.

"Cat? Cat!" came Lucy's cheer a moment before she tried to run into my arms, then tripped over nothing and ended up stumbling into me.

I sighed, tension bleeding off me as I let the cat in and then closed the door with a heel. Home at last.

The peace wouldn't last, but I'd take what I could when I could.

CHAPTER ONE

BLISS

There are seven megacities in North America. Cities so grand, so huge, that they're impossible to map fully, with populations in the hundreds of millions, and with enough drama and waste produced in them every hour to drown anyone that goes looking for it.

There's not a minute that passes where something terrible, and something just as magical, doesn't happen.

Keep your eyes open, or you'll miss out on all the fun.

—Three Swipes, 2037

"And then what?" Lucy asked.

She was tucked into my side, head heavy against my shoulder.

I had been enjoying that wonderful sensation of bare skin against bare skin, but then my arm fell asleep and all I could feel were tingles when Lucy played with my fingers.

My lips were also tingling, but in an entirely different, far more amusing way.

"Well, then I triggered the bombs. All of them at once. It was kinda cool. The whole tunnel caught on fire."

She shifted a little, head tilting back to stare at me. "The tunnel you were in?"

"Well, uh, technically?"

"Did you do any research at all about the explosive you were using?" she asked. "Because I've just googled it, and that stuff is supposed to be dangerous."

"It was. But mostly for the aliens."

Lucy huffed. "Catherine," she said. She never used my full name like that unless she was on the wrong side of miffed.

"What?"

"You're . . . you're a bit of an idiot."

"Hey!" I said. I couldn't help but chuckle. "I'm not an idiot. I'm, uh . . . inexperienced."

"You're going to blow yourself up," Lucy said as she shifted, turning onto her side and wrapping an arm across my chest so that her face was resting just below mine. "You know, I can't use you to satisfy my incredible lusts if you're dead. I'll have to settle for that nun friend of yours, and she looks all prudish."

I snorted. "I'd pay to see that. I think Gomorrah would faint at the first sight of a bare leg."

"I don't want you dying, so that means you need to jam some smarts into that thick skull of yours."

"Like some sort of education program?" I asked. "I think Myalis has something like that."

"I was thinking more . . . school," Lucy said.

"School."

"Yes! I told you I want to go to some fancy school, get all educated and all that. That way I can get a fancy job and be rich." She rose up, getting excited by the idea. Her leg dragged up mine and distracted me for a moment.

"Lucy, we're already rich . . . rich-ish," I said.

She flopped back down. "Boo! You're no fun. You just want me as some sort of trophy wife."

I laughed. "That would be hilarious. Can you imagine yourself meeting some fancy CEO types and trying to snob it up?"

She giggled. "Bet I could manage better than you. You'd punch someone."

"Hey! The rumors about my violent nature are heavily exaggerated." I leaned down and buried my nose in her hair, then relaxed there for a moment. "Do you really want to go to some fancy school?"

"Only if you come with me."

"I have samurai stuff to do," I said.

She snorted. "Oh yes, because the poor teachers will be so eager to scold you when you leave to save the planet for an afternoon."

I considered it for a while. "All right." If it made Lucy happy. And . . . yeah, I was a bit of a dumbass sometimes. So more thinking couldn't hurt any. "But only if it's one of those schools with a fancy uniform. With, like, skirts."

"You hate skirts," she said.

"*I'm* not going to be the one wearing the uniform."

Lucy laughed. "But what if we want to do some role—what is it?"

I frowned up at the ceiling as the augs in my eyes went off. I had an incoming call, and somehow it was marked urgent. With Myalis around, I figured this wasn't some telemarketer calling me about the urgent need to insure my nonexistent car with their extended warranty.

Gomorrah's name hovered over the call's number. "Gomorrah?" I asked aloud as I answered.

Lucy perked up, then glanced to the side where a fancy digital clock was reading the time as . . . a bit past midnight. If Lucy hadn't been keeping me up with fun, I would have been long asleep already.

"Cat?" Gomorrah replied, turning it into a question.

"What's up?" I asked. My arm finally freed from Lucy's weight, I started to run my fingers through Lucy's hair, scratching at her scalp in a way that had her falling back down onto me like a big bony cat.

I heard Gomorrah breathe, then pause. I had the impression she was rubbing her face. "This is . . . are you awake?"

"I'm talking to you, aren't I?"

"I mean, I don't want to . . . screw it. I need help?"

"You turned that into a question," I pointed out. Bending down, I gave Lucy a kiss on the head, then started to squirm my way to the edge of the bed. There was a lot of bed to squirm across. "Okay, what's up?"

"This is embarrassing," Gomorrah said.

"You just interrupted my postcoital bliss; trust me, the last thing I'm worried about is how embarrassed you are. What happened? Did someone fail to convert to whatever you're preaching? Did you stumble into atheism? Start a cult by accident?"

"Cat," she said.

I sobered up. "All right. Tell me about it."

"It's a long story."

"Do you need my emotional help or, like, my physical help? Do you want Lucy instead? She's better at feelings and shit." I fell back, legs over the edge, and landed with my head on Lucy's stomach. She coughed, then wiggled herself to be more comfortable and started to play with my mechanical ears.

"I think physical? Or maybe I just need advice. My friend's in trouble."

"What sort?" I asked.

"She . . . she has a habit of sneaking out of the convent and picking fights with troublesome people. Drug dealers near schools, pimps that try to recruit in the wrong places. She takes the whole 'fear of God' thing into her own hands."

"Sounds like a great person," I said. I'd heard of vigilantes and the like before. They were nearly always vilified by the corps and the news—unless some corp was trying to look hip by siding with the "rebels"—and what they did varied, but usually beating up the worst sort of people and blowing up the homes of some bureaucrats was to be applauded.

Gomorrah shifted on the other side. "She left sometime today. Didn't tell any of the sisters where she was going, and Atyacus can't track her. Her augs are offline."

I sat up straighter. "Oh. You're going around looking for her?" I asked.

"That's what I *was* doing," she said, obviously frustrated. "She's not at any of the places she usually hides in. None of her friends know, at least those I was able to get in contact with. Well, they said they didn't know. I scared one of them into spilling the beans."

"What's she doing?"

"She's attacking a gang, a bunch of idiots that call themselves the Sewer Dragons. They're based in the lower levels, usually just a bunch of jumped-up nobodies, but they started kidnapping people around the edges of the incursion zone. I think they took someone Franny knew."

"Okay, wait. Two things. First, Sewer Dragons? Really?"

"They live in the sewers. It's not as stupid as it sounds."

I snorted. "Sounds terrifically stupid to me. Okay, second, Franny?"

"That's her name," Gomorrah confirmed.

I had a mental image of a sixty-something woman with a crop and attitude.

I shook my head and got up, then started looking for some clothes. "So you need my help?"

"I can find her," she said with conviction. "I just don't know if I can find her before she gets herself killed. And I'm tired; I've been at it ever since Black Bear."

"Hey, hey, it's all right," I said. "I'm on my way, okay? We'll find your . . . whatever she is to you, and then you can scold her or whatever it is you nuns do behind closed doors. Quick in and out, it won't take more than twenty minutes."

"Thank you. I'll have Atyacus send Myalis my geo-location. Text me if you get lost. It's a mess down here."

"All right."

The line went dead, and I sighed as I bent over double, picked up my pants off the floor, then tossed them to the side. They were nasty.

"Heading out already?" Lucy asked.

"Yeah. Gomorrah's . . . Franny, whoever that is, is in trouble, and she needs help saving her. I . . . sorry?"

Lucy rolled around on the bed until she was facing me. She also pulled some covers around, turning herself into a cocoon with just her head poking out. "Don't be sorry. I'm not some bitch that'll whine when her girlfriend needs to go save the world again."

"Not the world, just some girl."

"Oh, in that case, I'm going to bitch endlessly," she said.

"All right, now help me find something to wear."

"We're buying clothes?" Lucy asked. She was suddenly out of bed. "Myalis! We're buying shit, come on!"

"Oh, for fuck's sake," I muttered, and then I laughed as Lucy grabbed on to me, and we both went crashing back onto the bed.

It was going to be hard getting to Gomorrah in anything like a hurry.

CHAPTER TWO

BECAUSE BEING A BAMF IS EASIER IN POWER ARMOR

Spacesuits evolved surprisingly slowly after their inception. For a long time, the same suits that were designed for the Apollo missions were being used by astronauts onboard humanity's fledgling space stations.

It wasn't until interest in space travel—and, more importantly, space defense—grew that the spacesuits started to evolve and change quite rapidly.

As with many other technologies originally developed for space exploration, this eventually meant that people on Earth had access to new technologies.

Of course, some military asshole had to weaponize our power armor!

—A Rant About Space Tech, WriteIt forums, 2026

"All right," I said. "We need a bunch of things for the new place, once we move over. And a bit of cash wouldn't hurt to pay for, like, contractors and such. Also, I do want to get to Gomorrah sooner rather than later."

Lucy nodded. "And none of those excuses will work to stop me from shopping," she said.

I sighed. "Damn. Fine. Myalis, want to get one of the Dumbasses over? We could probably use the projector."

Certainly. One of them is on the way. You might want to open the door, though.

I bounced off the bed and opened the door a crack, then shut it when one of my little drones scuttled in on all fours and installed itself in the middle of the room. "All right, I'm going to put my armor on," I said.

"Your armor wasn't enough," Lucy said.

"What? It was plenty!" I protested as I bent down and picked up the belt and neck pieces of my under armor. As soon as they were on, the armor itself started to melt onto me, connecting itself together and hardening over my important bits.

"Cat, your back has a bunch of blue splotches on it, and your arms, and your legs."

I shrugged. "I got tossed around a bit. The armor did a lot to help."

Your Mark IV TIGER-B armor did prevent you from dying. Some of the impacts you sustained would have been lethal otherwise. Not to mention its ability to protect your skin from all the acids in the air.

"See," I said.

"You didn't mention acids in the air!" Lucy said.

"I, uh, forgot?" Maybe that explained why my pants had melted a bit. They were just normal cargo pants.

Lucy rolled her eyes. "Proper armor," she said. "Like your new helmet." She pointed to where my new helmet was sitting on the floor. It was a nice piece, shaped like a cybernetic tiger of sorts, teeth barred and eyes set in a frown. I didn't know what it was made of, but it was tough, airtight, had its own air purification thing going on and a bottle of oxygen for when things got rough.

"I . . . guess?" I tried. I was well aware of time ticking by. "Okay, um, Gomorrah had this thing with modular armor. It was actually kind of cool."

"Then get something like that," Lucy said.

I nodded. "Right, right."

"And when you come back, we can shop some more, for other things you need. Your new arm is a first-tier one from your Sun Watcher catalog, and you have the second tier unlocked there. You could get something way better."

"How do you know that?" I asked.

"Myalis is a gossip. She texts a lot."

I turned and glared at the Dumbass drone since I couldn't exactly glare at Myalis when she was in my head. "Really?"

"Would you rather I not tell Lucy how you are? She gets worried," the AI said. "It's healthier for your relationship that she knows."

"And she can help you bully me into buying stuff."

"That too," Myalis admitted.

Lucy giggled at my distress. "We win!" she declared. "Now buy cool sexy armor!"

I shook my head but gave in to the inevitable. Lucy wanted to see new toys, but she did also want me to stay alive, so there was that. "Okay, fine. Myalis, can I do the modular armor thing?"

"You could. It would require a new catalog, but combined with your second-tier Sun Watcher Technologies, you could purchase some fairly impressive gear. Though it would mean discarding some of your equipment."

I looked at the pile of gear in the corner. I had my auto-reloading under-arm holsters, one with my Claw, another with my Trench Maker. And my back-mounted guns, with the plasma cat-tail and all.

My coat was kind of awesome, but the cloak was a bit much. It was unwieldy. And in terms of weaponry, my Icarus was nice, but my Whisper was a tiny bit clunky.

"All right," I said. "Get me a modular gear catalog."

"Consider it done!"

Class I Modular Equipment Unlocked!

Points Reduced from . . . 12,471 to . . . 12,371

An expensive catalog, but not much compared to what I had.

"Okay, so, armor. I want . . . uh."

"It needs to look cool," Lucy said.

"Yeah, obviously," I replied. "It needs to be stealthy. Silent, no smells, invisibility too. I'm tired of being partially invisible. I bet there are other senses we can mess with."

"A high priority for stealth. Noted," Myalis said.

Lucy bounced. "It needs to be tough! But not something like a walking tank. Those are cool, but they're not sexy cool."

I laughed. "Yeah, that works for me. Back-mounted weapons wouldn't be bad either. I've gotten used to having those."

"I think I have something that would fit," Myalis said. "Though it would come with a few compromises. The Lion's Mane, Mark XII. It's an expensive platform, but it should cover most of your bases."

Dumbass shifted, and soon an image was projected above it. The armor was pretty much what I imagined when thinking about stealthy cybernetic armor. Plates covered everything, with some sort of weave between them and glowing lines in between. The legs had a set of curved metal pieces at the back that joined up under the heel.

"Is that a boob-plate?" Lucy asked the pertinent question.

The way the chest was shaped did hint at . . . some . . . chest. It wasn't as egregious as some armor I'd seen, though. The way the abs were shaped was neat too.

"The armor is meant to be worn over an under armor like the one you already have. It can turn entirely invisible, has jump assists, and servos around every joint. Each section is hermetically sealed."

The image spun around so that we were looking at the back, which unfolded.

"There is room for small gun emplacements in the upper back. Or you might wish to install jump-jets. The amount of room is limited, which reduces the space for weapons and equipment. The plates themselves are reactive armor over a graphene weave. The armor is heavy; you might need to accustom yourself to the weight, even if the powered parts of the armor will make movement feel relatively natural."

"Neat," I said. "And bits can be replaced piecemeal?"

"Indeed! The full set costs nine hundred points."

I winced.

"That's not much if it means you get to live," Lucy said.

"Yeah, I guess," I said. "Anything better out there, Myalis?"

"Plainly put, yes, but the price would either be significantly higher, would require better tiers than you currently have, or would need different compromises. Larger armor would be safer but would limit your mobility and increase your mass."

"What kind of upgrades can it take?" I asked.

"I would suggest back-mounted weapons, seeing as how you enjoy those." The armor in the image spun and the ribs and chest unfolded. "There is room for multiple smaller systems. A nanite self-repair system, injectors for adrenals and an exterior healing system, maintenance subsystems, communication suites, more weapons . . ."

"Nice," I said. "Okay, get it."

"Wonderful!"

"That was fun!" Lucy cheered. "I was afraid I'd need to toss a ball of yarn down while Myalis and I talked about things."

"Hey!"

New Purchase: The Lion's Mane, Mark XII

Points Reduced from . . . 12,371 to . . . 11,471

The armor appeared standing in the center of the room, arms crossed and shoulders set. If it didn't lack a head, I might have thought someone was there. It had a tail behind it, because of course it did, but otherwise it was pretty un-catlike for something Myalis had suggested. Though there was the word "STRAY" stenciled on one pauldron and "CAT" on the other.

I walked over to it, then blinked. My nose came up to its shoulder. Sure, I wasn't wearing shoes, but still. "Tall," I said.

The armor unfolded, plates shifting aside then opening up to reveal an interior that would have a claustrophobe sweating.

"Okay, then," I said as I gingerly stepped in. It was only when I was awkwardly pressing myself into it that the armor closed up around me. My augs tingled, then I felt as if I had been dunked into cold water for a moment. I gasped.

"Are you okay?" Lucy asked.

"Oh, yeah, just . . ." I snapped the fingers on the glove of my left hand, and *felt* it. "Oh, that's messed up. There's some tactile thing going on."

"Really?" Lucy asked.

She got up, tugging a blanket around herself, then reached out a hand and grabbed the armor by the breast. She squeezed. "Did you feel that?"

I felt my cheeks warming just a bit. "Uh, yeah."

"Sensation levels can be tweaked. It shouldn't allow you to feel pain, but it is sensitive enough to feel changes in temperature."

"What about pleasure?" Lucy asked.

"That . . . that isn't part of the original package, but there may be modules for that sort of thing," Myalis admitted. The AI sounded reluctant there.

"Okay, so . . . put a pin on that one," I said. "Weapons, real fast, then Gomorrah. I don't want to be late, all right?"

"Sure thing!" Lucy said. "We can explore all the options later."

CHAPTER THREE

TAXI

The closer you are to ground level, the poorer you're likely to be.

It's the way it is, you know? Shit's dragged down, and down here is where it stops.

—Quote from a vagrant, Chicago Megacity Complex Four, 2039

"Guns!" I cheered.

"Guns!" Lucy cheered right back.

"The ability of humans to be amused by anything that can make a pro-jectile move fast is fascinating," Myalis said.

"Oh, come on, don't tell me you're not keen on weapons and the like, not with the amount you have available."

"Oh no, don't misunderstand. The Protectors are also keenly interested in weaponry in all its forms, but more from the viewpoint of someone who wishes to have the most effective tool at their disposal at any given time."

"That just sounds like an excuse to compare cannon sizes to me," I said. "Speaking of: modular guns, what do you have?"

"There are two slots on the back of your armor, over your shoulder blades. They are relatively small."

I shifted my shoulders around, the armor moving languidly along with the motion. No satisfying servo sounds either, which kinda sucked but made sense if the suit was supposed to be stealthy. "I need something with a bit more kick than my last shoulder-mounted guns. The railgun was all right, but the plasma casters were too bright, and they didn't have enough oomph to them."

"Ah yes, more oomph," Myalis agreed. "You seemed to enjoy the railgun. Perhaps two smaller rails, designed to fire silent rounds. The overall rate of fire would be lower, but each shot should mean a dead opponent as long as you're not fighting Antithesis that are too armored."

"Railguns use ammo, right?" Lucy asked. "Maybe we can use the fabri-cator to make you some! Save some points for later."

I nodded. "Genius. Yeah, two railguns, then. I liked the last one, it made things dead in a way that I liked."

"Might I suggest a railgun catalog, then? Your options are otherwise limited."

I nodded. "A cheaper catalog, maybe?"

"I think this should do!"

Class I Subsonic Rail Weaponry

Points Reduced from . . . 11,471 to . . . 11,401

"And two railguns."

New Purchase: Class I Stealthed Micro Rail Launcher (two units)

Points Reduced from . . . 11,401 to . . . 11,301

"That wasn't expensive," I said as two boxes appeared. I opened them to reveal . . . a mess of rods and pipes and little servos, all next to a sharp-looking gun painted a deep black.

"Lucy, could you lend Catherine your hands?" Myalis asked.

"Oh, I'd love to insert something into Cat's back," Lucy said.

I shook my head and turned while dropping carefully to one knee. My shoulder panel opened, and Lucy fiddled with the railgun for a moment before it slid into place. Like putting a square peg in a square hole.

Once both were in and connected to my augs, I had them deployed.

They weren't as imposing as my last railgun, but maybe that was for the best. They were certainly a lot sleeker, and they sat just over my shoulders when deployed. Also, they glowed pink from within, which was a plus.

"Nice!" I said, "Okay, we just wasted like, ten minutes, easy. I need to get going. Kiss?"

Lucy got onto her tiptoes, and we wasted another thirty seconds before I broke off and rushed to the last of my equipment.

There are holsters in your thighs. They should conceal your holdout weapons and reload them if you place some ammunition within.

That was cool. I slid my trusty old Trench Maker into a slot that opened on my right thigh, and then my Claw went into a similar opening on my left. I slung on the strap for my Icarus, then tossed my long coat on top of everything else. "Right, I'm off!"

"Helmet!" Lucy said. "And kiss!"

"Oh!"

I picked up my helmet and slid it on, then waved to Lucy as I squeezed out of the room, careful not to mess up the door.

The Twins were in the corridor, both of them holding on to juice boxes and what looked like bags of chips. They stared at me.

"Uh, gotta run for a bit," I said.

"A'ight," one of them said.

I felt awkward in my armor as I slunk out of the penthouse. It wasn't that it didn't move right or felt wrong, it was just . . . kind of strange. It felt like I had some tight clothes on, but at the same time I could feel the air moving around me as if I were in loose sweatpants and an oversized T-shirt.

Grabbing the handle was a bit strange; my hand wasn't exactly where I thought it was. Maybe that was it? My sense of where my limbs were was being thrown off.

I'd get used to it.

I made sure to close the door carefully behind me as I stepped into the hotel's corridor, then turned toward the elevators and noticed the two rotating guards next to it staring at me, wide-eyed.

"Probably looks a bit scary, huh?" I asked as I came closer.

"Yes, ma'am," the one on the left said.

Well, at least people were taking me seriously in this.

I flicked through my augs, then went fully invisible, my jacket following a moment later. I knew that my gun, between my jacket and armor, was still visible, but someone would need to be at just the right angle to see.

"What about now?" I asked.

The guard wasn't looking my way when he replied. "That's, uh, not much better, ma'am."

"Wonderful," I said.

The elevator door dinged open, and I stepped in before jabbing the button for the lobby.

Once I was on the ground floor, I switched on the muffling on my mask. Didn't need anyone to hear me speaking. "So, where's Gomorrah and how are we getting there?"

She's on the eastern side of the city. Unfortunately, none of the automated taxi services will drive someone there, and taking the public transportation services would both take a long time and be a needless risk.

"The subway's not that bad," I said.

The infrastructure hasn't been properly maintained since before your birth, and the amount of gun violence in the underground is so high that you are as likely to be shot while taking the night train as you are to be hit by friendly fire in an active incursion.

"So, how do we get there?" I asked before stifling a bit of a yawn. Maybe I needed a bit of sleep. Maybe I should have gone to sleep when I got home instead of messing with Lucy.

A non-automated taxi. One is waiting for you outside.

I nodded along as I moved across the lobby, then through one of the revolving doors onto the parking tarmac.

A car lit up in my vision, highlighted in pink until I started making my way to it. It was not an impressive ride. Some car from the early thirties, with a dented fender and one light that flickered intermittently.

Yes, that is the best they had.

"I'm going to need to look into getting my own ride one of these days," I muttered.

I'll add it to the list. You do have a somewhat significant number of points remaining.

"Might not have an incursion for a while, and besides, I want to spend a lot of those on the security of the museum-slash-orphanage." I moved around the cab, peeked through the window, and waved at the driver, who currently had a finger in his nose up to the knuckle.

I pulled the passenger-side door open and sat down carefully. I just barely fit.

The driver stared out the side, past me, and looked both confused and a bit scared.

I felt like an idiot a moment later and flicked off my invisibility. "Hey."

"Oh," he squeaked.

"Hey, don't worry," I said. "Just looking for a ride over to, uh . . . this address." I pointed to the computer jammed into the car's dash and held in place by what looked like a strip of tape. Myalis caught on and the screen flickered before showing a new address.

"Ah, right, yes. The client is supposed to sit at the back?"

I looked behind. The seat had a fist-sized hole in it and what looked like cigarette burns all over the pleather. "This seat looks more comfortable. And you don't need to be afraid or anything, I really do just need a ride."

"That place isn't very safe," he said with a gesture to the car's computer.

"I mean, no offense, but your setup here doesn't look like it's made to carry VIPs from one mansion to the other."

The driver squirmed. "You will have to leave fast. We land, you leave, I go. And I want payment up front."

I felt my eyebrows rising. "All right, but only if you tell me about the area on the way over. I'm not from the nicest part of this city, but even our neighborhood wouldn't warrant that kind of response."

"Yes, fine," he said. And then he slammed his foot on the gas, and we chugged along at a perfectly reasonable speed while making an unreasonable amount of noise.

CHAPTER FOUR

BELOW THE CITY

Hex-platforming is a technique that became popular in the late twenties. It involves creating a set of six large pillars to hold up the corners of a hex. The hex's size varies, but it's usually between 100 and 200 meters from point to point. Buildings are built above these, and the gap between the hex platforms and the ground allows for plenty of space where infrastructure can be laid out. Sewers, electrical grids, any kind of interconnecting system.

If a city is attacked and a building collapses above, the hex's pillars are designed to blow out, forcing that entire section to collapse beneath the main section of the city.

It almost guarantees that anyone there will die, but it also means that the destruction is contained.

This was wonderful on paper. By the midthirties, everyone realized it was a disaster in actuality. But by then, it was too late. Half of all new cities were hex-platformed, and it's not something that can be stopped halfway.

Now new cities are built to sprawl out more and have extensive aboveground piping and networking. It's not much better. At least in a hex city, the super-poor are entirely out of sight.

—*The Hex*, by Professor of Engineering Duskland, 2041

The taxi dove down, and down, and then even lower down, slowing all the while as the driver went from just a little nervous to an outright wreck, hunched over the wheel and with his eyes roving all over to look for danger.

I didn't blame him.

The orphanage where I'd done a lot of my growing up had been on the ground level, near the outskirts of the city. Ground level was, generally, bad news. It was where all the people who fell from above ended up. A lot of the chemicals in the air were heavy, and they tended to seep down too.

No one wanted to live so low, so those that did have to live there weren't often there by choice. They were the slums, built in and around the pillars holding up the massive towers that hid the sun from view.

Right now, we were below that.

The city had been an island, once, but that was decades ago. Someone had terraformed it, built a new "ground" onto which to build the rest of the city. Everything under that wasn't fit for living in; it was all pipes and earthquake absorption shocks and pillars dug deep into the earth to hold the weight of everything above.

When we started to dive, we'd been in a nicer area. Gomorrah didn't seem like a slum-raised kind of girl. Now, about thirty floors below that, we were in hell.

Horizontal smokestacks were spewing some vapors onto the road, the clouds of smoke being torn apart as cars that didn't look street legal raced past. Bigger trucks were moving by, some taking the ramps leading up to the ground level. Most of those were being escorted by little drones.

"It's a bit above this," the driver said. He gestured up to a hole in the ceiling that cut through the ground level but never reached the sky. The interior of a hollow skyscraper?

By the looks of it, it was one of those industrial ones. The sort that was a windowless box from the outside. I guess it made sense that they'd move things in and out where no one could see it happening.

The cab rose up, and we started to navigate through a maze of catwalks and suspended roads, the path marked out by rings of green light, at least where the lights hadn't been torn off and stolen.

"There it is," the driver said. I didn't know if that was relief in his voice or not. He pulled us up and around to a hole in the wall, the faded words "Employee Parking" next to it.

A bazaar had been tacked onto the sides of the hollow interior, catwalks leading to little booths and shops suspended over the void.

We came to a stop, not quite parking alongside the other cars. I guessed the driver wanted an easy path to rush out of if things went south.

"All right," I said as I pushed the door open. Judging by the way my helmet's augs flashed and switched to tanked air and the way the driver's nose wrinkled up, the place didn't smell rosy. "I'll give you a call if I need to get out," I said.

"My shift ends now," he said. "Not working tomorrow."

"Uh, all right?" I stepped out, boots squelching into some muck as I shifted my weight to move. "Myalis, can you give him a good tip?"

Certainly.

"See you around!" I said as the taxi driver put pedal to metal and rushed out of the parking area with a rumble of his car's engine.

"Bye," I said to the taxi's retreating back. I shifted my shoulders, resettling my coat on properly, then tapped my thighs where my guns were tucked away. Everything looked like it was in place. I moved out of the parking garage, then to the edge of one of the walkways.

I held on to one of the struts coming up from below, a big chunky thing that was supporting some structural stuff above, then leaned forward to look down. The ground, the actual ground, with dirt and mud and trash, was only some hundred or so meters below.

It had probably been a forest or something once, and there were some lots where plain old-school homes still stood in the shadow of the city, trash heaped up against their walls. Some little buildings rose up around the pillars, with windows that had lights on within casting some light across the dark.

I couldn't imagine it being much brighter in full daylight.

"Right, Myalis, where's Gomorrah?"

Tracking her now . . . she's three floors above, on an abandoned factory floor. To your right, then up. Follow the signs leading to Irregular Welding Co.

I nodded, then did as the AI said. The steps I climbed, all rust-covered corrugated steel, creaked as I moved up. There wasn't too much traffic. In fact, as I entered the bazaar one floor above and started to make my way to another staircase, I noticed that half the stalls were empty, and maybe a third had shitty AI behind them.

"Hey, hey! Do you need anything? Best shit you've ever seen, fresh from the trash cans of the rich fucks above!"

I paused at the voice; not at the pitch—it wasn't the best I'd heard—but at the age of it.

Turning a little at the next intersection, I found a little girl on a plastic crate, with what looked like a video game console over her head. "Look! A console, PlayStation Nine! Still functioning, three generations old! We can even hook you up with some DRM-cracked games!"

She had . . . trash behind her. That was the word for it. Knickknacks and broken toys and some exercise equipment. All of it a bit grimy, all of it obviously broken.

A dumpster diver, then.

I'd seen their sort before. Hell, I'd jumped into a few myself when I saw someone tossing something good away. They had their own little territories and rules. Where to dive, what to pick up, which places to avoid.

I moved on. Felt bad for the kid, but there was only so much I could do. It didn't look like she was hawking to the greatest customers either. It struck me just how few people there were around.

"Is there anything about why this place is so empty?" I asked Myalis.

Nothing on any news site. Homeless migration trackers show a three hundred percent increase in mortality rates over the last week.

"Holy crap, what . . . oh, the incursion?"

That's likely. The Antithesis would travel farther underground, though they usually prefer more access to sunlight. Most paramilitaries wouldn't stop them.

"Damn," I said. "Are there any left?"

It's likely. The Antithesis are difficult to root out. Though any large break-outs within the city would be noticed and purged. There are some Vanguard whose entire duty is to sit above a recent incursion site and wait for more Antithesis to appear.

Made sense to me. I continued along, up another staircase that I didn't trust, then past a large set of double doors with the words "Irregular Welding Co." next to them. The interior was a poorly lit mess of girders and cat-walks. There were supposed to be huge machines here, at least I assumed as much from the markings on the ground, but they were all long gone.

The hum from the neon lights above fought with a clunking air vent to be the more annoying sound filling the room.

It didn't take much to find Gomorrah. She was walking away from a group that was huddled next to a tarp lean-to, her steps conveying just how frustrated she was.

"Oh great, she looks like she's in a good mood," I muttered as I started after her.

Time to see what was up with my closest samurai friend.

CHAPTER FIVE

RAC

Hello. I'm Jeff Personen, and I'm the director of CPS. Child Protective Services. I was made director because of my ability to turn any organization once run by the government into one that can bring in a steady profit.

With CPS, I did this by hiring ex-military, psychologists, and lawyers, and using them to extend the reach of both what CPS does and how it acts. Now, for a small fee, a parent can protect their child from just about anything: psychological issues, legal issues, and even the other parent!

—Jeff Personen, director of CPS, in a 2029 interview

"Uh, heya!"

Gomorrah stopped midstomp and whipped around to stare at me, her expressionless mask not conveying any emotion, but her stance did a lot of the work. "Cat? You took your time in getting here."

"'Here' isn't exactly the most accessible place," I said. "The auto-taxis won't even come here, you know? Plus I was buying new gear."

"Nice armor," she said. "I'm thinking of getting an upgrade too . . . but that's beside the point. I'm glad you decided to show up."

"Wow, you're extra passive-aggressive this, uh, morning."

She shook her head. "I haven't slept. I'm running off adrenaline and two energy drinks. I've still got the shakes from them."

"All right," I said. "So you're looking for Franny. I'm assuming no luck so far?"

Gomorrah sighed, then looked around us for a bit. The ex–factory floor was still as empty as it had been when I arrived, but that did leave some prying eyes. "Come with me; we shouldn't talk out in the open."

I followed the nun as she moved to an exit, then slipped outside. The air was as foggy and cancerous as it had been moments ago. "What's the situation so far?"

"Right," Gomorrah said as she grabbed on to a nearby set of rails. "I arrived at the convent because Sister Darlene called and said that some friends of Franny were worried about her. I figured I'd find her with some bruised knuckles and maybe a black eye again."

"Again?"

"She takes the 'saving the lambs' things a little more literally than most," Gomorrah said. "She's a good person, just a bit zealous."

"I figured zealous was a pro in your line of work," I said.

"Usually," Gomorrah agreed. "Franny is a bit more violent than I think the average nun should be."

I paused, then pointed at her. "Don't you frequently set things on fire? Living things?"

"That's beside the point. I asked around, and she was here for a little bit. Usually she stays aboveground when she's going after some pimp or whatever. It's not like her to go down this deep. This isn't the safest place around."

"Who was she going after? You mentioned something about Sewer Dragons?"

"That's what one of Franny's friends said, but no one else will tell me anything about them. There's barely anything on the net except a few mentions and those don't tell me much."

"Right, so you lost her," I said. Gomorrah turned to protest, but I cut in first. "No idea where she is, no idea where she's heading. And neither of us knows much about this area. I'm poor . . . was poor, but not *this* poor." I gestured to the wide open space around us. "So . . . let's get help."

"Help? Wait, where are you going?"

I descended the nearest stairs and walked back into the bazaar, Gomorrah hot on my heels. The bazaar hadn't gotten better. Maybe some of that had to do with the time; it was very early in the morning. Most sane people would still be asleep, though I figured without any sunlight down here, there might not be anything like a natural circadian rhythm.

The girl hawking junk was still in place, sitting on the counter of her little stall while she rubbed at some old phone with a rag.

I gestured for Gomorrah to stay where she was as I moved up to the stall and coughed. It didn't make any noise. Frowning, I reached out and tapped the counter twice.

The girl didn't even turn around.

Was that not loud enough? I made sure my mask was set so that my voice was projected from it. "Hey."

The girl bounced up and spun around, staring at me with widening eyes. "H-hey! Welcome to Rac's Trash and Shit, uh, how can I help you?"

"Rac's?" I asked.

"My name's Raccoon," she said.

It kind of fit. She had these big goggles on with thick pads around them that gave the impression of rings around her eyes, and she certainly had the "rooting around in trash" part down.

"Cute name," I said. "Don't mean to bother you, Rac, but my nun friend here and I are looking for some information. You got any? Or if not, do you know any good local gossip?"

"Yeah, yeah," Raccoon said. She squinted, looking at me up and down. "Whoa, that's some nice armor. You must be from above. Like, way above."

"Not that far up," I said. "So, we're looking for someone called Franny. Uh. Gomorrah, you have a picture or something?"

"Sure," Gomorrah said. In a blink I got a message from her, a picture of an unmasked Gomorrah, looking as genetically privileged as usual, with a girl next to her. Franny was a tall redhead with a smattering of freckles across the bridge of her nose and cheeks. Bright green eyes, the sort of smile that I'd seen on the faces of plenty of kittens just before they did something unfortunate to someone.

"Okay, what the hell?" I asked. "Does your abbey or coven or whatever only take in cute girls?"

"Uh, no?" Gomorrah said. "I . . . guess there might be some overlap, though. We're all well fed, and we exercise a lot. Beauty tends to follow that often enough, I guess."

"Yeah, Lucy's not allowed to visit, okay?"

"Deal," Gomorrah said.

I turned back to Raccoon, then flicked through a few options with my augs. I found hers a moment later, the Cyberwarfare package I had making things a little bit too easy. The overlay basically let me see everything I could connect to with an outline, and focusing on anything just casually bypassed whatever there was as security. Raccoon's augs were . . . actually, better than what I had had pre-samurai-ing.

"Here, this is who we're looking for," I said. "Not the blonde, the redhead. Her name's Franny."

"Whoa, hey, that's fucky," Raccoon said as she turned her head this way and that. "Didn't know people could do that . . . did you fuck with my augs?"

"No viruses, I swear. Girl Scout's honor."

"You were not a Girl Scout," Gomorrah snapped.

"No, but I stole some cookies once," I said. "I figured I might have stolen some of their honor too, while I was at it."

"So, you're looking for that redhead? 'Cause I haven't seen her. But for a few credits, I could show you to someone who might have," Raccoon offered.

I laughed. "I think I can spare a credit or two. What about the Sewer Dragons? Know anything about them?"

Raccoon's expression shifted, instantly turning guarded. "I don't know anything about them," she said.

"That was a fast reply," I said. Leaning forward, I put my elbows on her counter and tilted my head to the side. "Come on. Our friend Franny's in trouble with them; we mean to help her a bit."

"Help her while wearing that?" Raccoon asked. "You look like . . . you look like a samurai."

"Do I?" I asked. I guess the armor finally tipped things in my favor there. "Nice. You've got to know something."

The girl looked left and right, checking for anyone watching us, but the few people I'd noticed were walking fast, and rarely our way. We probably looked like we were doing a shakedown. "A thousand—no, ten thousand credits."

Enough credits to buy food for a week for a single person. Not exactly asking for much. "Okay," I said. "Myalis, can you do the transfer?"

Done.

Raccoon blinked. Her eyes wandered around, obviously looking over things in her augs. "Oh, shit, uh, right. What . . . what do you want to know?" she asked.

"Everything you know? Mostly where they hang out."

"Yeah, that's easy. In the sewers. It's in the name."

"Yeah, okay," I said. "But which ones?"

Catherine, the money we just deposited was moved. Not all of it, but nearly eighty percent was removed from the account it was placed in. It wasn't done by Raccoon, so I found the transaction curious.

"Huh," I said. "Hey, Rac, who just took your cash?"

Raccoon blinked, then frowned a little, her lips puckering up in a pout. "That's . . . that's the Underground Kings. It's the local tax."

"Local tax, huh," I said. That wasn't uncommon. The orphanage had been hit once or twice for protection money, but we barely made enough to keep everyone fed, and we didn't have anything worth stealing. That, and stealing from literal orphans was a bad look. Most gangs at least tried to make themselves look a bit noble. "Think these Underground Kings might know a thing or two about the Sewer Dragons?"

"Yeah, I mean, they've been fighting a lot lately. Last couple of days, the Sewer Dragons have been a lot more active. Taking folk off the streets and all."

"What for?" I asked.

The girl shrugged. "Parts."

I looked back to Gomorrah. She seemed as unimpressed as I felt. "Tell you what, Rac, there has to be some place these Kings gather, right? How about you lead us there, and I'll give you another lump of cash. I'm pretty sure I can make it so they can't touch it."

Raccoon considered it for a bit, then nodded. "Yeah, all right. Let me close up shop."

I gave Gomorrah a thumbs-up. One step closer to getting to the bottom of things.

CHAPTER SIX

QUEEN TAKES PAWN

Name: George Orbad

Alias: King, The King of the Kings

Wanted for the minor crimes of: Racketeering, Assault, Smuggling of Contraband, Homicide.

Wanted for the major crimes of: Corporate Defamation, Pirating of Private Data, Corporate Espionage.

Suspect is presumed armed and dangerous.

Reward: 1,750,000Cr

—King of Kings bounty posting, 2057

The Underground Kings had their hideout in the same ring of buildings as we were in. The factory they occupied was an old cotton candy machine factory, of all things. Some of the signs on the outside were still bright and cheerful under the layer of grime that covered everything.

Of course, they'd covered it all with graffiti, mostly crude images of men with crowns on, sometimes just crowns, sometimes giant dicks with crowns on them. Very imaginative stuff. Some of the best bathroom-stall-type art I'd ever seen.

Raccoon, our guide, paused on one of the catwalks about a hundred meters away from the factory. "That's it," she said. "The King's King stays there sometimes."

"Sometimes?" Gomorrah asked.

"He doesn't live here," Raccoon said, as if it were the most obvious thing in the world. "No one that makes a bunch of credits stays underground."

"Makes sense," I said. "Other than robbing little girls, do these idiots do anything special?"

Raccoon shrugged. "They make drugs to sell to the people above. It's called syrup. You can smell it when they make it. It's nice."

"Syrup?" I asked. I'd heard of that. It was a sort of goopy liquid, golden and clear, and apparently really sweet. It was actually a bit of a classier street drug, the sort middle-class guys would buy for a party or something. "I didn't think they'd make that shit here."

"They have to make everything somewhere," Gomorrah said. "I imagine real estate down here isn't too pricey."

I shrugged. Didn't matter to me. I didn't come down here to rid the world of some party drugs. "Maybe the stink down here is the special ingredient," I muttered.

Raccoon giggled. "So, that's it? You guys are going to go ask them for stuff?"

"Just going to ask them about Gomorrah's girlfriend."

"Franny isn't my girlfriend," Gomorrah said, voice flatter than usual.

"Not with that attitude," I replied. "Rac, do you know who we should ask to see?"

"If they even let you in," the girl said. "Ask for one of the Bishops. They're, like, the important ones, I think."

I patted the girl atop the head, because that was what I'd do with a kitten, then pointed to the front of the factory. "Let's get this over with; they might not know what we want."

Raccoon followed Gomorrah and me as we approached the factory, but she took off once we were closer to the doors and the two guys standing next to them, who might have been guards, maybe.

They had guns and were wearing some ratty clothes that had crowns stitched into them like some sort of uniform. The full-faced masks they had looked like they'd been pulled from a bargain bin, not that I'd cast stones from my glass orphanage.

"Heya," I said as I walked over. My Cyberwarfare augs were still on, and they highlighted the doors and the electronic locks keeping them closed. I toggled the option to unlock them, because I was curious, and was only mildly surprised when they didn't fall apart.

"Hey, hey, stop right there!" one of the guards said. He brandished his gun around, some sawed-off shotgun thing held together with happy thoughts and duct tape. His finger was on the trigger already.

I stopped, both hands rising up to shoulder level. "Stopping," I said. I was pretty sure the gun couldn't hurt me, but then, I was on a catwalk bridge leading over to the factory entrance, and there was a hundred-meter fall next to me. One side didn't even have any railings. It wouldn't take much for the whole thing to collapse.

I'd probably be fine if it did, but it would be inconvenient and a waste of time.

"What you here for?" the guard asked.

"I've got questions. We heard some of your, uh, 'Kings' might have some answers." I was sure to make it obvious that there were some quotes around their title. "Think you two can help us out?"

The two guards looked at each other, considering things.

Myalis, being the gem that she was, tapped into their coms with the ease of an experienced porch pirate stealing someone's insulin package from their doorstep.

Pawn G: Tell Bish?

Pawn J: Y

Pawn G: I call. Keep gun > thm

Their names were Pawn? I was never too keen on joining any gang, but joining one where your title was literally "pawn" had to be some sort of Darwinian test for any potential recruit. "Just let us go see Bishop," I said. "Also, are you guys really going with a chess theme?"

"Chess is a game for intellectuals," Pawn J said.

"Yeah, that's why I'm wondering why you guys are using it as a theme."

"Cat," Gomorrah said aloud. "Don't antagonize the idiots."

Pawn G puffed up in anger and waved his gun around some more, but neither of us could be bothered to care, so with a frustrated grunt, he turned back and started sending more texts. I glanced at them as Myalis intercepted the lot, but for the most part he was just asking someone with any level of authority what to do.

"Yeah, you can come in," he said at last.

"Thanks," I replied.

We were met just inside by a big guy in a ratty suit, a tube tucked under his jacket where it ran down from his breathing mask. He had a little rook pin on his shoulder. We were climbing up the ranks, it seemed. "You two, follow me," he said.

I glanced at Gomorrah, but she didn't seem to have anything to say about how polite our hosts were being.

We didn't go very deep into the factory. The entrance was a grimy place, with a locker room filled with hazmat suits and masks to one side, and what looked like an office on the other side. We were led past those and into a lounge where a wide window overlooked the hole leading to the ground below, with the occasional flash of light as a car hovered through the maze of catwalks.

Two people were waiting for us.

Well, two people and a few guards that faded into the background.

One was wearing a black suit, the other a white one. Actual nice suits too, the sort I'd expect to see in an ad for some insurance agency or something. The small rebreather masks they wore didn't quite fit, but safety first and all that.

"Greetings, dear samurai," the guy in the white said. "It's not every day that we receive such distinguished guests, so please pardon our lack of preparedness."

"Uh, yo," I said. "It's fine. Are you the people in charge here?"

"No, no," the black-suited one said. "We are merely the King of the Kings' right- and left-hand men. I'm Black Bishop, and that's White Bishop."

They were both pastier than anything, but I chose not to insult our new info-broker buddies. "All right, cool. We're not actually here for anything related to the Kings. We're looking for someone." I sent them the image of Franny again. "And maybe we're looking for some information about this gang called the Sewer Dragons."

"I'm certain we can assist," Bishop Black said. I saw him blinking as he took in the image I sent him. "I think we know about this girl."

"What do you know?" Gomorrah said.

"Oh, this and that. I'd need to pull things up. It might take a little while. We don't store things digitally, for obvious reasons," he said. "It's time-consuming and expensive, but worth it."

"Uh-huh," I said. "Got a price?"

"Everything does!" White Bishop joined in. "We will make sure to provide you with a discount, of course, on account of the good work you samurai put in to improve our lives."

I snorted and was about to ask him something else when Myalis interrupted.

Catherine. I thought you might wish to know this. The girl, Raccoon, is currently being physically assaulted just outside the factory.

It took me a second to register that, and then I was out of the room and walking back out. Gomorrah kept up with me, and so did the two Bishops and some of their guards.

I arrived outside to see Pawn G kicking at a familiar bundle of cloth on the ground.

For just a moment I saw red. Then reason caught up with me and I realized I had a perfect solution. I tugged out my Trench Maker and shot the Pawn in the back. Then I shot the other, who was laughing, for good measure.

"What are you doing?" Bishop White yelled.

I slammed my gun back into its holster and stomped over to Raccoon. "Gomorrah, can you keep an eye on them for a minute?" I asked. I had more important things to take care of.

CHAPTER SEVEN

KNOCKING OVER THE BOARD

Information is a wonderful currency. Extracting data from customers is how modern media make a profit.

The information of some people is worth more than others, of course. The algorithm rates people on a scale from utterly insignificant to paramount importance.

Data about paramounts can be worth hundreds of thousands of credits.

The submission process is simple, and payments are sent electronically within ninety days of that information being validated.

—Infosec's submission page, 2041

Gomorrah's habit shifted as two flamethrowers unfolded over her shoulders; they burped, and two little licks of flame, no longer than an inch or so, burned merrily at the end of their soot-blackened barrels. "Don't move for a moment, please," Gomorrah asked politely.

I nodded and knelt next to Raccoon, reaching out to move her just a little.

I wasn't keen on medical stuff, but I knew that someone shouldn't be moved if they were injured. At least, that was what the ads for some of the medical services said. Sit tight, wait for the ambulance to arrive, and have a credit card at hand.

Didn't think I'd be needing that just yet. Not that any service with common sense would come all the way down here to help with anything. "Hey, are you okay?" I asked the girl.

Her mask had slipped off, and she was breathing hard. I gingerly moved some hair away from her face, then winced at the gash across her nose. One of the corpses had kicked her nose in before I introduced new holes in his skull.

The way she cradled her chest worried me more. She was hugging herself, but her hands shook and her breathing was rough, little gasps that I recognized as someone trying to catch their breath while their lungs refused to work.

"Myalis, we need something for this."

The damage seems fairly extensive. A Class I Nano-Regenerative Suite would be the minimum required to prevent further damage.

"Forget further damage," I said. "How can we get her back to full health? Hurry, she looks rough."

A Class II Nano-Regenerative Suite would repair most of the damage. Otherwise, you need a surgical suite. She has broken ribs, not to mention several failing organs. Those seem more like environmental issues than anything caused by her assault.

I cursed. "Get that second class in Medical. I have a few tokens to spare, right? Gimme something good, Myalis."

As you wish.

Class II Medical Utilities Unlocked!

Points Reduced from . . . 11,401 to . . . 11,001

That cost a single token. You have three remaining.

"Didn't I just have three left?"

You gained one in Black Bear.

New Purchase: Class II Nano-Regenerative Suite

Points Reduced from . . . 11,001 to . . . 10,901

The box that appeared next to me was . . . complicated. It had multiple flaps, and what looked like coils of tubing inside connected to semitransparent containers. There were more things too, but I didn't know where to start with any of it. "Myalis?" I asked.

Open the rightmost flap, take the tube within, and press the suction device on the end to the patient's skin, preferably somewhere close to a vein.

I reached out and grabbed the cloth of Raccoon's sleeve and pulled it apart. The new armor made ripping it open easy. Then I did as Myalis said, and tugged out a pinky-thick tube with a sucker on the end and pressed it to Raccoon's arm. It stuck, and the tube filled with a blackish liquid a moment later.

The second tube should be connected elsewhere. I would suggest her thigh. Also, move her onto her back. Her ribs need room for the suite to be able to push them back into place.

I didn't need much effort to open a hole over Raccoon's legs; her jeans were already ripped at the knees, and the patches there were holding on by a thread.

Then the box next to me burst open, and I stared as two pistons lifted out of it and then opened at the top, releasing a pair of spiders the size of my hand. They scuttled over to Raccoon where I'd laid her down on her back and, with a burst of light from their forelimbs, cut holes through her shirt and her skin beneath before burrowing in.

"Holy fuck, that was disgusting," I said.

The bones need setting. They won't move on their own.

"Will they, uh, come out?" The skin over the cuts hadn't bled, and the holes were already gone and healed over.

Eventually, yes.

I decided I didn't want more details.

Raccoon groaned, then shifted over a bit before I pushed her back down. "Don't move," I said. "You should be right as rain in a bit."

She could use a detoxification routine, and better, more nutritious food. Or any food at all.

"We'll get her a snack after," I said. "She's past the worst?"

No, but she would need massive traumatic damage to die right now, and she's healing at an extremely accelerated rate. In thirty minutes, she will only have to deal with some of the more esoteric damage she has. Given a few days, good nutrition, and time to defecate, she will be free of the heavy metal and chemical contamination currently killing her. The cancers will be repurposed as well.

"Right," I said.

I glanced at the nano suite and noticed that the containers full of slush were nearly empty. She had a soda can's worth of nano stuff in her.

Good enough.

"Cat, is she all right?" Gomorrah asked.

"She'll be fine," I said. I stood up, then spun on a heel and walked back toward the Underground Kings. Black Bishop and White Bishop seemed a little on the nervous side.

"Miss Samurai," White said. "Please, you must understand that the—"

Their moods didn't improve when I grabbed White by the collar of his suit, lifted him up, then pulled him to the side where I could hold him over a hundred-meter drop to the ground below.

"I have questions," I began, shaking the man a bit. "Also, I'm not in the kindest mood right no—"

White's eyes widened for a moment before his suit ripped and the man just disappeared.

I stared, then moved to the edge of the catwalk and looked down.

I could make out the bright white of his suit way, way below.

"Did you mean to kill him?" Gomorrah asked.

"No, I wanted to . . . you know, hold him over the edge and question him," I said. "Uh, I should have used my cybernetic arm; my other one's just not as strong. Could have grabbed him by the throat instead too."

"You, you killed White!" Black Bishop said.

"My bad," I said.

I stepped up to Black and grabbed him by the tie before he could run away.

"Don't worry, I'll use the right arm this time."

"No! No, no! No need for that, I'll talk, I'll talk!"

I held on to Black's tie for a bit. I . . . felt a bit bad about White. Sure, he worked with people who beat up kids, but maybe he didn't deserve to be dropped to death for that. It was a genuine mistake.

The two guards didn't even rattle my remorse. They were acting beyond the pale.

"Okay," I said as I lowered Black. "I'm not going to kill you." Glancing past Black, I looked at his guards, the dudes with rooks stitched on their suits. They had guns in hand but seemed really reluctant to start shooting. I was pretty sure at least one had run away already. I refocused on Black. "I do need you to talk, though."

The Bishop nodded up and down in a hurry.

"Right. Franny, the redhead, where is she?"

"Sublevel two! There's a bar called the Halfstar. She's there right now. Was asking questions to one of our Knights."

"Oh, what sort?" I asked.

"About the Sewer Dragons," he said.

"Well, well, they're the ones I was going to ask you about next."

"I'm calling the bar," Gomorrah said. "I bet I can convince the owner to hand a phone to Franny."

I nodded, then let go of Black Bishop. "Sewer Dragons: what can you tell me?"

"How much do you know?" he asked.

I tilted my head to the side a little. "They like sewers and dragons."

Black Bishop shuffled, hands twining together with none of the easy confidence he'd had ten minutes ago. "The Sewer Dragons live in the sewer systems across the entire city. The systems are a maze. They're impossible to navigate and the air is poisonous. But the Dragons live there with specialized augs. They work for the city, cleaning out the sewers. None of the corps will go after them; it's too dangerous."

"All right," I said. "Who's their boss? What are they up to?"

"We don't know! They don't act like a normal gang, and we don't know what they're planning. They've always been a place for outcasts to hide, but lately they've been heading out and kidnapping people."

"That sounds pretty normal for a gang," I said.

"No, no, a lot of people. Entire blocks."

"Oh," I said.

Well then, maybe we knew why Gomorrah's friend was looking into them.

CHAPTER EIGHT

THE BAR AT THE BOTTOM OF THE CITY

You want seedy? You want a grimy pisshole where the beer is definitely watered down and the inspectors have literally never reached the place?

You want to see homeless idiots beating on each other for a syringe full of nostalgia? Want some ass?

Then come to the Halfstar. The name's our rating.

You'll regret it in the best way.

—Ad for the Halfstar Bar, 2037

I watched Black Bishop stumble toward his buddies, and then the lot of them scampered back into the factory as if they were mice who'd just spotted a hungry tiger. It was kind of amusing. Probably not in a healthy way, but I'd never really stopped myself from doing something just because it was terribly unhealthy before.

"So, the Halfstar. Sublevel two," Gomorrah said. "The bartender agreed to keep Franny busy, but we don't have forever. Franny won't like being held back."

"All right," I said. I turned and moved past my favorite nun and knelt next to Raccoon. The girl had pushed herself back and was sitting up against the rusty rails of the catwalk. She looked a bit better. Her skin was healing well, the discoloration around her ribs and face fading already. "You okay?" I asked.

"You're a samurai," she said.

"Yeah. Are you all right?" I asked.

The girl's head bobbed up and down so fast her ponytail bounced. "I'm fine," she said. "I feel . . . uh, actually kind of good."

"That's great," I said, smiling even if she couldn't see it. There was something in the voice when someone smiled that made it obvious, regardless of whether their mouth was visible. "Let me just check on this, okay?" I tapped the machines still connected to her, and she nodded.

The Regenerative Suite has run out of nano slush, but that's expected. The current readouts from her body indicate that most of the bruising has faded, and her bones have been reset. The medical suite is doing what it can to repair the more long-term damage to her musculature, organs, and skeleton. They will continue operating until they run out of power.

"When will that happen?" I asked.

That would depend on the task. Within forty-eight hours, the last of the nanomachines will have run out of power.

I nodded, then gestured to the tubes poking into Rac's skin. "Can I?"

Retracting.

Raccoon gasped as the tube around her arm and leg popped, then reeled back into the box by her side with a zip. "Whoa."

"You should be right as rain," I said as I stood back up and extended a hand.

Rac hesitated for a moment, then picked up the Nano Regenerative Suite and grabbed my hand before bouncing to her feet. She hurried to put her mask on once she was up, for what little good it would do with the air around here.

"Are you ready to go, Cat?" Gomorrah asked.

"Yeah, sure thing," I said. "Will you be all right, Rac?"

"Let me come with you!" Raccoon said. "You're looking for stuff down here. I've been everywhere. I know people. I've stolen just about everyone's trash before. I can help."

"You know that we're pretty much just looking for one girl, right? And we know where she is."

"Then, then let me go with you that far; I'll help!" Raccoon said. It was verging on pleading.

Gomorrah looked at Rac, then back to me. "We . . . could bring her to the church, I suppose."

"The church?" I asked. "Why would we bring her there?"

"Because they'd feed and shelter her."

Well, there was that. I'd feel pretty awful if I just left the kid behind with nothing to show for it. My plan with Rac was to give her a good chunk of credits after everything was done, enough for her to get by for a while. But she wasn't an orphan, she was a street rat; that was, like, an entire level below what I'd once been.

There was always someone in a worse situation than you. It was one of those small-comfort things. Some of the people who worked at the orphanage would point out kids like Rac and remind us that we could be like her if we didn't want to enjoy their generosity.

"Rac," I started. "We're heading up a bit. Now, I'm not keen on charity and shit, but if you do a bit of work for Gomorrah and me, we'll pay you for it, all right?"

"Yes!" Rac said. "I'm ready to go now."

"Right," I said.

"I can find stuff for you; I'm good at that. And I know how to fix things, and give me three minutes and a screwdriver, and I can open any trash can ever made."

I laughed and rubbed the top of her head again. "If we run into any violent trash cans, you'll be the first I turn to," I said. "So, where'd you park?" I asked Gomorrah.

The nun pointed across the doughnut we were in, and I followed her finger toward a gray smudge moving through the air with frequent jukes and twists. It looked almost like a drunken fly the way it bounced around. Still, the car was making good time.

"Whoa," Rac said as God's Righteous Fury slid up next to us and hovered in place as if it were on solid ground. "Nice ride."

The car was nice, there was no denying that. I didn't know how Gomorrah's aesthetics resulted in what looked like a high-tech muscle car with more glowy bits than a rave DJ, but it did, and there was no denying that the Fury looked like it could punch through a skyscraper and come out the other side without a blemish.

The front door opened, and Gomorrah slid in without comment, and then the car backed up and spun around so that the passenger-side doors were facing us. They both slid open. "In the back," I told Rac.

She scrambled in without protest, wide eyes soaking up everything as I dropped down next to Gomorrah.

"So, the Halfstar next?"

"Before Franny gets some idea and runs off," Gomorrah said. The doors closed while I was still trying to get comfortable in the passenger seat. It wasn't designed for someone in armor, though the seat was moving and expanding and basically doing its best to accommodate.

Gomorrah spun up around and we shot out, only narrowly avoiding a few girders as Gomorrah juked us out of the way. "Franny won't stay put for long; she's too . . . active for that kind of thing."

We drove out of the doughnut that housed all of those factories, and Gomorrah shot across a few lanes of automated traffic, then up and out of a large opening in the metal sky above. We were back out and in the open, the sky no longer an oppressive ceiling. Well, if one didn't consider the smog oppressive. Rain battered at the windshield and was wicked off almost in the same moment as Gomorrah swept up around and back into a building.

The tunnel we flew through had a few other cars darting through it, but Gomorrah seemed content to dodge those at the last minute while poking at the screen in the middle of her console.

"Fast, fast!" Rac cheered from behind.

"Um," I said.

"Here," Gomorrah said just before turning the Fury around so that its bottom was facing where we were going. It slowed us down just in time for Gomorrah to drive us into what looked like a maintenance alley. At the end of it was an open area, with a tall ceiling and a parking space with a few boxy maintenance vehicles collecting dust.

"The bar is around here?" I asked. We were definitely still aboveground.

"No, there's access to the elevator banks going down from here. We could have walked from where we were, but this is faster," Gomorrah said. "At least, according to Atyacus."

Gomorrah set the Fury down and put it in park, then stepped out. Raccoon and I followed a moment later, though the girl had to figure out the handle. As soon as she was out, she glanced around, then nodded. "You're trying to get to the Halfstar?"

"Yep," I said.

"Then you don't want to take the big elevator. There's this other one, a service elevator that goes up the spine of one of the scrapers here. It's not for the public, but the keypad code is 1234 and people from above use that to get to the bar. I've used it to go trash hunting before."

I raised an eyebrow, moderately impressed. "People go there often?" I asked.

"It's a popular place, I guess," she said. "Big. They have fights and sometimes rich people come to bet on them."

"Well, then," I said. "Lead the way."

Raccoon nodded and zipped ahead of us.

"You sure bringing her along is wise?" Gomorrah asked, her voice transmitted directly to my augs.

I replied after flicking on a few options with my mask. "No, but it's better than leaving anyone down there, isn't it? I can't save everyone, but I'll save those I can, you know?"

"Hmm," Gomorrah replied. "You might do well in a convent after all."

I laughed and walked a bit faster to keep up.

CHAPTER NINE

HALFSTAR

Logistics are life.

Without them, you have no food, no water, no ammo, no materials. You're basically stuck with what you have on you. It's why, in times of crisis, one of the most important things is setting up a proper logistics train.

That gets complicated when the train needs to reach the undercity. The terrain is treacherous, the paths down are maze-like, and if cargo is unguarded, it's liable to never make it to its destination.

One popular trick is to just figure out where the destination is, then plow a hole through the building above it.

It's a bit unsubtle, but it's better than being shanked by a hobo.

—Sgt. Aaron Fenzer,
The True American Army's Logistics Division, 2048

The maintenance elevator might have been faster, but it was also cramped and jittery and *felt* like a place where someone could easily die.

"Oh, wow," I said after we hit a particularly jarring bump. "I had Myalis pull up the records, and this elevator was last inspected in 2045."

"I was like, three years old then," Raccoon said.

I nodded. "Next time, I think we can use the non-shortcut."

"We're in somewhat of a hurry," Gomorrah said. She was off to one side, hand wrapped around one of the metal poles reaching up to the ceiling. The elevator didn't have completed walls. Instead it was lined by a cage on four sides that ended at about hip height. It meant that we got to see the bare structure of the building as we slid down. Cracked concrete, exposed rebar, and the occasional open vent where glowing eyes watched us pass.

The elevator jerked to a stop, and the cage slid most of the way open just as the door squealed apart.

"This is it," Raccoon said as she squeezed out ahead and stepped into a dingy corridor. It was all graffiti-covered drywall, with the occasional hole punched into it. Lights hung from the ceilings, some of them working enough that they illuminated the boxes here and there where the homeless lived.

Had lived—none of those I saw had anyone in them.

"The Halfstar is one level down," Raccoon said.

"All right, lead on."

Gomorrah and I walked side-by-side behind Rac, the girl bouncing ahead with near-manic energy. "Has anything changed in this area recently?" Gomorrah asked.

"Yeah, there were aliens."

"Aliens?" I asked.

"You know, plant xenos. From the incursion. Some of them made it this far out, but then some samurai like you swept in. We had a whole lot of soldiers down here too, but only for a day or so before they left."

"And that's why there isn't anyone around?" I asked.

Rac shrugged. "I guess. When the incursion happened, I went topside, hid in one of the big shelters. They had free food. I bet a lot of homeless people did that too. Online, they say that there's a lot of opportunity right after an incursion. Lots of companies pick up new employees for the factories from all the people who lost their homes and stuff."

"Huh," I said. Likely easy pickings. Desperate people would grab on to any contract in a pinch. "You don't like that kind of work?"

"I'd love to work in a factory," Rac said. "Just doing the same thing all day. I could save up some credits, buy one of those story-generating machines. You know, with, like, an AI writing a story for you, then reading it aloud? Just zone out all day."

That sounded awful. "If that's what you want, then why didn't you try to find work?" Gomorrah asked.

"Too young. Most corporations are real careful about hiring anyone under eighteen, because there've been some samurai that kicked up a fuss about child labor, and no one wants their factory burned down."

"Maybe we can find you some better work, then," I said.

"Really?" Raccoon asked.

"Really?" Gomorrah repeated.

"Hey, I have a whole new building that needs cleaning and stuff. And we're basically rich, aren't we?" I asked. Plus, Raccoon reminded me a lot of my kittens. A bit dirtier (and that was saying something) but she had that same energy about her. She was tough.

"That would be incredible! I'll work really hard, and for cheap too. And I promise I won't sell most of your trash!"

"All right, all right," I said. "Let's get all of this stuff done first."

Raccoon brought us down a stairwell, then opened a door that led into a maintenance corridor, with a low ceiling covered in exposed pipes and dangling wires. "Don't touch the tubes, they're hot," she warned as she easily squeezed between two of them.

I had to contort myself through, the armor making it a lot harder, but at least it kept me from getting burned or anything.

Once we were through, we pushed into a much wider corridor, this one acting as a sort of street. There were a few booths along the sides, and some enclosed greenhouse planters that looked to be filled with oxygen-rich molds.

Doors with panels on them led off to apartments on both sides, and at the next corner, we passed a convenience store with barred windows. There were people around, at least. Some looking tired, others tipsy. Mostly, they looked like workers on their way back home after a night shift's work.

The corridor eventually tipped downward and we reached another intersection, one leading onto a road that was lit only by reddish lights.

Some kids with neon spray paint were designing a mural on one wall with quick strokes. Sharply drawn aliens, recognizable as Model Threes, racing up toward a figure that looked suspiciously like Deus Ex, with red slashes flowing out and away from her and through the aliens. The bottom half of the image looked like the undercity, though, and it was crawling with aliens.

Above it all, in that typical hard-to-read lettering graffiti artists liked, were some words: "GOD'S EYES DON'T SEE DEEP."

I snapped a pic while we walked past. Something to send to the pip-squeak later.

The Halfstar announced itself with all of the bluster and pride of a silent fart. It had a sign hanging off one wall, the lights in it burnt out. Its entrance was a plain metal door.

But there was a line leading in, and a bouncer by the front with a half mask and two cybernetic arms that looked like they belonged to a factory worker.

We skipped the line.

"Hey," I said to the bouncer. "Can pretty girls come in free?"

He eyed me, then Gomorrah, then Raccoon. "No," he said.

"Can pretty girls with very big guns come in free?" I asked next.

Gomorrah sighed. "We're samurai, here to speak with . . . someone within. Please let us in."

He looked at Gomorrah, then stepped to the side. "Right, of course. Go on in."

"Thank you, sir," she replied.

"*Sir?*" I repeated.

"Being polite can help things. And it's just common courtesy, something that I know you're unfamiliar with."

"I can be polite if I feel like it," I said. "I've just never felt like it."

The Halfstar's entrance was a dark place, filled with gauzy curtains of light-absorbing material that made it hard to guess how big things were. They might have done something to dampen down the sound, because as we moved in, the noise grew louder and louder. I adjusted my cat ears down a notch or two. Super hearing was great when it wasn't pounding noise into your skull.

And then we were in the bar proper.

It was obvious that the place had been something else at one point. Walls were torn out and the floor cut open. A second level below had chairs around a ring that someone could easily jump into from above. There weren't even rails around it on the top floor.

No fights on at the moment, but the place was still lively. The dance floor was occupied by two dozen bodies, rubbing and gyrating against each other, and the DJ, some guy in a sweat-stained shirt waving his arms around.

"There," Gomorrah said.

She was pointing across the room to where a nun was facing off against an obese man jabbing a finger toward her face.

"That's Franny," she said.

Franny looked pissed. Sure, she was as pretty as she was in the pictures Gomorrah had shared, but that beauty was twisted a bit as she sneered at the man blocking her path.

Still hot, though.

"Well, then, let's go say hi to your girlfriend," I said.

CHAPTER TEN

TENSIONS

Never let anyone tell you you're not valuable! You have organs, after all!

At Organ-do's, we turn some of that value into cold hard credits. It's as easy as stepping into one of our insured Organ-do booths, and leaving a few minutes later with a pocket full of spending money!*

*Organ sales are nonrefundable.

—Organ-do ad, 2051

Franny was a little different in person: a couple of years older than in the picture Gomorrah had shown me, and she wasn't quite as clean. Not that she was dirty or anything, but her clothes had a few dusty stains on them, and she was obviously not wearing any makeup.

She looked past the fat man blocking her path, just a glance, but one that turned into an outright stare as Gomorrah stepped up . . . then paused.

I slowed to a stop behind Gomorrah. There were still a half-dozen meters between her and Franny, and yet she seemed reluctant to move.

"What's going on?" Raccoon asked when the moment started to stretch.

"Your guess is as good as mine," I muttered back to her.

"Franny," Gomorrah said.

The fat man turned, his frown disappearing in an instant when he locked eyes on Gomorrah. "Ah, Miss Samurai, you're here at last. As you can see, I kept the girl here. I did as you asked."

"You made him hold me back?" Franny asked.

"I didn't want you running off before I could arrive."

"I'm not twelve, Delilah," Franny snapped. "I'm an adult."

"One who's currently in one of the worst establishments I've ever had the misfortune of laying eyes on," Gomorrah retorted.

I felt my eyebrows rising. There was a whole heap of tension between the two, and not the fun kind. I imagined that Delilah was Gomorrah's real name. A bit weird to have spent so much time with her without knowing, actually. "Are you two all right?" I asked.

"Who's that?" Franny asked with a nod my way. "You hired a bodyguard?"

"That's Stray Cat," Gomorrah said. "She's a samurai. A friend."

Franny crossed her arms, the gesture bunching up the black cloth of her robes. She was wearing a mostly nunlike outfit, though her robes ended near her knees, which I was pretty sure wasn't standard, nor were the jeans underneath, or the all-black combat boots and choker. "So, you're making friends with more people playing God? I'm impressed you're even managing to make friends at all."

I raised my hand. "I'm not playing God. I wish I could play God. Right now I'm stuck in a permanent game of hide-and-go-seek but with high explosives. So, Gomorrah, this is the girl you ran halfway across the city to save? Because she doesn't look like she needs saving."

"I've never needed saving," Franny said with the snap and bluster of someone who had very much needed saving at one time or another and who didn't appreciate it.

"Yes, Cat, this is Franny. Now that the introductions are over with, let's go home, Franny."

Franny shook her head. "No, Delilah, I'm not just going to let you drag me back home like I'm some unruly kid. The old bags can live without someone to bitch at for an evening."

My "unresolved issues" radar was pinging like mad, but I decided not to poke at it. "Can we sit down?" I asked. "Maybe get a drink?"

"I don't drink—"

"I don't drink—"

Gomorrah and Franny turned to each other, then snapped their attention away and back onto me. "Uh, hey, I bet they have cola here? Rac, you like soda, right?"

"Fuck yeah," Raccoon said.

"See, you'd be depriving the poor homeless girl of a free drink," I said. "And you can spend the time educating her about the glories of proper language or whatever the fuck it is two nuns who need to get laid talk about around impressionable children."

"Where did you find this one, Delilah?" Franny asked.

"I almost lit her on fire."

"Have you maybe reconsidered the 'almost'?"

I laughed. "Oh good, that's where all of Gomorrah's snark went. Come on, it's . . . about six in the morning. Damn. I want to sit down and eat some breakfast, maybe get a few hours of sleep. But seeing as we're here, I'll settle for a bottle of something."

I stepped between and past the two nuns on my way toward a corner of the room where a few booths sat empty. I guessed that even this place was quieter at this hour. Then again, the dance floor was nearly full.

Gomorrah let out an audible sigh and followed after me.

I gestured Raccoon ahead, and the girl slipped across the bench before I sat down. Gomorrah took her seat across from me, then scooted over to make room for Franny, who stood by the side of our table.

She had a baseball bat.

I wasn't sure when or how I'd missed it. The bat was an old wooden thing, poorly spray-painted a flat black, with some peeling tape around the handle. "Nice bat," I said.

She scoffed and planted herself next to Gomorrah. "Yeah, well, it works. Not everyone can call down weapons from the heavens."

"Fair enough," I said. There was a screen in the middle of the table, one smudged with . . . liquids. I shook a napkin dispenser, found it to be empty, then reached over to the booth behind ours to steal a few from theirs to wipe the screen. "Order whatever, Rac. And grab me a Shock Soda. I need a sugar substitute."

There are healthier alternatives, with no microplastics and less radioactive waste used as a water substitute.

I made sure no one could hear me as I answered. "Don't need to alienate people right now," I said. "Franny here seems touchy."

She does seem somewhat nervous.

I leaned back into the bench and watched as Raccoon placed first my order, then two orders of water from Gomorrah and Franny. She moved over to the foods list and paused to look up at me. I nodded and made a "go on" gesture, and she started adding one of everything to the order.

It was a good thing I was rich, because Raccoon seemed determined to sample everything.

Then again, she had been injured, and the nanites needed her fed.

Probably couldn't expect much from the food here, but it was better than nothing, and she still had some healing stuff in her. When she was done, I connected to the screen through my augs, noted the number of viruses and junk my new augs just brushed off, and made the payment.

"So, Franny, Gomorrah here was stupidly worried about you."

Franny scoffed. "She didn't have to be."

"Yeah, well, she interrupted me mid-happy-time with my girlfriend to come rescue you." I enjoyed the incensed insult on Franny's face, as if it were enough to disguise the reddening of her cheeks. "Now, I'm always willing to help a friend out, but that doesn't mean I won't be obnoxious and ask questions, like 'Why didn't you answer your calls?' and 'What were you doing here anyway?'"

"The old bags are the sort to spend the day preaching about being good rather than doing good," Franny said.

She paused while pointing at me with a finger when a robot rolled over and crashed into the edge of our table. It was little more than an oversized

Roomba with some servos and a pitcher of ice where our drinks were waiting.

I served us all. "So you cut them off. All right. Didn't have to cut Gomorrah here off."

"I took out my augs," Franny said. "It's safer that way."

"Safer?" I asked.

"You wouldn't understand."

I shrugged. "Okay. And what were you doing here? You don't drink, and something tells me that while you'd like to look, the holographic strippers aren't why you're here."

Franny looked to Gomorrah, then at me. "I'm not going to sit back and do nothing, all right."

"All right, so what were you doing?"

"While you were hanging out with Delilah and playing tourist, I was down here looking for people. There have been disappearances. Lots of them."

"The incursion nearby probably accounts for some of that," I said.

"Some, but not this many. No one pays much attention when nobodies disappear. But I know some of them. Or at least I know people who know them. A lot of them are too poor to move farther out, and some have left families behind. That's *after* the incursion."

I leaned forward. "And what's that got to do with the Sewer Dragons?" I asked.

"How do you know about them?"

"I really don't know much," I said.

Franny licked her lips, but she did spill. "They're the ones doing the kidnappings. I couldn't get any answers yesterday. I . . . uh, persuaded some people to let me see their security camera footage, but all the video from where the kidnappings happened was either wiped or a loop. No clues there, and no other witnesses, at least none that I found. So I started to map things out."

"Okay," I said with a nod.

She reached out and grabbed some of the leftover napkins I had, then laid them out on the table. "The kidnappings happened in different buildings, but always on the same floor." She poured some of her water into her hand, then started pressing dots onto the napkins. "And there was a pattern."

There was a pattern now, all the wet smudges grouped together in a long trail. "The sewers, I guess."

"Yeah, concentrated around openings. No specific target either, just anyone. Young, old. Inside their house or standing outside. It took some work to figure out the who, by the way."

"That's impressive work," Gomorrah said, talking at last. "We can tell people, tell the authorities."

Franny slapped the table. "They won't do anything."

I sighed. This was going to be one of those discussions.

CHAPTER ELEVEN

PLAYING WITH GOMORRAH'S FRANNY

With the proper augmentations, even the least hospitable environment can become a comfortable paradise!

—Exos ad, 2049

Franny's rant about the injustice of things and the authorities not doing anything hit close to home.

At least, it did for the first couple of minutes.

As she went on and on, though, I found myself getting a little bored with the whole thing. Yes, life sucked. Yeah, corruption was everywhere, and people were assholes who didn't help those in worse situations than them. The corporations and whatever passed for a government around here were shit.

At least Rac was making the best of it, shoveling food down hand over fist while occasionally nodding at whatever Franny was spouting.

"Okay," I said, a hand raised. I was surprised that I was the one interrupting Franny. Gomorrah didn't seem like the kind of girl who would sit down and take a rant like that.

Then again . . . she was just staring at the redhead—staring and not saying anything.

I held back a grin. I couldn't jump to conclusions, but I really wanted to. Maybe my teasing wasn't so far off the mark after all. "Okay, so these Sewer Dragons, where are they?"

"Why? So you can tell the police and watch them not do anything?" Franny asked.

"What? No, I've never called the police in my life and I'm not about to start now. I want to know where they're at so I can poke holes into them."

Gomorrah sighed. "I knew it would come to this," she said. "I am curious as to *why* the Sewer Dragons are acting up now, though. What they're doing is being brushed off as losses to the incursion, but they could have done this at any time before now too."

Franny looked confused for a moment before snapping out of it. "I don't think this is new. I think they've been stepping up their game. Used to be they only grabbed hobos and sometimes maintenance people who were sent down to the sewers. Now they're going all out."

"Yeah, that doesn't make sense. Kidnap a dozen nobodies a year and no one will care, but . . . do you have a list of the people that went missing?"

"I do, here," Franny said.

I received a ping from her, with an unencrypted file at the end. I supposed a list of names and addresses wasn't anything worth keeping safe. "Myalis, can you check on these people's whereabouts?"

Certainly. Of the one hundred and seventeen, twelve recently made purchases or were seen in locations throughout the city. Three are outside New Montreal. The other one hundred and two have no clear electronic trail that I am able to detect. However, my resources and access are limited at this time.

"One hundred and two of those people are still MIA. Yeah, no, that's too damned many." I started to shift to the side to get up. "Rac, you done eating?"

Raccoon was currently lying back in the seat, her mouth half-open and her stomach distended from all the grub she'd shoveled down. "Huh? Oh, are we going?"

"Yeah," I said. "You can stay in the car while Gomorrah and I go say hi to those sewer people."

"I'm coming too," Franny said.

"There's no way you're coming," Gomorrah said. "It's dangerous."

Franny scoffed. "Delilah, I'm the one always saving you from danger; it's not like I'm unfamiliar with getting into a fight."

"It's not the same," Gomorrah said.

Franny's jaw set. "What, just because you're a samurai now? Because you're a saint?" She pointed at Gomorrah. "Under all that fancy gear, you're still the girl I had to keep safe for all those years."

"Franny," Gomorrah said. There was a lot of subtext in that one word, but it was way too early for me to even start trying to figure it out.

I stood up. "If you two are done arguing, we should get going. We don't know how active they are at night, but I bet those Sewer Dragons aren't sitting around picking their noses while we wait around here. If we're going to save people, we should get to it sooner rather than later."

Franny nodded and stood up. She picked up her bat and leaned it against her shoulder. "I know a few of the places where they have their bases."

"More than one?" I asked.

"They're only technically a gang. It's more like . . . I don't know, a sort of country that lives in the sewers. They have their own councils and towns, basically. Most gangs, when they're done doing their dirty work for the day, go back home. Even if that means some dirty apartment somewhere. The Sewer Dragons' territory *is* their home."

"I guess that makes sense," I said. "So, other than kidnapping folk, do they sell stuff?"

"Smuggling, mostly," Franny said. "None of the corps dare go into the sewers, and none of the cops will follow them in either. Half the gases in there are lethal. They control the ventilation systems and can redirect water from different plants to different areas."

"Water?" I asked.

"More like acid," Franny said. "Some gases are explosive, and they can move those around too. I heard that the last team sent in was blown up. The survivors got too many infections from open wounds to be saved."

"Shit," I said.

"Yeah, the sewer folk are real fucked up that way," Rac said.

All three of us older girls turned to her. "What do you know about them?" I asked.

She raised her hands in surrender. "Just what everyone knows."

"I didn't know they existed five hours ago," I said. "Come on, spill."

The girl shrugged, hands dropping to her sides. "They've got a big entrance to their place over by the water filtration plant on sub four. They call it the Oasis. Good place to sell any filtration stuff you find in the trash. Once, I picked up this really nice aquarium from one of the upper levels. None of the other trash divers wanted it, but it looked like it was real expensive. The sewer folk bought that thing for good money."

"Filtration stuff, huh?" I asked. "No, I guess that makes sense." If they had homes in the sewers, then they needed every bit of filtration they could get.

"Folk there don't live long," Raccoon said. "Mostly it's these people that can't live elsewhere. Not homeless people, just, like, people in a lot of debt, or who are running away from something. There're a lot of people like that."

"Is the Oasis the biggest entrance to the sewers?" I asked.

"It's the biggest that's easily accessible," Franny said. "Kind of like their public entrance. There are a few others, at waste management plants, but those are guarded a bit more. If you want to deal with the Sewer Dragons directly, you go to the Oasis."

"Then let's head over. I'd like to get this done sooner rather than later. Get home, take a shower, sleep."

Franny shifted, her mouth working and her brows meeting together in a frown.

"You look pissed that Gom and I are helping," I said.

"I'm not. It's just . . . Well, there's only two of you."

"Two samurai. Two slightly annoyed samurai. Pretty sure that's enough to break an army."

She glared.

"That's it, let the anger build. Soon you'll be able to let it all out on some unsuspecting gang members."

Franny turned to Gomorrah. "Your friend is awful."

"She is," Gomorrah said, tossing me under the bus. "But, she does, on occasion, get the work done."

I laughed as I turned and started for the door. The Halfstar's bartender seemed relieved to see us go. Poor guy probably thought we'd trash the place while we were here. Or that someone would pick a fight.

I saw a few guys poking at each other, jock-looking sorts who were eyeing our group up, but I think accidentally revealing that I had a grenade launcher under my coat scared them off a bit.

"We're not taking that maintenance elevator again," I said. "I don't think it could handle four of us."

Gomorrah somehow ended up at the back of the group, with Raccoon and me in the lead and Franny a little to the side, her arms hooked over her bat, which she'd slung over her shoulders. I got a call from Gomorrah almost as soon as I exited the bar. "I can't believe we're doing this."

I made sure my mask wouldn't let my voice escape before I answered. "You mean helping your girl get rid of some fucked-up gang so you can score brownie points at . . . just past of six in the morning?"

"That's not what's happening."

"You know, I consider you a good friend, G-girl. I'm there for you and your weird nun-ish sub-dom relationship."

"I hate you."

Raccoon looked up to me when my shoulders shook, but I just gestured for her to keep going.

Had to have some fun where I could.

CHAPTER TWELVE

STP-44 THE OASIS

Water is necessary for life.

It goes without saying that good water is necessary for good living, then.

At the lower levels, and lower costs, you have water services that will provide cheaper water. This water is poorly filtered, usually tainted and brackish, with microplastics and bacterial colonies giving it a pungent odor and color.

In better neighborhoods, where the community has agreed to pay for a better quality of water, you'll find near-distilled water. It may have some traces of industrial decontaminants within it, but it is entirely possible to drink this water without getting sick (in the short or medium term).

Many buildings have their own filtration system as well, but these are expensive, and usually reserved for industrial applications.

The best water, the water found only in the penthouses and the places where the ultra-rich live, is carried over to local cisterns from outside of any megacity. It is tailored to have a good taste, a clear coloration, and no plastics, oils, or any other chemical contaminants.

—On Watering, S. Cing

The non-maintenance elevator was probably safer, but holy fuck it was slow. The entire thing hummed as it rose up, and its LEDs flickered every so often. It made some of the ads plastered to the walls look cool for the split second they were in the dark. The glow-in-the-dark ink was probably worth it.

"So," I asked as I debated leaning against one of the walls. Would it hold? I didn't normally have to consider whether things could handle my weight. "How did you two meet?"

Franny turned my way. "I assume you're talking about Delilah and me?"

"Yeah," I said. "I was there when Gom—Delilah met Rac here, so that only leaves you two, right?"

Franny crossed her arms, her bat left next to her, the lump at the end of the handle pushing against her side. "I joined the convent when I was . . .

nine? Ten years old? I met Gomorrah the year after that. She wouldn't stop crying until I became her friend, and then she followed me around nonstop."

"I was terrified," Gomorrah said. She looked my way, and probably guessed that I was missing some context. "The convent has a few programs in it; some of them basically act as a sort of . . . babysitting-slash-summer-camp. It's not too expensive, and it means your daughter gets to go to a decent private school afterward."

"Like a scholarship?" I asked.

"Something like that," Gomorrah said. "They train girls to be well-behaved and on how to carry out basic duties, and we get to attend one of the city's better schools for a lot less. It's also one of the stricter schools, but the results are usually pretty good."

"I wouldn't know," I said. "Half of my schooling was online, and when I did go to a class, it wasn't exactly ritzy."

"Oh, my family couldn't afford anything too nice," Gomorrah said. "Hence the convent. But it . . . well, I'm not close to my parents, let's say. A lot of the girls there aren't."

"What, like abandonment issues?"

Gomorrah shrugged, and I decided not to poke at it any more than that.

"The place isn't so bad," Franny said. She picked up her bat and twirled it around. "They're strict, but that's better than being tossed out on the street, and they're big on morals and such."

"Never could afford morals," I said.

Raccoon nodded. "Those are rich-people things."

I raised my hand her way, and she slapped it in a quick high five. "Yeah, moral-less gang, rise up!"

"You're terrible," Gomorrah said.

The elevator ground to a halt, and the doors slid open. Raccoon slipped past the rest of us and took the lead, doing what I think she thought of as her job in leading us through the underground. Either her sense of direction was really keen, or she just knew her way around—either way, we soon exited into the parking space where Gomorrah's Fury was waiting.

"Dibs on the front," I said.

"You want to sit up front?" Franny asked. "I've been friends with Delilah longer."

"Oh, this is a competition?" I asked. "Well, I've fought by Gomorrah's side before."

"You don't even call her by her real name," she said.

"We have cute nicknames for each other. She calls me Stray Cat, as if I'm some mangy mutt off the street, and I call her Gomorrah, after a city that was burned down or whatever."

"I don't think that fits the usual definition of cute," Franny said.

Grinning, I leaned down so that I was closer to Franny. "If you want to sit next to your girl, you just have to ask. I'm sure she's appreciating you fighting for the right already."

She sputtered, then with a huff moved over to the rear of the Fury and jumped into the back seat. Raccoon followed her in without any fuss.

"What did you tell her?" Gomorrah asked over a secured line.

"Just poked fun at her obvious romantic feelings for you."

"Franny isn't like that," Gomorrah said. "And if she were, it wouldn't be for me . . . You don't actually think she's . . . you know?"

I stared at Gomorrah over the roof of the car and noticed she was gazing at the ground. "I mean, call me a hopeless romantic, but she used to protect you, right? Your redheaded knight? And now the balance of power is all twisted around and she's not sure what's going on anymore, and you're both upset at each other because you both care a lot, but things aren't the way they used to be?"

"You're taking a lot of this out of context."

"Lucy would be sighing right now at how romantic everything is," I said.

Gomorrah groaned. "Lucy is dating *you*. Her romantic abilities are very much up for debate, and her taste is unquestionably poor."

I laughed as I slid into the passenger seat. She wasn't wrong; Lucy could do better. I was just lucky, and clever enough not to tell Lucy as much. "Come on, let's go see about killing some dragons," I said as I flicked out of the private channel.

"I thought nuns didn't like killing things," Raccoon said.

"We don't," Franny said.

"Aren't there dragons in the Bible?" I asked.

"No, not the way you're thinking," Franny said.

"The fuck would you read it, then?"

Gomorrah spun up the Fury, and we pivoted before taking off out of the alley at a speed I think Franny wasn't comfortable with.

"When did you learn how to drive, Del?"

"This week," Gomorrah said as she shot out into oncoming traffic, wove over a truck, then flipped us over into the right lane. There was a speedometer sign against one wall, large green digits telling drivers how fast they were going over or under the limit. It flashed red when we roared past.

"So, what's the plan once we get to the Sewer Dragons?" I asked. "Because I have a plan, but I'm not sure it's a good one."

"Does your plan involve copious amounts of explosives?" Gomorrah asked.

"You know me so well," I said.

"I . . . actually haven't considered it that far," Franny said. "If I caught a few of them in the act, I could beat them up, make them regret taking people the way they have. But I'm not equipped to assault their front door. There'll be dozens of them, at least."

"So, we try the diplomatic method," I said. "Gomorrah, you talk to them, maybe ask that they . . . I don't know, give up on their evil ways and such."

"And what will you do?"

I flicked on the invisibility on my coat and my new armor, and in the time it took for someone to blink, I was gone. "I'll be sneaky!" I said.

"That's so cool," Raccoon said.

"I know, right?"

"No one would be able to see me stealing their trash with something like that," she said.

"Not . . . exactly what I had in mind, but hey, good for you."

I held on to one of the handles above the door as Gomorrah took a turn at a speed that was pretty far from advisable, and then I refocused on what was going on outside as we slowed down before a large gate with the words "SEWAGE TREATMENT 44" stenciled across them in fading paint.

"Give me a minute," Gomorrah said. She did something that locked the car in place, hovering before the doorway while she wiggled her fingers in the air, the strange gestures of someone fingering their way through complex menus on their augs. "Yeah, this is the one. The section beyond this technically belongs to the city, but it's all being rented out by a few companies that are in charge of the water filtration and sewage treatment. They have things divided up, based on where in the city the waste is coming from and where it's going."

The gate thumped, dust peeling off it in a rain of rusty flakes before the entire thing slid aside. When the path was finally clear, Gomorrah drove us in slowly, the headlights on the Fury doing more than the lights on the ceiling to illuminate the tunnels.

The walls here weren't walls at all, but huge pipes and tubes, all of them wide enough that I was sure the Fury could fit into them, if tightly.

We moved down a long, narrow passage that opened up at the end on a large balcony that circled halfway around a lower level. It was like walking out of one of those entrances in a stadium, only instead of benches all around there were stations with pipes and little buildings with flickering lights, as well as other passages heading off every which way.

The lower level had a cement arch over a much wider tunnel. There were smaller buildings all around the entrance, made of steel plates and scrapped cars. Stalls and shops and little areas where people were sitting around drums with fires burning merrily within. The entire area was lit up in the familiar blues and pinks and greens of stolen neon ads, most of them strung onto towers covered in wires to brighten the place up a little, like psychedelic trees.

"I guess this is where the Sewer Dragons come from," Gomorrah said. "Let's find a place to park before we go say hello."

CHAPTER THIRTEEN

WHAT OLD PEOPLE SAY

With the Great Tinder Crash of 2024, the world of online dating suffered terribly, with people suddenly forced to try finding people to date and meet out in meatspace.

Paradoxically, the number of children born in 2025 was twelve percent higher than the previous year.

—Excerpt from *Dating in the Modern World*, 2027

The Fury lurched as Gomorrah put it in park and shut the car down. "All right," I said. "Raccoon, Franny, stay in the car."

"You need me!" Raccoon said before I'd even reached for the handle.

"And I'm coming too," Franny said.

I shifted so that I was looking back, which wasn't easy to do while in power armor. "All right, Rac first. Why would we need you here?"

Raccoon swallowed, but she was a brave sort, so she tightened her fists and stared me in the eye. Or my helmet's eyes—close enough. "You don't know much about the Sewer Dragons. Some of them are assholes, some of them are a bunch of cunts, but some of them are all right. So you need someone to tell you which ones to off."

I considered it for a moment. "I was just going to walk over there, threaten some people, then murderize my way to victory. It's really late . . . early, whatever."

Gomorrah sighed, the long-suffering sort when a more adult-y person knows a kid's right and doesn't want to do something about it. She reached down to the console between the chairs and pulled open a lid with a hiss of compressed air.

A whitish haze floated out of the compartment she opened, and Gomorrah reached in to pull out a thin can with the words "ENERGY DRINK" stenciled on the side. "Here, one for each person coming," she said as she handed me a can, then tossed one to Raccoon.

Franny, pointedly, didn't get one.

"Where's mine?" she asked.

"We haven't determined if you're coming yet," I said, guessing at Gomorrah's intentions. Hell, if Franny were Lucy, I wouldn't bring her into some den of depraved lunatics either.

"So I'm coming?" Raccoon asked over any protests Franny could make.

I slid the energy drink between my legs, glad the armor kept the chill at bay—beyond a vague impression of coolness—and reached up to undo my helmet. "Yeah, you can come. We'll get you a better mask, though. You're not equipped for this kind of thing. Actually, maybe we could give her a screen, let her do overwatch instead of walking into trouble with us?"

"Holy fuck, what happened to your face?" Raccoon asked.

I blinked.

Usually, if people had issues with the scarring on the side of my face, they made it known when I met them. Then again, I wasn't usually wearing a full-face helmet. "Fire shit," I said.

"Cool! Like from an alien?" she asked.

"Sure, let's go with that," I said. "Lost my eye and everything. This one's a cybernetic one."

"That's pog as fuck."

I stared. "Where'd you pick up 'pog'?"

"I thought that's what people your age said," Raccoon said.

"Well, that's horrific," Gomorrah said.

Franny cleared her throat and leaned forward until she was on the edge of her seat. "Why, exactly, can't I come?" she asked.

"Because you need to keep Raccoon company," I said. "Rac, we'll let you use, uh . . . there's a screen somewhere in this car. You can use it to see what's going on. Gomorrah and I, I at least, will feed you video."

"Awesome," Raccoon said.

"I'm not a babysitter," Franny hissed. "And you can hardly keep me here."

"We can literally keep you here," I said.

"Cat," Gomorrah warned. She turned toward Franny while I popped the tab on my drink and took a sip. It was . . . really plain. Water with a tiny hint of a fruity aftertaste. Then I felt an electric shiver run down my spine, and I blinked my eyes feeling fully awake. "Franny, I'm . . . I'm not just Delilah."

"You've hardly changed that much," Franny said. "It's been what, three months?"

"Yes, Franny, three months. A very long three months, where I became a saint, and where I've done a lot. I'm not the same Delilah, dammit."

"If Sister Clarice heard you now," Franny said.

"Sister Clarice had to be convinced not to kiss the ground I walk on," Gomorrah said. "I'm glad, really glad, that you're not like that. But still, can't you just . . . I don't know, accept that I don't need . . . urgh, whatever."

Gomorrah downed her can in a single pull, let it drop into the freezer, then shoved her way out of the car while slipping her helmet on.

"Myalis, can you . . ." I gestured between my eyes and the car's interior. The ceiling and windshield flickered and were soon replaced with a feed from my cybernetic eye, which of course created a mirroring effect. "Thanks. Raccoon, I think the car has a microphone, we should be able to hear you."

"Cool, cool," Raccoon said.

I leaned back and pointed a finger at Franny. "Stay."

"I'm not a dog," she snapped.

"No, you're Gomorrah's friend, and she cares about you. Possibly even in a platonic way, which would be impressive if she's still willing to put up with your bitchiness. So, you stay in the car."

I slapped my helmet on, then shoved the door open and stepped out. I closed it fast. Neither of the girls within had masks on, and I figured the air out here wasn't the greatest, though I imagine the Fury had decent filters.

"You okay?" I asked Gomorrah over a private channel. Switching channels on the fly was going to be a pain, I just knew it.

Gomorrah took a deep breath, then moved to the back of her car. "Yeah, I'm fine," she said as she opened the trunk. I blinked at the gun within. It was a lot smaller than her usual flamethrower. Then she pulled out a backpack and shrugged it on. It was all black, with golden crosses and silver gilding over the sides.

She connected a hose from the pack into the stock of her new gun while a pair of back-mounted flamethrowers unfolded.

"Nice new gear," I said.

"Thanks," she said. "Come on, we should get this done."

"We don't have to, if you're not up to it," I said. I was wired as hell, though. That energy drink had some kick.

"No, no, I want to do it. Franny's right to want to stop these kidnappings, and if no one's doing anything about it, then it kind of falls to us to take care of it."

"All right."

Gomorrah started walking ahead of me, and I figured I'd give her a bit to settle before asking her about our plans.

"Franny was supposed to be there," Gomorrah said. "It was a trip to some lakeside forest thing. With the school. Franny had to stay back. She busted up her hand and broke a few bones, and the sisters kept her away as a sort of punishment."

"Okay?" I said. I wasn't sure where she was going with it.

"The incursion was small. Like, really small. And we were on the edges. So we started moving toward a shelter outside the forest. Then we were hit by some Model Threes. I was next to a canister full of fuel, I had a lighter on me. Next thing I knew, Atyacus was offering to help me."

"That's how you became a samurai?" I asked.

She nodded. "It wasn't exactly glorious. There wasn't much to do after that. Rallied the others, killed a few more aliens. Not many, mind. I stuck around and tried to help after, but all the Vanguard that showed up knew what they were doing, and I didn't. Maybe I was a little shell-shocked, I guess. Came home and nothing was the same, you know?"

"I guess. And Franny didn't care for it?"

"Not at all. She's been distant. I've been distant too. I'm an adult, dammit, I shouldn't be following another girl around like some . . . some puppy or something, but Franny meant, means, a lot to me."

"I'm not actually sure what to say."

"Nothing, I don't think," Gomorrah said. "It'll work out, or it won't. I'm mature enough to concede that much."

"Well, if it were Lucy, and I'd somehow changed in a way she didn't understand, I think I'd talk to her about it?"

"I've tried" was Gomorrah's flat response.

"Fair enough. Should have figured you'd give it a try." I gestured aimlessly ahead. "I guess you can prove to her that you don't need her anymore, not to keep you safe, but then she might drift off, you know? Think that since you don't need her, you don't like her anymore."

"That's ridiculous."

"Probably doesn't feel that way to her," I said. "I'm a bit worried that Lucy will start thinking I don't need her either, which is stupid. Or maybe now she's better and I'm not always going to be around, she'll find someone nicer than me. Someone with more fleshy bits . . . and probably a nicer ass."

Was there something I could buy for that? Had to be.

A problem for later.

"I don't think it's quite the same. This is entirely platonic," Gomorrah said.

I nodded along, not believing her one whit. "Yeah, totally. Now, let's at least get the proving-you're-badass part down."

CHAPTER FOURTEEN

MALLY

You can't survive in the sewers. Those who work within them can only survive thanks to their extremely robust survival equipment.

The kinds of augmentations (augs) required to survive and work without restrictions within these environments are often disfiguring, requiring massive modifications to a person's skeletal frame, musculature, and brain.

It will be impossible, or impractical, to convince normal people to work in these conditions. I suggest that the board find a way to improve our existing robotic infrastructure to care for the maintenance of these sewer systems. It would be more expensive, but the cost in lives would be worse otherwise.

—Report to the board of Infracorp, 2032

I twisted my head left and right to crack my neck. That energy drink had given me a kick in the rear, but I still felt as if I should be in bed. I wouldn't be able to sleep, and I'd probably be restless as hell, but still.

Gomorrah was going to owe me for messing up my sleep schedule.

Or I could spend the next couple of days napping here and there. Had to live up to the "cat" part of my name.

"All right," I said as I switched channels. "Rac, tell us what we have to know."

Gomorrah and I paused at the top of the last landing before the "ground" level of the sewer opening. There was a single working neon sign, large and piss-yellow, with a green blow-up palm tree next to it. It read "THE OASIS!" in letters taller than I was.

Below that were the stalls and roads leading into the sewers. I could make out plenty of amateur artwork staining the cement walls. Long eastern-style dragons, often made to look like they were diving out of manholes.

I tried a quick head count. Maybe fifty people in all. Most of them looked . . . pretty normal. Vagrant chic, with maybe a few more augs than I'd expect from homeless people. Lots of prosthetics going around, and a lot of people were wearing long, brown coats that hung low on their frames.

"Right, right!" Raccoon's voice came in my ear. "Okay, see that place at the back, on the right? Looks like a sort of watch room, with the windows?"

I looked that way and made out a control room set above and next to the large entrance into the sewers. It had angled windows overlooking the Oasis. Mirrored windows, so I couldn't make out anything within. "Yeah, I see it."

"That's where some of the people in charge of the Oasis stay. There's like, a place with rooms and stuff in there. That's what I was told, anyway."

"So we'll find the Sewer Dragons there?" I asked.

"Well, yeah and nah. The people here are sewer people, but they might not be Sewer Dragons, you know? A lot of them are just hiding out in the sewers 'cause they're safe, in a way. But pretty much everyone works for the Sewer Dragons in one way or another."

"Huh," I said. "So we . . . don't gun them all down?"

"Yeah, just some of them," Rac said.

"I would rather you didn't go in and kill everyone," Franny snapped.

I frowned ahead. "Weren't you going to go in with a bat? I can't picture you dropping the bat for a Bible to go all gospel on them."

Gomorrah placed a hand up on my shoulder. "We'll try to employ some discretion," she said. "I'm sure Cat wouldn't mind purchasing something less lethal for the occasion?"

"Yeah, fine," I said. "Myalis? Sell me on something decent?"

I see three simple options; you might even consider using all three. Your Icarus can use foam grenades. They fire a rapidly expanding, breathing foam that turns into a cementlike substance a few moments after expanding. This cement breaks apart rapidly, though it takes hours to weaken and days to fully melt away on contact with oxygen. As for other options . . . Your Cyber-warfare augmentations can disable some prosthetics and augmentations, and your Trench Maker can easily accept electrified gel rounds.

"Electrified gel rounds?" I repeated.

"That sounds so cool," Rac said.

I'd forgotten to switch channels. Oops?

They're small impact-dissolving gel capsules. They will not penetrate, but will disperse kinetic energy against any surface they hit. They're also electrified, similar to a modern Taser, though the shock isn't long-lasting. They should be capable of disabling organics.

I nodded. "Let's gear up, then. Gomorrah, you, uh, going to tone down the fire or something?"

"Foam," Gomorrah said.

I slid my Trench Maker out of my thigh holster, then slid the magazine out of it. Soon enough, I'd replaced it with some gel rounds, and I did the same with my Icarus. The extra grenades I gave to Gomorrah, who had some room in her pack, which she said was explosive enough already that some more wouldn't matter.

Current Point Total: 10,851

"All right," I said as I adjusted my coat. "Let's go in."

"You should talk to Mally first," Rac said. "She's this lady, left side of the Oasis. She makes really good food, for cheap too."

I shrugged. "Good enough for me," I said.

"It's a place to start," Gomorrah replied. "Are you going in stealthy?"

Usually I wouldn't, but I was basically acting as the camera-cat here, and Gomorrah's maybe-crush was watching. I wasn't going to beaver dam my wingnun. "Yeah, I'll be right behind you. Same setup as in those mines? For friendly fire and all that."

"Sounds good to me," Gomorrah said.

Myalis and Atyacus worked things out while we went around and found a staircase leading to the floor below. I flicked on my invisibility between one step and the next. And when I glanced down at my hand, all I could see was the grimy floor below.

"That is so fucking rad," Raccoon said.

"It's got its uses," I said. I kept close to Gomorrah as she reached the ground floor and looked around. There were people coming and going. Vans parked to the side and unloading boxes, people coming over, sometimes with boxes or crates, others in little groups carrying more weapons than was likely legal.

There was life here. Dirty life, but life.

Gomorrah went left, and I kept after her as she moved toward a line of tents. "MALLY'S" was painted on one wall in fat graffiti letters, little hearts and flowers through the name.

Gomorrah moved around to the front of the tent, where the curtains were pulled back. The rear of the tent was an air-sealed room. Clear plastic let us see into a small kitchen area where a pair of people were working some pots and pans. From the overfull trash can at the back, they were cooking from two dozen different sorts of canned food and some microwavable meals.

There was someone at the front, next to a counter covered in torn linoleum. She was rubbing the surface with some cloth, mechanical arm moving in little circles.

Mally, or the person I guessed was Mally, had a half mask on, her mouth entirely hidden by it and twin tubes coming out of the mask and diving into her flesh between neck and collarbone. Her arms were both long, thin things, servos at the elbows and wrists, and hands that were all actuators and chrome.

She was hunched over, long mechanical legs folded in on themselves so she could fit under the tent, but it was obvious they were designed to extend and make her much taller than she was now.

I guess she'd be over nine feet tall standing up with everything extended and her three-padded feet deployed. Her long coat, all black but decorated with colorful stickers of flowers and suns, hung over her frame, hiding her torso entirely.

"Hello," Gomorrah said.

Mally looked up, organic eyes blinking to take in Gomorrah. "Oh, hello, dearie," she said. "I don't recognize you, but you're welcome, as all are."

Her voice had a croak to it. Old age and rough air, I guessed.

"Thank you," Gomorrah said. "I'm a little bit . . . lost, I suppose. I'm here looking for some people, maybe you could help me?"

"Certainly. Are you hungry? We're not quite done with breakfast, but if you take a seat it'll be ready in no time."

"No, but thank you. I appreciate it."

"Oh, no need for that. I do charge. It's just good business. Are you from one of the convents? You have the outfit for it, but it's not often that we see your sort this far down."

"Yes, but I'm here on my own business," Gomorrah said. "I'm looking for some people, quite a few of them. They've gone missing recently."

Mally's cleaning stopped for a moment, and then she resumed. "People go missing," she said. "It's a terrible thing, isn't it? But it's a big sewer, and there are plenty of nooks and crannies."

"Right. Maybe you could help me find them? Or maybe the Sewer Dragons could help. I hear that they know this place fairly well."

"I . . . that might not be good business, sweetie."

Gomorrah sighed audibly. "Yes, I know. But it's my business now. Please? Can you help me?"

CHAPTER FIFTEEN

THE CULTURES BENEATH

You'll find good people anywhere.
You just won't find a lot of them.

—Sewer Dragon proverb

Mally turned her eyes down and stared at her counter, her hand resuming its slow circles, rubbing away at some grime that seemed determined not to leave.

"Miss Mally is nice," Raccoon repeated in my ear. She was speaking in a hushed tone, as if worried she'd be heard. "She makes sure everyone has something to eat."

I supposed that was important in a place like this, where food had to be scarce, or at least harder to come by. Kind people weren't too uncommon. I could remember soup kitchens and vans set up by folks who'd given away meals. Some were pretty decent.

People were, I found, not mean by nature. Just greedy, and it was easy to forget to look down and remember that those beneath you didn't need much to be helped. Some folks didn't forget; they helped where they could. Maybe it was selfish, maybe they did it for the praise, but I figured that was fine. It was some of the only actual praise that was deserved.

"Miss Mally?" Gomorrah asked.

The woman's mechanical hand tightened, squeezing her rag. "What do you need to know, dearie?"

I moved off to the side to make sure I wouldn't be in the way if anyone stepped into the room. It let me keep a better eye on the two still in the kitchen mixing stuff in a pot.

Gomorrah stood a little taller. "I need to know where the people who have been kidnapped are being kept. And I need to know who's doing it. Everyone is pointing fingers at the Sewer Dragons, but it's a big group; I don't want to be indiscriminate."

"Ah, I . . . thank you," Mally said. "We're not all bad people down here, you know. Jeff and Cynthia back there were middle management for a nice little company. When they closed up, some accounts came back crooked, and someone had to be blamed. So now they're here."

"Okay?" Gomorrah said.

Was she going on a tangent on purpose?

"I was a manager at Nimbletainment once. Then I slept with the wrong man, and the next thing I knew, his wife tried to bury me. I had nowhere to go. My story isn't so special, I don't think. Most of the people here are like that."

"I see," Gomorrah said. "I just need to know where to look."

Mally's hand shot out, faster than I expected, and grabbed Gomorrah by the arm, metal fingers pinching the material of her habit. "You should leave. We have nothing left to take. And less to lose."

Gomorrah tore her arm free. "Miss, I don't *care*."

"Those people are lost already," Mally said, her arm retracting. It had stretched out, growing longer with her little lunge.

"Then I'll find those responsible and stop them from trying again."

"You'll get yourself killed. Please, if you want to help, then there are other ways." She gestured around, eyes jittering around as if she were nearing a panic attack. "There're so many things you could be doing to help."

"Gomorrah," I said, my voice sent to her and the two in the Fury. "I think it's time to go."

Gomorrah nodded and stepped back from Mally. She exited the tent, the woman staring after her as she held the flap open for a moment.

"So, that was a bust," I said as I slid out after her.

"Yeah. Still, we learned some things."

"That some of the people here are nuts?" I asked.

Gomorrah shook her head. "I had Atyacus break into her augs. Rooted around for a moment. She actually keeps good records of her transactions. Money spent on food, how much of what she bought, equipment expenses. I think she's not lying when she says she had a corporate job."

"You violated her privacy," Franny said.

I snorted. "You'd have violated her brainspace with your bat, wouldn't you?"

"I'm not some violent sociopath," Franny shot back.

"Girls," Gomorrah snapped. It was a good snap. "Let's stay focused. If I found nothing, then I wouldn't mind making reparations, maybe slip her a few credits for forgiveness, but I did find something."

"Oh?" I asked.

Gomorrah nodded, then gestured ahead. "Let's not stay on the edge here; we'll attract attention." She moved over to some stalls, one of which had weapons on racks and a man slumped behind the counter, sleeping. "Mally buys food. Recently she's been buying a lot more. More equipment for cooking it too. Either she's expanding her little business by a lot, or she's supplying food to someone."

"The kidnapped," I said.

"That's what I was thinking too," Gomorrah agreed.

I glanced around. The little stalls near the entrance didn't provide much cover. There were people I'd call guards, or maybe thugs, standing around next to the entrance of the Oasis. Long, stalklike legs, with hunched bodies and what was obviously an arsenal of guns under their coats. "We could find a place to jack into the local network; there might be more out there to learn. Cameras, maybe?"

I'm afraid that the local security network has been entirely disconnected. I can relay the position of some augmentations, but only to a certain depth within the sewer network. Many of the walls are made of lead to prevent radiological contamination from spreading out of the facility, and that makes communication impossible within the sewers themselves.

"Will *we* be able to communicate?"

Of course. With Atyacus's assistance I can use the Fury as a relay. We are not limited to things like waveform communication methods.

"So, that's a bust," I said.

"What's a bust?" Raccoon asked.

"Uh, I was talking to Myalis. They don't have security for us to tap into."

Gomorrah raised a handgun; it looked positively ancient, with wooden parts and a nice patina of rust. The label on its side called it an Oberez. She stared at it for a moment, then placed it back down onto the rack, next to other shitty-looking guns. I was pretty sure Myalis would throw a fit if I started using something like that. "We need to figure out something else."

"We could . . . you know, walk in guns blazing."

"That would be cool," Raccoon said. "But some people aren't mean."

I sighed. "I miss killing aliens. There's no moral shit to wade through, you know? They look like evil plants: you shoot them. Nice and simple."

"If the Sewer Dragons themselves are as crude as I suspect, I don't think you'll need to worry too much. Now . . . maybe we find someone important to question?" Gomorrah tilted her head back and looked to the tower next to the entrance.

"That works for me," I said.

We started crossing the Oasis but had hardly made it more than a dozen meters before Gomorrah was stopped. The culprit was a boy wearing a hoodie under one of those long coats. He had normal-seeming legs, though their bottom halves were all bare metal and plastic-covered servos.

His hood covered a full-face mask made of reflective glass on the outside. "Hey, babe," he said.

"What?" Gomorrah asked.

"I said, 'Hey, babe,'" the guy repeated, louder.

"I'm not hard of hearing," Gomorrah replied. "My question was more in the lines of 'What are you doing?' Perhaps 'What do you think will happen if you don't get out of my way?'"

"Hey, nothing like that," he said. "Just saw an unfamiliar face, so to speak. Thought I'd say hi. You can't believe how hard it is to meet new, ah, friends down here. Say, you bio under those robes?"

"I'm what?" Gomorrah asked.

"Bio? Meat, still got the curves your mama gave you."

Gomorrah and I stared for a while. I knew he couldn't see me, but still. "I'm a nun."

"That's cool."

"No, no, it's . . . go away, please."

"Wait," I said. "He might know something."

Gomorrah half turned to look in my general direction. "You have got to be kidding me."

"He thinks you're hot. Use it," I said.

"That is both demeaning and disgusting," Franny said.

"I agree," Gomorrah replied.

"Uh, you okay, babe?" our new idiot buddy asked. "Cat got your tongue?"

Gomorrah sighed, then grabbed the idiot by the arm and tugged him along. "Follow me," she said as she aimed for the back of the Oasis, where a few signs indicated the bathrooms. "And don't talk until I tell you to."

"Yes, ma'am!" he said.

Poor fucker.

CHAPTER SIXTEEN

FUN IN THE WASHROOM

The article looked wonderful.

The Sewer Dragons are an interesting enough society from a purely anthropological viewpoint that the university would never pass up an opportunity to study them.

So, they send in a team of five graduate students, and (apparently) after conferring with the Sewer Dragons they met, three of them agreed—with the university's approval—to go through the extensive procedures needed to join the group on a temporary basis.

I was really eager to read their publication and look through the initial findings, but the paper is just "fuck you" written over and over. The graduates discovered that the university insurance wouldn't cover their retransformation into people able to return to normal society.

Why can't I get a refund on the paper I bought?

—Excerpt from the Anthrough Journal Customer Support Forums, 2052

Gomorrah pulled our favorite new boy toy to a washroom. "Hey, hey, this is a bit fast for me," he said as his back bumped into the door and shoved it open.

I followed them in, ears twitching to make sure we were alone. If there was anyone in one of the stalls, they were real quiet shitters. I pushed the door closed and pressed the heel of a boot against it.

The bathroom was a shit hole. Busted doors on the stalls, a cracked mirror against the wall. Of the three sinks, only one was free of yellow tape, and that one was currently leaking brownish sludge water into a basin already half-full of the stuff. Some of the non-penis art was nice, though.

Gomorrah let go of flirty boy and wiped her hand against the side of her robes. "I'm happy you came up to me," she said.

"Uh, yeah," the idiot said.

"Yes. I have questions. I doubt you'll be able to answer them. Atyacus, shut off his coms."

"My coms? Oh, fuck, how'd you do that?" He reached up, rubbing the side of his head in the way a lot of people did when their augs were on the fritz. "Hey, I wasn't going to record everything, and if I had, it's not like I'd resell it."

Gomorrah reeled back. "That's disgusting," she said.

"It is," Franny agreed over the line.

"I don't get it," Raccoon added.

"That's fine," I said. "Franny can explain. Gomorrah, question away."

"I'm not entirely sure where to start," Gomorrah said. She tilted her head to both sides, stretching her neck. When she next spoke, her voice filled the bathroom. "Are you part of the Sewer Dragons?"

"Hey, babe, I'll be anyone's dragon if they ask nice enough," he said, some of his confidence returning.

Gomorrah looked at him. A pair of flamethrowers slid out from her habit over her shoulders and pointed themselves at his face. "Do you work for the Sewer Dragons?" she asked again.

"Oh shit, what are those?" he asked, two mechanical fingers pointing at the flamethrowers.

"Flamethrowers," Gomorrah said.

"I wouldn't have expected to see Delilah threatening someone," Franny said.

"What, and you carry that bat around as a walking stick?" I asked.

Our new friend squirmed a bit. "Like, that's hot, but I'm not into whatever kink that is."

Gomorrah grabbed him by the front of his jacket and pulled him closer. "You will stop messing around and answer my questions, or you'll regret it by ten."

"Ten what?" he asked.

"One," Gomorrah said.

"What?"

"Two." Her flamethrowers burped, and two licks of flame danced on their ends.

His eyes went wide. "Oh shit."

"Three."

"We're all Sewer Dragons," he said. "Everyone here."

I shifted. "What's that mean?" I asked.

"Explain," Gomorrah said.

"Look, everyone who lives here, in the Oasis, is a Dragon. All of us. I don't know what you want, babe."

"I want the location of the people the Sewer Dragons have been kidnapping," Gomorrah said. "And I want to find out who is responsible so I can bring them to justice."

"Oh, fuck, you're a samurai." The realization had the guy trembling. "We're not going to fuck, are we?"

"No . . . we aren't," Gomorrah said. "Just answer my questions."

I shook my head. "This is why people don't talk to each other live anymore. It's such a bitch to get answers."

"Oh man, right, so the Sewer Dragons: we're an anarcho communist commune. We don't really have leaders, you know. Just a lot of freethinking people, doing our own things, and sharing based on what we need," he said.

"Does sharing include kidnapping people off the streets?" Gomorrah asked.

"I don't know anything about that!" he said, both hands raised in surrender.

"Atyacus, check his location data and cross-reference it with the kidnapping locations," Gomorrah said. We all waited for a moment, and then Gomorrah nodded. "You might be telling the truth. So, if some of you were taking people, where would you take them, and what would you do with them?"

"Hey, hey, I don't know," he said.

Gomorrah's flamethrowers shifted, the flames on the ends growing brighter and longer. "Are you certain about that?"

"Oh shit. Uh. Look, I'm sure there's some folks that know all of that. But I'm not one of them. I've been doing nothing but robbing vending machines and trying to get ass for the past two weeks."

"Seriously?" Gomorrah asked. She paused. "Oh, wow. Atyacus confirms it. That's . . . kind of disgusting, actually."

"Hey, babe, I have needs," he said.

I sighed. "This idiot doesn't seem to know anything. Let's rip any maps he has. I don't think we'll be getting much more out of him."

Done. If you want, I can chart out the most likely location where you'll find a large group of people within the sewer system based on the little map data I do have.

I nodded. "Thanks, Myalis. Send it to Gom and the others; it might be useful."

Gomorrah didn't seem quite done with her new friend. "A few last questions," she said. "You say there's no one in charge, but there has to be some sort of hierarchy. And how do the Sewer Dragons operate? You can't be this much of a black box."

"Hey, hey, it's real simple," he said, and then he started to gesture, hands coming around as if moving a little ball though the air. "Everyone that joins the commune has skills. Even if it's just manual stuff. If someone brings someone new in, or someone joins up, they're brought to Doc Hack, and he fixes you up."

"Fixes how?" I asked.

Gomorrah repeated the question to our pal, who gestured to himself. "Makes it so that you can live down here. You need filters over your air intake; that means replacing some of your throat. You can't have legs in the sewers, not for long. And you need some other things, augs that let you know what the air's like."

That explained some of his extensive modifications. I'd seen a few aug-junkies before, idiots who went really deep into cybernetics. Usually they wanted high-tech stuff, not the rust-chic aesthetic the Sewer Dragons I'd seen had going for them.

"So, you get fixed up, then you get a nook to live in. Nicer ones have better air, are farther from the ins than the outs."

"The whats?" Gomorrah asked.

"Intake or outtake tunnels," he explained. "Once you're set up, you do your part. That's it. We keep each other safe, sorta. There's no police down here, no bossmans, no leaders. We have community halls and game nights."

"Cute," Gomorrah said. "We have the same at the convent, but without the hideous self-mutilation and kidnapping." She growled. "Where does your money come from? You can't live off nothing."

"I dunno. We take care of the sewers, keep it running. Without us, people will have to shit in buckets and fling it out the windows."

"That's it?" Gomorrah asked.

He nodded. "Yeah. Been a right nightmare this last week too. I've been, uh, not around for added work shifts because of other preoccupations, but lately everyone's working a lot more."

"How many of you are there?" Gomorrah asked.

"We don't exactly have a census," he said. "But, uh, maybe twenty K? Thirty maybe? Less now; a lot of us died last week. Lost, like, a whole housing area to the xenos and a bunch of good folks besides when the aliens dipped into the sewers."

"Are there any left? Antithesis, I mean?"

"Some other samurai came in, gave the sewers a look, said it was fine. Haven't heard of any, but we've been on high alert for that shit for a few days."

"There are a lot less of them around," Raccoon said. "Usually there's a lot of Sewer Dragons near the Oasis, and today it looked a bit empty."

I unjammed my foot from the edge of the door. "Anything else you want to ask Casanova here?"

"No, I'm done," Gomorrah said. She let go of the guy and backed off, then pointed a finger right at him. "Stay here. I don't need you running into the crossfire."

"Yes, ma'am!" he said. His eyes widened as I opened the door for Gomorrah and followed her out.

"Didn't learn much," Franny said.

I saw Gomorrah's shoulders tensing up. "We did learn some things. Mostly that we're not fighting anything organized."

"What do you think is happening? Kidnapping people to feed pet aliens? More bodies for some corporation or another?"

"Nah," Raccoon said. "When a corp wants bodies, they just put a bounty out."

"That's disturbing," Gomorrah muttered. "As for the Antithesis, it would be significantly cheaper to feed one with just about any other biomass. Buying a ton of potatoes is easier than kidnapping a ton's worth of people."

"Well, then," I said. "I'm stumped."

CHAPTER SEVENTEEN

SHIT BUREAUCRACY

New Montréal is an interesting city for many reasons, one of which is its government. Originally a city in Quebec, after the Great Split, Montréal declared itself a city-state and was rechristened New Montréal.

Its fledgling government discovered an immediate issue when its mixed-language groups both started to wrestle for power within the city. The end result is a municipal government that's nearly entirely French, serving a population that's nearly entirely English, while in actuality being run by an upper crust that is entirely non-Canadian.

—Excerpt from the *Guide Touristique du Nouveau Montréal,*
2049 édition

"I figure we walk in and just go straight to them," I said with a gesture to the Oasis's entrance. We'd wasted enough time asking questions and trying to get to the bottom of things, but the Sewer Dragons seemed about as organized as my kittens halfway into a pillow fight. There was some semblance of a hierarchy, maybe, but there wasn't a boss, and no one quite knew what the others were thinking except that they were all thinking along the same chaotic lines.

Gomorrah nodded. "Might as well. Either we'll find someone to help us or we'll find the people we're looking for. Do you think we need anything special to head in?"

"I guess we'll need masks and things that will keep us alive in there. Does your armor cover you entirely?"

"Did you think I was nude under my robes?" Gomorrah asked.

I raised my arms in surrender. "I wasn't even thinking it. I thought you had some sort of under armor on. But . . . now that I'm imagining it, it's not a bad mental image."

Gomorrah's hand snapped back, and she smacked my arm with the back of her hand. "Pervert," she said.

"Are you always this horny?" Franny asked.

I grinned. "Your Delilah's the one who started it . . . this time. But before we start talking too much, we really do need a gear check. Myalis, we going to be okay in there?"

If by we you mean you and I, then yes. Your under armor is intact, reading at ninety-nine percent integrity. It should prevent most chemical or radiological contaminants from touching your skin. Your Lion's Mane's structural integrity is still replicator-perfect. Your helmet's filtration system should allow you to breathe in nearly any environment, and with the stored air, you could survive in a vacuum for up to a quarter of an hour.

"So, no dying from fart air. Nice," I said.

"A disgusting way to put it," Gomorrah said. "But not entirely wrong. I'm ready as well, although . . . I think I might need to disrobe."

I blinked. "Huh?"

Gomorrah tugged at the front of her black robes. "These won't be great in what might be a wet environment."

Made sense. Gomorrah and I looked for a place for her to change, and we ended up sneaking into an alley between two small maintenance buildings off to the side of the Oasis. I stood by the entrance, making sure no one was around, and then I looked back in.

Gomorrah shifted her shoulders, then carefully reached up and tugged at the edge of her collar. It loosened and she tugged down the outer hood of her habit. She had a tighter, white hood beneath, one stuck to the sides of a helmet that looked about as high-tech as my own. Well, it had little glowy bits and was made of metal, so I was guessing.

She placed a leg forward, then bent down and swept the robes off in a single, languid motion, the cloth riding up along her legs and back and revealing the Gomorrah underneath until she straightened, a bundle of cloth in her hands. She started to casually fold the robes while I stared.

I thought my armor was a bit . . . feminine, but Gomorrah's was on another level. Tight, fitting to her calves and thighs and butt, with armored plates and some sort of blacker-than-black weave over the parts that needed any flexibility. Her back-mounted flamethrowers rested below her shoulders like a pair of folded wings, and there was a cross-shaped cutout under her bust.

"Fuck me."

I blinked. The whispered words weren't my own. They were Franny's. I doubt anyone else picked them up, though.

"Right, so that's—yeah. Ready to go?" I asked.

"I'm ready," Gomorrah said. She placed her folded robes next to a box on the ground, then picked up her flamethrower. She slid a strap over her shoulder.

She looked a lot smaller without the volume of her robes making her bigger.

"What?" she asked.

"Nothing," I said. "We heading out?"

The Oasis loomed large above us as we moved toward it. Gomorrah didn't have the advantage of being invisible, and I couldn't help but notice a few of the people near the sewer entrance looking her way.

Something told me they weren't staring to check her out, exactly.

"Myalis, can we have a map of the sewers?" I asked. "And highlight any places big enough to house a bunch of civilians."

Myalis was quick to create a small hovering map at the edge of my vision, and when I tried to peek at it, it grew larger before me. The three-dimensional wireframe was a confusing mess of tunnels, side passages, more tunnels, and a few boxy buildings. Some of those were flashing slowly.

The map expanded, and then expanded further. I frowned as it continued to grow, mostly getting wider and longer, but occasionally there were sections that rose or fell below. Fortunately, the map became smaller, zooming out as it covered more territory.

"What the hell," I said once it finally stopped.

"That's the entire sewer system," Franny said. It sounded like she was guessing, though it was an educated guess. "The system for the entire city."

Which meant its footprint covered the whole city too. A city with nigh on a hundred million living in it.

"Fuck," I said. "Covering this on foot is just not going to happen."

Gomorrah paused. "You're right. I didn't expect it to be quite this large. Atyacus, can you overlay the locations of the kidnappings on the map?"

Dots appeared, a couple hundred of them sprinkled atop the sewer lines. "Oh, that's better," I said. For the most part, the abductions were happening in an area that was more or less oval shaped. There were lots of tunnels beneath that, but they mostly joined up to one or two larger passages.

"Do the Sewer Dragons have vehicles?" I asked.

"Likely," Gomorrah said. "I imagine there's something that can travel through the large sewers, at least."

I nodded. That made it more complicated. Still . . . "Let's start with the places nearest the kidnappings." There were two larger locations being highlighted there. "If I were a creepy sewer-living person who wanted to . . . I dunno, eat surface-dwelling hobos, I wouldn't want to travel far for my lunch."

"Disturbing, but probably not wrong."

"I don't think the whole 'don't shit where you eat' thing applies down here," I said as I minimized the map back to a square in the corner of my vision.

Raccoon giggled, and I heard her feet patting against . . . what was likely the front seat in the Fury. Gomorrah groaned. "And now you went from disturbing to disgusting."

"I do that," I said.

No one stopped us—or at least Gomorrah, who was the only one visible—from entering the facility. I was expecting a sewer. Like, a large tunnel half-filled with shit water. Instead, it was all cinder-block walls and a cement floor, with lights hung from the ceiling, most of them functional enough to brighten the place up.

Crates were pressed against one wall, some shipping containers against another, and on either end was a long tunnel that curved around.

A few metal doors at the far end seemed to open up into some offices, of all things.

"Not what I expected," I said.

"This is an access area," Gomorrah said. "The map . . . isn't terribly clear."

"Hey, miss, whatcha doing here?" someone asked.

It was a rotund man, with a ketchup-stained button-up and slacks. He had a helmet on, like a large glass bubble with the bottom half over his mouth covered in filters, but otherwise he could have been any midlevel factory foreman. At least, I figured he was a foreman; that was what the tag on his shirt said.

"Hello," Gomorrah said. "I'm . . . who are you?"

"I'm Bob," he said. "Who're you?"

"I'm Gomorrah. I'm looking for access to . . . this area."

Bob frowned the frown of someone who had been interrupted—there was some sauce on his patchy mustache—and of someone who'd been sent a pile of data that they didn't want. "That's a ways from here. Do you have permission to be down here, miss?"

Gomorrah gestured to some of the others in the large room. Sewer Dragons, with their long coats and metallic limbs. Some were looking our way; others were fiddling with tablets or pushing crates along or just minding their own business. "Do they?" she asked.

"Yes," he said. "They do. They're all commission-based, temp-contract workers for the city of STE New Montreal."

"STE?" I muttered.

The department in charge of the city's sewerage: Société de transport des égouts du Nouveau Montréal.

"Oh, fuck me," I said.

Bureaucrats.

I'd rather have my legs eaten by an alien than deal with that kind of shit.

CHAPTER EIGHTEEN

FLUSH PRIME

In 2034, Wallace Everyman, rich tycoon and owner of Theracore, discovered his London penthouse filled with a foot of untreated sewer water. It was an act of vandalism caused by some activists fighting against his new proposal that would tax employees based on the number of hours worked.

As the news went around, the ultra-rich and top-percenters became worried that such an attack could be carried out against their own homes.

Then, middle-management officer J. Grimm proposed Flush Prime, a service whereupon the undesirables of the rich would be treated with the respect they deserved . . . for a small monthly fee.

In 2047 it was discovered that Flush Prime never actually existed as anything more than a very expensive pipe dream.

—Excerpt from *The Great Scams*, 2052

Bob was actually pretty nice, I decided.

"C'mon," he said once it became clear we didn't have a clue what we were doing. The man turned and led us through one of the doors at the end of the room where an admin area was laid out. There were a few desks in neat cubicles and posters on the wall, mostly maps of the sewers or blueprints of some sewage plants, but there were a few nude women with spread legs and the sort of proportions that were only possible with extensive surgery, or in cartoons. Classy place.

The far end of the room had a few screens with the camera feeds overlooking what looked like a really complex command center.

"Right this way," Bob said. He opened a second door into a small office and plopped himself down behind a chair with a heavy thump. "Close the door, please."

I slid in before Gomorrah, then found a spot by the corner. I felt like the world's most boring voyeur.

Bob gestured to a grubby seat across from his desk. It was the only seat in the room not covered in papers or soda cans. Once everything was settled, he reached up and removed his helmet. "Now, what's a samurai doing down here?"

"You knew I was a samurai?" Gomorrah asked.

"Kinda obvious, isn't it?"

"And you're not . . . worried?"

Bob shrugged. "Might've lied on a few reports here and there. Taken a bribe or two in my day. But I never did nothing worth that sort of attention. I'm responsible for making sure the three-odd billion tons of sewage getting pumped by here don't explode and get processed well enough. It's boring work, but the pay's all right, and someone's gotta do it."

"I . . . see. You don't mind the Sewer Dragons?"

"Them? Course not. I run this plant, that's it. The Sewer Dragons take care of their home. Mighty thankful for it too. No one else will do what they do."

"And what's that?" Gomorrah asked.

"Everything," Bob said. "They know how every machine works, can tell something's fucked by the noise or smell alone. They'll dive in sludge to fix valves, and run down lines that'll kill a normal man from the smell alone just to kick at a clog."

"Huh," Gomorrah said.

Bob nodded. "Folks don't know it, but without the Dragons, this city would go to shit. So I don't mind them, nor does anyone else up top. You wouldn't imagine how much it would cost to replace them with 'normal' folk. Billions, trillions, even."

Bob gestured, and Gomorrah leaned back as she received a file. It was shared my way almost immediately.

I opened it, curious (and trusting that Myalis was right and that it wasn't some virus-filled thing). The entire document was text. Thick, boring text, occasionally broken up with a wonderful graph that was entirely incomprehensible. "What am I looking at?" I asked.

A cost-analysis breakdown, done in 2050 by the city of New Montreal, estimating the cost of hiring civilian contractors and additional city workers in order to operate the sewer systems. The final tally is in the order of several billion credits. A month.

That . . . probably made some sense. No wonder the city was happy to keep the Sewer Dragons around.

"Interesting," Gomorrah said. "Maybe you can assist me. I'm looking for a group of people that were abducted by the Sewer Dragons. We suspect they're in one of these locations."

I imagined that Gomorrah sent Bob a copy of the map. The foreman nodded along. "All right. Most of 'em are good enough folk. Weird, but not all bad. Might have a few bad apples here taking people off the street. It's something they've done before."

"Why?" Gomorrah asked.

"Parts, because they're horny, because they need more hands working on the shit they do. Who knows?" Bob said.

I grimaced. Not the nicest reasoning, there. And how little he cared wasn't pleasant either. Then again, most people wouldn't give two shits about some homeless.

"Do you know how we can reach that section?" Gomorrah asked.

"That's past the edge of SPT-44," Bob said. "But I think I can show you a way over. You'll want to go down the east corridor a good ways, then you'll see a sign on an embankment labeled 'Ratways.' Get in there, and head to . . . is that . . . yeah, you'll want sludge line 537. The place you're looking for, the nearest one, should be off of junction 6H-dash-5K."

Gomorrah nodded slowly. "I have it mapped."

"You'll want to be careful down there. The sludge lines aren't bad, but they're not safe either. Shit-skimmer accidents happen, and you can't swim in sludge. It'll suck you right in, like quicksand. And the Ratways have some nasty folk in them, but usually they'll be pretty far from the more civilized parts of the sewer."

"Thank you," Gomorrah said.

"No problem. Anything, as long as it doesn't have me filling out more paperwork."

Gomorrah stood up, then extended her hand to Bob.

"No, no, we don't shake down here," he said.

"I see. Well, in either case, thank you for the directions."

Gomorrah headed to the door and held it open for just a moment so that I could follow her out. I got a call almost as soon as we were back in the offices. "He was distracting us. He sent a message to some server warning them that a samurai was down here," Gomorrah said.

"Oh, great," I responded.

"Yeah, he looked like the sleazy sort," Raccoon said.

"Because he was fat and dirty?" I asked.

"Huh? Nah, because he does paperwork stuff," she replied.

A fair and just point. "Think his directions are worth following?" I asked.

"They're pretty straightforward," Gomorrah said. My map flashed and updated, a yellow line cutting through it toward one of the flashing buildings. "I think it's similar to what Atyacus projected as a route."

"Is there a way to get to those places overland? Like, without being in the sewers?"

Some locations can be reached from the exterior. The sewer system is mostly suspended beneath the structure holding the city in place, and large portions of it should be accessible from the exterior. But some areas are buried inside the hexplate, and others are within the basements of the structures above.

"Right," I said. "That's how they kidnapped people; every building is linked to the sewers. Damn, if they try to run away, we'll never catch anyone."

Gomorrah nodded as she stepped out into the main corridor again. The Sewer Dragons who had been around earlier were conspicuously missing.

"Well, fuck."

"No choice about it," Gomorrah said. "Let's keep moving. It shouldn't be easy for them to hide as many people as they've abducted."

"It's not like they can just flush them away," I grumbled.

We were quiet after that, walking down the surprisingly loud corridor, Gomorrah's footfalls echoing ahead of us along with the rumble of the working ventilation. The corridor straightened after the curve, though the floor wasn't level. It took me a few steps to realize there was a slight uphill tilt to it.

Weird. And also annoying to walk on.

The passage went on and on, with alcoves on the sides and places where the walls would open up and large pipes with QR-coded labels ran through.

"That's the Ratways," Gomorrah said a little ways down. She gestured ahead to an alcove that was very obviously surrounded by a knee-high wall. There were spikes on the inside of the wall, each about half a foot long.

"What the hell is up with that?" I asked.

"I'm assuming it has to do with the rats," she said.

"Rats tall enough you'd place the spikes this high off the ground?" I asked. "No, don't answer. I've seen some big rats before." But never any that required spike walls.

"Yeah, they're real fucking big," Rac said. "I saw one the size of a dog once. Like, a decent-sized dog. Some of them are covered in boils and, like, tumors and shit, because they're not smart and they'll eat anything. You hear stories about packs of them pouring out of sewer grates and eating homeless people or people carrying food that's not sealed right."

I was beginning to suspect that Gomorrah and I were in for a fun morning.

CHAPTER NINETEEN

HUMANITY DEGRADED

When cybernetic replacements became more common, there was this prevalent fear that they would make a person less human.

The notion that having a bionic heart or a mechanical hand makes a person any less greedy, vain, prideful, and dumb, is entirely wrong, of course.

—Excerpt from a VoidFight Forum post, 2033

"So, where are we going?" I asked as we pushed past the entrance into . . . I guessed it was the Ratways, at least judging by the stencils on the nearest wall.

"Down this passage until that large junction ahead into sludge line 537. It looks like it's a big tunnel that goes on for . . . a few kilometers actually. It might be a long walk," Gomorrah said.

"If I may interject," Myalis said, speaking through my coms so everyone could hear. "The locals use vehicles to travel across the larger lines, including sludge line 537."

"Who's that?" Rac asked.

I heard Franny inhaling. "That was a saint's companion," she said with a weird amount of reverence."

"That's just Myalis, my AI," I said.

"'Just'?" Myalis asked.

"She's very arrogant for a bunch of ones and zeroes," I added.

Myalis was quiet for a while. "I won't argue, except to correct you on two mistakes you have made. First, it isn't arrogance if it is entirely earned. Second, I'm hardly made of something as primitive as *binary*."

"Your AI is a lot more vocal than Atyacus," Gomorrah said. She ducked under a low-hanging pipe, and I did the same right after her.

"You mean Myalis is more interesting than Atyacus," I shot back.

The Ratways really deserved their names. The passageway was a long series of corridors, cut apart by large bulkhead doors that were usually left wide open. Each segment was filled with pipes, either vertical along the sides or straight horizontal pipes that cut across the ceiling. QR labels were slapped onto all of them, though I imagined some of the pipes weren't being used for much, especially those that looked like they were rusted through.

There was a nice sludge of decomposing detritus in the corners, though I did recognize some of the trash. Cups and straws and brightly colored boxes from a few fast-food joints I knew.

"People ahead."

I blinked out of my reverie and focused. Gomorrah wouldn't say something like that for shits and giggles.

I tapped Gomorrah on the shoulder. "Let me check," I said.

She nodded, then shifted to the side where part of the cement wall that jutted out would cover her a little better. Her flamethrower came up, ready to spray whatever goop she had in there.

Walking carefully, I moved up to the next bulkhead. The door was all metal and about as thick as my thumb. It had some instructions stickered to it and a complicated wheel lock. I made sure not to touch it as I peeked into the next room over.

It was a larger segment. The ceiling was still low, but the room was wider, with cement half walls spaced out evenly across. There was a bulkhead at the end but also one to the right, between two cement half arches that reached the ceiling.

I couldn't see anyone, but it wasn't hard to hear the shuffling of cloth and the slow sound of people breathing.

Three of them? No, more than that. Five, with two of them hiding behind one air vent that was rattling loud enough to wake the dead.

I reached under my coat and grabbed my Icarus's handle. The moment I pulled the launcher out, it would be visible.

"Five dudes," I said, voice low. I trusted my helmet's voice dampening, but I wasn't taking chances. "One to the right, three at the rear, one more to the left, behind that vent thing."

"All right," Gomorrah said. "How do you want to do this?"

"I'll move in, then foam our two buddies to the left from the back; that way I can take out the next three, then the last two. If I do it right, they'll never have time to react or figure anything out."

"Not a terrible plan," Gomorrah said. She moved up next to me, footfalls light on the cement floor. She had the door between her and the other side. "I'll move in when it all goes terribly wrong."

"It's not going to go terribly wrong," I said.

Then I stepped in and everything went terribly wrong.

"The air shifted," one of them said. It was a whisper that I heard repeated from all the others. Shitty headsets, maybe? They were organized enough to have coms, at least.

I started to move to the left, intent on skirting around the edge of the room.

Then one of them tossed something over their barricade, and I crouched down and winced, waiting for the explosion as the thing . . . thumped to the ground with barely any noise?

I turned and stared at what looked like a large wet bundle of rolled-up socks. "Huh?" I asked.

Then the bundle started to hiss, and a faint smoke poured out of it and across the room.

That's just a plain smoke grenade.

"How do you know?" I asked.

Your helmet's filtration system can detect potassium chlorate, lactose, and other components in the smoke.

The smoke was rising, coming out faster now, and I could see it swirling around my feet. "Is something moving there?" one of the ambushers asked.

That was good enough for me to start the party.

I whipped my Icarus up and placed the gun's red arc over the heads of the nearest group, then fired. Turning, I aimed toward the back where my targets conveniently stood up, guns rising as they aimed in my general direction.

I was expecting some bangs, but instead the air filled with loud thumps that sounded more like a pneumatic hammer than a gun going off. Still, something clattered off the walls behind me, and I ducked while squeezing my Icarus's trigger.

The next four shots I took went wide, one smacking into the barricade they were using for cover, and then I finally hit one of the assholes shooting at me, right in the face.

He gurgled something that sounded like a curse before foam expanded around his face and upper torso. "Got one!" I cheered.

A pair of rounds rammed into my side, and I winced reflexively before my mind caught up and I realized that it hadn't actually hurt.

Gomorrah stepped into the room and put an end to the little shoot-out: one spray to the right, then an arc of foam sent splashing across the far end of the room, off-white goop splattering everything and expanding in seconds to swallow up any of the idiots around us.

I stood up from my half crouch and searched for more targets, but the room was cleared. The most any of the five could do was kick with their legs while their torsos were glued to the ground.

"Well done," I said.

"That's three for me, two for you," Gomorrah said.

I blinked. Was she being competitive all of a sudden? We'd worked together for a few days, and I'd never really had the impression that she cared about getting more kills or anything of the sort. Then again, we had never fought with an audience watching over us. "You know what my aim is like," I said.

Gomorrah hummed something noncommittal and moved over to one of the ambushers, who was stuck in the foam in such a way that the top of his head was still partially visible. His eyes were darting around madly, and he was twitching from side to side to try to free himself. Gomorrah pointed the end of her flamethrower's nozzle into his face. "We have questions," she said.

Then she fired.

I'd half expected fire, and from the gasp I overheard, so had Franny. Instead, a yellowish liquid splattered onto the guy's face and the foam melted away, revealing his entire head. "Whaa!" he shouted.

I had to hold back a snort at that. Seeing as how there wasn't anyone around, I flicked off my cloaking. "Hey there, pal," I said. "Myalis, shut off their coms, please. And can you root around and see what they were thinking?"

Five guys with what looked like pneumatic guns trying to take out even a single samurai was suicidal, at least by most standards.

"Who are you, and why were you trying to ambush me?" Gomorrah asked.

"Didn't know you were a samurai!" he said. "We heard some corpo-types were here making noise."

"And your first idea was to attack?"

"This is our home!" he shouted.

I shook my head. This guy sounded like he was on the wrong end of zealous. "Who told you we were here?" I asked.

"The doc! The doc pays attention to that kind of thing."

I do have some messages from a contact calling itself Doc Hack. They claim a single corporate agent would be at our current location and they should be killed and disposed of.

I shut off my helmet coms. "Any sign that the good doc knew we were samurai?"

No obvious signs, no.

"Anything about the folk we're looking for?" I asked.

Not directly. But there might be some oblique references. Doc Hack has been putting out requests on what's essentially a community bounty board for cybernetic parts. It seemed quite urgent.

"Huh," I said. "Can you figure anything out from the sort of parts they're looking for?" I asked.

At a guess, they are converting more people into Sewer Dragons. Notably, a group was praised for breaking into a factory from its sewer connection and stealing a crate full of commercial-grade cybernetic lung replacements.

"Fuck," I said.

That didn't bode well.

CHAPTER TWENTY

UP SHIT'S CREEK

They tried, you know. Way back in the late 2020s, there was this whole thing where they tried to cut down on drug use. It wasn't all that great. The world was going to shit; what did they expect, people to inject less shit into themselves?

Nah, we still made bank. It became harder to move materials around, but then, no one ever really checked the sewers.

—Excerpt from a 2049 autobiography

One thing became increasingly clear as Gomorrah questioned our ambushers. They didn't know jack shit.

If they did know something, then they weren't spilling. Myalis and Atyacus both took a turn rooting around in their augments to see if there was anything worth finding, but other than some questionable kinks, a few bits of potential blackmail, and a lot of mundane messages, there wasn't really anything worth our time.

One of them knew about the kidnappings. A younger member had been helping transport some people grabbed from the upper levels. He was a ferry driver, and that meant he had seen the kidnapped people being shifted to one of the locations Myalis had tagged as a likely spot for the kidnapped to be housed in.

But as for the why, he had nothing.

"This is such a waste of time," I muttered as I stood up from a crouch. Talking to our new buddies was made more complicated when all of them were glued to the floors and walls in rather awkward positions.

The goop was starting to melt off, though. Given another four or five hours, they'd be able to start fighting their way free. I didn't plan on being around for that.

"I think I agree," Gomorrah said. "Any ideas, Raccoon, Franny?"

"No. These people seem like . . . pardon the term, but they seem like lowlifes. They're not at the top of the food chain."

"The way they put it, there's no food chain around here," I said. I reached up to rub at my nose, then sighed and let my hand drop. Masks were annoying. "I think we might need to go pay this Doc Hack guy a visit, though. He doesn't seem to be quite in charge, but he is giving out orders, which is close enough."

"I think I've heard of him," Rac said. "He's, like, this super-smart guy who used to be a bigwig in some company, but then he did something sleazy and he came down into the sewers to be left alone. He's been there forever, though. Some people say he's like a bogeyman."

"Oh, great," I said. I loved the idea of a sewer-dwelling bogeyman. The name Doc Hack inspired such great imagery too. I could imagine telling the kittens to shut up and go to sleep, or else Doc Hack would show up and gut them.

"Should we keep moving?" Gomorrah asked. "I have the codes for one of their vehicles."

"That'll save us some points," I muttered. "Yeah, let's move on. These guys can chill out over here. Do a bit of thinking about all of their, uh, sins or whatever."

"Being glued to the floor isn't exactly like visiting a confessional," Franny said.

I laughed as I gestured to the end of the room. "We're continuing down that way?"

Gomorrah took the lead with a nod, and I fell in behind her while turning my stealth systems back on. We still had a little ways to go.

The Ratways earned their name in the very next room. Gomorrah and I both froze as we came face to face with a rat the size of a small dog. It stared at Gomorrah with its two beady eyes, and then its whiskers twitched and it skittered off and into an open grate it really shouldn't have been able to fit through.

"I'm gonna go back and close the doors. I don't want our buddies to be eaten by one of those," I said.

"Good idea."

I jogged back into the room, checked around for rats, and, on seeing none, closed the massive steel bulkheads. I even picked up one of those airguns and placed it in the arms of one of the guys who had a bit of mobility. "For the rats," I explained.

He swore at me, but I think he understood what I meant.

I closed the last door from the other side as I rejoined Gomorrah. "Right, let's keep moving," I said.

I made sure my railguns were ready to deploy at a moment's notice. If we got buried by a pile of those rats, I wanted the firepower to kill them dead.

"I'm really not fond of this place," I said. "It's a shit hole."

"Is that some sort of pun?" Gomorrah asked.

"No, it's a fact."

We crossed a few smaller rooms, occasionally after something scurried out of the way. There were enough droppings around to guess what.

And then, at long last, we reached the next junction, a space where the room ended with a staircase going up and onto an airlock. The airlock wasn't anything impressive. Two bulkheads with a rod system in the middle made it so that opening one door closed the other.

We crossed through and into the sludge line.

"Fuck," I said as I took it in.

Sludge line 537 was a long tunnel, set at a slight angle so the sludge could flow down and toward us. It was wider than some highways, with an arched ceiling with LED lights casting their glow onto the river of shit below.

This wasn't some brownish water, but a thick paste of stuff, like one of those store-bought cream of whatever soups. Small bits of detritus stood out in the muck, making it easier to see the gentle flow of it.

Pipes stuck out of the walls at even intervals, occasionally disgorging a downpour of sludge like a frat kid vomiting out his last Mexican-alcohol fusion meals.

"Those have to be their vehicles," Gomorrah said.

I followed her gaze to a makeshift dock set into the side of the tunnel, accessible from a ramp. Three boats were parked there. I think they were pontoon boats, but my knowledge of nautical things started and ended with what I'd picked up from rerun cartoons.

"They don't look so reliable," I said.

Of the three, two looked like they'd been scavenged from one time too many, which meant there really was just one boat we could use.

The third was about as big as a minivan, with hip-high walls around it covered in a nice spray of shit over off-white plastic boards. There was a small cabin in the center, with a window and a wheel next to some levers that no doubt operated the whole thing.

"That's our ride?" I asked.

"It's that or we swim," Gomorrah said. "Or you could buy something."

"I'm not buying a vehicle specifically made to navigate through shit," I said. "That's . . . such a waste of points. No, let's use that thing."

I started to regret my choice the moment I walked down the ramp leading to the dock. The boat was even worse from up close, with a few holes in its bottom and some obvious decay all over. Even the bits that looked like they were made of aluminum looked like they were starting to fall apart.

"I don't believe this thing was made for these conditions," Gomorrah said as she leapt onto the boat. It bobbed in place, sending a few quick-fading ripples through the sludge.

"I pity the poor idiot who discovered that their boat was stolen and brought over here," I said.

Gomorrah installed herself behind the wheel and looked over the controls. There was a small onboard computer on the dashboard, with a touch screen that was entirely dark. She poked at it, then the obvious "on" button next to it. Predictably it did nothing. "There's nothing on here to start the engine," Gomorrah said.

I shifted over to the back and grimaced at the onboard. "I think it's electric?" There wasn't an obvious gas tank or an exhaust. The latches to the side of the engine were undone, so I tugged them open, then stared at the stuff within. "There's a gun here," I said. "And . . . I think those are batteries?"

There was a thick wire with a metal loop on the end dangling next to a battery post. I grabbed the wire and touched it to the post, then shifted my legs for balance as the engine whined to life and started to push the boat forward—while we were still connected to the dock.

"That worked," Gomorrah said. She throttled down and the boat stopped bobbing quite so badly.

"Great," I said as I slammed the case shut. I walked over to the nearest line holding the boat in place and, after a moment of staring, recalled that I had a super suit that had very sharp nails. The shitty ropes holding us in place didn't last long.

The boat moved over toward the middle of the sludge line, and Gomorrah spun it around to face the direction we had to go. There weren't any seats on the boat, so I gravitated to the middle and hung on to the cabin.

"Let's get going, then," Gomorrah said.

"I'm real happy I'm here and not there," Rac said.

I didn't say anything, but I wished I were back there.

CHAPTER TWENTY-ONE

DISPOSAL

Want your biological junk gone? Call Want-Not today!
Safe and sanitary biowaste disposal since 2023!
—Excerpt from an ad for the biological waste and pseudo-meat
production company Want-Not, Inc., 2034

The pontoon boat moved like one of those little four-wheeled scooters that walking whales used when they were shopping in the bigger discount stores. That's to say, it was slow as hell, and, judging from the engine's whine, it was having a hard time even keeping up this pace.

"This is like the world's worst amusement park ride," I said as I looked around. The walls were all arched up, with large struts every dozen meters, and lights hanging off them to brighten things up a little. But only a little.

"Something tells me you haven't ever been to an amusement park," Gomorrah said.

"I have, actually. The orphanage got this cheap trip to this amusement park, just outside the city. Big rides, lots of tourists and middle-class sorts. We were there for some photo-shoot thing. You know, bunch of kids who can all smile, most of them obviously disabled in some way so the place looks like it's inclusive and shit."

"That sounds . . . nice?" Gomorrah tried.

"Eh, we weren't allowed on the rides, but we got lots of free food and stuff. I'm pretty sure Lucy stole a shirt too. She might still have it somewhere."

Gomorrah shook her head, but she kept her attention fixed on the waters ahead. The trip was going to be a dull one, I figured.

"I hear places like that have the best trash if you're looking for food and stuff," Rac said. "There's this man on sub six. He buys any meat you can pick up. Ten credits per pound. I bet you could make thousands just from the stuff they throw away at a park."

"What does he do with the meat?" I asked.

"Sausages."

Made sense.

"That's disgusting," Franny said.

"Don't you love street food?" Gomorrah asked.

"Not anymore" was Franny's quick reply.

I laughed. At least we had good conversation to make the ride a little less dull. Then I heard something ahead, a low rumble that was growing louder. It didn't sound like the gurgle of shit water coming out from some of the smaller pipes either.

"Gom, someone's heading this way," I said. I pulled out my Icarus and checked its ammo count. Down to five rounds. Good enough for something small, probably.

"Could just be normal traffic down here," Gomorrah said. Her shoulder-mounted flamethrowers deployed anyway, which said a lot about how confident she was in that statement.

I tucked my launcher under my coat and made my way to the front of the boat, careful about the part of the floor that looked corroded through. We were bobbing along hard enough that some of the slush we were cutting across splashed up and onto the sides of the boat, painting it in a fresh coat of brackish brown.

I really, really didn't want to fall into the sludge.

The rumble grew louder, and I leaned around, ready to draw my gun at a moment's notice.

Gomorrah moved us off to the side so that we were riding next to the rightmost wall. I figured that normal traffic laws might apply down here. The tunnel curved ahead; I wouldn't be able to see what was coming until we were nearly in the middle of the bend.

A ship came rushing by us. Not a pontoon boat like the one we were on, but a proper boat with a tall, shit-covered hull, old rubber tires hanging off the sides, and a cabin at the rear. There were three Sewer Dragons sitting at the front, one of them behind a mounted gun.

They stared at us as we moved past.

We were nearing the middle of the curve, bobbing up and down in the wake of their passage, when I heard the ship come to a stop and start to turn around.

"Shit," I said as I moved to the back of the boat. "I'll keep them busy. Can you go any faster in this thing?" I asked.

"Not much," Gomorrah said. She pushed the throttle up, and the electric engine hummed a notch louder. It didn't feel like we were moving faster.

The boat chasing after us rumbled around the bend, the three gang members at the front aiming ahead of them, obviously ready to fire. I tightened my grip around my gun and waited. They didn't fire yet.

They sped up, quickly approaching while bouncing along through the sludge.

Grinning, I flicked off my invisibility and raised my Icarus, starting to squeeze the trigger even as I aimed the glowing target line over the front of the ship.

All three Sewer Dragons started screaming. "Wait! Wait!"

I paused, and I saw Gomorrah glancing back. They weren't pointing their guns our way, at least, and most were waving their arms around like mad.

"What?" I called back.

They were coming closer. "Does that thing explode?" one of them asked, his free hand pointing at my Icarus.

"Uh, it can," I said.

"Methane's at seven percent!" the guy behind the gun screamed. "Are you trying to kill us all?"

"Huh?" I asked.

I think he's referring to the fact that the current composition of the air around you is made up of seven point two percent methane. There's also a decently dangerous percentage of hydrogen sulfide, as well as trace elements of a dozen other highly flammable chemicals.

"Don't you guys have guns?" I asked.

"We use compressed air!" one of them shouted. He raised his gun, revealing a rather bulbous stock that had what looked like a tank stuck in it.

"Cool," I said. "I'm firing expanding foam grenades. They're non-explosive, and I don't think they launch using an explosion either. No fire."

I wiggled my Icarus around.

We both stared at each other, still bobbing along at a decent clip over the dirty waters. "So we can shoot at each other?" one of them asked.

"I guess so," I replied. "Uh. Why were you going to shoot at us in the first place?"

"You're from the government! Here to kidnap some of us!"

"What?" I asked. "Do I look like a fed?"

The guys stared at me, then at each other.

"I'm a samurai, for fuck's sake," I shouted back. "I'm here to look for kidnapped people."

"The people Doc took?" one of them shot back.

I really didn't know what to say to that. "Yes?"

"Shoot her!"

"Are you fucking—" I ducked down as a spray of pellets zipped through the air above me. They might not have been shooting proper guns, but it was hard to tell when being shot at.

Gomorrah spun the wheel, throwing us across to the other side of the tunnel and casting a wake behind us that had the faster boat chopping up and down through the wastewater. "You're terrible at negotiations!" she screamed.

"Oh, shut up. Watch them negotiate this!"

Standing on wobbly legs, I brought my launcher around and fired, five squeezes of the trigger that sent an equal number of glittering shells toward the Sewer Dragon boat. The first two missed, but the other three were dead on. One even slugged one of the Dragons in the arm, and, when the shell burst, it glued him to the deck.

His pals weren't too pleased with that.

"Fuck!" I shouted as I felt a dozen little pinpricks across my chest. The heavier gun was firing as if ammo wasn't a concern, and I winced as it left little pinholes all across the surface of the pontoon.

Dipping to one knee, I let go of my Icarus so it dangled by my side and reached for my Trench Maker, then paused. That did use an explosive to fire, didn't it?

"Myalis, rails?"

Entirely safe.

My railguns deployed from over my shoulder and my vision filled with twin reticles that I locked onto the ship's rear, about where I figured the pilot was.

Two thumps tugged my shoulders back as a pair of railgun rounds shot out and punched a pair of holes into the hull.

Didn't seem to do much. "Dammit!" I shouted.

"This is so fucking cool," Rac said.

"You're taking on water," Franny replied.

I blinked, then looked down. The nun was right—the bottom of the boat was filling with sludge, some of it pouring through the holes in the floor. Our pontoon was starting to fill up.

"Shit," I said. "Gom! Ram them! We're taking their boat."

"We're what?" Gomorrah asked.

I moved up, a foot on the edge bent so I'd be ready to jump. "We're going pirate!" I shouted back. Then, as Gomorrah veered us into the other boat's path, I jumped.

CHAPTER TWENTY-TWO

PIRACY ACROSS THE SHITTY SEAS

It can't just be about choosing people who aren't asses. There's something else to it.

I don't know what it is, though. The numbers are hard to grab, but it's something like ninety percent of all samurai who turn around and start fighting to help people, but only in a very narrow, select way that won't entirely destabilize society at large.

Selection bias is a factor, sure, but there has to be more to it than that. We ran the numbers, entering every last bit of information we could about people, and we have access to their media feeds. The best our machine-learning algorithms could pull up was some weird correlation between time spent reading on the shitter and people who become samurai.

It's not just about people with a certain mindset. People are too muta-ble. There's something else at play, and I can't figure out what it is.

—Intercepted message between CIA analysts, 2024

I was never very acrobatic. For that matter, I was never all that strong either. Fortunately, I had badass power armor to make up for some of my deficiencies.

My jump over the edge of the boat wasn't perfect. A larger wave and maybe some faster reactions from the pilot, and there was no way I would have made it aboard. As it was, I banged both shins on the edge of the boat and rolled forward into it.

I was pitched to the bottom, but I tucked at the last moment and landed shoulder-first, which meant I could roll and crash onto the bottom back-first.

Which left me near the pointed front of the boat, on my back, between the legs of the two Sewer Dragons who weren't glued down.

The one on the big mounted turret swung his gun around to point at me, only for the gun to stop before reaching the angle needed to shoot me. It couldn't depress low enough.

I didn't have any such issues as I kicked out, heel first, and rammed him in the shin hard enough that I heard something snap.

His pant leg tore and a metallic bar pierced through the tough fabric where his obviously prosthetic leg had broken. He tumbled down onto his ass, the entire boat shifting with the sudden motion.

Dragon number two jumped down onto me and grasped for joints in my armor. I think he'd done the mental math and figured shooting me wasn't cutting it. Maybe he planned on tossing me overboard?

I wrestled with him for a moment until I got one arm free and had enough room to swing a punch into his face. The first made him wobble. The second cracked against his jaw and he went stiff and collapsed onto me.

Swearing under my breath, I shoved him to the bottom of the boat, then wobbled onto my feet. The idiot on the ground who'd been behind the fixed gun pulled out a small handgun he aimed at my chest.

He fired.

The bullets went clink-clink.

I kicked at him. I intended to hit the gun, but the awful footing and bumpy ride had me kicking higher. I hit him in the wrist. I couldn't hold back a wince as I saw his clearly mechanical hand detach from his arm and go flying overboard. No one was retrieving that anytime soon.

I kept myself low as I moved toward the back of the ship and the little cabin there.

The guy in it stared at me coming, wide-eyed, until I tore the door open and grabbed him by the front of his shirt. "Throttle down," I asked, politely.

Almost meekly, he reached over to a lever in the ship's console and carefully lowered it to the sound of the boat's engine slowing down.

I kept a hold of him as I looked behind us. Gomorrah was still in our shitty little pontoon boat, puttering along and getting closer at a decent clip. "Don't do anything stupid," I warned the pilot before I moved to the back of the boat.

Gomorrah slowed down so that when she inevitably bumped into us, it was just a small lurch, the tires along the edges of both boats squeaking with the impact.

"What do we do with them?" Gomorrah asked as she casually stepped up and onto our new ride.

"Uh, toss them in the shit?" I asked with a gesture to the flowing river of sludge next to us. I had the impression it was moving along faster now. Could have been wrong about that, though.

"They'll drown," Franny said with all the indignity a nun could muster.

I shrugged. "They were shooting us," I said. "And don't tell me that bat of yours has a nonlethal setting on it."

"I'm sure there are other options," Gomorrah said. She moved into the cabin, opened the door, then stared at the trembling idiot within. "Out."

"All right, fine," I said. She was taking her girl's side, which, while annoying, was entirely fair. "Hey, idiot, help me load your idiot friends up onto the other boat."

"The one that's sinking?" Gomorrah asked.

"They'll have five minutes to get somewhere," I replied. "Less if this guy's slow about it."

As it turned out, he might've been an idiot, but he was a highly motivated one. We flung his one-armed, one-legged buddy aboard, and then the guy I conked on the chin woke up and managed to stumble onto the boat too. The only idiot who proved a challenge was the one I'd glued to the back of the boat, but I solved that by breaking off the prosthetic arm I'd glued to the hull with a few well-placed kicks.

"You didn't want to keep them around for questioning?" Gomorrah asked as we watched the four of them move off. The pontoon boat was sitting noticeably lower in the water. I didn't think they had all that much time left.

"Nah. I figure they know fuck-all, and at this point it's pretty clear what we're doing here isn't an investigation."

"What is it, then?" Gomorrah asked.

"This is a good old-fashioned un-kidnapping," I replied before I cocked my head to the side. "I can hear something else coming. We might have more company on the way."

"I'll get us moving."

Nodding, I moved to the front of the boat again and sat down on a plank that seemed to serve as a bench. "Myalis, more sticky ammo, please," I said.

New Purchase: Nonlethal Explosive Ammunition
Points Reduced from . . . 10,891 to . . . 10,881

I reloaded my gun while the boat picked up speed. Then, once that was done, I eyed my map. Myalis was kind enough to mark the route we had to take in green, with the path we'd already taken grayed out behind us. Our little adventure so far had taken us about halfway there.

Good enough.

I moved to the very front of the boat when the noise of something moving up ahead became even louder. I slid down, one knee wedged into the tip of the boat and my Icarus up to my shoulder. I turned on my invisibility. Someone might be able to see my gun, but that was it.

"Is it always like that?" Rac asked.

"Like what?" I asked.

"You know, running around, scaring the hell out of idiots. Shooting shit?"

I laughed. "Nah. Usually it's aliens. They're a lot trickier than people. Not that I have a ton of experience, you know. I'm not the kind of girl who's had a lot of jobs, but so far, this one's not bad. Good exercise, you get some great perks, visit fascinating new places." I gestured to the shitty tunnels around us.

"I bet! That's, like, the coolest job ever," Rac said.

I shrugged. "It's not too bad, honestly. Dangerous, but so far the pay's been worth it. You get to save people, you know? Sure, you're putting your neck on the line, but it's worth it sometimes. Depending on the people you're saving."

"You think of yourself as a hero?" Franny asked. There was surprisingly little judgment there.

"Nah. I'm no hero," I said.

The tunnel had a bend ahead, and as we came to it, a pair of speedy little boats came around. They had guys in familiar augs with guns out. I raised my Icarus, lining up the firing arc with the first ship, then fired. Three shots, and then I moved on to the next boat and fired again.

By the time we crossed them properly, the foam covering the boats was expanding and the two were veering off course and bumping into the walls while their occupants screamed and cursed.

"I'm not a hero," I repeated. "Just a girl with a bit of luck, a lot of guns, and . . . I guess it's the willingness not to let good folks get fucked over."

"Nice speech," Gomorrah said. "Can you focus on the road ahead?"

"Yeah, sure," I said. "You just don't want us to start talking about your philosophy on the whole samurai thing."

"What philosophy?" Franny asked.

I could almost feel the daggers being glared into my back.

CHAPTER TWENTY-THREE

SURPRISE!

Every generation complains about the music of the next generation. It's just how it works. Older folk don't get new music.

But my music? It transcends genre. BeepBoopCore is the future of noise!

—Excerpt from an interview with the European samurai Mix, 2031

Our trek down sludge line 537 continued uneventfully. Gomorrah didn't want to press us into going too quickly, and I was entirely fine with moving along at a slow but steady pace. I kept an eye on the waters ahead and stayed low and out of the way in case we ran into any surprises.

The little green icon that represented us on our map plinked along neatly, moving closer and closer to the intersection where we'd be getting off. Junction 6H. A nice, auspicious name, full of history and class.

"We're getting close," I said.

"We are," Gomorrah said. "The water's different."

I glanced back at her, then down to the sludge, which seemed to be the same almost-greenish brown as it had been the entire time. Maybe there were fewer chunks in it? I couldn't recall seeing as many used sanitary pads floating by as before. Still wasn't tempted to take a dip in it.

"You know, I don't know how to swim," I said.

"You mention that now?" Gomorrah asked.

"What was I going to do? Buy some floaties?"

Gomorrah shook her head. "I don't know, but I'm quite certain there's at least one flotation device available in your catalogs. Or an implant to teach you how to swim, at least."

"This armor's heavy. I'm pretty sure I'd swim like a brick in this. Also, a teaching implant?"

"You need a small implant in your brain. It connects to . . . well, your brain. Then you can download some lessons and, over a few hours, they'll teach you something. It's . . . not exactly pleasant? It feels like being on a sugar high the entire time. You keep getting weird flashes, as if you're . . .

have you ever forgotten something, like it was on the tip of your tongue, then it hit you for a moment, but it wasn't important anymore?"

"Yeah, sure," I said. "I can't remember birthdays. Lucy's been real miffed about it a few times, when I remember that hers was a week ago and I didn't get her anything."

"Right, well . . . I suppose it's something like that for a few hours. Mildly annoying, because even as you're doing other things, you keep having stray thoughts that aren't exactly yours. But it does work."

"Huh. What've you learned with that so far?" I asked.

"Driving was the big one," Gomorrah said. "I haven't really invested in any others yet. They're on the pricier side."

I grimaced. "I'm a bit cheap, you know."

"Yes, because you want to be cheap with your brain implants," Gomorrah said, her tone very flat.

"It is a difficult battle," Myalis said, because of course she had something snarky to say.

That was a fair point. I wasn't too keen on the idea of having stuff jammed in my head like that, but I could see how it might be useful. "Yeah, all right," I said. "Something's coming up ahead, by the way. The sounds are different."

"Different how?" Gomorrah asked.

I shrugged. "More echoey? Like it's a bigger room or something."

"Different acoustics, then."

"That's what I said."

The tunnel didn't widen ahead, at least not the part of it where the shit flowed. Instead, the top of the tunnel opened up into a huge circular room, with a tower in the middle and some bridges leading to openings in the sides, four of them, one for each cardinal direction. The sludge was flowing faster here, even as more of the stuff came down from another large sludge line and was unceremoniously shoved down the same passageway.

The section ahead looked a little different, large mechanical fencelike things dropping into the water, then raking through it before shifting to the side. They were covered with all sorts of thicker crap they were picking out from the sludge.

"There's a dock there," Gomorrah said.

I looked to the right, toward that towerlike section in the center, and noticed a pier extending into the waters. It wasn't too far from the place where it all sped up. I imagined that missing it might mean running a boat into those large raking machines, which I imagined wouldn't be amusing for anyone involved.

It was only when we came closer that I noticed the ropes across the surface of the water.

Gomorrah, being the decent pilot she was, brought us over to an empty pier at a pace that was almost glacial, but it did mean that when it came time to stop we did so with barely more than a slight lurch.

"No one around," I said as I looked about. There was another pontoon boat docked there, but it didn't look like it had been used recently. Not that I really knew what to look for.

Cement steps at the end of the pier led up a level to a section around the base of the tower. There were some windows there, looking into what I guessed was some sort of maintenance or control room.

I hopped off our borrowed ride and wobbled as I landed on the pier. It didn't shake, but I did. I guessed that I'd spent enough time on the waters that I had something like sea legs. But for sewer water. Shit legs? No, better not say that aloud. Rac would laugh, but the other two wouldn't enjoy my incredible humor, so they didn't deserve it.

Gomorrah made a humming noise behind me, and I saw her eyeing the space between the boat and the pier. I gave her my hand and pulled her across. "Do you know how to swim?" I asked.

"Of course I do," she said. "I spent time in the countryside, doing camping stuff. You can only swim in the Great Lakes on some days, but it's enough to learn. I would . . . very much appreciate not swimming in this, though."

"I bet it's nice and warm, though. Warmed up by the bodies of countless New Montrealers."

"Urgh," she said.

Laughing, I moved up the steps and closer to the tower. There was a large door at its base, worn-off instructions next to it, and some rusty rails running around the edge of the sludge line. The handle on the door was one of those big latches. I tugged it open and it revealed a small airlock-like space, with shower hoses on the sides.

"A decontamination shower?" I asked as I carefully stepped inside.

"Looks like it," Gomorrah said as she followed.

I had to close the entrance door to open the other one, which meant Gomorrah and I were practically rubbing shoulders when the shower came on and drizzled water onto us with all the pressure of a drunkard losing his lunch on the sidewalk.

"I feel very decontaminated," I said when it ended some twenty seconds later.

Gomorrah shook herself a little, and I made sure to look her way. For Franny's sake, of course. "It's barely lukewarm," she said.

"I literally have shit on my shins," I grumbled as I looked down. The splash from the boats, I guessed. It was running off me in little rivulets. At least the armor was mostly hydrophobic.

Opening the second door led us into a small room, a spiral staircase on one side, an industrial elevator with ropes across it on the other. There was a small table with some random crap left on it. Mostly delivery boxes.

"Do they deliver food down here?" I asked, incredulous.

"People would eat in this place?" Gomorrah asked.

"The air," Myalis said aloud, "is technically breathable in this location. Though I would advise against it. There are several carcinogens, and the ambient levels of oxygen and other life-sustaining chemicals are lower than would be desirable."

I nodded. "Won't need to tell me twice. I can't imagine the smell here." There were a lot of mask filters in an overflowing trash can to one side, and some small silver bottles in a rack with "O_2" stenciled on their sides. So this place was more like a refilling station before anyone headed out, then? Or something like that.

"We need to go up," Gomorrah said.

I moved to the stairs and bounced on the first step. It creaked, but it didn't seem as badly rusted as the things on the outside of the tower. Maybe being somewhat airtight had advantages.

We climbed up, going around and around until my calves started to burn. I was feeling the exercise in my lungs by the time we reached the next floor up. "These Sewer Dragons are probably pretty fit," I muttered.

"With the amount of prosthetics they have, I doubt that," Gomorrah muttered.

"Which way now?" I asked as I looked around. The next floor up was more of the same. Windows overlooked the sewers below, but judging by the number of pipes in the ceiling, we were still in the thick of things. There were four airlocks around the room.

"That way," Gomorrah said with a gesture to one of the airlocks.

We both got a second terrible shower, this time with a few rare suds in the water. Still not enough water or pressure to do more than make me mildly wet.

The second airlock door opened, and something punched me in the chest. I coughed, the air kicked out of my lungs as my armor locked.

And then I stumbled and fell on my back.

I was suddenly very awake.

CHAPTER TWENTY-FOUR

INGENIOUS

Trash Island is probably the most famous location filled with human waste, but there are other, larger deposits. Notable examples are the Cambodian trash castle, Malaysia, and the Philippines.

There are also super-landfills closer to home.

Such as Florida.

—"Where's the Trash?," *Death Magazine* article, 2046

"Ouch," I said to the dirty ceiling of the decontamination room.

Something banged against my shin, and I folded my knee so that whatever it was could get past.

The door closed, and the room thumped as it locked. "Cat! Are you okay?"

I swallowed, then raised my head. Gomorrah was standing next to the heavy door, a hand on the handle. She'd closed it, which, all things considered, was pretty clever. I looked lower, toward my chest. There was something flat and shiny squished under one breast.

Reaching over, I tugged at it, then inspected the almost flower-shaped disk that must have been a bullet a moment ago. "Oh," I said. "That's what hit me."

My armor had a small smear, the paint over that area scuffed. No dents, though, which was nice. "Are you injured?" Gomorrah asked.

"I don't think so," I said. I climbed onto my elbows. "What the fuck was that?"

"A gun. I think it's a turret—I didn't exactly stop to stare," Gomorrah said.

"Not the nicest welcome," I said.

"I can't detect any electronic switches, or any program designed to fire a weapon in the vicinity. It's possible that the trap is entirely mechanical," Myalis said for our benefit.

Grunting, I half turned, then stumbled to my feet as the shower started to spit and gush water back down onto us. "Great," I said. "Should we try again?"

"You want to get shot again?" Gomorrah asked.

I chuckled. "No. I'm standing to the side this time."

Gomorrah did the same, stepping back so she was pressed up against the wall. I reached over and tugged the door open, the massive thing creaking even as the water from the decontamination shower finally stopped.

Nothing happened.

"All right," I said. "Myalis, do my shoulder guns have cameras?"

They do.

I deployed one of my railguns, then leaned over so that it could poke out around the corner. Myalis helpfully filled the vision of my cybernetic eye with the fish-eyed sight from my gun's camera sight. There was a plain corridor, relatively wide, with pipes here and there and a lot of fifty-five-gallon drums to the side. In the middle of it was a rickety table, one with fold-out legs, and atop that a gun in some homemade rack.

"That thing looks like it was put together by a kid," I said as I flicked my railgun back off and moved into the corridor.

A glance to the side revealed the trigger. A bit of rebar, held in place by a few nails welded into the wall next to the door. A piece of cardboard was taped on the end. Opening the door shoved the cardboard aside and made the rebar drop, which tugged at what looked like a piece of fishing line that ran through some rings all the way over to the gun.

Gomorrah inspected the booby trap, then hummed. "Primitive," she said.

"It worked, though," Rac said.

I rubbed at my chest. "Yeah, it did. Very creative. I'd give the asshole that put this together a gold star if I could find him."

"I don't know if this alerted anyone," Gomorrah said. "It looks like the kind of trap that you just need to know about to avoid." She reached into the decontamination airlock and pulled out a long bar with a crude hook on the end. Something to disarm the trap from within, I guessed.

"There are marks on the walls," Franny said.

"Where?" I asked as I looked around.

"In the airlock," she said. "I thought they were graffiti."

The nun was right; there were some marks painted against the inner edge of the door. "Warnings, then," I said. "They've got their own little codes and shit."

"It's a thieves' cant," Rac said. "Us trash people have something like it. Marks that tell you where good trash is, where the trash cans are watched, which ones are bad, and where to go to get away from the cops."

"Do the Sewer Dragons get attacked often enough to need traps like this?" I asked.

Franny hummed. "They probably do. Most of the gangs in New Montreal are pretty small. One, two buildings. Maybe a district at most. If they get too big, they become a problem, and then someone fixes that problem because it hits their bottom line. Or they start making enough money that a corp steps in and replaces them. The Sewer Dragons are basically the exception to a lot of rules. Their territory is huge, the entire city."

"And that means they bump into every gang, not to mention every corporation, being dicks and wanting to use the sewers for shady shit," I said. "At the same time, they're a necessary evil."

"So it's complicated," Rac said succinctly.

I nodded, then gestured deeper down the corridor. "Shall we?"

"You first," Gomorrah said.

I did have a whole heap more armor on. Still, I took my time as I moved ahead, eyes roving across the walls and ceiling and floor. I was expecting pressure plates and hidden lasers and maybe one of those giant boulders ready to roll down a slight incline.

I wasn't exactly well-versed when it came to traps.

The next section of the corridor was somewhat distinctive. The wall to our right was made of stone. Not cement but rock that had been cut into and chopped apart, the marks left by some no-doubt-massive machine still left over after however much time had passed since they dug this part out.

"How deep are we?" I asked.

"You should be at about sub four," Rac said. "Myalis let me play with the map. So you're pretty deep. There are these big mountain and hill bits that reach up from the dirt-ground and all the way up to the underside of the city in some places."

"All right," I said.

I glanced at my own map, just to have an idea of where we were. There were a lot of corridors ahead, a whole maze of passages, with some ending in elevators that ran up into the sub-basements of the buildings above. We were, if I zoomed out, pretty close to the dead center of New Montreal, the place with the tallest towers and where the richest folk lived.

Our destination was only a couple of hundred meters away, a section filled with small rooms and a few larger areas that might have been factories once. Not necessarily part of the sewers, I didn't think, but connected all the same.

At the next door, both Gomorrah and I paused, then looked around for marks and obvious traps. "There," Gomorrah said; she spotted the little painted symbols first.

"Rac, you know what these mean?" I asked as I stared at them closer. They looked like . . . a house, some squiggles, and what might have been a mask? They were blue, blue, and green, respectively.

"I've no fucking clue," Rac said. "I don't do sewer cant, I do trash cant."

"So you can't understand these?" I asked while restraining a giggle . . . poorly.

Gomorrah sighed. "Why do I even put up with you?" she muttered while Rac giggled over the line. She reached out and opened the door a notch, then looked around it for triggers. "Nothing I can see," she said.

I nodded, then took her place behind the door and opened it carefully. Nothing exploded, so that was nice. At least until Myalis piped up. "There are lingering traces of . . . quite a few toxic chemicals in the air. I suspect this airlock is meant to kill anyone using it without the proper precautions."

"Anything we should worry about?" I asked.

"Atyacus has disabled the air exchange already," Myalis replied. "The area past the airlock seems like another short passage, followed by an area with more activity."

"How much more?" I asked.

"I count twenty-two active augmentations."

"Any guards?" I asked as I stepped in.

Myalis took just a second to respond. "One augmentation in the next room. The user is currently distracted observing some adult material."

I shook my head. "Well, let's not interrupt our new pal's alone time," I said as I turned on my invisibility. "Gomorrah, do you mind if I check out the next area solo? I need to do something with all of this stealth gear. You can back-seat samurai and not-flirt with Franny."

Gomorrah sniffed. "Fine. Do try not to get yourself shot any more than you need to."

"You know I don't live a life where people try to not shoot me. That's how you know you're doing things right. Or very wrong."

"You're so terribly wise," she deadpanned.

I was grinning as I pushed the door open a crack, then snuck into the next room over. Time to see what was up at last.

CHAPTER TWENTY-FIVE

SNEAKY GHILLIE LEMON SQUEEZY

The pornography industry is nearly always at the forefront of technological changes. Video playback, online streaming, VR, augmented reality [. . .] it's not surprising that when new tech became available, alien technology at that, it was immediately put to carnal uses.

Also, alien porn was an interesting development for the industry.

—Excerpt from an article on TheHub.com, 2023

I knew I didn't need to move stealthily in order to not make any noise. My armor's boots were silent, and it wasn't like I was wearing some of those cheap nylon clothes that make swishing sounds when they rub together.

Still, it would be wrong to casually walk in while stealthed.

I kept low, eyes and ears peeled for any trouble, and it didn't take much for me to find some.

There was, as Myalis had warned, a guard in the room. He was sitting behind a desk, head bent back, looking toward the ceiling. I could have imagined that he was taking a nap if it weren't for Myalis telling me what he was watching at that moment. The jerky movement of his forearms didn't help any.

"Weirdo," I muttered.

"At least he's all alone," Rac said.

"Close your eyes, you," I said. Didn't need her seeing any of this. "Myalis, can we just shut off all of his augs?"

Not being able to see anything might calm the idiot down a notch.

Certainly, but shutting down all of them would terminate him. He has respiratory augmentations, and some that assist with blood circulation, likely because of the way his arms and legs were disconnected.

"Can you be selective?" I asked. I navigated through the menus of my Cyberwarfare suite and found a way to connect to his augs. Then I saw a flash of what he was looking at before I shut it off in a hurry. "Wow," I muttered.

People living in sewers were pretty dirty.

That should be easy enough to do. Shutting down all nonessential augmentations in three . . . two . . .

My new pal jerked on his chair, then looked around. It was pretty clear that he couldn't see anything, though, judging by the way he moved his arm around as if searching for stuff. He bounced to his feet, did up his zipper, then stumbled toward the door at the back. "John! John, my eyes have fucked up again!" he shouted.

I followed him.

According to the map I had, the next area over was a wide passageway that overlooked another corridor one floor down.

I kept close to my blind masturbator buddy as he moved in. There was a catwalk that ran all along the corridor, with some passages leading off it to the left. A rail kept people safe on the right, and below that I could see down to another corridor with crates and boxes. There were some tables with games, a few TVs on the wall, even a bed tucked in a corner. It was a living space.

"Davie, you stupid fuck, close the fucking door!" someone shouted from below. "You're letting the good air out."

Davie stumbled backward, swearing under his breath the entire time. "My arms are all screwed up," he said as he tried to find the handle. "My fingers are numb, I can't feel my joints, and my eyes are off."

"What were you doing?"

The dude talking walked out of one of the side rooms. He was a tall guy, with a good chunk of his face from cheekbones up missing and replaced with a set of embedded augmentations. His arms and legs were prosthetic as well, the sort I'd seen on plenty of Sewer Dragons, though maybe a notch nicer.

"C'mon, John, you know I was just checking my media feeds," Davie said.

"Uh-huh. What kind of porn were you watching?" John asked.

I stepped to the side so that I was next to the wall and out of the way.

"I wasn't watching anything like that—don't be disgusting. Now fix my eyes, I can't see shit!"

I snuck around John while he grabbed a hold of his pal's head, then continued on deeper down the corridor. It was strange, being entirely invisible to people. "Myalis, how's the air in here?"

There continue to be trace elements and small quantities of various chemicals. Long-term exposure is more harmful than would be advised, but the air is otherwise close to standard.

"Great," I said. I tapped on my thigh and opened the holster that held my Trench Maker. It would be in easy reach if I needed it.

The room that John had been in looked like a combination office and bedroom. So this entire area had to be some sort of living space. Or at least an area where this lot spent a good deal of time. I passed by the entrance to a short corridor with the stairs in it so that I could check out the other rooms on this level, but for the most part, they weren't much more than storage and what looked like a small barracks with two people sleeping in it.

It was . . . I glanced at a clock on my HUD. Nearly eight in the morning. "We've been down here forever," I muttered. If I wanted to get to the hotel and take six showers before Lucy woke up, then I'd have to wrap things up in . . . Lucy and I'd had a busy night, so I probably had until noon before she woke up.

I refocused. The top section didn't seem to have anything too out of the ordinary. Certainly no room full of kidnapped people.

Making my way downstairs, I resisted the urge to hum; that was, until Rac started to make commentary. "It's a nice place," she said.

"This place?" I asked.

The decor was a bit industrial for my liking. Too much rust and flaking paint and signage that dated all the way back to the thirties hanging on the walls.

"Yeah. It's safe, got some air, probably water. Bet they can sneak out from a bunch of places too. And it's safe."

"You said that twice," Franny said.

"Yeah, 'cause it's important," Rac said. "Really sucks to have your house blown up, or mowed away by some corp. Or just . . . taken, you know? You arrive home and you find out some gang needed a place for a lab, so now you need to move out. S'not fun."

"Hey, you'll be fine from now on, you know," I said.

Rac was silent for a long while. "Thanks," she said at last. "But, uh, I don't need charity. I can look out for myself."

"Sure," I said. "But I look out for my friends, so you'll have to deal."

She chuckled, and I figured I'd have a hard time convincing her to be anything like one of the kittens.

The bottom floor wasn't all that weird. Cement walls made more cramped by boxes and crates and stacks of those plastic pallets used to carry stuff around. Some enterprising people had stacked them in such a way as to create little cubbyholes where they could sleep, but otherwise, there really wasn't much worth poking at.

One guy was sitting at a desk, an IV tube poking out of his jacket and connected to a syringe that he was slowly, ever so slowly, plunging down.

Judging by the way he was twitching every few seconds, whatever he was juicing himself with wasn't healthy. I left him to it.

There were plenty more Sewer Dragons in the rooms here and there, most of them sleeping, but a few were gesturing in the air as though working through media feeds. They could have been any number of people I'd seen waiting on the sides of stores and streets—background people minding their own business. Except these were in some fucky underground pit, and none of them had much of their original bodies left.

At the end of the corridor was a large door. It had a wheel in its middle, and, strangely enough, a bunch of wires running across it. "Is that a trap?" I asked.

"It's not live," Gomorrah said. "Look, bottom left: there's nothing at the end of the wire."

"Huh," I said as I knelt down and stared. The wires were bare in some spots, but still in their plastic sheaths in others. "What is it?"

"I suspect that it's a rudimentary Faraday cage," Myalis said.

"The things that make it hard to connect to the internet?" I asked. A few stores had them. You needed to use the local Wi-fi or nothing at all. That way they could datamine you while you shopped.

"Makes sense," Franny said, "if that's where they're keeping the people they kidnapped."

"Well, then," I said. I gripped the wheel and spun. If anyone heard, I had plenty of ammo to tell them to calm down.

CHAPTER TWENTY-SIX

BIP BAP BAM

Here at CAGE—a subsidiary of ImmigraTech!—we do our very best to ensure that all beings captured while attempting illegal border crossings are treated humanely and with the care and attention they deserve.

Our state-of-the-art housing and lockdown facilities guarantee that cases of physical harm, sexual harm, suicide, and child mismanagement are kept to a tolerable minimum, while also encouraging and re-educating any future citizens on the benefits of joining the workforce of any corporation looking for new employees!

—*The Collateral Acquisition and Gatekeeping Enforcement Handbook*, page 759, 2048 edition

I grunted as I shoved the door aside. The folk who made it probably wouldn't be happy I'd jammed a hand against the Faraday netting and fucked it up, but then I didn't really care all that much about those folk.

The corridor past the doorway led to a bright room with a ceiling five meters up. It was pretty wide too, and I assumed it was just as deep.

I glanced at my map, but it didn't match what was there at all. Someone had gone around and modified the room a good deal. Not too surprising.

The walls were entirely white, that kind of near-fluorescent white they painted on asphalt. Combined with the dozens of lights hanging from the ceiling, it made for a room that might have been too bright to look at if it weren't for the visor on my helmet darkening itself.

The walls were covered in wired mesh, or at least the exterior walls.

In the center of the room were some enclosures. Just walls without any roofs, and with one door leading in.

"What do you think?" I asked.

"Looks like a cage, for people," Gomorrah said. "Like something you'd see at the borders."

"Yeah," I said. "I guess we might've found our missing people." I moved over to the doorway and fiddled with the latch keeping it shut. It was a rusty metal bar, nothing fancy, but likely enough to keep anyone without tools or good leverage from breaking through.

I pushed the door open and peeked past it. There was a small room, with a fridge, of all things, and a second gate, this one made of fencing mesh. A table, with some trays stacked on it and a microwave on the end, sat off to one side.

"Likely for food," Gomorrah said. "To feed their prisoners."

The fridge was filled to the brim with cheap microwavable meals that anyone could afford. Mostly flavored cardboard and some cheap vat-grown veggies. The brownies always tasted good, though.

I moved over to the next door and unlocked it. The enclosure was split down the middle. One large cage on the left, another on the right. "Shit," I muttered.

The folks we were looking for were there. Some of them, at least. Poor, decrepit people, lounging on the floor, some sleeping, others huddled against the walls. A few were pacing back and forth.

They'd at least had the common decency to split them up, men on one side, women on the other.

It struck me as a little strange that they only had buckets and a small corner with a curtain to take care of their business. They were being held here by Sewer Dragons. Of all the people able to furnish usable plumbing . . .

"Can you ping their augs?" Gomorrah asked. "We could identify them."

"That's a good idea. Myalis?" I said.

"Of the forty-two people here, thirty-nine are on the list of missing people we previously created," Myalis said.

Franny hummed. "We missed a few. Where are the rest?"

"Unknown," Myalis replied. "Though some have recordings on their augmentations of other captives being escorted away, from which I've identified twelve more individuals. As for those present who were not on the list, they are without prior documentation or housing, or are from far outside the search range attributed to this scenario."

"People from outside New Montreal," I said.

"Essentially, yes."

"We're going to need to evacuate all of these people," Gomorrah said. "Atyacus, I need a route back to the surface."

I nodded as I crossed the room. The people here seemed to cover the entire spectrum, young and old, male and female, and there were plenty of skin tones and nationalities on display. Whatever anyone said about the Sewer Dragons, they couldn't be called discriminatory when it came to picking kidnapping victims.

I noticed one guy standing by the edge of the enclosure fence. He had a clean button-up shirt; only the bottom half had a chunk missing. It was tied around the lower half of his face. A real shitty mask, but an attempt anyway. He was staring at the still-open doorway behind me.

Bringing up the options for my Cyberwarfare augs, I aimed them at the guy and found the option to take over the speaker built into his system. "Hey," I said.

The guy jumped and glanced around, eyes darting this way and that to search for the source of my voice. He reached up and touched his ear eventually.

"Yeah, sorry for the scare," I said. "I'm standing right in front of you, but you can't see me. My name's Cat, I'm a samurai, and I'm here to get you folks out. Had a few questions, though."

He settled down, still scanning the room, but without any obvious panic. Dude had a cool head on his shoulders. "Ask away," he muttered.

"You don't need to talk loud, I've got good ears," I said. "Anyway, how did you end up here, and what can you tell me about the place? Where are the others?"

"I was taken off the street while heading out to visit a student," he muttered. "Three guys grabbed me, took my things, then dumped me here. That was yesterday. There were more of us then, but they've been moving people out all day. One or two at a time."

"And new people keep coming in?" I asked.

He nodded slowly.

I checked his augs for his name. He had a couple of social media accounts, all linked to the name Shaun Gregory. "All right, Shaun," I said as I resisted the urge to snoop. I didn't need to know the dude's hobbies to know that getting him out of here was the right thing to do. "I'm going to be opening up the gates around this place in a moment. We need to clear the path for all of you to be able to get out of here—think you can help me keep everyone calm?"

"I'll do what I can," Shaun said. He stood a little taller, some of the wariness leaving him.

"Good man," I said. "Did they tell you anything about where they were bringing the others?"

"They mentioned a Doctor Hack. I've been trying to send messages out every time they open the door, but the signal down here is trash."

"Doc Hack again, huh? Right, hold tight, Shaun." I backed up and moved to the gate to swing it open wider. "Gom, got a plan?"

"Something of a plan, yes," Gomorrah said. "It's going to require your explosives."

My eyebrows perked. "I'm listening real hard," I said.

"We're currently under some buildings. There are a lot of access and maintenance corridors above this level. Getting to them naturally requires navigating a maze, and I bet half of it is trapped, but at some places the floors are right above."

"So we blow up the ceiling and just keep bursting onto the floor above until we see the sun?"

"We're maybe four floors below street level here," Gomorrah said. "There's a stairwell two floors up that leads right to the ground floor of what looks like an office building."

"Great," I said. I reached down to my thigh and unholstered my Trench Maker. "Let me give these folk an inspirational speech, and then we can get a move on."

"Oh, I can't wait to hear this," Franny muttered.

I sniffed. Someone was doubting my ability to give a good speech. I was about to start talking shit when I heard the room's heavy door creaking open. "Someone opened the door," a voice said from outside the enclosure.

Two sets of feet ran over, and I backed away from the entrance so I was in the middle of the passageway when a pair of Sewer Dragons burst onto the scene. They had rifles tucked close to their sides and had their heads on a swivel looking for escaped prisoners.

Their arrival woke people up, had them paying attention again.

Which was great for me. I raised my Trench Maker and pointed it at the face of the nearest Sewer Dragon.

They both stared at the very much not-invisible gun. "What the fuck?" the Sewer Dragon asked.

I answered by shooting him in the face, the bullet impacting with a meaty thump followed by a sparking electrical discharge. He hit the ground writhing with wild twitches.

"Oh shi—" his buddy said. I hit him twice in the face.

I lowered my handgun, noticed all the people starting at it, then flicked off my invisibility. "All right, y'all motherfuckers, listen to me. I'm about to save all of your asses, but only if you're real good about following orders."

CHAPTER TWENTY-SEVEN

A GOOD JOB

Fashion, the ever-changing monster. Trends come and go all the time, but there's no doubt the current meta involves integrating the tech necessary to living into your apparel. Accessories are the name of the game now.

Nothing encapsulates that more than the samurai, who, by necessity, tend to be normal people under all the gear. So, of course, we emulate and copy that very same equipment, that aesthetic.

—Coco Model, *Memories of the Changes*, a 2045 autobiography

"Gomorrah, I think I might need a distraction at the far end of this place," I said.

The map with the path Gomorrah had given me was relatively simple. I had to take these people to one of the rooms just down the corridor leading here. That would mean, for a good stretch of the way, anyone on the floor above would be able to see the kidnapped people, not to mention anyone on the bottommost floor.

Then I had to blow apart a wall once inside that room, which would likely wake anyone who wasn't already up. The noise of dozens of people moving by wouldn't help.

While I considered my options, I moved over to the nearest door and looked at the padlock keeping it shut. It was a big thing, all heavy steel, with a metal loop as thick as my thumb. I'd need something to blow it up.

"That guy has the keys," Shaun said. He was pointing to one of the Sewer Dragons who was busy twitching on the ground behind me.

"Oh, that's nice," I said. I scooped the keys out of the guy's jacket pocket, then fiddled with the lock. "All right, Shaun, I need you to keep an eye on everyone here. You're going to stay in this room for the next five minutes or so. If any of you know how to handle a weapon, then there's two shit guns on the floor there. A bit dirty, but I'm sure they work."

"Where will you be?" Shaun asked.

"Me? I'm going to be in the corridor doing some remodeling. If you hear gunshots and explosions, that's because it's working."

"All right?" Shaun said. He didn't sound entirely on board with everything. He was probably too normal to be used to the speed at which samurai worked.

The lock came apart with a satisfying clunk and I tossed it away to the side before walking over to the other side. The women were climbing to their feet, some of them helping the others. There was an air of cautious optimism. "We're saved. Oh, thank the saints, we're saved," one woman was muttering to herself while worrying her hands together.

I undid the last padlock and let it fall. "Okay. Everyone, follow Shaun over there. My partner—another samurai—and I will be making a lot of noise. When I come and get you, move fast, and keep your heads low."

I moved into the little room at the entrance of the enclosures while turning on my invisibility. I caught a few gasps as I disappeared, then the sound of the gates opening and people shuffling out, slow and cautious.

"Gomorrah?" I asked as I headed over to the bulkhead. The two who entered had closed it behind them.

"I'm standing by the entrance," Gomorrah said. "I've glued down your chronic masturbator friend. He decided to return to his post."

"He's not my friend," I said. "Just someone I met one morning—you know how it is."

Gomorrah snorted. "Sure. I'm ready to make a scene."

I shoved my Trench Maker away. "All right. Let's see what kind of trouble we can cause."

I pulled the door aside and stepped into the corridor, my Icarus rising as I pulled it out from under my jacket.

John was standing nearby, staring at a tablet next to some other Sewer Dragon.

They got to see my gun for all of a second before I lined it up with John's head and fired. The canister sailed through the air and smashed the Sewer Dragon in the nose before bursting apart and sending a cascade of foam across his front. The second canister I fired erupted against the other Sewer Dragon's chest.

"Two down," I said.

Someone screamed from above, and I heard a powerful whooshing sound. Pure-white foam spilled down through the catwalks above. "That's one here," Gomorrah said.

The panic started about then, which did wonders to wake up the Sewer Dragons who were still asleep. I nailed one of them while he was only halfway out of his bed, gluing him while I moved deeper into the corridor.

"Feds! It's the feds!" someone screamed.

Not quite right, but I gave them points for trying to warn the others.

I considered gluing the door to one of the rooms I passed shut. It would have locked a few Dragons in, but they could shoot out of those rooms and that might put the civvies at risk.

Best to let them exit and remove them from the fight entirely.

Screaming idiots burst out of side rooms, some waving guns around, others with long knives attached to their prosthetic arms. A few of the faster ones took potshots in my direction, but they were poorly aimed and trying to hit the only part of me they could see: my gun. It wasn't working well for them.

I winced as a Sewer Dragon tagged another in the neck and he went down gurgling. Tight spaces, with fire coming from every direction, meant that everything was going to shit real fast-like.

"Upper floor is clear!" Gomorrah said. "I'm foaming up the passages here. That should slow them down."

"Nearly done here," I said. I was already past the room where I'd need to plant a bomb; I just had to take out the last few idiots. I fired another round from my Icarus, clicked on empty a couple of times, then pulled out my Trench Maker.

The remaining two Sewer Dragons were hiding behind some crates. They were bringing their guns around and firing wildly above the boxes, which meant they weren't hitting jack.

I walked past the crate and fired twice, sending them both to the floor as squirming messes. "I think we're clear below," I said. "Can you keep an eye on the corridor? I'm going to go renovate us an exit."

Gomorrah came down the stairs two at a time, then searched the passage for things to shoot at. "I'll keep it safe," she said.

I nodded as I swung past her and into the room that was soon going to get an expansion. It was an office space, of sorts. A few computers here and there, a small bookshelf with ancient paper books. Lots of spectacularly terrible wire management, with cords strewn across the floor.

"So, the back wall," I muttered. A glance at the wire-mesh map showed that there was about ten centimeters of concrete between the wall and a room on the other side, one that was a bit higher up than this room. "Myalis, I need something that'll blow this wall apart."

You can't imagine how many options that leaves you with.

"Ah, let's go for something old-school?"

Certainly.

New Purchase: Remote Detonated Plastic Explosive

Points Reduced from . . . 10,881 to . . . 10,880

"Cheap," I said as I picked up the little box that appeared by my feet. There was a small disk inside, with a plasticky thing in its middle with a few small lights. My augs connected to it and gave me a new menu with a few options. I toggled on the "click to detonate" then pressed it to the wall. It stuck fast.

I decided not to stand next to the explosive as it went off, because I liked my remaining limbs and Lucy would be miffed.

Stepping out of the room, I moved closer to Gomorrah's side. She was next to the bulkhead door. "Is it done?" she asked.

I glanced back, then selected the "detonate" option on my aug's menu.

The ground shook, and there was a nice bassy bang. Dust shot out of the doorway leading into the freshly renovated room. "It is now," I said.

I kind of regretted not being able to see that, but I could imagine it well enough.

"In that case," Gomorrah said, "let's get people moving. We still have quite a few people unaccounted for."

"I think, for those, we'll need to find Doc Hack and ask him some questions. The fun sort."

"That can wait until the people we can save now are safe," Gomorrah said.

I glanced around at all the Sewer Dragons currently stuck to the floors and walls and to each other. One of them had their arm sticking out of the white foam, so they gave us the middle finger. "I love my job," I muttered.

CHAPTER TWENTY-EIGHT

STEPPING UP AND OUT

Air filtration technology has changed significantly in the past decades. Most of this change was pushed by the increasing need for unpolluted, pure air that won't ruin your lungs and fill your brain with lead and mercury. It's why HVAC specialists are some of the best-paid people in the infrastructure industry.

—Extract from *What to Be When You Grow Up!*, a job-guide pamphlet, 2056

The civvies in the enclosure looked ready to go, or as ready to go as a dozen underfed, slightly traumatized civilians could be under the circumstances. Shaun had one of the guns hanging by his hip, and I noticed that the other was in the arms of a young woman who looked tense enough I figured she'd jump and shoot at the first thing she saw.

I didn't ask about the two Sewer Dragons that had been left in one of the enclosures. I suspected they'd been used to bleed off some unhealthy emotions.

I stepped back from the enclosure, flicked off my invisibility, then walked back in, making sure to rattle the gates a bit. Didn't need to freak anyone out. "Hey," I said as I walked in. I had a lot of eyes on me. Somehow, knowing they saw me as some sort of savior made the tension of so many people looking at me worse.

"Cat," Shaun said. "I think we're ready to move."

I scanned the group. A few looked rough. Some of them, I imagined, were going through withdrawal or hadn't taken the meds they needed, but they were all on their feet.

Was it better to heal them up now or move out and take care of them outside?

"We're going to move now. We'll be using the buddy system. Find someone, and stay next to them. If anyone's injured, we'll pair them with somebody in better shape," I said. I couldn't sound uncertain. If convincing these people to move was anything like herding my kittens, then hesitation would mean trouble for me.

"We can do that," Shaun said. He moved back, tapping shoulders and telling people to partner up. It was nice having someone who could help while I just did my best to look cool.

"How are things coming along?" Gomorrah asked.

"Fine on my end," I said. "We'll be out in a minute or two. A lot of normal folks, and some of them haven't enjoyed the Sewer Dragons' five-star treatment."

"Understood," Gomorrah said.

Once everyone was partnered up, I nodded and then gestured to the exit. "There's another samurai out there. The girl with the big flamethrower. She's on our side. Anyone else you see isn't."

I spun around and led them out. I kept myself visible too. They'd need someone to see, someone to reassure them they were safe.

It was often like that with the kittens too. If one of them got hurt, it helped to see someone nearby who could protect them.

We moved into the corridor and I noticed the folk behind me slowing down. Were they afraid of leaving the enclosure room?

Gomorrah stood nearby, a leg shaking with obvious impatience. "I checked out the room you cleared. It's safe."

"Cool," I said. "Want to take the front, or the rear?"

Rac giggled, and I held back a laugh of my own when I realized what I'd said.

"You take the Vanguard," Gomorrah replied, unamused.

"Okay, people, follow me," I called over my shoulder. I tugged my Icarus out from under my jacket and popped the spent magazine. "Myalis," I muttered.

New Purchase: Nonlethal Explosive Ammunition
Points Reduced from . . . 10,880 to . . . 10,870

The ammo wasn't too expensive, but I could only afford a thousand or so new magazines. That was a good amount, but I didn't know when I'd get another bounty of points. The blueprint for the ammo was definitely going on my "to buy" list if I was going to use more of it. That way I'd get plenty more for essentially nothing.

Maybe I could hire Rac to work the printer? It used trash, as far as I knew.

The room I'd partially exploded was in shambles. Dust still clung to the air, and the ground was covered in smaller stones and chunks of cement.

There was also a huge-ass hole in the far wall. The other side was higher, so we'd need to step up to climb to it, but it wasn't so bad as to need a ladder or anything.

I entered the hole and stared around the room. It was some sort of storage space, with boxes rotting in the corners and a distinct lack of light. My helmet's visor compensated, but I imagined it wouldn't be pleasant for the folk behind me. Then I noticed the light switch near the door.

"All right, come on up," I said as I leaned down and helped Shaun. He turned and helped the next person, and they did the same. The weakest of them were hoisted, and some of those more hale bounced through without difficulty.

"How far is the surface, ma'am?" Shaun asked.

"Not too far, I think," I said. "A kilometer, maybe. Lots of stairs, and we don't exactly have a straight-line path out of here."

Shaun nodded. "Good, good. That's not too bad. I don't know if everyone here is in the shape to walk that much."

I glanced back and noticed a few of the civvies panting with hands on knees; some of them looked a little yellow. Shaun might be right. "We'll take it slow," I said. "If anyone flags too much, tell me, all right?"

"Okay," he said.

Gomorrah was the last one to climb up. She stood, turned, then sprayed a layer of foam over the hole in the wall. "That won't stop someone determined, but it might slow them down," she explained. "Besides, it masks the direction we moved in."

I nodded, then moved to the door at the far end of the room. It led to a long, low corridor. More pipes on the ceiling, but these looked less like massive industrial things and more like standard air vents and plain old water stuff.

I glanced at the map Myalis had put up for me, then started forward. I heard the folk we were rescuing lining up behind me. "Once you're done bringing those people to the surface, what will you do?" Franny asked.

"I don't know," I admitted. "We're missing a lot of them, which means we need to head back down. But . . . I don't know what to do or say to these people. They'll be safer, at least."

"I . . . don't know what I'd do either," Franny admitted. "But we can't just leave them all on the side of the road somewhere."

"Well, what do you want to do?" I asked.

"We could contact local law enforcement," Gomorrah said.

"The cops? What in the world would they do to help? Shoot the minorities and the poor? I don't know if you noticed, but none of these people are upper-class white men."

Gomorrah sighed. "You're not used to dealing with the police from the position you're in. You'll find that they're very polite and helpful to anyone who's a samurai. They'll help. EMTs as well. They can write off the losses easily enough."

I didn't like it, but . . . Gomorrah hadn't steered me wrong yet. "All right, but you call them. I'm liable to toss in a few slurs too many. Don't need the cops that show up to be angry because I kept calling them pigs or something."

"Sure," Gomorrah said.

I glanced back. We were at the first set of stairs we'd need to climb. So far everyone seemed fine. If anything, moving around might have made them feel a little better.

I started to jog ahead. The power armor made the stairs easier to climb, and if we were going to run into any traps, I wanted to be the one to trigger them. I wasn't invincible, but I was a damn sight harder to kill than the people behind me.

There weren't any traps, just more corridors and passages, with a few doors to barge through along the way. Gomorrah didn't notice anyone following us, and neither of our AI caught any interesting chatter.

In the span of thirty minutes, we were out of the maintenance areas and into a plainer corridor, one with beige walls and fluorescent lights. An old lady with a few bags, likely heading home, stared at us as we moved past to the double doors at the end.

Outside.

I stepped onto the sidewalk, then took a few steps forward so I was under the warm glow of the morning sun. Cars zipped overhead, and a few self-driving trucks rumbled by on the road.

"Oh, this is nice," I said.

"Lady, you fuckin' reek," a hobo said from his spot on the ground.

"Get fucked," I replied with all due respect.

There were giggles and a few hearty laughs as the folk behind me poured out onto the street, and then Gomorrah followed them and nodded to me. "EMTs should be here within five, police two or three minutes after them."

"Should we wait?" I asked.

She shrugged. "If you want. I think it would be wise."

"Cool." I pointed to a fire hydrant. "I'm going to pop that open, then stand in the water."

"I . . . might join you," Gomorrah said.

CHAPTER TWENTY-NINE

THE PO-PO

Most inner-city police forces can be divided into four broad categories. These might overlap, being controlled by the same corporations, or they might be their own entities. This depends on the city, or even the area within a city.

Detectives: charged with solving crimes in the way best suited for the entity they work for.

Beat cops: charged with keeping the peace and solving low-level disputes.

Max tactical: charged with high-stakes, high-risk situations. Often similar to mercenaries or paramilitary groups in appearance, equipment, and policy.

Traffic: charged with keeping the peace in the air and on the roads.

Knowing how to approach each of these is what this pamphlet aims to teach you!

—A Good Citizen's Guide to Your Armed Protectors!, 2023

"Uh, ma'am?"

I opened my eyes and looked around. It was hard to see, on account of the wall of water splashing against my front with enough pressure to send a normal, non-power-armored person flying back.

I knew I wasn't the only one benefiting from the splashing water. The civilians we'd saved took turns standing nearby, allowing the spray to wash off some of the grime. It left them wet and even more bedraggled than they had been, but at least they were clean. Gomorrah had used the hydrant water to clean herself off too. I think her suit was just as hydrophobic as my own.

I was standing there because there was something very enjoyable about the noise and feel of so much water beating against me.

"Ma'am?"

I sighed and turned to the man calling out for me. A police officer was standing there, wearing a blue uniform and white body armor over his chest, legs, and arms, made of hard plastic and likely reinforced enough to take a low-caliber shot or two.

A beat cop. The sort with an uncovered face and who carried no more than a handgun. Not a tactical police officer or a detective; just a normal, almost-friendly face that would only beat up minorities, the homeless, and likely his wife.

Stepping to the side, I let the water move past to bathe the sidewalk and clean it off for the first time since . . . likely forever. "Yes?" I asked as I dripped water like a cat pulled out of a tub.

The officer shifted on the spot. His trousers were wet up to the shins. "We wanted some direction, ma'am," he said with a gesture behind him.

The side of the street was a busy place today. Some six or so paramedic vans were parked half on the sidewalk, their large turbines humming as they idled, and the auto-turrets mounted above them scanned the street for potential threats.

The police cars were parked in a semicircle around the area, lights strobing red and blue and sirens blaring with the occasional pause for an audio advertisement. The few hobos hanging around the street were long gone. This many cops in one place was bad for their business.

The civilians we'd liberated were being looked over by some EMTs. Blood pressure was being taken, skin swabs, maybe blood samples to check for whatever they'd caught while down in the sewers. Basically, the EMTs were running every test they could without bringing anyone back to a proper hospital.

Likely for the best.

"We've secured the perimeter, ma'am," the officer said. "The other, ah, samurai is communicating with the EMTs. I thought we could discuss things with you."

I winced. Now was the part where they'd ask if I had anti-crime insurance or the like. We were the ones to call the police, so we were responsible for their wages. "All right, what's up?"

"We have the addresses of most of the, ah, civilians. Some of them don't have homes on record, but we obtained the locations where they wish to be dropped off. We're ready to set out with the first batch. Ah, we don't have enough squad cars to bring all of them back in one trip. We might have to split the group in two and leave a few cars behind as protection while we bring the first batch home."

"Oh," I said. "Yeah, that sounds reasonable. Gomorrah and I will be around for another few minutes, so I doubt anyone will try anything. We might be going back down soon."

"Are there more civilians down there?" he asked. "If you don't mind the question, that is."

"Yeah, another group—a bit bigger than this one, I think."

"In that case, if you call us ahead of time, we can arrange for transportation to be there. Given enough notice, we can ensure that there will be enough cars to bring everyone back home safely."

I nodded, slowly. "Thanks, you're being real helpful," I said.

"Anything for one of our fine city's samurai," he said. "I'll be organizing things here. If you have any questions, feel free to contact me, or if you wish, the home office. The operators know to expect your call and give it the highest priority." He saluted me, then jogged back to where the rest of the cars were waiting.

I couldn't get over the absolute weirdness of talking to a cop and them not being an absolute jackass. It was like waking up to discover that the sky was, and always had been, yellow.

"Fucking strange shit," I muttered as I walked over to where Gomorrah was standing. She was talking to a paramedic, but the conversation ended as I arrived. "Feeling cleaner?" she asked.

"Barely," I said. "I don't think there are enough showers in the world for that. But I'll live with it. How about you? Done here?"

"I am," she said. "Most of the people we pulled out of there had some sort of infection. Never the same twice. They'll need to burn their clothes and maybe take a few long showers, but for the most part, they should be okay."

"That's good to hear," I said. I noticed Shaun climbing into the front passenger seat of a squad car, the officers all smiling as they laid down plastic sheets onto their seats. "I guess calling the cops was the right move."

"They're not the same when you're in a different part of the hierarchy," Gomorrah said.

"Tell me about it. So, we're diving back down?"

She sighed. "We are. Franny, Raccoon, how are you two holding up?"

"We're fine," Franny said. "Though I wouldn't mind standing and taking a walk."

"You're not in a very safe location," Gomorrah said. "And I doubt that the Sewer Dragons failed to notice the Fury after this much time. There are drinks in the middle console. And some food."

"Yeah, this food is kickass," Rac said. "But I'm going to need to use a washroom sooner or later, you know?"

"Ah," Gomorrah said.

"Is your awesome car not equipped with an in-built bathroom?" I asked.

She smacked me in the stomach with the back of her hand. "Don't be an idiot, Cat. I can have the Fury move. There has to be a restaurant or a gas station somewhere in the area."

"Right, that'll give Franny her walk too," I said. "Stick together, don't get kidnapped, and . . . the Fury is armed, right?"

"Obviously."

"Then let the Fury do any shooting if it comes to that," I said. "We'll be diving back down into the shit hole again."

"You're going to find that Doc Hack guy?" Rac asked.

"That's the plan," I said. "He seems linked to everything else, somehow. I'm hoping it won't be too hard to figure out where he's hiding."

"Atyacus has a location for his base," Gomorrah said. "A few of the Sewer Dragons we took out had it marked on their augs."

Not the best information security, but I suppose it made sense. They had so many other things keeping their home under the city safe that hiding things probably felt like overkill to them. Myalis added the location to my own map, a red box a few blocks away and maybe six floors down from ground level.

"Can we reach that from above?" I asked. "Instead of navigating through the sewers again."

"We can," Gomorrah said. "Fancy a bit of a walk?"

"I'd rather walk here than in the sewers again. In fact, I think I've spent enough time in the sewers that I'm good for the rest of my life."

"We could ride along with the police. I'm sure they wouldn't mind."

"And have every cop watcher in the neighborhood tell the Dragons we're coming? Nah, let's walk over. No one will pay attention to a single person walking on street level."

"Going invisible on me again?"

I shrugged, then flickered away from visibility. "It makes things easier."

Gomorrah started walking along the sidewalk, undisturbed by any of the cops or the EMTs who were busy wrapping things up.

It felt as if we needed some background music. I bet there were samurai out there who had that sort of thing all figured out. Maybe Cause Player? It sounded like something he'd do.

CHAPTER THIRTY

BYPASS

How many times do I have to repeat myself?

Don't antagonize the nutjobs with literal aliens in their heads and very large guns!

It's like you people want to die!

—Former CFO of Nimbletainment after the July 2044 incident

Our trek across the city was uneventful. Unexpectedly so.

Maybe it was the way Gomorrah was dressed. In full, high-tech gear, her flamethrower hanging close by her side. Maybe it was the way she was walking, as if she owned the damn place. Or maybe anyone who would cause trouble knew something was going on and they all just collectively decided to mind their own damned business for the morning.

It was still super damned early. I didn't think I'd ever gone out at this hour to cause trouble. I guessed that troublemakers weren't the sort to wake up at the crack of dawn.

From the ground, it was hard to tell which tower housed the rich and affluent and which was built to make them richer and more affluent. They were all the same lifeless gray, with the occasional splash of color—graffiti and painted rebellion that hadn't been wiped out by the automated sweepers yet.

"The nearest entrance to the sewers might be off-limits," Gomorrah said.

I shook myself out of my daydreams. "Why's that?" I asked. A glance at my own map indicated we were getting closer to the building where we could get to the sewers from the basement. It didn't seem different from any of the others around it.

"The entire bottom half of the building is owned by a pharmaceutical company. They make drugs there, and the security is pretty tight."

"So we ask them nicely to let us into the sewers. It's not like we're there to steal their overpriced insulin or whatever," I said.

"They might not be so understanding," Gomorrah said.

I blinked. "The fucking cops were willing to play nice with us. Why wouldn't some legal pill-pushers do the same?"

Gomorrah gestured vaguely ahead. "They're hardasses. I think I've heard other samurai complain about them before. The thing is, it's the one industry that's well backed by samurai. Easy money, and all the company needs to do is produce some drugs for cheap."

"Yeah, I don't get it."

"A lot of samurai sold the recipes for meds to these big companies. They expect the companies to sell them, almost at cost. That means curing people of a lot of things relatively cheaply. It's why we're not going through the twelfth iteration of some plague. Those same companies use that backing to sell their own drugs on the side. It's a big industry, with plenty of cash to be made."

"And because they're basically helped by samurai, they think they can just do whatever?"

"Not whatever," Gomorrah said. "But they might try to flex a little if we don't approach things the right way."

"Sound like a bunch of dicks," Rac interjected. I'd almost forgotten she was there. Then there was a loud slurping sound followed by a smack and a whine. "Fuck, my brain."

"I warned you," Franny said.

"Uh, what's going on?" I asked. I knew that Franny and Rac had left to visit the bathrooms, but that was it.

Rac moaned, and I was a little worried before she replied. "Aunt Franny got me a slushie, and now my brain hurts."

"She drank it too fast, and please, please don't call me that."

"All right," I said. At least the kid was having fun.

"Man, it's been an hour since you've shot at anyone," Rac complained.

Maybe too much fun, even. "Calm your tits, we're going to go see the boss in a bit. I bet there'll be plenty of people to shoot at."

We came around the corner and Gomorrah pointed to a building across the street. Our destination. It looked the same as all the rest, with a few doors at street level and an opening that had a ramp where self-driven trucks could slip into the building.

There were spikes all around the base of the building, little ones, no longer than a finger, and with a blunted edge. Probably to keep out the homeless, I figured.

We looked both ways before crossing, especially since I was invisible and didn't particularly feel like getting splattered by anything going a hundred kilometers an hour.

We crossed at a jog, and then Gomorrah beelined for the ramp. There was a garage door at the top, and Gomorrah paused next to it. "Are you certain you don't mind?" she asked.

"I don't mind what? Telling these people that we're using their sewer access? The worst that happens is they say no, then we threaten them, then we get in anyway."

"Yes, that's what I mean," she said. There was a small door next to the larger one. Maintenance access, I guessed. Or maybe a way for people to walk to work? Though I doubted that anyone living so close to the ground worked in a place like this. Gomorrah stared at the door for a moment, then stepped back. "I sent a message to the building's security."

"I'm not going to spend forever waiting," I said.

"I'll let them know we're in something of a hurry. I'm sure . . ." The door clicked and we both turned toward it as it opened.

It remained open, the room within lit by bright fluorescent lights.

Gomorrah gestured with her head, and, catching the drift, I moved in first.

It looked like the security here was pretty fast. They'd gotten a stooge out to stand a dozen paces from the door, armed and armored in some high-tech shit that probably cost a year's wages in credits.

The area was a simple parking garage, broken up by large pillars supporting a ceiling that felt heavy, if only because I knew how much mass was hanging above me. A few trucks were waiting at the end of the facility, and there was a parking space with some rather ordinary cars along one wall.

I started looking for more threatening things, and that was how I noticed the ceiling-mounted turret emplacements, and, with some help from Myalis, the dozen guards in full armor rushing to get ready behind what looked like a security booth.

"Looks safe enough," I said.

Gomorrah stepped in, head tilted back as she looked around the place, and then she focused on the guard.

"Welcome, we wish to know wh—"

"I need access to your maintenance sublevels," Gomorrah said. "Specifically, sublevel three."

"Ah," the security stooge said. "Ma'am, do you have the right building?"

"Obviously," Gomorrah said.

"We can't just let anyone into our sub-basements, you understand," he said. His tone had shifted, turning from confused corpo spokesidiot to male Karen with some perceived reason to be offended.

"Good, you can lead me there, then," Gomorrah said.

Of course, that was when the idiot's idiot friends ran out of the security room at the back and lined up behind him. A full dozen guards, in heavy armor with obvious servos and pistons and artificial muscles keeping everything working. They had guns that looked like they were torn off the sides of helicopters, and their helmets glowed from within. The fuckers meant business.

"I don't need twelve escorts," Gomorrah said. To me, she added, "I don't know if I can take all of these guards, you know."

"Ma'am, I will have to ask that you leave our property."

I walked up to the Karen, my new pal, and turned off my invisibility with my face an inch from his. His eyes went wide. "My samurai friend over there said we needed to get to your basement," I replied in a calm, even tone. As if he'd just asked for the manager, and I was the manager.

"Ah," he said. "Who are you?"

"Stray Cat," I replied. "Pleasure to meet you, buddy. I'm a stealth-specialized samurai. I mostly use explosives. Nice building you have."

"Was that a, ah, threat?"

"I could be more obvious, if you want."

"Cat, please don't blow up the building," Gomorrah said. "People live around here."

"Yeah, yeah," I said. I stepped back from the Karen. "I'll be on my way down, then." I flicked my invisibility back on, and then, just to be sure, walked past the row of guards while they glanced around and tried to spot me.

"Hmm, I can make my way down by myself, then," Gomorrah said. "I appreciate the greeting."

"Wait, uh, I mean . . ."

CHAPTER THIRTY-ONE

SAYING HELLO
TO THE GOOD DOCTOR

You want to be doctor?
Get real medical degree! Cheap! Six easy paiments!
—A pop-up ad on the University of New Montreal home page, 2027

"We don't have far to go," I said as we walked down yet another maintenance corridor. It was becoming a habit to spend time in cramped spaces with a bunch of pipes and terrible ventilation. At least it was better than the actual sewers, though not by much.

"How do you want to do this?" Gomorrah asked. "The way I see it, we have a few potential approaches. Doc Hack's . . . I can't believe that's their name."

"I'm called Stray Cat and you're named after a city," I said. "Glass stones."

"Glass . . . the expression is casting stones from a glass house. There's nothing about glass stones," Gomorrah said.

I shrugged. "Sure. I just figured stones made of glass would suck to deal with. All that shrapnel, you know?"

"I suppose," Gomorrah said. "We're getting off-topic."

"Right, you want to know how to deal with Doc Hack?" I asked.

"More like I want to know how we'll reach him. He's not terribly far from here. A couple of levels down. But the route to get to his . . . lab, I guess, isn't exactly straightforward."

She wasn't wrong. The fastest path Myalis had outlined involved going into the sewers again, traveling uphill a ways, cutting into a maintenance elevator, then up to the level where Doc Hack was from below.

"Are you thinking what I'm thinking?" I asked.

"Are you imagining unreasonably powerful explosives being used in confined spaces in defiance of all common sense?"

I nodded. "I wasn't going to say it with such a negative tone, but essentially that, yeah."

Gomorrah nodded, and my map flickered as it updated. Our path now went through two floors as if there weren't several feet of concrete in the way. "We should be able to bypass any traps if we demolish our way to the heart of the enemy's installation. I think it's our big advantage in fighting a foe that wants to use the terrain against us."

"I like it," I said.

"Are you two certain that this Doc Hack is so antagonistic?" Franny asked.

"I mean, he's called Doc Hack."

"Yes," she said with the strained patience of someone dealing with a brat, which I found rather insulting. "But other than his association with the Sewer Dragons, you don't know that he's really the person who ordered all of the kidnappings. For all we know, he could be at least somewhat innocent in all of this."

"That sounds real unlikely," I said. "But we're packing nonlethals, and I don't plan on blowing that big a hole in this place. We'll try to ensure he stays alive enough to answer some questions."

"Aren't you afraid you're sounding like exactly the kind of person a saint would despise?" Franny asked.

I paused and thought about it. "Nah." I was way too cool for any samurai to despise me. Besides, something in my gut was telling me that Doc Hack wasn't all rainbows and sunshine. No one with a name like that living in the sewers was going to be a friendly old man who handed out lollipops to orphans and only wanted good in the world. Best-case scenario, I could imagine him being chased down here for fucking up and somehow acting like the local doctor, but that was a big ask.

"You're very confident in yourself, aren't you?" Franny asked. I didn't miss the bite in her words.

"Franny, for a long-ass time, all I had going for me was a heap of confidence and a lack of shits to give. I don't see why becoming a samurai should change any of that."

"You would think those are some traits that might fade when given so much power," she said.

"I don't think I was given any power with the expectation it'd change me that much," I shot back. "At least, that's the impression I got."

Gomorrah nodded, though it was reluctant. "I think Cat is essentially correct. The people chosen to become saints aren't the ones likely to change too much from the act of becoming a saint."

"If the cool aliens wanted people who acted one way, they could just hire people to be samurai," Raccoon said. Something about the way she spoke gave me the impression she was sitting in a very comfortable, back-breaking posture. "Or they could send down, like, robots or something.

Like those androids that some places have, but more people-like . . . unless Cat and Gom are androids, which would still be really cool."

"I'm afraid that I'm at least eighty percent human," I said. We reached a passageway that was fairly close to right on top of Doc Hack's place. "Gom, should we drop down from here? It looks like there's . . . some sort of large room over the doc's place, but there's a passage under us now."

"You don't want to drop directly on top of him?" Gomorrah asked.

I shook my head. "What if he's an actual doctor? He might have patients and shit around. Dropping the ceiling on some poor injured guy would suck. It might piss people off too. There's a reason you only bomb hospitals when you know you can get away with it."

I leaned down and took a moment to survey the spot. This was a corridor that technically connected the basements of two larger skyscrapers. Technically, because the corridor ended at a bricked-up wall. Someone had likely blocked things off to prevent people from passing at some point, though there was still access to the sewers below.

Weird, but all right.

The passage was about large enough that two forklifts could drive past each other if they squeezed in tight. Concrete walls, a floor covered in plasticky shit with some tile pattern printed onto it.

You'll likely want an explosive with a fairly low yield and an easily controlled cone of destruction. Aimed downward, naturally. Alternatively, if you want to create a passage directly, you can use an applied detonation that will burn out the edges of a hole into the floor.

"I think that might be best," I agreed. Big explosions were cool, but we did want to limit the property damage somewhat. I didn't know which wall was load-bearing, but I figured it was safest to assume all of them were. "Give me the bomb, Myalis."

New Purchase: Shaped Burn-Through Charge
Points Reduced from . . . 10,870 to . . . 10,865

The box that appeared next to me had a well-folded cord within it, as well as a small brick that the cord was connected to at both ends.

I pulled it out and stared for a second before catching on. I started to lay the cord down in a circle on the ground.

The detonator goes in the center.

I nodded and placed the brick in the middle, the black-ropy cord coming out of it and forming a loop on the ground that was about the size of a proper manhole. "Should we move over to the next room?" I asked.

That is not necessary. This will burn rather than explode, and the amount of light produced, while dangerous to the naked eye, won't harm you as long as you don't remove your helmet. Gomorrah's equipment is likewise sufficient to keep her safe. Though I would strongly advise not standing on the hole you've marked, or touching the wire with any limbs you intend to keep.

I nodded and backed up a good few meters, just in case. Gomorrah, the more cautious one between us, stood even farther back. I found the controls for the detonator in my aug menus and tapped the "detonate" button with great relish.

The room lit up, the lights hanging from the ceiling entirely eclipsed. A rough circle of light burned, tracing the path I'd laid the cord on. I blinked just as the brick in the center blew up with a low *whump.*

The floor caved in, the circle cracking in half and falling down and out of sight even as the cord winked out and left us in the comparative darkness of the corridor.

"Well, then," I said. "Ladies first?"

Gomorrah stared at me. "You're a woman, last I checked."

I grinned. "So you're saying you've been checking me out? Besides, you're a lot fleshier than I am, so technically you're a little bit more lady, aren't you?"

"You have a very strange mind. And no, that's not a compliment," Gomorrah said as she stepped past. She leveled her flamethrower at the hole and peered inside, then tapped the edge with her foot. "Cool already."

"How can you tell?" I asked. There was no way her boots were thin enough to let her feel the ground.

"Heat vision," she muttered before dropping into the hole with a little hop.

I moved over to the edge, then stared down. That was deeper than I was comfortable leaping, so I sat myself on the edge of the hole and scooted forward until I dropped. The servos in my armor's knees bent with a hiss I felt rather than heard.

"Dark in here," I muttered.

"Come on, we need to do the same trick all over again," Gomorrah said. "And then we can say hello to the good doctor."

CHAPTER THIRTY-TWO

THE DOCTOR'S IN THE HOUSE

There are hundreds of ways the installation of an augmentation can go wrong. You get these backyard non-companies that'll do installs for cheap, but half the time you don't get what you paid for.

Then there's stuff like infections, both physical and malware, piracy things. Some folk, and it's not just girls, will be put to sleep for a simple op and wake up in some underground black market.

I'm not a company shill. I don't give half a fuck where you get your augs. Just get them from a reputable source.

—WriteIt LifeProTips board, 2047

"We're one level up," Gomorrah said. "Another hole through the floor?"

I glanced around the room we'd burst into. I couldn't see much until my helmet's visor adjusted for the near-darkness, but my ears let me feel the room just fine. It was a storage room . . . maybe? It was hard to tell, exactly.

"Yeah, we . . ." I paused, ears twitching within my helmet. Raising a hand, I made the universal "one second" gesture and shuffled over toward the far end of the room. There was a door there, one that, according to the maps Myalis had laid out for me, would lead into a passageway connecting a bunch of smaller rooms together. Our next push down was supposed to be a couple of rooms over, where we'd be dropping right into the spot where Doc Hack had his lab.

"What is it?" Gomorrah whispered. We were still talking over our coms, but I guessed that kind of habit didn't die.

"There's noise in the next room over," I said. Once I was next to the door, I leaned down and brought my head closer. The sounds were mechanical. Something like a grinder, whirling and . . . grinding at something. There were other sounds too: air hissing through something, the gurgle of water, and the constant beeping of what had to be some sort of medical device.

Gomorrah stepped closer, boots crunching through the floor bits we'd blown up.

"I think the next room over is Doc's place," I said. "They might've done some renovating."

"Then the place isn't going to be the size and shape we expect it to be," Gomorrah said.

"I don't know about you all," Raccoon said. "But I was thinking evil bad-guy lair. Like in one of those movies."

I wasn't going to admit it, but I had the same idea. "We'll just have to see," I muttered as I reached up to the door handle and carefully, slowly, spun it around. The door wasn't locked, and the reason why became clear enough as soon as I peeked through.

Doc Hack's lab was a messy, uneven room, mostly rectangular, but with segments to the sides that didn't mirror their opposites. Obviously, they'd torn out walls wherever to make more room.

Still, someone had been at least a little clever about it. Large concrete pillars rose up from the ground floor and all the way up to the ceiling. Obvious additions to keep things from collapsing down.

The space past the door wasn't all that big. A segment of floor maybe a meter wide, with no rails to the side and a fall down two floors of empty space to the ground below. There were some catwalks and multiple levels on the end opposite us, each one reachable by a metal staircase built around one of the pillars.

"I think we're mostly out of sight up here," I whispered. There were lights in the room below, but most of them hung from the ceiling at a level lower than the one we were on; anyone looking up would need to see us in the shadows behind a light. Also, they'd need to be able to see me while I was invisible.

I opened the door a little wider after ensuring there wasn't anything connected to it. I didn't want another dollar-store trap going off and alerting everyone.

"Want me to scout ahead again?" I asked.

"Go ahead," Gomorrah muttered.

I nodded and stepped onto the overhang. It was really a balcony at this point. One without a railing, and overlooking what was obviously some sort of cheapo hospital setup. I made sure I was properly invisible before moving closer to the edge to look down.

I'd gotten augs once, in my eye. Just the standard crap that everyone got. It had required going to a specialty clinic where I sat down in a plush chair and was given some options. I'd opted out of the local anesthetic because that shit was expensive. Then some bored undereducated guy had stuck my head in a vise and, a lot of held-back screaming later, I had my first aug. Quick and easy and just a little painful. Like getting earrings.

That was for a simple, run-of-the-mill augmentation that everyone and their grandma had.

What was happening below was on a whole other level.

There were three baths, old cast-iron-looking things, too small for any-one to be properly comfortable in. Each of them was currently filled with someone.

Most of someone.

Someone from the torso up.

Tubes leading into baths were probably keeping the three down there alive.

Off to the far end of the room was a pile of clear plastic trash bags, cur-rently filled with discarded limbs, but very little blood.

There were more people down there. A couple hanging off metal racks, prosthetic arms and legs dangling as they were held up by hooks that passed under their arms.

"Well, this is exceptionally fucky," I said.

"Super fucked," Rac agreed.

"You probably shouldn't be seeing this," I said as I looked away. I didn't need to scar the kid.

"Eh, it's not the first time I've seen most of someone in a trash bag. Never seen that many, but then, that's just, like . . . a matter of scale, you know?" Raccoon said.

"You worry me sometimes, kid," I said.

She laughed, and I couldn't help but shake my head at it all. We had to make our way down there and figure out a way to help those people. That was five of the missing; there had to be more of them somewhere. Though the size of the limb pile did suggest that these five weren't the first to get operated on.

"What in God's name are we going to do with them?" Gomorrah asked.

"Save them?" I tried.

"I don't know how to replace people's limbs," Gomorrah said. "And the point cost to give the number of people I suspect are here a semblance of a normal life . . . it's more than either of us can afford, Cat."

I shrugged, even if she couldn't see. "Then we do what we can. Look, we need to find the fucker who did this and ask him to explain. Or maybe we can extract that from his augs. Just going to have to be careful not to blow his brains out while we murderize him."

"Speak of the devil," Gomorrah muttered.

I snapped my head around and searched the ground floor. Three people had just walked in. Two of them were very obviously Sewer Dragons. Metal feet clicked on the concrete floor and they both wore those familiar long coats that hid most of their bodies. One of them had four arms, the second set ending in what looked like a suite of surgical tools.

I didn't peg him as Doc Hack—that went to the third guy.

Doc Hack was a wide, large fellow who walked with all the grace of a beached whale. He barely fit in the white coat he had hanging over his shoulders, the doctor's smock beneath straining.

I didn't think it was all fat, though. There were some strange angles under there. Modifications?

The good doc walked over to one of the baths while his pals moved around the room. Tools came to stand on the other side of the tub, while Four Arms moved to a bench off to the side and sat down with the nonchalance of someone already bored out of their mind.

"What are his readings?" Doc Hack asked.

"BP's a bit low," the . . . I decided to assume it was an assistant, said. "Anesthetic is starting to wear off."

"Give him another . . . no, best not. We're running out as is. We'll have to act fast." Doc Hack leaned over the body in the tub and a clearly mechanical hand snaked out from the sleeve of his coat and smacked the guy's face. "Wake up, my boy."

"He's coming to," the assistant said.

I watched as the guy's eyes flickered open. "What?" he asked. He looked around, then started to move.

"Stay, stay, you shouldn't move just yet," Doc Hack said.

"Who? You're that . . . where's?" The man raised his arms and stared at the stumps. Then he glanced down. "What the fuck? What the fuck?" he screamed.

"I explained it to you already," Doc Hack said, his voice way too fucking calm. "We need you. The whole city needs you. It's a delicate machine, and many of its most precious cogs are missing."

"What the fuck did you do to me! Put them back! Put them back!"

"Now, now, no need to worry, you'll have new limbs soon, entirely suited to a whole new biome! A miracle of innovation and science, impossible even a century ago!"

"Where the fuck is my cock?"

"Right," I said. "Votes that we just go full samurai on Doctor Hacks-a-Lot down there?"

"He's disgusting," Franny said.

"Let me switch to a more flammable fuel," Gomorrah said.

That was a yes in my books.

CHAPTER THIRTY-THREE

NO SURRENDER

It is in the opinion of the General Inspector that, without immediate action, the water treatment systems keeping the city functional will fail within six to nine months.

This situation is a ticking time bomb. The system currently in place was designed for civilian use, and the number of corporate entities piggybacking on it is causing shortages, backups, and pressure issues across the entire mechanism.

If we do not immediately begin to repair this damage, this city might soon find itself without water or sewerage.

At least the sewage issues will be alleviated once the population no longer has access to water.

—A note to the city council of New Montreal, 2047

The first step in my plan, which I was officially dubbing "Operation Fuck the Doc" required that Gomorrah and I be able to reach the doc so we could, in a figurative sense, fuck him.

The problem was that we were three floors up and I didn't trust my power armor that much. Not enough to risk a plunge from this height, at least. "We need to get down there," I muttered.

Gomorrah stepped next to me, then looked around. "There's a rope right there," she said, pointing.

There was a cord, thick steel wire running from the ceiling all the way down to the ground level. It had lights hanging off it every meter or so. "Yeah, I guess I could use that," I said. Like sliding down one of those stripper poles in a firefighter station. "Aren't you worried you might give yourself friction burns?" I asked.

"Cat . . . I don't know why you think that something like a rope would be able to burn me, but . . . I suppose I appreciate the concern, but it's not necessary."

"Fair enough," I said. The rope was a good ways away, definitely out of reach unless I jumped.

So I jumped.

My cybernetic hand wrapped around the metal cord and clamped shut. The entire thing swung, and me with it, lights rattling below me even as the rope started to screech past and I went from a swing to a barely assisted fall.

Falling, I discovered, happened fast. I didn't have much time to react except to point my legs down as I rammed through light housings and sent them clattering down below me.

The doc, his assistant, and the guard jumped up, and the dude in the tub squirmed around to look at the spot where I made my grand entrance.

I landed in a crouch, my entire body jarring within my suit, but it didn't hurt. I wouldn't do it for fun, but the suit definitely absorbed the impact. I stood, slow and careful, then faced the doc and his pals.

"What the fuck?" the assistant said. "What made the lights fall?"

Oh, right, I was still invisible.

Ruined my own big entrance.

At least when I was invisible, no one could tell how embarrassed I was.

Nice landing.

"The suit did most of the work," I said as I stepped out from the pile of broken light fixtures. As stealthy as my boots were, there was no stopping the crunch of glass and tin underfoot.

A sibilant hiss sounded, ending in a crunch as Gomorrah landed behind me. She stood, then picked up her launcher and aimed in Doc Hack's general direction. "Back away from the man in the tub and raise your arms," Gomorrah demanded.

"Who in the fuck are you?" Doc Hack asked.

I stepped to the side, my invisibility turning off. I wasn't going to miss a second opportunity to be intimidating and cool. "We're two girls who have spent far too many hours trawling through shit to get to you."

I should warn you. I was trawling through Doc Hack's systems and files for information. He has shut off his exterior connections. I intercepted every signal he sent out, but I no longer have direct access to his systems.

I made sure my next line wouldn't be heard aloud. "Can't hack back in?"

He disconnected by literally disconnecting any wireless systems in his body. A simple but efficient method to prevent tampering.

"Pulled the plug, huh," I said.

"Which corp are you two from?" Doc Hack asked. His head turned his head my way, then back to Gomorrah. His face was some uncanny-valley shit. Like a mannequin's face with some shitty mechanism giving it motion. It didn't quite move in time with his voice.

"We're not from any corporation," Gomorrah said. "Now, please surrender. It would make all of this infinitely simpler."

Doc Hack nodded. "So, the reports were correct. You are samurai. To think that the very guardians of humanity would interfere with the work we are doing here. Or . . . perhaps you don't know better. Yes, that's far more likely."

Had he lost his mind? . . . That was probably not the cleverest thought I'd had all day. The dude was chopping people up while living in a sewer.

"Look, Doc, you're doing some pretty fucked-up shit, so we're going to . . . you know, stop you from doing that. Permanently, if need be."

Doc Hack raised his hands and gestured, as if telling us to calm down. It didn't work all that well when the guy in the tub next to him started screaming again. "Please, dear samurai, you misunderstand what is happening here."

"So you're not kidnapping people off the streets, chopping off their limbs, then turning them into . . . actually, why in the fuck are you cutting people up? Unless you're getting off on it."

"Him getting off on it would be enough to explain all of this for you?" Gomorrah asked.

I shrugged. "People will do some weird shit if you let them. Wouldn't make me shoot him any less."

"Fair enough, I suppose," Gomorrah conceded.

Doc Hack shook his head. "No, no, please, let me explain. This place—the sewers, the underground—it is the beating heart of this city. Its lifeblood pumps through day and night, every moment of the year. And we are the guardians of that heart, just as you are the guardians of humanity."

"I don't recall chopping people up while guarding humanity," I said.

"That . . . that is a failure on my, on our, part," Doc Hack said. He gestured to the rest of the room, but I had the impression he was trying to encompass the entirety of the sewers. "We failed to predict the future, to plan for the loss of so many of our members. And now the whole system suffers. Entire sections have been closed down and are being repaired, but in that time, the rest of the heart bleeds. We need more people, more valiant men and women on the front lines, fighting back against the rust and degradation that put the entire city at risk."

"Wait, wait," I said. "You're trying to get more members? That's why you're kidnapping people?"

"We will have new, voluntary members as time goes on. We always do. The lost, the homeless, those who, like myself, seek to hide from the oppression of the world above and find solace in the honest work here. But alas, those numbers are slow to come. We need more hands."

"And you thought you'd just grab folks off the streets?" I asked.

Doc Hack nodded. "If we do nothing, the city dies. Already the water systems are falling apart, already the imbalances caused by the loss of entire districts are trickling down to the areas around them. Monsters inhabited the sewers for a time, and though they are gone, you guardians were not gentle in your exterminations."

"Fucking hell, just put an ad out on the net if you need more workers!"

"Are you so naïve that you think people would want to come to a place like this? To become mutilated and defaced? To lose their humanity in order to save this city?" Doc Hack asked. He was becoming increasingly louder as he spoke. "This is a place of great sacrifice, where none will ever acknowledge the work that is done!"

"Sure, whatever, that doesn't mean you can just . . . take people. For fuck's sake," I said.

"Who will do the work that needs doing if not us? We don't expect much. We are the liquidators of this city's filth and the providers of its life! It is thankless, but no one else will do it. End me, and this city crumbles."

My analysis suggests that he may be correct. The city's water and sewer infrastructure have been due for an overhaul for nearly a decade. Without that overhaul, and with what little maintenance the system has been receiving so far, it is likely a chain collapse will occur at any moment. The Sewer Dragons seem to be working to postpone this.

"That doesn't mean we won't do something about this guy." I glanced at the man in the tub before turning my glare to Doc Hack. "I . . . can't allow this kind of thing in my city."

"You can't allow it?" Doc Hack asked.

I . . . might have forgotten to turn off the helmet's speakers there.

"Not . . . allow it? Then you would bring ruin to this city and all that we've done to protect it!" Doc Hack's jacket burst open and a pair of arms moved out from a mass of metallic limbs, all of them holding handguns.

"Ah, shit," I said.

CHAPTER THIRTY-FOUR

THE EDGE OF THE SWORD

Why?

Because it's cool as shit!

—Three Swipes, 2037

Things happened fast.

Gomorrah opened up with a surge of flames so hot I felt them through my suit. It was a spitting bar of fire wider than a person's head, and it instantly started to melt everything within a meter of it.

Doc Hack was just as quick. Three arms tore out from his body and grabbed his assistant to place the poor idiot between the doc and the flames. The man screamed as he cooked.

Doc Hack drowned the screams out in return fire, the guns held by three of the arms he'd deployed spraying bullets across the lab.

There was no grace in the way he fired, just a wild spray of shots that pinged off empty tubs and cracked into cement pillars.

Gomorrah rolled to the side, the wash of her flames ending as easily as it had begun. She hid behind a pillar while weathering the storm.

My turn, I supposed. I whipped out my Trench Maker and sighted down the barrel even as my finger squeezed the trigger.

Doc Hack looked worse for wear, the front of his smock still alight, but beneath it were layers and layers of prosthetics, all shifting into place. He stumbled back even as thicker, armored arms rose to intercept my shots. Electrified bullets crashed into steel plates with a snapping buzz and did fuck-all.

"You are making a mistake!" Doc Hack roared, his face twisted into a mockery of anger, plastic teeth bared.

"You don't have room to talk about mistakes," I shot back.

The doc fell onto his rear with a heavy crash.

I paused. Was it over?

The back of his smock tore apart and long multijointed legs slammed into the ground. He started to scuttle backward.

There was only so fast a body that size could move.

I grunted and aimed to fire again, and then motion caught my attention from the edge of my vision. The guard.

He screamed something incoherent and loud as he raised a gun to his hip and fired.

I winced back as a trio of shots clattered against my helmet. It rang, but the pain wasn't any worse than being hit with a rolled-up newspaper.

"Shut up!" I shouted at him before putting two in his chest.

"Cat!" Gomorrah called. "He's moving out!"

I whipped my head around to see Doc Hack slamming through the doors at the end of the lab. I swore and bolted after him, Gomorrah a step behind me.

We arrived in a long passageway, the doc already halfway down it. "You would bring this city down with your greed and naïveté!" Doc Hack screamed.

I took two steps into the room, then raised my Trench Maker up and fired.

Doc Hack's head exploded, plastic and servos flying back.

"I was the solution to all of your ills!" Doc Hack roared via the mouth in his chest.

"God damn it!" I shouted as I started to run and fire center of mass. I wasn't sure if anything actually hit; I could barely aim standing still.

"I got him!" Gomorrah said. She fell to one knee and raised her flamethrower.

I ducked away and activated my railguns.

Doc Hack must have seen it coming. "Then I'll take the place and burn it down with me!"

I hadn't noticed the pipes in the walls and the ceilings. They were everywhere, in every corridor we crossed and every wall we passed. The O_2 signs and the methane warnings were like ads in my periphery. Easily ignored.

Doc Hack fired. This time it wasn't a wild spray, but something more calculated.

I saw the holes punched through the rusty old pipes as if they were paper.

There was a hiss, and Gomorrah's flames raced across the room.

The world went white, white and warm, and I felt myself being thrown back into the nearest wall. I didn't hear a damned thing, but the alerts across my vision warned me my ears were off.

I stumbled away from the wall and shook my head.

Everything was on fire. The walls were blackened and fire poured out of pipes in long jets.

Doc Hack was gone.

My hearing returned with a pop, and I was introduced to the sound of the world burning and crumbling apart.

"Gom!" I shouted.

"I'm fine!" Gomorrah said. She picked herself up off the floor and surveyed the room. "Keep going. I'll take care of this," she growled. "Kill him for me, would you?"

"Yeah," I said.

The floor had collapsed, the ceiling too. Large slabs of concrete with crooked, rebar-like grasping fingers poking through.

Where was that fucker?

I leapt over the hole, vaguely aware that the collapse had gone deeper than I'd initially thought. This was going to be costly.

The corridor bent, and I found Doc Hack running while tearing off broken limbs. The lost mass was lying across the floor, discarded arms and legs trailing behind the doc, who was running all the faster now.

"Wait!" I screamed as I took off after him. I whipped out my Icarus, Trench Maker slammed into my thigh holster. "I need to kill you!"

"I died for the cause a long time ago, girl! There's no killing me now!" Doc Hack screamed right back.

He stopped running, spinning around with a screech of metal-ended limbs on grated flooring.

His chest opened up, and two of his arms tore something out from within. A long barrel, covered in rings.

Cat, that's a Tier One Vanguard weapon. A railgun.

My own railguns fired, twin tracers punching holes into and through Doc Hack.

I squeezed the trigger on my launcher.

He fired.

It felt like someone had just landed a jumping kick right in my short ribs.

My forward momentum turned into a backward flip, one that ended with my crashing onto all fours after somersaulting through the air. I gasped as a warning flashed up on my HUD.

ARMOR INTEGRITY DOWN TO 99%

"Shit," I groaned as I jumped back to my feet. I didn't have time to process the pain. The doc was too big a problem for that.

I stared. The bastard had left a foot behind, glued to the floor by my launcher. A launcher that was a dozen paces behind me.

No time for that.

I sprinted after him again.

The corridor ended at a pair of double doors, steps beyond them leading down.

I leapt over the steps while taking in the room. Not a normal room. A passageway next to one of those large open tunnels filled with shit. Windows along the edges showed the crap flowing past a floor down.

There were idiots in the room—trench coats, metal limbs, guns. Doc Hack was at the far end, tossing his railgun to one of the grunts. "Your sword has been blunted already, samurai!" he shouted. "Let's not end this in your demise."

I whipped out my Claw and fired as soon as the reticle was over the bastard.

He screamed, for the first time in actual pain, as a spinning blender appeared in his innards.

The fire from the grunts distracted me right after. There were six of them, at a quick count, pneumatic rifles in hand.

I didn't have time for them.

Twisting around, I fired first at one, then another, emptying my Claw into them while my railguns took care of the rest.

Doc Hack didn't stick around.

I ran to the edge of the room and saw him below. He was boarding a boat, the engine already on, a Sewer Dragon at the wheel throttling up.

He would pass right in front of me on his way to some other shit hole.

The other boats were sinking.

"No," I growled.

I swung forward, fist meeting safety glass with all of the strength and weight of my armor behind it. The glass didn't shatter, but the plates holding it in place did, rusted strips tearing off with a squelch of old rubber as the entire thing fell away and ruined the room's seal.

"Myalis, I need a fucking sword."

Understood.

New Purchase: Fixed-Point, Lethal Transition Melee Weaponry

Points Reduced from . . . 10,865 to . . . 10,815

New Purchase: Class I Void Terminus Hiss

Points Reduced from . . . 10,815 to . . . 10,715

A sword appeared by my side. I didn't have time to consider how very stupid it was to ask for that, specifically. I was too busy placing a foot on the edge of the ledge created by the missing window.

The sword requires an activation phrase to turn on. Do you wish to set one now?

I jumped.

Doc Hack turned, and I could see his face, his actual face, in his chest, buried behind prosthetics. Just a pair of eyes, metal grafted to his exposed bones, his mouth nothing more than a tube. His eyes focused on me.

I crashed into the boat a meter in front of him, knees bending with the impact even as a tide of shit splashed up around the boat.

I grabbed the sword in one hand, the other grabbing the sheath. "Fuck,"
I began.

I tore the sword out of its sheath. It was a metal rod, with a few rings
along its length. I was confused, but I trusted Myalis.

"You!" I finished.

Activation name set. Activating!

The sword hissed, like a cat met in a dark alley. The blade snapped into
place, a dark bar sucking in the air around it. I swore I could see stars within.

I twisted with the swing. The air screamed blade as it moved, a banner
trailing after the edge.

It touched Doc Hack's side, and he tried to grab at me.

It didn't help him.

The sword sliced through him in a single swipe, and everywhere it
passed, the meat inside Doc Hack's mechanical body was dragged into it.
Metal rent and vacuumed into the black edge.

Then it was over and I stood there, deck wobbling under me, as Doc
Hack's remains fell apart. I saw a piece of his face splash into the shit.

A fitting end for him.

CHAPTER THIRTY-FIVE

VOID TERMINUS

We do what we can. Most of us are hard workers, and you'd be hard-pressed to find a samurai that wouldn't do some horrible things to keep people safe. It's not just about killing aliens; it's about trying to make the world we live in a better place.

Some days it feels like we're swimming against the current to achieve anything, but on some days things work out.

This isn't the nicest world we live in, but dammit, it's ours too.

—*Good Morning New America* interview with Rising Tide, 2034

The boat bobbed in the water, and I had to sway with it not to fall ass-first into the shit stream. Once I had my balance I shifted to get a better footing and turned toward the Sewer Dragon piloting the boat.

We weren't moving, which was probably because the guy was too busy staring at me, wide-eyed. "Turn us around and park back at the docks," I said.

He glanced past me and down to the lower half of Doc Hack's body, which was currently leaking all over the deck. He spun the wheel around and we started to head back.

I stared at the blade that Myalis had chosen for me. It had a metal rod at the back, straight, with a sharp cap on the end, and all along that rod, not touching it but almost, was a paper-thin slice of nothing that seemed to be sucking in the air around it with a constant hiss.

Deactivating.

The black slice disappeared with a snap.

"What was that?" I asked. "I swear I saw stars in there."

The Void Terminus Hiss is a melee weapon whose main function is to create a temporary rift. Objects entering that rift are transported to a location in empty space. The edges of the rift are, in layman's terms, very sharp.

I stared at the sword, which was currently just a metal stick. I didn't miss the fact that it had one of those Japanese-looking hilts, with the round guard thing. Though the guard on this one looked like a cat's paw, and there was a small plastic cat dangling from a loop at the very bottom, like one of those toys people used to hook onto old-school phones. "So . . . it murders people by teleporting a slice of them elsewhere."

Essentially, yes. It is obscenely dangerous, but the requirements for that rift to exist make that particular kind of technology unwieldy and unviable in most combat situations. It so happens that as a melee weapon it is quite lethal.

"Fucking awesome," I said. "If I swear while this thing is dangling by my side, will I cut my own leg off?"

I will do my best to prevent you from cutting your own limbs off. Though I am merely a millennia-old hyper-intelligent machine with unfathomable powers. There's only so much I can do to counter human idiocy.

"You're sassy today," I said.

You've essentially won, as far as I can tell. All that remains is the tedious work of cleaning up and assessing the situation, which I suspect will be somewhat complex. Giving you a moment to relax will help you manage the stress, and for some reason you find insulting banter amusing.

I didn't know what to say to that, exactly. "That's nice to know?" I tried.

The boat came around and lurched as it hit the edge of the docks. I jumped up and onto the nearest pier, then walked over to the tower. The Sewer Dragon I left behind looked around, confused, but he stayed put.

Honestly, I didn't care what he did; as far as I was concerned, I was done here.

The tower had the usual airlock set up, though the decontamination shower here actually seemed to have some pressure to it, which was nice.

I stepped up the staircase and came upon the room where I'd killed a few of Doc Hack's buddies. It wasn't a pretty sight. My Claw wasn't a delicate weapon, and I think the blender bit was wider than most people, which meant that the blended hole it left in them had a place to leak out of.

Didn't feel like sticking around the mess much, so I moved on past it all and shoved my way into the corridors leading back to Doc Hack's lab.

I found Gomorrah jogging over to me. "Hey," I said.

"You're alive. Did he get away?" she asked.

"Oh man, you didn't see it!" Raccoon said over the line. "It was awesome! Cat was like 'fuck you!' and her sword was like, hisschaw! Then he fell into the shit."

I blinked. "You were watching this whole time and you only spoke up now?" I asked.

"You were being all broody and cool, like heroes are after they kill the big bad. I wasn't gonna interrupt your Batman moment."

"Thanks, I guess," I said. I sighed. "Rac's right. Doc Hack's very dead. Unless he can survive with only half his brain, I don't think we'll need to worry about him anymore. I think we've won?"

Gomorrah shook her head. "We took out the source of the problem; now we need to deal with the problem itself."

"What do you mean?" I asked.

"There are a lot of people who were turned into Sewer Dragons. Not to mention the people still in the lab. We need to rescue them," Gomorrah said.

"And," Franny interjected, "you can't forget what Doc Hack said. About the sewers needing the Sewer Dragons. You've killed a number of them, taken out the person who made more of them, and I imagine that the people they turned were put to work. If you remove all of them, then maybe the Sewer Dragons really will collapse."

I groaned. "And then everything would go to shit."

Rac snorted, and I made an effort to ignore it.

"We . . . we can . . . fuck, what can we do?" I asked. The problem was a lot bigger than I was used to, even as a samurai. You couldn't explode a sewer system better.

"We need to rescue those stuck down here," Gomorrah said. "That'll be our first priority. The sewers . . . aren't really our responsibility. Not directly. Our job is to make sure that humanity is safe, which does include things like infrastructure, but I don't think we're equipped for this."

"Myalis, do we have anything for sewer maintenance?" I asked.

"There are catalogs designed around that, yes. Though the total point cost to repair the sewer system as it is would exceed the points you and Gomorrah have. To bring the system up to par would cost a prohibitive number of points. I'm afraid the Vanguard's point system isn't designed for use on that scale."

"Yeah, I can imagine," I said. "Crap, we're not equipped for this."

"You can't take everything on your shoulders," Gomorrah said.

I barked a laugh. "Trust me, I'm good at only caring for me and mine. But this might fuck up the whole city, and me and mine live here."

"We can tell the government. It is their job to take care of this," Franny said.

"As if," Rac said.

"Raccoon's right. They'll panic, then cover their asses," I said.

"Not everyone is that incompetent," Gomorrah said. "Especially when samurai show up at their office and deliver the news personally. After we save the people down here."

"Right, after," I said. "So how do we go about it?"

"Can you check on the people in the lab? I'll question that guard Doc Hack had. The Sewer Dragons have to have some way to communicate. I think we can convince them to bring anyone who wants to be . . . returned to normal to the lab."

"And can we do that?" I asked.

"It's easier than fixing the entire sewers," Gomorrah said. "But . . . I'm not sure? Maybe? We can at least get them looked at by actual doctors."

"Right, right," I said. I really wanted to rub my face, but there was armor in the way. "Well, nothing for it. Let's get this over with."

Gomorrah nodded and shifted her shoulders. "We're nearly done, I think. Don't worry, it won't be so bad."

"I hope not," I said.

The patch of corridor that Doc Hack had oh-so-helpfully blown up was now covered in white foam, courtesy of Gomorrah, I guessed. She stepped up before me and crossed a bulbous bridge of the stuff that spanned the gap left in the floor.

"Ah, shit, we're going to need to tell someone about this too, aren't we?" I asked.

"At least this part we can blame on Doc Hack . . . in fact, I think we should blame everything on him. It will make things easier," Gomorrah said.

"How saintly," Franny shot back.

"Yes, yes, I think that's exactly what it is."

CHAPTER THIRTY-SIX

WRAPPING SHIT UP

It's not true. There aren't people living underground, it's all some bullshit urban legend. Some punk saw a hobo and didn't know better and then when he told his buddies they exaggerated the story.

This is Bigfoot all over.

There's no such thing as a "sewer dragon." It's stupid.

—WriteIt Post, June 2040

There was a lot of shit to wrap up, metaphorically speaking.

Gomorrah was, somehow, worse than me when it came to sweet-talking folk, so I got the dubious honor of being the one to talk to the people currently stuck in bathtubs with no limbs.

It took proving that we were both samurai to convince them to calm down, that and six points' worth of alien painkillers. The folk currently pinned to racks were somewhat mobile, though they reminded me of some videos Lucy'd shown me of cloned baby giraffes taking their first steps. Awkward and unwieldy, and they tended to crash into everything around them.

At least we didn't need to carry them.

Doc Hack, as it turned out, had a clever system in place to communicate across the sewers. Morse, transmitted over signals that ran along the network of pipes. I didn't get into the finer details of it, but once Gomorrah figured it out from his stuff, it wasn't hard for her and Atyacus to tap into the entire communication system the Sewer Dragons had.

Its simplicity actually served it well. We could swamp it with random data, but there was no real way to hack into a communication system that could be powered by someone with a pair of booster cables and a stolen car battery.

Still, Gomorrah managed to get the message across, and before we knew it, Sewer Dragons were congregating. Not at Doc Hack's lab—the place was currently a mess—but at the Oasis.

We left the lab the same way we came in, out the top. Carrying our new limbless friends made that somewhat complicated, but we managed, even if it took well over an hour to trace back a path that had initially taken us ten minutes to walk.

By the time we were outdoors and meeting a team of EMTs, I was dead on my feet.

And it wasn't over.

"Jesus, Mary, and Joseph," Franny swore as she walked closer.

We didn't stray far from the entrance of the pharmaceutical building, no matter how much it annoyed the guards. Seeing us come up with the quasi Sewer Dragons had made an impression, I think.

The Fury parked itself right on the sidewalk. Rac and Franny hopped out, the younger of the two with a mouth stained blue by slushie, and stopped half a dozen meters away.

"You fucking reek," Raccoon said.

"We do?" I asked. "I can't actually smell anything."

"You're lucky, because if you smelled yourself, you'd off yourself like a corpo after too many months of overtime." Rac nodded at her own sage words.

I snorted. "Right, I can imagine. The EMTs were giving us looks too. They didn't say anything, though."

"You're covered in shit and blood," Rac pointed out. "And you're wearing nutso samurai stuff. They'd be mental to try anything."

She had a point.

Gomorrah sighed, then looked me up and down in a way that had me very worried. "How fireproof is your armor?" she asked.

"That's not a question I'm very keen on hearing," I said.

"It'll remove the smell."

"It'll remove my fucking skin," I countered.

In the end, Myalis assured me that I was, for the most part, fireproof. As long as Gomorrah held back and used a reasonable amount of fire on me.

A few gawkers filmed us, and the few cars that were piloted by people stopped on the roadside to stare as Gomorrah hosed me down with her flamethrower. I was warm, uncomfortably so where my armor was thinner, but she was moving fast and it didn't exactly hurt, so I didn't complain.

Then it was my turn to flame her, which was a lot more enjoyable. Though her armor was, predictably, very fireproof.

After cleaning off our tools with a few spurts from her shoulder-mounted guns and a sniff check from Rac, who confirmed that we smelled more like exhaust than outhouse, we got into the Fury and took off with the usual amount of alacrity.

The ride wasn't long, but it did allow me to grab another one of those energy drinks and text Lucy.

Cat: Hey Lulu, I'm safe. Going 2 b a while b4 I get home

I didn't have time to lean back and relax before Lucy replied.

Lulu the greatest: What happened?

Cat: Long story. Fought in the sewers. Weird monster doctor

Cat: Still some people to save. Will try to head home after

Cat: Might have to make a stop before that.

Lulu the greatest: Are u hurt?

Cat: Nope! I'm fine. Tired tho

Cat: And I want a shower

Lulu the greatest: We'll have a nice warm one once you get back!!

I was grinning so hard I think the two in the back thought I was losing my mind.

I wanted to keep talking to Lucy, to convince her things really were all right, but Gomorrah pulled into the lot before the Oasis and I had to say goodbye and refocus. Things weren't over just yet.

There were at least a hundred Sewer Dragons gathered around the front of the Oasis.

Unlike last time, Gomorrah parked us in front, the sleek car looking out of place against the cement and rust.

"You two stay inside," I said. "They might not take kindly to what we're going to tell them, and I don't want to have to patch up any more bullet holes than I have to today."

"I'm not an idiot," Franny said. "I know better than to get in front of an angry mob."

The crowd did look pretty mob-like. A lot of the Sewer Dragons were standing there with arms crossed and heads bowed. Plenty had weapons of some form at hand. There was a large group that was standing apart, though. They looked awkward—not just their body language, but the way they moved. They lacked the fluid, almost mechanical grace of the other Sewer Dragons.

Our missing people, I guessed.

Gomorrah and I stepped out of the Fury and instantly we became the center of attention. "So, you wanna be the one who does the talking, or do I get the honors?" I asked.

"On the one hand, the likelihood of there being a riot rises exponentially if you're the one to talk. On the other, I'm . . . reluctantly weary of public speaking."

"Really?" I asked, glancing over to the nun. She didn't seem shy, at least body-language-wise. "You have a pretty voice."

"I don't think the beauty of one's voice matters all that much when it comes to deciding whether you're good at orating."

That sounded fair. "Have you tried imagining them all naked?"

"Have you?" she shot back.

I looked at the Sewer Dragons, all in their long coats, metal bits shining beneath. A number of them had a nice coating of shit on their pant legs. I imagined the place smelled like a convention held in a pig farm.

Tilting my head from side to side, I cracked my neck and stepped up to the edge of the entranceway to the Oasis, right where a few steps led down into the main area with the tents and little shacks the Sewer Dragons had put up.

Adjusting the volume on my helmet's microphone, I pushed it all the way up. "All right!" I said. My voice boomed across the vast concrete hall and I only just managed to hold back a wince. "Some of you might have heard of us. I'm Stray Cat, this is Gomorrah, and for the past few hours we've been running around your sewers and kicking your asses."

I think I had their attention. Now I just had to avoid fucking it all up.

"We came down here because we learned that a whole lot of people were missing from above. Sewer Dragons were responsible for it, but we wanted to get to the bottom of all that mess and rescue those people." Some of the Sewer Dragons below started to look excited, the unarmed, awkward ones. "Doc Hack's dead," I said. "He didn't cooperate, so now he's swimming in some pipe somewhere. I know that the city needs you, but that doesn't excuse kidnappings. We'll be twisting the government's arm later today to get them to act."

I settled my hand over the hilt of my sword. Somehow, that really helped with the nerves.

"If you're one of the people who were transformed against their will, then gather up here. We'll be doing what we can to turn you back. If you want to stay the way you are, then all the best to you."

CHAPTER THIRTY-SEVEN

HEADING FOR GREENER PASTURES

The standard 9 a.m. to 5 p.m. workday (with weekends off) proved entirely inefficient as travel time increased and working from home became standard across many industries. Now workers can look forward to daytime work hours that better reflect the needs of modern corporations, such as 8 a.m. to 6 p.m. shifts that occasionally include one day off per week!"

[. . .]

Your employees are going to kill themselves anyway; might as well make the best of it while they're still work-capable!

—Excerpt from "A New Standard for a Brighter Future! How to Make the Best of Workplace Suicides!," a *Business Outsider* article, 2031

"I'm going to be real honest here," I said as I stared out across the crowd. As it turned out, the Sewer Dragons at the Oasis when we'd shown up were just those who made it there in time to hear my speech. There were supposed to be something like twenty thousand of them, and I was starting to believe that number.

"I'm listening," Gomorrah said. She was eyeing the crowd. The crowd that didn't stop growing. There had to be five hundred of them by then.

"I don't want to be here." I gestured to all of the people before us—a sea of humanity, despite all of the modifications and prosthetics and the shit. Actually, the shit was pretty human too. "I want to go home."

"We still have a lot of work ahead of us," Gomorrah said.

I sighed. "Yeah, I know. Just complaining."

"You have the right."

I chuckled. "I hope so. You know, I've been a samurai for . . . has it been four days now? It's been pretty nonstop."

"Need a break?"

I pressed my hands into the small of my back—it was a bit awkward with the armor there—and then I pushed and stretched as best I could. "I think I do," I said.

Gomorrah shifted her shoulders. "I could take care of the rest here."

"What are you even going to do with this many people?" I asked. "We promised to help them, and I intend to, but . . . there's a lot of them."

"We have the church," Franny piped in. She was still in the Fury with Rac. Things didn't seem dangerous, but still, I didn't exactly trust the people I'd spent the morning shooting at and being shot by.

"The church?" Gomorrah repeated. "They'd never accept this many. One or two, certainly."

"There's room for this many. We have that entire shelter thing set up to take in refugees. It filled up after the incursion, but I think it's nearly empty now. It was temporary housing."

Gomorrah tilted her head. Bit creepy, with her mask and suit giving the impression she had a longer neck. "That could work," she said. "I think we have enough shuttle buses that it won't take too many trips."

"They'll stink," I warned.

"We can set up a decontamination system," Gomorrah said.

"Huh," I replied. "That won't exactly un-fuckedupify these people, though."

"No, but it's a better step than leaving them here."

That was a fair point. "Well, while you do that . . . urgh, what else do we need to do?"

"Inform the city about the impending disaster."

I considered it. "Would a strongly worded email do?"

"I very much doubt it," Gomorrah said.

"Fuck me. Okay, you stay here. I'll go . . . tell the mayor or whatever that he might be shitting in a bucket for the next couple of weeks."

Gomorrah chuckled darkly. "I kind of wish I could be there for that. It's amusing to see people's expressions as they come to grips with a new situation. Perhaps not a healthy sort of amusement, but still."

"Right, I'll call a cab. Rac, you want to come with?"

"Fuck yeah!" was the immediate response. Gomorrah glanced my way, but I shrugged. The girl wouldn't be any safer at her church or whatever. All I was going to do was threaten some politicians.

I moved over to the Fury and called up a cab, then leaned against the car to wait. It didn't seem as if anyone came down here all that often for pickups, but this wasn't the undercity where Rac lived. It wasn't safe, but it was an industrial area. I imagined most pickups around the area were just folks heading to and from work.

Gomorrah fielded questions from some Sewer Dragons while I looked on. She had things well in hand. Her nun-ness made her perfectly intimidating to anyone with particularly dumb ideas. Or maybe it was the armor and flamethrower and the deployed cannons on the hood of her car.

Our ride arrived half an hour later. A shitty little car with a sticker on the door for the cab company. The guy behind the wheel looked like some college-aged dude who needed whatever cash he was making. A gig job, then?

I opened the Fury's door to let Rac out, and we both walked over to the cab. When I opened the passenger-side door, a few soft drink cups and some burger boxes fell to the ground. Didn't even make it dirtier. "Hey," I said as I squeezed in.

"What the fuck," he said.

"It stinks better in here than out there," Rac said.

The driver looked to me, then to Rac, then at the crowd of Sewer Dragons outside. "The fuck is going on here?"

"Nothing," I said. "Just drive and everything will be fine."

"Uh, right," he said as he reached for the controls and pulled us up and away from the ground. The car listed to my side, my weight likely throwing it off a tad. He compensated without complaint. "So, where are we going?"

"I set the address on the app, didn't I?" I asked.

"Well, yeah, but that's all autopilot stuff. I don't actually know where it's taking us."

"We're going to city hall," I said. "Going to go say hi to the mayor."

"Uh, okay," he said, then reached for the console and flicked on the AC. "Sorry, but it, ah . . ."

"Smells like we just ripped a fat one?" Rac asked.

"Basically that," he admitted.

I chuckled. "I don't think the Sewer Dragons back there do showers all that often. For that matter, I don't think they leave their tunnels all that often either. Today's a special day."

"All right," he said. We paused next to a road while his car's autopilot loaded, and then he let go of the wheel and the car moved up, merging into traffic and tailgating a larger van. We got to see a constant stream of ads from the rear of the truck, but I supposed the slipstream saved on power or whatever.

I tugged my Trench Maker out and removed the magazine. "Myalis," I said. "Something with a bang. Some ammo for the Claw too."

A box thumped into place on the dash ahead of me and I started to reload. Myalis sent me a text, just the number *10,705*. Was she napping or something?

"Oh, shit," the driver said.

"Not going to shoot you. Or steal from you or your awesome car," I said. "No no, I mean . . . you're a, ah."

"She's a samurai," Rac said, obviously relishing being the one to spill the beans.

Our driver nodded and pulled out some wireless earbuds from his pocket. "I'm going to listen to some audiobooks and shut up now," he said.

"Clever guy," I said. I could respect someone who didn't stick their neck into trouble. I cocked my Trench Maker and shoved it away, then reloaded my Claw. My railguns still had eighty percent of their ammo, and my Icarus was in Gomorrah's car. Didn't think I'd need a grenade launcher to talk to some snobby politician sorts . . . then again.

We moved out of the lower parts of the city and merged into morning traffic. It was approaching nine in the morning, which meant the roads were congested with idiots heading to work.

"Just fly under them," I said. "I don't want this to take all day."

"Uh, that's . . . illegal?"

"Yes, and?" I asked. "Myalis, can you tell any cops or whatever to leave us alone on the way over?"

That should be easy enough to do.

The driver grinned as he flicked off his autopilot and darted under the thick columns of air traffic. "Always wanted to do this. Fly past all the chumps with an eight-to-six."

"One of the perks of the job," I said. "Then again, that job meant I was fighting monsters in the sewers all night, so eh."

"Yeah, yeah," he agreed. He was staring ahead, and we weren't moving all that fast. I guessed he didn't have Gomorrah's confidence in his own driving, which was probably for the best, actually. I don't think his rust bucket could do what the Fury did with casual ease.

We were in the older part of the city, where there were fewer skyscrapers. The buildings were all the fancy expensive sort that law firms and banks used for their headquarters. City hall stood out against those. Old and made of big bricks, with pillars by the entrance.

"Drop us off at the front," I said.

"That's not a parking spot," he said. There were, in fact, large pillars to prevent cars from ramming into the front of the building. A smaller building next to city hall had the entrance to a parking garage in its front.

"Don't really care," I said. "I want to get this over with."

"All right, then," he said.

We shifted down and slid to a lurching stop. "Thanks, bud," I said. I transferred the money we owed him, then a generous tip on top of that while opening the door.

Rac scrambled out and stood next to me.

"Come on, Rac, let's do some politics!"

CHAPTER THIRTY-EIGHT

THE RAT AND THE HUNGRY TIGER

The System started in 2022.

It's not really surprising. We'll rank anything; it's a species-wide fixation. The best car, the highest-ranking web serial, the most popular creators. Give us a dataset, and people will organize it from best to worst.

The System is complex, though. There are a lot of things to take into account with it, and some of those are very much speculative.

Fortunately, we like speculating too!

—Documentary except from an interview
with the creator of the System, 2029

The city hall's entrance was a grand and ostentatious place, tax-paid marble, bribe-paid paintings, a few repossessed statues on plinths. It was genuinely nice. Very intimidating.

I walked past men and women in suits, who often stopped to stare. I don't know if it was my armor or Rac's Racness. It was sort of disappointing that I wasn't making any noise as I moved. It would have been appropriate to clang and clunk with every step.

There was a small line before the reception desk, a long counter with inch-thick glass over it and some secretaries behind. Three of them currently served some forty-odd people in three columns.

I considered cutting to the front, but that was just rude. I was here to scare big important politicians, and most of those in line looked like normal folk. Middle-class people in their Sunday best, clutching paper documents and staring off into space with the boredom appropriate for someone waiting in line.

The woman behind the bulletproof glass was overweight, her third chin decorated by a couple of gaudy infomercial necklaces, and her eyes were very obviously focused on anything but the man standing before her.

"Why're we waiting?" Raccoon asked.

"Because it might make things easier in the long run," I said. I couldn't help but notice the security guards gathering on the edges of the room. They were eyeing me the way a rat might eye a hungry tiger.

The guy at the very front moved out of the way, walking off with a huff. One of the people ahead of us spotted me, then stepped aside and shifted to the next line over. Awfully kind of them. That left us one person behind the front.

"What?" the man asked in a low hiss.

The fat woman behind the desk spoke with the low drone of someone who had no shits to give. "You brought the document in duplicate, but it needs to be in triplicate, and these are dated for today. The deadline is today, which means that it's too late."

"Isn't it inclusive?" the man asked. "This is unreasonable! If I don't have this, where will I stay?"

"There is a nine-month waiting period for an affordable housing unit. Please see form AF80. Can I help you with anything else?"

"You . . . argh," he groaned before stomping off.

I looked at Rac and she shrugged. "I ain't ever filled out any paperwork before."

Fair enough. I stepped up to the counter.

"How may I help you?"

"I'm looking for . . . whoever's in charge here," I said.

"That's not this department," she replied.

"Well then, which department would know where the mayor's office is?" I asked.

She frowned. "The mayor's office is on floor eight. You need an appointment to visit him, which you can obtain from the—"

"Okay, cool," I cut in. "Look, the city's about to be in a heap of shit, and I'm trying to stop that from happening. Can you buzz the mayor and tell him I'm coming? That might smooth things over."

"Miss, this isn't the department for that."

I was pretty sure shooting her would complicate things. "You're real useful, aren't you?"

"Insulting a government agent is an offense," she droned.

I wasn't allowed to insult the people here? "Um, go fuck yourself?"

"I could call the guards," she snapped.

I blinked. She still wasn't looking at me. A twitch of my augs and I was in her system and . . . she was watching a soap opera. I flicked that off, and she jumped a little, blinked, then refocused on me. "Fuck your guards too," I said. "What are they going to do? Shoot me? I have a space sword, bitch. Come on, Rac."

I took off, heading toward an elevator bank at the far end of the room.

"You lost that one," Rac said with obvious good humor.

"I didn't summon a live grenade in her lap, which is a victory for my self-control," I said to soothe my pride.

A guard stepped up before us, still a dozen meters ahead. He looked a pinch nervous, but ready to try to stop me.

"Get in the elevator," I said. Rac nodded, so I stepped away from her, angling slightly off to the right.

The guard moved to stand where I'd be walking now.

So I turned invisible and sidestepped back to Rac.

The guards started to panic a little, so out of the kindness of my heart—and because I thought it was funny—I reappeared by Rac's side as we entered a waiting elevator. "Myalis, can we get to the eighth floor, please?"

Is the button panel too complex?

"Yeah, it's got all these numbers and shit," I said. "Plus I'd need to raise my arm. I'd ask Rac, but she might press all of them." I really just didn't want the guards stopping the elevator halfway up.

The door shut with a *ding* and we started to rise. Rac bounced from foot to foot to the beat of the copyright-free music playing while the floor ticker counted up. We hit the eighth floor and the door remained closed.

Four potential hostiles on the other side.

"Noted," I said. "Rac, go stand in the corner. Make yourself small."

"I'm pretty small already," she said as she moved to the side near the door and squeezed herself in. "Didn't eat enough as a kid."

"Work for me and you'll be able to afford all sorts of grub," I said. I reached out and tapped the "door open" button at the same time as I went invisible.

The door opened into another lobby, this one much smaller, but no less rich. A desk took up the end of the room, with two corridors stretching out behind it on either side, offices and rooms all along it.

A pair of guards were huddled on two sides, partially hidden by some large pillars. Another was to the right, next to a doorway, and the last was right before the elevator. He stared within. "It's empty."

"The target could teleport," one of them said. "Check it."

The guard before me moved to enter the elevator, so I stepped up and grabbed him by the collar. He let out a rather undignified squeak as I lifted him off the ground, then carried him over to the counter, his feet brushing the floor as he kicked out.

There was a young secretary-looking guy behind the counter. He wasn't watching any soap operas, but he was filming.

I shut off my invisibility, aware of the guns pointed my way by the three other guards. "Hi," I said. "I'd like to make an appointment to speak with the mayor."

"Uh," the secretary said.

"Right now, please," I said. Being polite was tiring.

"Put me down!" the guard I was holding up screamed. The other three were shouting too.

"Fine," I said as I let go of the guard. "Tell the mayor that Stray Cat is here to see him."

"Stray Cat," the secretary said. He looked at something on a nearby screen, and then blanched. "Oh. S-stand down, stand down, everyone!" he said as he stood, both arms waving up and down.

The guards paused in their useless screaming and glanced his way.

"Miss Stray Cat here is a samurai who is coming to, ah, visit the mayor."

"I should have opened with that," I muttered.

"We wouldn't want to insult one of the top fifty thousand," the secretary replied.

"What?" I asked.

He blanched even further, if that was at all possible. "It's, ah, just your ranking . . . miss?"

I frowned. "My ranking on what?"

"The ranking?"

He has a screen opened to a site that ranks Vanguards. Specifically those in the North American continent. You are currently ranked number 48,094th. Out of nearly fifty thousand active Vanguards in the region. Your international ranking is significantly worse.

"There's rankings?" I asked. "Based on what?"

The system is relatively complex. Active-duty time, level of perceived threat, some popularity polls.

"Huh," I said. "Where's Gomorrah?"

Currently at 47,947.

I frowned harder. "And Deus Ex?"

2,581st place. The higher rankings move less often.

"Well . . . let's go see the mayor and get those rank numbers down, shall we?" I asked. "Come on Rac, no one's going to hurt you without getting shot right after."

CHAPTER THIRTY-NINE

MEETINGUS INTERRUPTUS

Cheating? No, no, I would never. My wife and I have been in a loving relationship for nearly a decade now—more, maybe. She's the one that tans my hide when I forget the date of our anniversary! Hah!

No, Tom, I won't be paying those sorts of accusations any mind. They're just a loser's attempt to throw dirt on my good name.

Now, my competition seem like good folk at first glance, but I think if the wise, voting citizens of our fine city start to dig a little deeper, they'll learn that things aren't quite as they seem.

Why . . .

—Excerpt from an interview with Mayor Dupont, 2056

The secretary jumped out of his seat and darted down the corridor ahead of me. "Th-this way, miss," he said. "I've sent a message to the mayor to expect you, but, ah, he's preparing for an important meeting."

"What about?" I asked. We soon took a turn in the passageway and were crossing down the middle of a room filled with cubicles. Office drones were clicking away behind screens, some few leaning back while jacked into the net.

"Ah, it's with the city council? There's a meeting at ten this morning."

I glanced at my aug clock and held back a wince. It was past nine already? At the rate we were going, I wouldn't get to sleep until the afternoon. "What's the meeting's agenda?" I asked. "Is it an emergency meeting?"

"Ah, no? Just an ordinary meeting."

"Huh, all right," I said. I considered crashing the meeting instead, but we were already here, and there was no way I could just sit around and wait. Maybe I could have planned things a little better, but then, I wasn't all that keen on planning things.

The mayor would be . . . interesting to handle. I didn't know anything about him. I think I'd seen his face on some posters slapped onto walls and maybe a few ads between two posts.

"Hey, wait up!"

I stopped and glanced over my shoulder. Rac wasn't next to me any-more, and I had no idea when she'd moved away. I spotted her a few meters back, tossing aside bits of paper and junk off her shirt. She had a stapler in hand, and there was an office worker staring at her from next to a tipped-over trash can.

"What's that?" I asked.

"Stapler. Slightly used. Probably a broken spring or something," Rac said. She stuffed it into one of her bigger pockets, and it clunked against something else she had in there. Then her arm darted out and she added a pen to her collection.

"That wasn't in the trash," I said.

"Meh, they won't miss it," she replied.

Fair enough.

"Uh, here," the secretary said. He gestured down at the end of the room. There were some steps leading up to a landing with a mirrored wall beyond that. I bet that it was there so that anyone in the room could overlook their sea of keyboard monkeys.

"So, you know the mayor, right?" I asked.

"In passing," the secretary said. "I've been an intern here for two years now. Just a bit more and I'll be on the payroll! But yeah, I've seen the mayor before. Mr. Dupont is . . . nice enough. I'm not his secretary, I'm just at the front lobby."

"Uh-huh, so how do you figure he's going to react if I tell him there's a threat to the city that needs his immediate action to fix?"

The secretary winced.

"Right, got it," I said. "Rac, stay close, and if you see me pulling a gun, cover your ears. I don't want to hurt your hearing."

"Aww, thanks!"

I walked up the steps and right up to the mayor's door. There was a plaque next to it with "Mayor Dupont" written on it in big blocky letters. I turned the handle, then frowned as it jiggled in place. He left his door locked?

I checked with my augs, but there didn't seem to be any electronic lock on the door. I knocked instead.

"I'm busy here," someone said. "Come back in a moment."

I heard shuffling, and with a twitch of my ears I could make out some of what was happening on the other side. The mayor had to be the big guy behind a bigger desk. The woman on her knees before him was probably not the mayor.

I shrugged and brought my foot up.

"Want me to pick the lock?" Rac asked.

I considered it. "No, but thanks. It's nice of you to offer." My foot rammed into the door right next to the handle with all the force I and my very expensive power armor could put into it.

The real wood wall next to the door cracked and the entire thing crashed back into the room.

I glanced around as I walked in. The mirror really was a window. Knew it! There were some plinths with pots on them, and a few old knickknacks in glass cases. The desk was pretty impressive, a huge wooden thing that looked older than most of the buildings in the city, the kind that had probably broken someone's back when they tried to fit it into the room. The far wall had another window, this one overlooking the front of the city hall and the streets before it.

"Who the fuck are you?" the mayor asked as he stood up.

My hand snapped out and covered Rac's face.

"Might wanna put away your little electoral device there," I said.

The mayor's face went red, but he put things away and zipped up his pants while a pretty young woman in office chic wear climbed to her feet and stared daggers. Not at me, but at the secretary who had led me here. "Fuck off, Tim," she snapped.

"I didn't say anything," Tim the intern said, his hands raised.

"Okay, the drama's cute, but could you two . . . you know, do this somewhere else? I need to talk with the mayor."

The two secretaries moved out of the room while Mayor Dupont slammed his hands on his fancy desk. "Who are you, and why hasn't security stopped you?"

"I'm Stray Cat, or just Cat. Apparently I'm ranked 48,094th most . . . something samurai, which is really unimpressive. Also, they didn't stop me because of either common sense, or a sense of self-preservation. Toss-up, really."

The mayor swallowed, eyes widening a moment before they narrowed and his glare reset itself. "I don't care if you're the head of the Family itself. You can't just . . . barge in here!"

"She literally just did," Raccoon said. "Can I?" she asked, pointing with both hands at the wastebasket next to his desk.

"Who's that?" he asked, pointing to Raccoon.

"That's Raccoon," I said. "She, uh, likes trash. Don't ask. I'm here to talk."

"So you broke my door? That's oak!"

"I thought you'd be more pissed because I interrupted your pre-meeting BJ," I said. "I would be."

Rac stood up, a pair of very lacy underthings held up by a string in her hands. "I don't know, fatso here seems to get it on a lot. That, or he's got really small hips." She held the panties out by the band and raised them, as if judging if he'd fit in them.

"Don't touch that, Rac. You don't know where it's been."

"I can guess," she said.

I shook my head, then stepped up and pulled out one of the chairs before the mayor's desk. "Come on, let's sit down. We have a lot to talk about, and I feel like I've made a bad first impression."

The mayor glared for a moment more, then stepped back and sat down. "I'm Mayor Dupont, the rightfully elected official in charge of the city of New Montreal," he said.

"Brilliant," I said. "I was hoping that if I started at the top I might be able to get things done. We have a problem, both of us."

He eyed me up and down, not in a dirty way, just judging. "I imagine it has something to do with the faint odor of shit wafting off you?"

"Are you guessing?" I asked. "Because that would be somewhat impressive."

"No, I received reports that two samurai were causing trouble in the sewers sometime very early this morning." He gestured to me, then Rac. Did he think she was a samurai? She was certainly weird enough.

"Yeah. A lot of citizens were kidnapped by the Sewer Dragons." No recognition on his face. "A gang living in the sewers. They maintained the sewers and kept them running; it also made them somewhat untouchable. Plus, their home is a death trap."

"You're using the past tense," he noted. "I imagine they're no longer an issue."

"Maybe. We freed the civilians they'd taken and . . . we'll take care of them, I guess. There're probably some remnants of the gang down there. Our problem is that they kept the sewers working."

"And that's *our* problem?" he asked.

"I like hot showers and running water as much as the next girl. And when I flush, I like it when my toilet doesn't vomit shit all over. Now, I'm no expert in matters of sewage, but I know something's fucky when I see it, and the entire city's sewage system is very fucky."

CHAPTER FORTY

REAL POLITICS

I don't know when it happened, but somewhere along the way, people split along two lines. And yeah, I know, that's a generalization, which means it's generally wrong. Anyway, on the one side, you got those that understood the more pragmatic side of politics, the realpolitik and the reasoning behind some of the bullshit.

Only some of it, mind you. There's some bullshit that's just people being dumb.

On the other side of that line you have the fanatics. Wildly devoted to whatever echo-chambered message they've been fed over and over again until it's all they know, and they live in this constant state of thinking they're right.

Anyway, I don't have time for all that political stuff.

—Jerry Grant, political commentator, 2045

Mayor Dupont looked at me for a long moment before saying anything. "Is that why you're here? To ask that the city do something about this mess you caused in the sewers?"

"Two things," I said, my hand coming up in a peace symbol. "First, I didn't cause the mess. The lack of foresight in letting a literal gang of self-mutilating lunatics take care of the sewage caused the mess. Second, I'm not here to ask, I'm here to inform you, personally, that shit's about to hit the fan."

"And that's a concern for me?"

I blinked. "Are you dumb?" I asked. "No, you can't be. Not if you got this fancy office and morning blowjobs. I'll bet you're corrupt as fuck, but you need to be able to put two and two together."

Dupont placed his fists on his desk and glared before leaning back. "Let's presume that this sewer problem isn't your fault, which I'll only treat as a hypothetical. What do you expect the city to do?"

"Isn't the entire goal of the city to take care of . . . you know, the city? Roads and power lines and building permits and sewage?"

"No, the purpose of the city as a governmental institution is to make a profit by means of taxation and regulation. Punishing those who fail to comply with our rules and lubricating the economic machine for those who require assistance."

"What?" I asked.

"That means that yes, we take care of infrastructure, because we are better situated to take care of that infrastructure than the companies that need it to exist."

I shook my head. "All right, I don't get it."

He sighed. "Then go take a civics course and get out of my office."

"No, and no," I said. I tried to cross one leg over the other, but that wasn't exactly possible in power armor. "Come on, explain it to me using small words."

The mayor rolled his eyes. I liked him better when he was less sarcastic and more scared shitless. "Imagine a road. That road needs to be built, which costs money. It needs to be maintained, which also costs money. Hundreds of thousands of credits, all poured into this road. If it's never used, then it's a loss. But if it is used, then that money *might* not be lost."

"Lot of emphasis there," I said.

"It depends on who uses it, doesn't it? Some normal citizens? Do you know how much we make in taxes from the average citizen in this city? Barely enough to cover the expenses in this building alone. The real money comes from taxing the important players who use the city's infrastructure. The companies and corporations that need those roads to make their businesses work."

I nodded. I got the gist of it, at least. "And that's why you won't fix the sewers?"

"Oh, if things are as fucked as you imply, then of course the good city of New Montreal will make an effort to maintain and repair what we can. We provide a service to the corporations that inhabit this city. We take care of things so they don't have to, and because the cost of those things is defrayed across the entire population and across every company based on their use of said infrastructure, it's a fair cost. There's always some grumbling and cheating, but I'm not a fucking moron—I can tell when someone's cutting me short, and I know how to put the squeeze on their bottom line."

He chuckled darkly.

"You can't imagine how quickly a company will turn around and pay up when they can't move any cargo from one factory to the next because every road around them is under permanent construction, or if their internet is cut off for a day or two."

I sighed and shook my head. Was he trying to waste my time? Not that the discussion wasn't interesting; it actually was. I could see why Dupont got the seat. It wasn't his looks or his incredible slut powers, that was for sure. The guy just had a lot of charisma once he got going . . . somehow. "You know, every minute we spend not acting is another minute that passes with the entire water system for the city on the verge of collapsing."

"And every credit that isn't taxed is a worthless one. Are you going to cover the cost of repairing the system?"

"Fuck no," I said.

"Then who will?" he asked.

I gestured around, trying to encompass the city as a whole. "The people who need water to live? You know, the same ones paying taxes and shit?"

"As I said, their contributions don't amount to much. Maybe enough to maintain things, at a guess, but I'm assuming the entire thing will need repairs if you've shown up."

"Then what do you expect to happen? People will be okay tomorrow when they can't flush and their taps give them fuck-all?" I asked. "You're going to have riots."

He shrugged. "Someone will make a fortune selling bottled water? A few people will be inconvenienced, and then some corporation will realize they need water to run their operation and will invest in the city in order to get things running again."

That sounded so backward to me.

"We can help things along, of course," Dupont said. He sat down in his big plush seat. "A few tax breaks here and there, maybe a favor to one company or another. As long as it's worthwhile in the long term, then the problem will get fixed. In the end, though, it's just shit."

"Are you going to pipe it out to the ocean, then?" I asked.

"We could," he said.

"Aren't there environmental agencies that'll throw a fit?"

Dupont laughed. "Girl, we *are* those agencies. And we only throw a fit when it means we can extort more cash from some corp that doesn't know to pay the bribes before the problem becomes obvious."

I shifted in my seat, thinking. I didn't quite know what to do, which was really annoying. So I leaned on my elbows and asked a dumb question to pass the time while I mulled things over. "You're being very open about all of this. I could be recording you. Actually, I am literally recording you, there's no 'could' about it."

"Oh, I don't particularly care," Dupont said. "In my time as mayor I have made a lot of the right people very happy. They know that any replacement might rock the boat. The voters could line up to suck my knob and I still wouldn't care about their opinions. They can clamor and scream and riot all they want."

"Can you talk about your knob a bit less? There's a kid in the room," I said.

"Talk realpolitik, not dick," Rac singsonged. Then she grinned. "Realpolidick."

"Please never repeat that again," I said. I refocused on the mayor. "You know, I came in here expecting to threaten the shit out of you, not to get lectured about the benefits of corruption. I haven't even pulled out my awesome new sword to skewer anything yet. I'm kind of disappointed."

"You wanted to solve everything with violence?" Dupont asked. "In that case, politics might not be the right line of work for you, Stray Cat. Here the violence is either delivered verbally or through an accidental car bomb."

"So, you won't do anything to help until literally millions of people are fucked over?" I asked.

"I'll do something to help when the right people are fucked over," Dupont corrected.

I stood up. "Right, then," I said. "Thanks for your time. I still think you're a sleazy fuck, though."

"Are you going to do anything about my doorframe?" he asked. From the tone I think it was just a parting jab.

"Fuck your doorframe," I said. "Come on, Rac, we're going to have to fix our problems ourselves."

And by ourselves, I meant that I had to make some new friends.

But first, I needed a shower and about ten hours of sleep.

CHAPTER FORTY-ONE

PHYSICAL COMFORT IN THE PRESENCE OF ANOTHER

It's a strange quirk of human nature that no matter the culture, there is nearly always something that will be considered an intimate, or even taboo, subject or action. For many Western cultures this was depictions of sexual intercourse and images of breasts and genitals. For other cultures the taboos were other things.

As humanity entered the twenty-first century, however, titillating materials became the tools of advertisers who wished to shock and intrigue, and because of their overuse of such salacious materials, they became commonplace.

Now, images that might once have been considered downright pornographic inspire little more interest than passing notice. Instead, what has become the new subject of enticement is something beyond the reach of many: Physical comfort in the presence of another.

—Excerpt from *Handholding and Other Carnal Desires*, 2050

"So whatcha gonna do?" Rac asked.

No one tried to stop me or even slow me down as I headed out of the city hall building and back onto the street. I absently called up another Uber ride, this time aiming for the hotel. "I have an idea or two," I said. "But nothing concrete."

"Surprised you didn't just cut the mayor in half."

"It was tempting," I said. "But that wouldn't fix our problem."

"It'd feel good, though," Rac said.

I couldn't fault her there. The mayor was, in a word, a shitsack. He was making a terrible situation worse just by being himself. It was frustrating as hell. I didn't think that killing him would improve things either. The mayor was a product of a system, someone who was good at playing a fucked-up game. He reminded me of Doc Hack a little.

Then again, I did cut Doc Hack in half. But that . . . felt different. It was violence in response to violence. An escalation, where the mayor wasn't.

"If it really comes down to it, I don't think I'd have a problem introducing the mayor to my sword," I said with a tap to the hilt by my hip. "But I think there might be other things we can do first."

Our ride arrived a moment later. A driverless car that hovered near the ground and waited for Rac and me to board before taking off and merging back into the traffic above. I didn't even bother trying to make it move faster.

"Where're we going now?" Rac asked.

"I have a home . . . but it's under construction right now. We'll be going to a hotel. That's where the kittens are, and Lucy, my girlfriend. You can stay the night, if you want."

"I can take care of myself," Rac said.

I nodded. "I know. I won't force you, but . . . well, wait until tomorrow? I have something that you might like. A job, of sorts, you might be really good with. Plus we have room service."

"Okay," Rac said.

I leaned forward, elbows on knees, and ignored the incessant beeping of the car trying to tell me to buckle my seat belt. I needed to figure this sewer thing out.

Gomorrah and I could take over the operation, I was sure. Some of those matter-reconfiguring machines, a few hundred drones, and a steady supply of materials, and probably a whole heap of stuff I wasn't thinking about and we'd control the sewers. They'd probably run better, and we wouldn't need a mutilated sewer gang to do things for us.

But that was a huge responsibility, the sort of commitment I wasn't ready to take up, not by a long shot. Hell, I hadn't even asked Lucy to be more than girlfriends yet; I couldn't turn around and take over the critical infrastructure for a city with a population over a hundred million.

So, if we didn't do it, then who would?

The city had proven unable or unwilling to act until it was way too fucking late. That left . . . some corps? The Family, maybe. They had to have a few samurai who could handle big infrastructure things in their ranks.

"Myalis, can you write something for me?"

I likely can, yes.

I leaned back into the seat. "I need a summary of everything we've learned about the Sewer Dragons and the water system for the city. How soon it's likely to fail, what needs to be prioritized, all that stuff."

Done.

"Right. Can you send that to Deus Ex and Longbow? Tell them that I have no fucking clue what to do with this whole thing."

Message sent. I assume you're aware that you could do something to allevi-ate this situation, though at great cost to yourself?

"Yeah, I know," I said. "I don't like it, and I'm pretty sure I wouldn't do a good job of it. Let's look into other solutions before we get locked into becoming some sort of . . . sewer samurai."

Understood. I think there are a few avenues that you haven't yet considered.

"Oh?" I asked. Trust Myalis to have a hundred solutions to my none. I should have asked her earlier.

Before you take any such step, you should rest. You're not in a physical state to act just yet. You're likely to make some critical mistakes if you don't take time to sleep. Unless you wish for a method to remove the need to sleep entirely?

I snorted. "I like sleeping," I said.

It didn't take long for the car to pull up into the hotel. Rac had her face pressed up against the window as we arrived. "Fancy" was her only reply.

"Yeah," I agreed as I pulled open the door and stepped out. A small pop-up informed me of the credits I'd just spent on the ride, and it was only the fresh knowledge that I was rich that kept me from wincing at the number of zeros.

Rac scrambled after me and we headed for the front entrance.

I noticed plenty of people looking our way, and plenty more of them recoiling or touching their noses once we passed them.

Right, the smell.

Rac followed me into an elevator, and I pressed the "door close" button. "Myalis, I need something for the smell," I said.

There are some low-cost antibacterial decontamination sprays available in your Medical catalog, in aerosolized form. They should remove the major-ity of the stench.

"That sounds perfect," I said.

My points dropped to 10,704 and I received a small box with a can within it, one that had a big plastic nozzle on the top and some very basic instructions on the side. I sprayed down my side, then up the center of my body, and hoped that the spray was getting everywhere.

"Do I still stink?" I asked Rac.

"I guess," she said. "I'm used to it."

Fair enough. I gestured for her to turn around. "Close your eyes and T-pose for me while I spray you down. You can do me after."

Rac nodded and did as I asked. "Can is running out," she said after a bit. The entire elevator had a haze to it, which I figured was for the best, all things considered. "Can I keep it?"

"Sure," I said as I reached out and pressed the button to our floor. I mostly didn't want Lucy to find me smelling like shit.

The elevator doors dinged open and Rac and I stepped out and into the corridor leading to my kittens and Lucy. I felt like I had a weight lifted off my shoulders.

Still, I had some sense of responsibility. I sent off a text to Gomorrah, telling her that I was home, and that I needed a few hours of sleep. She replied with a thumbs-up emoji, so I figured we were cool.

I knocked.

"This is where you are staying?" Rac asked.

"For now. I bought the top floor of a building not too far from here. But we're still fixing that up."

"Neat," Rac said just as the door opened.

Lucy was standing there, in a T-shirt and ripped-up jeans, her hair a messy wet poof above her head. She stared, then grinned before noticing Rac. "Oh hey, you brought another one home."

I stumbled forward and pulled her into a hug.

Lucy laughed, and I felt her hands sliding over my armor to return the hug. "Missed you too," she said. "Where do you want to start?"

Where did I want to start? A rant about stupid people, a long discussion about what to do? Maybe some fucking? Food? Those would all feel great.

"I want a shower," I decided.

Lucy giggled. "I just came out of it. Should still be nice and warm. Come on."

"Uh, this is Rac," I said with a gesture to the girl who had followed me in. She was staring at the other kittens, who were perked up and staring right back. She also glanced at the cat mecha currently acting like a sphynx before the fridge. I bet there was a story there.

"Hey," Rac said, one hand rising to wave. "Sup?"

"Hi, Rac! Junior, can you take care of Rac, please?" Lucy asked. "She looks like she could use something to eat, and a shower too."

Junior looked up from where she was zoning out on the couch, sighed, then bounced to her feet. "Why can't you ask Daniel?" she muttered as she approached Rac.

"Come on, kitty Cat," Lucy murmured. "Let's get you all cleaned up."

She pulled me after her, and despite the armor and all the gear, there was nothing I could do to resist her tug.

CHAPTER FORTY-TWO

R&R

It's an unfortunate fact that humans can't operate at full capacity at all times.

If you don't allow your workers a minimum of time to decompress and destress, the quality of their work will sharply decrease.

—Excerpt from *Minimums and Maximums:*
A Guide to the Workforce, 2024

I couldn't remember most of the events of the afternoon. There was a shower that lasted until my entire body was a wrinkled mess. Then I remembered Lucy helping me dress (which probably explained why I was only wearing a T-shirt and socks) and then a blissful fall into a deep sleep.

I yawned, toes stretching out under the blankets. The screen-windows to one side showed that it was still dark out, maybe approaching midnight? It was hard to tell. I was never exactly a very punctual "up with the sun" kind of girl, but I wasn't used to waking up so damned early.

My arms rose and I spread my legs so that I was splayed out across the entire bed. It was nice. I might have been able to fall asleep again, but I had the nagging impression that I still had a lot of work to do.

Also, there was no Lucy in bed, which was somewhat discouraging.

With a bone-deep sigh I rolled over to the side of the bed, rubbed at my face for a bit, then climbed to my feet. I had to visit the washroom, which, as usual, was a great way to ruin any mood.

I found my power armor laying on a heap at the bottom of the shower. I vaguely remembered leaving it there. Probably for the best. It looked dry now, but I wouldn't mind hosing it down again, just in case.

Exiting the en suite, I shuffled out of the room. The penthouse was quiet, which was nice. A peek into one of the rooms on the way to the kitchen revealed a few of the kittens sleeping in a heap on one bed. Though I did find that Nose was awake and playing some game. I didn't particularly mind as long as he wasn't being loud.

"Cat?" Lucy asked.

I grinned and looked up to find the most beautiful girl in the world waiting for me by the kitchen island. She smiled right back and pulled me into a hug. Not a sexy hug, just a warm, soft hold that made me want to melt. "Hey," I muttered.

"There's cereal and milk," Lucy said. "And did you know that the theater room has a lock on the door?

I groaned. Sexier words had never been uttered.

Lucy laughed and squeezed me tighter before letting go. "Give me two minutes," she said. I leaned against the island while Lucy scrambled for bowls and spoons, then tucked a milk carton under one arm and an entire box of Longb'O's under her chin. "Come on, kitty Cat," she said.

I followed after her, partly amused, and partly because I really was hungry. It didn't stop my eyes from straying down to the way her hips moved. "Are you trying to strut?" I asked.

"Is it working?" she replied.

I snorted. "Not really, no, you look like a grandma who just had her hip replaced."

Lucy sniffed, but she soon broke out into giggles. "Yeah, I'm still getting used to walking. I'm not ready for catwalks just yet, I don't think."

"I'd love to see you practice," I replied.

She turned so that she could open a door from behind. "I'm sure you would," she replied.

The theater room was the same place Daniel and I had dived into the Mesh in. The far wall had a massive screen on it, and the room was filled with a few plush couches arranged so that they all more or less faced the screen.

"Sit, sit," Lucy ordered. She gestured to one of the bigger, more plush seats.

I sat; the leather was cool against my bare legs, but I could live with it. Lucy filled two bowls with milk and cereal, then handed one to me before she paused next to the seat. It was a couch for one, but I couldn't imagine her not sitting on or right next to me.

She sighed and placed her bowl on the seat next to mine. Then she reached under her T-shirt and undid the front of her pants before dropping them. "Uh," I said.

"It's not fair that you're the only one not wearing pants," Lucy said before retrieving her bowl and sitting wedged right up against me. "Isn't this better?" she asked.

Her skin was warm against my own, and I felt the blood rushing to my cheeks. "Yeah, this is much better," I said.

It was a bit awkward to eat while Lucy used me as a seat, but we both managed to start crunching through what was no doubt the least healthy meal we could manage to make on such short notice. "So," Lucy said after swallowing a bite. "Did you want to talk, or do you want to watch a movie and snuggle instead?"

"Hmm. I think . . . I'd rather relax, but I feel like I need to talk. Does that make sense?"

Lucy nodded. "Yeah, of course. Just don't talk during the movie."

"That would be a sin," I said. Not that I minded, but Lucy got unreasonably annoyed at anyone who spoke during a movie. It was always nice to cuddle while watching some pirated cartoons, but Lucy tended to hyperfocus on whatever she was watching, so it never really went beyond cuddles. Not that I really minded. Sex was nice but tiring, and I was all tired out.

Lucy nodded. "You spent the day in the sewers?"

"Yeah. Did I tell you that much?"

She shook her head. "Media feeds told me. I'm following the people following you."

"I have people following me?" I asked.

"Oh yeah. Not that many yet, though. You're not super-popular. Gomorrah has a lot more. Sexy nun is just hard to pass up, you know?"

I snorted. "All right, fair. So yeah, spent the morning in the sewers. Can't say it was fun. Things . . . honestly, they're still not done. We need to figure things out. A bunch of people are in really shitty situations, and I feel like if I don't try to do something, they'll be fucked. Not to mention the rest of the city."

You don't need to worry that much. I have been monitoring the situation, and I believe you still have some time to react.

"Hi, Myalis," Lucy said. Had Myalis sent that to her too? "Hey, can you help us find a good movie?"

That would be trivially easy. I'll load the movie onto the screen. When you're ready to start, just say so.

"You're a sweetheart," Lucy said.

I huffed and contented myself with another bite. "Mm, Myalis, we need to call people, don't we?"

I have organized the replies you've received from Gomorrah, Longbow, and Deus Ex. They will be ready for your attention once you're done relaxing.

"Once I'm done relaxing?" I asked.

You don't yet have the capability to overlook the amount of mental and physical strain you have put yourself through over the past days. If you don't take some time to destress, you risk harming yourself. If I judged things pressing enough, I would suggest that you forgo relaxation in order to tackle the next issue, but matters as they stand are not critical enough to justify that much risk.

"What Myalis is saying," Lucy translated, "is that you need a break." She dipped her bowl up and finished off the last of her milk. "Ah, so we're going to watch a movie, and maybe after that I'll give you a massage." Her hand came down on my thigh and I hissed at the contact. Her fingers were so cold!

I finished my cereal, tossed the bowl and spoon onto the next couch over, then wrapped my arms around Lucy and pulled her closer. "Fine," I muttered into the nook of her neck. "But if we're going to do that, then the least you can do is be a bit warmer."

"Hey, I'm plenty hot," Lucy said. She wiggled around until she was comfortable, and then I reached down and reclined the sofa and we spent an enjoyable couple of seconds resettling in place. Lucy reached over and pulled a blanket over, then snapped it open and covered the both of us in it.

"Thanks," I said.

Lucy sighed. "I love you, you know."

"I love you too," I said. I couldn't keep the grin off my face.

"We have a whole bunch of things to do tomorrow," Lucy said. "We need to get the museum-house ready, we need to do something about Rac and the kittens, and you need to save the world some more, but right now, you belong to me."

"Oh?" I asked. "I belong to you now, huh?" I pulled her closer, hands wrapped over her stomach.

She nodded and placed her hands over mine. "You do. Property of Lucy. I'm going to have that tattooed on your butt."

I laughed. "Wouldn't that mean that only my ass would be yours?"

"Two tattoos, then," Lucy said. "I've got two hands, after all."

"Pervert," I said.

She chuckled. "I'm not a pervert. But these legs, they're mine too. Myalis, start the movie; Cat's running out of banter."

"I am not!"

CHAPTER FORTY-THREE

NOTHING BUT CUDDLES

Ain't no one getting between me and my cuddle time! Uwu.
—Quote attributed to Neon Girl Happy-Chan, 2029

I woke up feeling both warm and content. It didn't take long to realize why.

Lucy was turned on her side, wedged between me and the edge of the couch. She had a hand pressed under her chin, which squished her cheek up, and her other hand was balled into a fist over my chest.

I shifted my leg just a little, and Lucy shifted in turn, her own leg moving up and down, soft skin against mine. She was snoring, and it wasn't the cute kind of snore that the girls in the movies had.

I smiled and leaned my head over to peck her on the forehead. She didn't react at all, entirely oblivious to the world at large.

That was fine. I tugged the blanket she'd covered us in higher so that it was tucked up near her neck and settled in to wait. I was trapped, of course, and there was no escaping this one—not that I wanted to.

I didn't want to speak aloud; that might wake Lucy up, and that would be a sin. So I took some pictures of her face, line of drool and squished cheeks and all, and saved them for later. Blackmail was always handy to have.

Opening a messenger app with my augs, I sent a message to Myalis. "Hey. Any news on the stuff?"

How very eloquently put. Yes, there has been some news about the conditions and changes with regards to the stuff.

I let out a huff of laughter before replying. "Cute. Did Longbow and Deus Ex reply? Any news from Gomorrah?"

You received replies from both. Neither was visual or audible, though. Do you wish to see the replies?

"Sure," I sent.

A new box appeared before me, my augs printing it on the air.

> *"The situation with the sewers is a problem, but it's not as critical as other issues we have. I'll send what you sent me to the Family. They'll put some pressure on the city to fix things. I'm too busy to interfere myself. Take care of it.*
> *—Deus Ex"*

"Fucking callous little pipsqueak, isn't she?" I asked.

She has proven her worth as a Vanguard. I trust that her claims of currently working on more pressing concerns are truthful.

"Hmm," I hummed. Lucy moved her head up and tucked it in the nook of my neck, so I tilted my head down and rested my cheek on the poofy mess that was her hair. "All right, so that's one avenue that's basically gone. The Family thing might help, but the mayor's a cunt, so I doubt it. What did Longbow say?"

Displaying now.

Deus Ex's reply was minimized and was replaced by a longer one.

> *"Stray Cat—*
> *Hey little sister, heard you had fun playing in the mud. Digging the Two Girls One Flamer memes, by the way. Not too sure if I can help much. I'm spread a bit thin as is, and I don't know if I want to concentrate that many resources in one city. Still, I think I can help in another way.*
> *There's a politician who's not that much of a twat (I know, they're all twats to one degree or another) who could probably use the kind of boost that comes from having a friendly samurai breathing down his neck. He's not an idiot, and I think he might actually mean well.*
> *His name's Jeff Burringham. Bit of a narcissist upper-crust type. Ivy league, rich parents, you know the sort. Still, my psych profiles suggest that he does want to help, if only to make himself look better.*
> *I'll send him a small intro. He's going to be running against the mayor in a bit. He might have the clout to fix your problem.*
> *Also, I gave a call to Peter Silverbloom. He runs a nonprofit. He might be able to help with your ex-Sewer Dragons.*
> *XOXO*
> *The best big bro,*
> *—Longbow"*

"Huh," I said. "Can you add those two to my contacts? Once I'm, ah, free, I'll give them a call . . . actually, before that, do you have anything on either of them?"

I do. Longbow seems to have extensive security systems in place across a few cities. These have been set to surveil Jeff Burringham in order to create a full psychological profile. He sent this profile along with the man's contact information.

"That seems a bit excessive," I wrote.

He is a normal human citizen trying to enter the political spectrum with the assistance of some Vanguard. It is only properly cautious that a Vanguard would verify such a person's past and present.

A bit much in my opinion, but I wasn't going to stop Longbow from doing what he wanted, especially not when it served me just fine. "So, what's the profile say about Jeff boy?"

To summarize, he is educated in politics and has had lifelong ties with the leadership of several midsized corporations. He has lived a life mostly devoid of major hardships but has nonetheless developed some empathy for those currently facing greater difficulty. An uncommon trait among the more privileged.

"So he's a good guy?"

Relatively.

I nodded, cheek rubbing against Lucy's head. "Okay. Do you think he can help?

You are ill-suited to solve the issues you currently wish to solve, not without a great shift in your future plans and ambitions. You also lack the contacts to press society itself toward solving its own issues. Currently, Jeff Burringham might be more capable than you are in this situation if given the proper incentive.

"Does Jeff's profile have his schedule for tomorrow . . . no, later today," I wrote. A quick glance at the time revealed that it was morning already, though still very early in the a.m.

It does. He currently has several activities on his itinerary, though this afternoon is meant to be used for clothes shopping at a specific mall.

"Let's crash that," I said. "I want to meet him. What about the other dude?"

Peter Silverbloom. His profile isn't as deep, though he does have a public record. He is a noted activist and philanthropist. He had founded several nonprofits and been a member of dozens. His history as a volunteer stretches back to when he was an older teenager. He was responsible for the social-outreach club at Lawson's All Girls Academy.

"Sounds way too good to be true," I wrote back. "Also, all girls?"

He was a woman then.

"Okay. Still too good to be true."

Good folks existed. We had a few at the orphanage who were genuinely nice people who really did seem to only want to help. But they were the exception, the one percent.

"Send him a message to call me sometime later," I sent. "We can chat. Does he have any organizations that might help the Sewer Dragons?"

He does run a nonprofit that raises funds to purchase cybernetics for victims of street crimes. It is likely that they would assist individuals who were kidnapped by the Sewer Dragons and forcibly modified. From the public records available, though, it is exceptionally unlikely that the organization would be able to assist the number of people who were rescued.

"Yeah, figures," I wrote. I sighed and cuddled closer to Lucy, mostly because that was my favorite way to get rid of any lingering negative thoughts.

I closed my eyes and zoned out for a moment. When I opened them again it was with a heavy yawn. Somehow an hour had slipped past.

"Gomorrah," I said.

Has expressed a desire to speak when you have the time to do so. She has also noted that the people you have saved are currently secure and housed at the church where she resides. The accommodations can last some time before they will need to begin addressing the issue of the survivors being rehabilitated and returned to their previous lives.

The people there were probably just happy that an actual samurai was looking into things. But that happiness wouldn't last if no one gave them a proper solution.

"Can you remind me to call Gomorrah later?" I wrote.

Added to your agenda for the day.

I chuckled. Me, having an agenda. It sounded like a joke. Still . . . "Thank you, Myalis," I whispered.

You're welcome, Catherine. You should sleep some more, you have a busy day ahead of you.

I nodded and ignored the way my arm was tingling after having Lucy's weight on it for so long, and I shifted so that I could wrap my other arm around her in a protective hug.

"Thanks," I muttered again.

CHAPTER FORTY-FOUR

SWORD TALK

The term "samurai" was, for the most part, a meme that became part of the standard lexicon. Early Vanguards—as they're appropriately called—were compared to feudal warriors, a new caste of expert combatants against the Antithesis threat.

Someone made the comparison to the ancient samurai, and despite some glaring inconsistencies between the actual samurai and the Vanguard (notably, the Vanguard don't answer to any lords or government) the term stuck.

Interestingly enough, there are a number of Vanguard who gravitate toward a self-image very similar to the pop culture depictions of actual samurai. From carrying swords to cultivating a "gentleman warrior" personality, they mimic the legends of the past to further their own image in the present.

—Lecture on the Cultural History of the Ancient Warrior,
Professor Hickmen, 2040

"Hey, Rac," I said as I sat down in the kitchen.

The girl pulled her head out of the fridge, a block of cheese in her mouth, a loaf of bread tucked under her arm, and I think every bottle of condiment in the fridge was pressed against her side. "Hmh," was her reply.

I watched as she navigated over to the table and dumped everything onto it, then returned to the fridge to scavenge out more stuff. "Whatcha making?" I asked.

"Sandwich," she replied, her voice made echoey on account of her being halfway in the fridge.

"Cool," I said. "Guess I'll make one too."

Rac returned with three packages of food, while I found some plates and some knives from one of the drawers. For some reason likely related to the kittens, there were no sharp knives left in any of the drawers, just butter knives.

Rac and I made sandwiches. It was nice.

"The ham's the best," Raccoon said between large bites.

I hummed. "I like the turkey better," I replied. We had made a few sandwiches from all the meats available. Real meats too, at least according to what was written on their packages.

"So," Rac said. She reached over and grabbed a juice box, tore the straw off the back, and jammed it through the top. She slurped loudly before speaking again. "When do you want me to leave?"

"You don't have to," I said. I shoved the end of my current sandwich down my mouth, then slapped a piece of bread down on my plate and reached over for the tomato paste.

"I'm not going to stick around and be one of your kittens," Rac said. "I'm my own girl, and I can take care of myself. Also, pass the mayo."

I passed her the mayo. "That's all right too. But if you ever need a place to spend the night, then we're around. And if you're looking for work . . ."

"You said that already. What kind of work? All I know how to do is pick up trash."

"Well, it happens that that's exactly what the job I'm thinking of needs," I said.

"What job?"

I looked up as Lucy walked into the kitchen. Her hair was a wet mop above her head, dragged down and looking kind of pitiful. She was in fresh clothes, which is to say torn-up cargo pants and a stained T-shirt.

"I'm hiring Rac for a thing. Also, we need to go clothes shopping."

"We do," Lucy agreed.

"Later today . . . maybe?"

She grinned. "If the world doesn't catch fire between now and then, sure."

"I'll tell the world to chill the fuck out for a bit." I placed some meat down, then some slices of cheese, which I covered in some brownish sauce that tasted sweet. Then the final bit of bread. "Want half?" I asked.

"Hell yeah," Lucy said. She sat across from me, and for a moment there was peaceful quiet as everyone at the kitchen island chowed down. "What are we doing today?" Lucy asked.

"Myalis called some contractors this morning," I said. "If you want, we can pop over to the museum and decide how to lay things out with someone there who, you know, does that kind of stuff."

"Oh," Lucy said. "That does sound nice."

I nodded. "After that. Uh, depends? I have a few calls to make, and some important people to annoy. I think you could come along for some of that, but it's a little dangerous. I'd rather you were home."

Lucy stared, one eyebrow rising.

"Not because I don't think you could help, I just don't want you to get hurt, and you don't have armor like I do, or Myalis. And you can watch over the kittens, uh," I said. I had the distinct impression that Lucy was letting me talk more so that I could dig myself deeper than to actually hear what I had to say.

She grinned. "You're lucky that you're so cute," she said.

"What's that mean?"

Lucy shook her head. "I can come back here before you go and get all dangered up."

I nodded. "Cool." We finished up, and then I went over to our bedroom to grab something to wear. I couldn't go out in nothing but a T-shirt if I wanted to be taken seriously.

I slid on my under armor after giving it a sniff—still clean enough—then stared at my armor in the shower.

It was a little bulky for everyday wear, I figured. Instead I tossed on my long trench coat and put on some of my slightly older gear. I wouldn't be as bulletproof, but we were literally just going to meet some people here and there. Nothing dangerous. And if it came to that, I could just buy more armor on the fly.

Probably one of the reasons samurai were so damned dangerous themselves.

I returned to the main room of the penthouse to find most of the kittens making an absolute mess of everything in the name of breakfast. Rac looked deeply uncomfortable as she guarded her sandwich from the others.

"You leaving again?" Junior asked.

I reached over and ruffled her hair for the split second it took her to smack my hand away. "Yep. And I'm taking Lucy and Rac with me."

"'Kay," Junior said. "So I'm in charge."

"How do you figure that?"

"Seniority," Junior said.

"I'm older than you!" Daniel called out from next to the stove. I suspected he was trying to make scrambled eggs.

Junior scoffed. "I've been an orphan longer."

"That's not a proper way to measure time," Daniel said. "Nor is it how anyone should elect a temporary leader."

"I don't know, time since parental demise sounds like a better system than some of the ways politicians get elected," I said.

One of my cat mechas walked into the room. "There have, historically, been stranger methods to elect a leader," Myalis said through the mecha.

I snapped my fingers. "That's it. Junior, you're in charge while we're gone. Myalis is your lieutenant."

"Cool," Junior said. "Can I buy weapons and shit?"

"Wait, what?" Daniel asked. "Are you serious?"

"Do you *want* to babysit?" I asked him.

He froze for a moment until his eggs started to hiss in the pan. "I retract my objections," he said.

"You ready?" Lucy asked. She was waiting by the door, a knowing smile in place and her hand on the handle. She seemed eager to get going, and I didn't have any good reason to slow her down.

"Yeah," I said before adjusting my coat with one hand. The other was busy holding on to the sheath of my sword.

Rac and I followed Lucy out into the corridor, the girl next to me still stuffing her pockets full of packaged meat and some stuff she'd swiped from the pantry.

"Why do you have a sword?" Lucy asked.

"Because it's cool," I said. "Besides, I don't want to leave this thing with the kittens."

"Okay, but it's a sword. You have guns. You have railguns, even. And a rocket launcher," Lucy pointed out.

"And now I have a sword," I said.

Lucy stared at it, then back up to me. "You need a belt for that," she said. "Or at least something to hold it. You can't walk around with a sword in hand all day."

"I mean, I can, it would just be really inconvenient."

"Why a sword anyway?" Lucy asked.

"I dunno, but I like it? It looks cool."

Lucy slid her arm around mine and held on close. "So it makes you feel powerful? Like a giant phallic symbol, then?"

"It's not like that," I said.

"Oh, Cat, maybe later we can play with your sword together," Lucy murmured next to my ear.

I felt my cheeks warming. "I said it's not like that."

"Sounds like it's like that," Rac said.

"Shush, you. No mocking my sword."

"I'd never," Lucy said. "Don't worry, I'm sure your sword is a lot more impressive than most other swords. It certainly looks a lot bigger."

"Dammit, Lucy."

"It's one of those Japanese-looking ones," Rac said. "So it's probably not good for thrusting."

"I hate both of you."

CHAPTER FORTY-FIVE

MALL DAY

Malls were an interesting idea before the turn of the century. A place where stores could be jammed in and where people could gather. They nearly became an artifact of a more peaceful time.

Terrorist attacks, a few plagues, the increasing digitalization of marketplaces, and the rising cost of physical marketplaces nearly killed the entire idea of a mall.

Nearly.

Now malls still exist, but more as a grand experience where those with more money than sense can be surrounded and cuddled in consumerist bliss, at least until they run out of cash to spend.

—Excerpt from *The Past Today: A Look at the Artifacts of Old America*, 2055

Lucy, Rac, and I arrived at the museum sometime before ten, which I figured was pretty good, considering how lazy Lucy and I could be if we wanted.

We showed Rac the matter recombobulator in what would be my armory, and the girl practically worshipped the machine. Its ability to turn useless trash into samurai-grade stuff was like a small religious revelation to her.

When I told her that my job for her was basically to collect trash and chuck it in the machine to make stuff with, she immediately took off and said she would take care of it.

Honestly, I was a bit worried, but I had Myalis track her, and she was mostly making the rounds of all the nearest dumpsters looking for preem refuse.

Lucy and I had a quick conversation with the contractor when he finally showed up. It ended with the man shooting down some of Lucy's more outrageous ideas before we settled on a plan for the renovations that was a bit more reasonable.

Once I dropped some cash for a deposit and warned the man about Rac and the very dangerous machine guarded by a few more-dangerous mecha-cats, Lucy and I found ourselves with a heap of time at our disposal.

"Now what?" Lucy asked. We were sitting on the edge of our floor's parking space, that overhang at the very top of the building where cars could come in to unload passengers into the more ostentatious entrance to the museum.

"I have . . . a couple of things to do," I said.

"So I should go home?" Lucy asked.

I frowned. "I think you can come along for the first one? I need to meet this guy called Jeff Burringham. He's a politician."

"Oh, yuck," Lucy said. "Think you'll find him getting blown?"

"I doubt it, but it's not impossible," I said. "He has the afternoon penciled for clothes shopping. So I thought it would be nice and natural to show up at whatever shop he's at to say hello and talk about stuff."

"Oh, an ambush," Lucy said. "You don't think it's going to be dangerous?"

"I mean, if he's not an idiot he'll have a couple of guards, at least, but nah, I think it should be relatively safe. You still have that gun I gave you?"

Lucy nodded and tapped a hand against her ribs. She had a dangerous glint in her eyes. "I'm armed and ready," she said.

I snorted. "I hope you don't need to use it, but you know. In case?" I didn't expect her to be able to fight off any real amount of resistance, but maybe knowing that she was armed would be enough to discourage some level of fuckery. "Myalis, can you call us a ride over?" I asked.

Certainly.

I leaned to the side and wrapped an arm around Lucy's shoulders. She let out a happy sigh and leaned right back into me. I sat there, eyes closed, until the whine of a hovercar approaching ended the moment.

Our ride wasn't anything special. An auto-taxi that parked with the precision of a bot. I helped Lucy in, then sat next to her in the back. The area around our new home was still underpopulated. There were fewer cars around than just about anywhere else in New Montreal.

Still, there was plenty of strange traffic. PMCs moved by in force, and there was a constant patrol of different police units on the outskirts of the incursion-impacted area. A constant stream of dump trucks were moving out of the area too, loaded with cargos of scrapped materials headed for parts unknown. Not nearly as many trucks with new materials coming in, though.

"I wonder if the city's going to recover," I muttered.

"Yeah, it will," Lucy said. "Folk around here are like cockroaches, but in a good way. We'll tough through it."

"If it helps, the city is likely to recover." Myalis's voice came through the car's speaker, cutting off a constant drone of background advertising that I'd barely really noticed. "The incursion that hit New Montreal was one of the softest to hit any major city in several years. The death toll was also relatively low. Likely owing to some public planning, the presence of shelters and vaults, and the rapid response of local Vanguard."

"Huh," I said. "I didn't think the shelters we had were worth jack shit."

"The shelters provided more than just physical protection, as little protection as they did. They were a gathering place for civilians and a method to keep people calm. In a situation like an incursion, the tendency for humans to panic and the various ways in which said panic feeds into itself can cause more harm than whatever triggered the initial response."

"Like distracting the kittens just before some inspector sort showed up," Lucy said.

I nodded along. It made some sense, I supposed.

Our flight across the city soon moved past the more damaged sections and toward the north end, where the older parts of the city were, and where the high-rises tended to take on a more artistic approach to cramping a lot of space up vertically.

We dipped out of the flow of traffic and dove down toward one building in particular. It looked like a tall pyramid, four-sided and covered in darkened glass. Our taxi dove past the entire building on a winding path that took us past the four dozen floors of the pyramid and toward an opening near the ground floor.

The taxi stopped in front of an unloading area and I opened the door and reached back to help Lucy out.

The air thrummed with ventilated air and the smell of running cars stank the place up.

The entrance was a series of revolving doors that people were funneling into in twos and threes while others exited and milled around, waiting for their rides or venturing deeper into the bowels of the parking garage.

Lucy entwined her fingers with mine and we ran up to the back of the line.

The people here skewed toward the younger, so much so that Lucy and I were about average. Teens in little cliques, some college students, plenty of upper-middle-class "Daddy's money" vibes going around.

I glanced over to Lucy, who grinned back.

The lines moved in toward the doors, and I noticed a ping on my augs. The mall was trying to connect to me to send me some maps and about a terabyte of ads mixed in with malware. Myalis was likely having a great time tearing apart whatever system had sent that.

We crossed through the revolving doorway and stepped into a smaller lobby area: cement half walls with security behind them, automated guns tucked away in large stainless crates, and rows of metal detectors that mall-goers were stepping through one at a time before being accosted by a guard who checked their temperatures and papers before letting them in. All to the tune of some shitty jingles played on crackly speakers.

"So much for this place looking fancy," I muttered.

"There's a 'no guns allowed' sign there," Lucy said, pointing to a large plastic board over the security stations.

"That's cute," I said. "Myalis, can you make us less conspicuous?"

Actually attempting subterfuge? How strange.

When our time came to pass through the metal detectors they came back clean, and when the guard checked our IDs by tagging our augs, we came back with nothing but flying colors. I noticed one of the guards staring at the very obvious sword hooked to a loop of my pants, but he didn't comment.

"So much for all that security," Lucy said as she leaned against me again.

"Yeah, well, fancy samurai tech beats half-assed mall security," I said.

"And if they caught on anyway?" Lucy asked.

"Then fancy samurai weaponry trumps mall security's Tasers," I said. "This whole samurai gig is a bit like cheating."

"A bit?" Lucy asked.

I smiled, a bit sheepish. "All right, so a lot."

The entrance led up a slight incline and around a corner, then into the center of the pyramid.

It was hollow, with a great big pillar filled with elevators in its center and all the floors of the mall ringing around the middle in ever-tightening circles.

"Right, now we just need to figure out where the fancy fucker is," I said.

CHAPTER FORTY-SIX

A BIT FANCY

Discovering alien, nonhuman life did interesting things to the field of psychology. The field, as esoteric and vague as it already was, didn't know how people would react to extraterrestrial life.

As it turns out, we as humans mostly want to either kill it (in the case of the Antithesis) or fuck it (in the case of all the rest).

—Cedric Richmond, PhD in psychology, 2031

"So, where's our dude?" I asked.

"How would I know?" Lucy replied. "Never exactly been here."

I chuckled. "I was asking Myalis, actually. But yeah, the place is a bit fancy, huh?"

The mall had that clean modern look of places with too much money poured into PR and advertising. Clean stainless steel decoration, holographic ads so well-crafted they almost looked real, and most importantly of all, a constant stream of bona fide middle-class losers buying shit.

There was no advertising like having clients.

Jeff Burringham hasn't yet arrived, though his appointment is in only an hour.

"Neat. Where's the appointment at?"

He's meant to be at a store called the Boutique de Beau Vêtements. It's on the third floor. Though I should inform you that the floors on this building are numbered in the reverse to most human buildings.

"The topmost floor is number one?" I asked.

Exactly. I suspect it's a marketing ploy to convince people to discuss the building more.

"Clever," I said.

Then I noticed Lucy pouting. "If you're going to take me on a date with another girl, then you could at least let me be part of the conversation," she said.

"This is a date?" I asked.

"It isn't?" Lucy asked right back. "We're out, we're shopping, we're going to go threaten some politician with possible bodily harm. We literally just snuck into a place while packing. Sounds like a date to me."

I laughed. "Well, sorry, I wasn't thinking and didn't realize. Look, once we find a quiet spot, I'll buy you some fancy augs, and Myalis can talk to you directly."

Lucy grinned. "Nice. Myalis would make a great girlfriend, you know."

I'm afraid that I'm not available.

"You're not?" I asked. Somehow it had never occurred to me to ask Myalis about . . . anything of that sort.

I'm married to my job, as it were.

Lucy laughed, and I realized that she had to have overheard. She saw my look of momentary confusion and pointed to her eye. "She's texting me."

"Huh," I said. I didn't really mind at all; Myalis was . . . a friend. "All right, well, should we go up to floor three? I'm kind of curious about where this dude buys his fancy-pants clothes."

We shuffled past a few fountains and a food court and over to the elevator banks in the middle of the giant room. They were all glass-walled and steel-flowed things, with hovering no-touch displays and interactive map overlays floating over the walls.

Lucy oohed and ahhed at all the shiny bells and whistles while I leaned back against one of the walls and watched, quite content just to see her having fun.

The elevator stopped to pick up and drop off a few people, but it unerringly made its way up until, finally, we reached the third floor from the top.

We stepped out into an area even more lavishly decorated than the floors below, with potted plants dotting the sides and barely any advertising past the names of the stores around us. There wasn't as much room up here, I imagined. The entire building being a pyramid of sorts meant that space became a premium the higher up a floor was.

I didn't know why that meant that the nicest stores were up here. A wedding dress shop, which I studiously ignored, a nice restaurant, and finally, wedged between the two, the Boutique de Beau Vêtements. There were a few more on the opposite end of the floor, but they didn't really matter.

"Oh," Lucy said. "Pretty!"

She was eyeing the mannequins at the front of the shop: full-motion animatronics that were walking on stationary treadmills and only pausing to flex and twist to show off the clothes they were wearing. Mostly they were business-y outfits, but the sorts I could imagine a CEO wearing. Nice patterns, soft-looking materials, and a lot of strange cuts.

I followed Lucy into the store, only for both of us to pause in the entrance. It was blocked off by a small red-velvet gate with a butler-looking guy behind it. "Bonjour," he said. "Do you have a reservation?"

"We don't," I said. "My name's Stray Cat, I'm here to talk to one of your clients in a few minutes."

One of the butler guy's eyebrows rose. "Is this an urgent matter? I would like to confirm things with my supervisor. Of course, if you'd be willing to wait, we can serve you some light refreshments."

"Sure," I said. I wasn't in a big hurry, and I didn't feel like shooting the place up.

He nodded, then stepped back and I saw his eyes glaze over. No doubt he was texting someone right there and then.

Lucy tugged me over to a love seat set off to the side, and I sat with an arm around her shoulder while we waited. Not thirty seconds later a second butler appeared with a tray covered in colorful macarons and with a pitcher filled with what looked like genuine strawberries and ice.

"This place is too fancy for my blood," I said after he left.

"I know!" Lucy replied past a mouthful of macarons. She'd taken one of every color, but I doubted she'd be able to tell the difference between their taste, the way she was shoving them into her mouth by the fistful.

"Madam Stray Cat?" the butler asked.

Lucy choked on her pastry.

"Yeah?" I replied.

"We would like to cordially invite you into la Boutique de Beau Vête-ments. Please, browse at your leisure, and if anything catches your eye, you need only inform a member of our staff. If you find yourself uncertain about anything, then don't hesitate to ask for assistance as well. Every member on the floor has a doctorate in fashion design."

"Thanks," I said.

The store didn't have racks of clothing. Instead it had little booths and stands with mannequins dressed in suits and nice summer wear; others had dresses or streetwear on.

Lucy gasped and pulled me into the front of a booth. "I've heard of these," she said before stepping up into the booth. The inner wall was a mirror, at least for a moment. A scan later and there was a color swatch that matched Lucy's darker skin to one side, and another for her hair, and then her image split and her reflection was wearing three different outfits, all from the same brand whose understated logo adorned a corner of the booth.

"Oh, I like this one," she said, pointing to one off to the side. The dress became the center of focus, and the next three Lucy models were all wear-ing similar but not identical versions of the dress. Different trim, slightly different colors, with and without complementing accessories.

"That's kind of cool," I said.

"I wonder how they did the models," Lucy said.

The entrance area had several high-resolution cameras at different angles. It wouldn't be difficult to build a three-dimensional model from that information alone. Also, take note that the models are being somewhat complimentary when it comes to Lucy's actual size.

Lucy sighed; she was half turned to the mirror. "Yeah, my ass isn't that nice," she said.

"Your ass is very nice," I said.

"Thank you, Cat," Lucy said. She smacked herself playfully, then laughed at the expression I made. "Come on, we should find something pretty for you to wear. You'd look awesome in a suit."

"As long as you don't try to fit me into a skirt," I said.

"Wouldn't suit you," Lucy said. "I, on the other hand, have these new and improved legs to show off. And to shave, urgh."

Lucy and I moved to another booth, this one more business oriented. I got to see what Lucy would look like in a blouse and pencil skirt, thick-rimmed secretary glasses and all, and then she forced me in front to try on different suits. I had to admit that I cut an intimidating figure in an all-black three-piece with a sword by my hip.

Cat. Jeff Burringham has entered the shop.

I half turned and looked toward the entrance. Somehow Lucy had dragged us a good ways into the store. It meant that I could snoop on Burringham from afar in peace.

Jeff didn't come alone. He had a pair of bodyguards who immediately stationed themselves next to the entrance, and a petite secretary-type who was stuck to his side like a bureaucratic limpet. The man himself was pretty handsome, for a guy.

"Well well, about damned time. Did you want to come?"

"You know I always do," Lucy said.

CHAPTER FORTY-SEVEN

IN WHICH LUCY DOES POLITICS

The cost of a vote?

Currently, a single citizen's vote is averaging out at approximately 1,245 credits each, at the going rate. That can change a lot.

Last election cycle the cost dropped when a mobile game company traded votes for waifus. It was one of the most popular elections in a while!

—Interview with Nimbletainment's CPO, 2035

Burringham—I don't know why, but some people just had a sort of . . . family-name-only kind of face, and Jeff here was definitely one of those—took a moment to glance around the store while standing in the entrance. His gaze swept right by me without ever lingering before his attention was caught by one of the butler-looking guys.

He started to chat with the butler, an easy, happy chatter that seemed to put even the uptight butler at ease. The two of them started to move toward a booth that the butler was gesturing at—Burringham's secretary in tow—when Lucy and I intercepted them.

"Hey there," I said with an easy grin. "You're Burringham, right?"

"Jeff Burringham," he said with a handsome smile. "A pleasure. I didn't expect to meet anyone who knew me here!" He glanced at the store clerk, one eyebrow raised in an obvious question.

The man cleared his throat. "This is Miss Stray Cat and her companion; she is a local samurai."

Burringham's other eyebrow joined the first. "A samurai! That's wonderful! To think that I shop at the same place as one of our protectors." He extended a hand my way, and without really thinking I shook it. "A pleasure to meet you, Miss Stray Cat. Ah, it is Miss, correct? She-slash-her?"

"Yeah," I said. "Actually, I'm here because you are."

"Really? I'm hardly that famous, at least not yet. I hope nothing I've done has been so abhorrent as to require the intervention of a samurai."

I shook my head. "No, not what you've done. Come on, if you still want to shop or whatever, then that's fine. I want to chat, not interrogate you."

I knew that no matter what, the guy would be on edge. It reminded me a bit of the very, very infrequent visits by psychiatrists and social workers of that sort at the orphanage. They never directly questioned the kittens who thought weirdly; they always tried to play the "I'm actually your friend" card before that. This time I was playing the part of the corporate-paid shrink, though.

"Certainly, though first I would love to introduce myself to your lovely friend here." He smiled at Lucy and extended a hand to her. Instead of shaking it, though, he bowed over it and kissed the air over her knuckles. "You must be Miss Stray Cat's girlfriend, I presume?"

"Yeah, I'm Lucy," Lucy said. She had a bit of a flush to her cheeks, but it disappeared almost as soon as it had appeared. "How'd you know? Good augs?"

"No no, augs won't tell you that kind of thing, not at first glance," he said. "But body language, that will. You two seem close. After that, it was all an educated guess. So! Clothing!"

We all moved over to one of the booths that was nearest. It was wider than some of the others, and without the more concealing walls to the sides. Perfect for a smaller group like ours to chat next to. The butler-clerk faded into the background, as did Burringham's secretary.

"I'm looking for an outfit for a gala I'm holding tomorrow night. It's a big affair. Lots of folk from a few industries, some political types, plenty of paparazzi and those sorts. You know the kind of event I'm talking about. Really shouldn't have put off finding an outfit until this late, but I've been run ragged these past few weeks, and when the incursion happened, well, that ruined more than one plan, I think."

"I can imagine," I said.

"It's going to be memorable, I hope." He stepped up before the wall of the booth, and the image of him before us was suddenly wearing a well-tailored suit. "A bit too plain, don't you think?"

I looked at the suit, then shrugged. "I guess. Black goes with everything."

"Including the background—you won't stand out in that," Lucy said.

Burringham laughed. "Good point! So, I've been chatting for a bit, but that's hardly fair to you, I imagine your time is important."

"It's . . . somewhat urgent, yeah, but the kind of urgent that's best considered. If that makes any sense."

"It makes plenty of sense," he said. "Miss Lucy, do you think I could do black with a brighter shirt and tie underneath, or should I try something entirely different?"

"Feels like undercompensating," Lucy said as she eyed the display.

Burringham nodded and with a swipe of his hand the outfit disappeared. "Let's try some more color, then. What kind of urgent but not situation are you dealing with here?"

I considered where to start for a moment before I jumped into it. "The sewers. I don't know if it made it to any of the important media feeds, but the entire city's sewer system is . . . basically fucked. We have a day or two, I think, before it starts to collapse. Then it'll probably go all Jenga tower on us."

"That is somewhat urgent, yes," Burringham agreed. He frowned at his own image, and I noticed that he was only idly switching tie patterns while he thought. "All right, so we have an issue on our hands. I'm going to assume that repairing the entire sewage system won't be all that easy?"

"The people who used to take care of it have probably disbanded," I said. "I don't actually know. Maybe they're still down there working to give us all a bit more time, but I doubt we're that lucky."

"I see," he said. "So, you have this incredible problem on your shoulders, and on your quest to solve it . . . you reach out to me."

"Yup."

He nodded. "Because I'm running to be mayor. Which means you've spoken to the last mayor."

"I did. He didn't seem to give much of a shit. I had killed my share of people that day, so I just left." I tapped my hand on the hilt of the sword poking from my hip.

"Killing him wouldn't have helped, I don't think. I commend you on your restraint."

"It was pretty close," I said. "But now you're running for mayor. I'm curious about your stance on the city-not-having-any-water thing."

Burringham hummed. "I'll be entirely honest with you, Miss Stray Cat. This is the first I've heard of this situation." He turned toward his secretary. "Did we know about it at all?"

"It was a low-priority situation on our docket for the week. Filed in with a few other infrastructure issues," the secretary said. "We did receive some news about a couple of samurai in the sewers yesterday, but it wasn't flagged as overly important. I can also confirm that the mayor spoke to a samurai yesterday, presumably Miss Stray Cat."

"Interesting," Burringham said. "How many people are likely to be impacted by this? I know the question is a little callous, but it's something I need to know."

"Anyone who has a toilet in their home, or who likes running water," I said.

Burringham's frown grew. "And what did the mayor say?"

"Mostly he seemed to think that bottled water sales would go up," I said.

Burringham crossed his arms. "The election is in four days. A few people have tried to postpone it, myself included, but the mayor and his party insisted that we hold it at its scheduled time anyway. We wanted to push it back because in times of crisis, politics aren't on people's minds, and keeping the status quo is often easier than moving people around. But this might change things."

"Not for the better," I said. "It's the poor folk who are going to get fucked over the most."

"I can imagine, yes." Burringham swiped his hand before him, and the screen started to play some generic footage of models in nice clothes. "All right. People need water. I agree with you on that, and besides, it's such an obviously good stance to take that I'd be an idiot not to. But that doesn't mean that I'll be able to do all that much, even if I do slip into the position of mayor. There are a lot of entrenched groups to move."

"Like who?" I asked.

He shook his head. "Miss Stray Cat, can I make a proposition?"

"You can try."

"The gala I'm holding tomorrow. Would you be willing to show up? Bring your beautiful friend as well, of course. If you help me gain the mayor's seat, then I'll turn the revamping of the sewage system into my highest-priority issue."

His secretary looked up. "Sir, that might be an unpopular stance to take."

"No, it won't," he said. "Not the moment people start to run out of water. The mayor's going to try to pin the failure on me, saying I'm sabotaging it to make my cause look better, but with Miss Stray Cat saying otherwise, people won't believe him."

"I don't know how keen I am on doing politics," I said.

Burringham laughed. "Miss Stray Cat, your being here means that you're already doing politics. Congratulations!"

CHAPTER FORTY-EIGHT

FAMILY MATTERS

Family's important.

We used to live in Florida, before the ocean took it. We weren't all that close as a family, not until the waves rose and all of a sudden everything was being swallowed up by more and more water.

We had to move. Lost everything, just like millions of others. All because like, ten companies decided to fuck humanity and the only planet we have.

Family's important.

And if saving my family means that I need to kill some shareholders, then fuck 'em.

—Guilty plea of Hernandez Smith, accused of multiple counts of homicide, 2027

"What do you think?" I asked Lucy while Burringham left. He had a bag by his side, and one of his bodyguards came up to take his new suit, wrapped in a layer of clear plastic and hanging on a coat hanger.

"He was charming," she said. "Handsome too. I think he knows that he's both, and he's used to leveraging it. But I guess that's pretty normal for a politician."

"Makes sense, yeah," I said. "He's a career politician, at least that's the way Myalis put it."

"She gave you a report?" Lucy asked.

I nodded. "It was pretty detailed."

"Can I see it? I won't read it now, but it might be interesting to know," Lucy asked.

I shrugged. "Yeah, sure. So, the gala thing, want to be my plus-one?"

"Oh, what a casual way to ask someone out," Lucy said. She grabbed my arm and leaned her head down onto my shoulder. "You know, it's going to be a real fancy gala thing. We can't just show up wearing whatever. Well, actually, you might be able to, as long as the whatever is samurai-ish enough, but poor little Lucy needs to wear something to blend in a little better."

"You just want a pretty dress," I said.

"No, I want to *buy* a pretty dress."

I could assist here.

I decided to ignore Myalis because she'd get Lucy something with a cat print and ears and Lucy would take it just to make me suffer.

"I really don't see how that's any different than what I said. Also, aren't you going to buy the dress with my money?"

Lucy looked up to me, and I could get lost in those eyes, even if they looked at my pityingly. "You are such a useless lesbian," she said.

"What?"

"Entirely useless," she declared.

"I am not!"

"If I didn't sit you down and tell you that we were girlfriends, you'd still be wondering now," Lucy said.

"That's not true," I said.

"We went on like, three dates before you realized we were dating." She shook her head, climbed to the tips of her feet, and pecked me on the cheek. "Now, let's look at pretty clothes to wear at the nice politician's party."

I rolled my eyes but followed Lucy over to one of the nearest booths. "My uselessness as a lesbian aside," I griped, "what do you think of Burringham's promise?"

"He'll keep it," Lucy said. She gestured at her reflection on the screen in the booth, and her image was soon wearing a long, flowing dress. It was nice, a beige that worked well with her skin, little gems woven near the hem flashing prettily.

"You think?" I asked. "It's a lot of money."

"He hasn't been in politics for very long, right?" Lucy asked.

"No, I don't think so."

She nodded. "Yeah, he was a bit too . . . you know, cocky? Like, he was quick to show off how good a politician he'd be. Kind of giving me some daddy-issue vibes."

I snorted. "Wow, and here I thought you thought he was attractive."

"I said he was handsome and charismatic, and he's both, and he knows it. Bet you he got training for both."

"You can train to be handsome?" I asked.

Lucy looked away from the dresses before her to nod seriously. "You can learn how not to be a twat while also not being all limp and beta-ish, and the other half of being handsome is mostly eating well and doing squats. You're halfway there already."

I bumped my shoulder against hers. "So, should I go with a dress too? Bet Myalis could find something. A pretty dress catalog."

Let's not touch the Pretty Dress catalog, please.

"I was thinking more . . . you'd look dashing with a masculine look?" Lucy said, though there was a hint of a question there.

I rubbed at my nose while I thought. "Yeah, I don't do skirts well."

"You really don't," Lucy agreed. "You always look uncomfortable with them on, and if it's an event with a bunch of important people, then we probably want you to look imposing and serious. You could go in your armor?"

"Isn't the armor a bit bulky?" I asked.

"Yeah, but it makes you look scary. Big sword by your hip, maybe a different coat? And I can play the part of the pretty gold digger hanging off your arm. Although, maybe the armor is too much?"

"A pretty gold digger, huh?" I asked.

Lucy nodded. "Now buy me a nice dress, please, sugar momma."

I laughed. "Sure. Something appropriately revealing?"

"But not too easy to break. I never had a pretty dress before; I want this thing to last." She flicked past a few that were very nice on her simulated body. With cuts so low they exposed her navel and flowing, silky lace.

"That's a nice one," I said.

"It's a bit old-fashioned," Lucy said. "And it wouldn't match your armor, if that's what you're going in."

"I do like having it, in case things go sideways. Better bulletproof when you don't need it than fleshy when you do."

"Wow, that's a big change for you," Lucy said. "Weren't you running headfirst into danger wearing barely any armor just two days ago?"

"I really like the armor. It's kind of awesome to get shot and have it only feel like someone poking you with a finger."

"Well, don't get used to standing in the way of bullets, all right?" she said.

I laughed. "Fine, fine. Actually . . . we should get you some armor for the gala."

"Do you really want to miss seeing me in a pretty dress?" Lucy asked.

"Maybe something like my armored suit, then? The one under the big, bulky armor."

"Oh, well in that case I'll need a whole different style of dress. Something more corpo-chic. You know, shoulder pads and a few contrasting layers. That way the undersuit just looks like it's part of the rest."

"I'd worry less if you were equipped like that," I said.

"Hmph, hypocrite," Lucy said.

I nodded. "You know it." I watched her flip through a dozen dresses, then back again. She was clearly looking for a specific style, something kind of blocky and formal. It wasn't as sexy, but it would have room to conceal a gun or two, which was pretty hot. "How are the kittens, by the way? I feel like I only see them in passing."

"Depends on the kitten. Spark and Bargain and Tim are fine. They're having a lot of fun just messing around in the penthouse. The Twins are more quiet than usual. I think they're spending a lot of time online. We might need to ask Myalis to check on them, you know how echo-feeds are. And Nose is . . . confused, I think?"

"By what?" I asked. "Oh, the gold is pretty."

She nodded, and the next dozen dresses all had golden highlights to them, or golden cloth on their inner layers; mostly the dresses were all black, though, maybe to fit with my armor? I didn't know fashion like Lucy did. "I think he expected to be dead soon, and now he'll be fine. It could be some sort of weird reverse depression thing? I'll keep an eye on him, make sure the others include him more. He was always a bit quiet."

"When he wasn't sniffling all over, yeah."

"Daniel might leave one day, but I think he's pretty happy just being lazy right now. And he's still bad at walking, but he's getting better. I think he's spending half the day flirting with girls online."

I snorted. I couldn't imagine him flirting, not well at least. "Junior? Katerine?"

"Getting along well with each other," Lucy said. "I think they really clicked."

"Like, click-clicked, or they're just friends?"

"Just friends," Lucy said. "I think Junior wants to go out and have adventures and start shit, like any girl her age, but Katerine is a lot more level-headed. She'd want to bring her dog too."

"Yeah, that's good. If they ever get into any trouble . . ."

Lucy giggled. "I'll tell you right away."

I hugged her from the side, then sighed. "How long does it take to find a dress anyway?"

"You can't rush perfection, Cat. Myalis has been spoiling you."

CHAPTER FORTY-NINE

PETER

Certain companies discovered that they could extract greater revenue from their clients in the form of services as opposed to products. Adobe pioneered some of this in the software market, but many other companies followed suit.

To oversimplify the matter: a company would provide the client with a rented, unowned version of whatever software the client needed in order to operate. That means that at any time the company owning the software can pull it away from their clients. Algorithms were pioneered that allowed the service provider to do just that at the most optimal time so that their clients would more easily surrender additional money in the form of fee payments and service costs.

Essentially, by turning a buy-and-sell economy into a rent-and-blackmail one, a company can earn much greater profits, though at the expense of losing the occasional client, and putting their CEOs at higher risk of sudden life termination events.

—*A Guide to Modern Business*, 2034

After Lucy and I met with Burringham, we had one last chore to take care of. Peter Silverbloom.

According to Myalis—who I just assumed was right about this kind of thing—Peter was currently working out of some building on the edges of the more residential part of New Montreal, insofar as the city could really be divided into parts so cleanly.

Lucy and I left the clothes store, one of the butlers promising us that her dress would be on our doorstep by the morning, and my wallet feeling a tiny fraction lighter (though the price of Lucy's dress had me reeling a bit, it was the most expensive thing I'd ever bought, house aside). We dropped back down to the ground floor of the building, then hopped into a taxi.

"So, who's this dude?" Lucy asked.

"Apparently he's some big-shot volunteer sort of guy. He might be able to help us with the whole Sewer Dragons thing."

"I guess they can't stay at Gomorrah's place forever."

"They can't," I agreed. "And they shouldn't be left the way they are. All prosthetic'd up, I mean. They at least deserve to have proper replacements for all of their limbs and shit." Which would be wildly expensive. I'd looked into artificial limbs before, what with my arm being missing for . . . most of my life really.

The cheaper ones cost half a year's rent in a shack, and that was for a simple, three-jointed arm that didn't have any servos or complex mechanical parts, just cheap Taiwanese plastics and a few recycled metal joints.

Something that could move and articulate simply was a whole lot more expensive, and one of those fancy better-than-flesh models cost as much as a brand-new car, and that was without the brain implants needed to run it, the constant software updates, and the other little expenses that came with it.

Most of those weren't even properly sold, they were rented to people.

Basically, it would be a bitch and a half to get enough arms and legs and other shit to outfit as many as Gomorrah and I had pulled from the sewers.

It actually made what Doc Hack did a little impressive, in retrospect. No less fucked up, but still impressive. He cobbled together prosthetics from what looked like nothing, maybe with a few aftermarket parts jammed in here and there. And by all accounts, they worked. The Sewer Dragons were able to move and fight. Probably not as well as someone running off their human 1.0 hardware, but they were better suited to life in the sewers than a normie.

"What're you thinking about?" Lucy asked.

"Just . . . stuff. How do you think this guy can help us anyway?"

"Don't you know that?" Lucy asked. She leaned into my side, her hands idly tugging at the fingers on my prosthetic arm.

"Not really. Been light on the details so far."

Lucy shrugged. "If he can help because he's like, a nice guy who really does want to help, then we should probably just be nice."

I chuckled. "Sure," I said. I made a mental note not to be a bitch.

The taxi nosed down and soon we were slipping lower into the city until we merged with the traffic on ground level. The taxi pulled up to the sidewalk almost immediately.

"We're pretty low," Lucy said.

"Yeah," I agreed. "Myalis, can we get directions from here?"

Certainly.

"Oh, that is convenient," Lucy said. "Myalis, you're like the best maps software ever."

I imagined that Myalis had interpreted "we" as meaning the two of us. Good enough for me. The map pointed up into the side entrance of one of the nearest buildings, a residential megabuilding, some one hundred and fifty floors' worth of shoebox apartments, only broken up by a few chain stores. Someone could live their entire life in a place like this without ever stepping outside to see that this one was set in a row of a dozen identical buildings.

"Come on," I said, hand reaching out toward Lucy, who grabbed on.

We slid into the building, and I couldn't help but notice the graffiti scratched into the paint-proof walls. Tight corridors branched out almost immediately into a maze of passages cut through by the main lane we were on. We moved in deeper with the confidence of two people who didn't care to be fucked with, and no one seemed eager to test us.

I did notice some hoodlum-looking fucks in tracksuits and with e-cigs loitering on a corner, but they chose not to interrupt us as we moved past.

Maybe it was the jackets? Or the obvious gear under them.

Or the sword?

I chose to believe that it was the very big, very samurai-looking sword hanging by my hip. No one wanted to fuck with someone cocky enough to bring a sword to a gunfight.

We stepped into a little elevator whose interior was entirely tagged with stickers and posters for all sorts of shit. Pandemic warnings about an out-break in this building a year ago had mustaches drawn on the faces of the corpo-art mascots, and there were brand stickers covering the entirety of the button panel.

The elevator pinged my augs to ask me which floor to go to, and it tried to dump about twelve viruses into my augs at the same time. Myalis gave me a little tally in the corner of my vision of the infections she ripped apart and the number of nanoseconds it took her to do so, like a really weird scoreboard in a shooter.

The elevator buckled and we started to rise.

"Nice place," Lucy said.

"Very," I agreed. It was actually kind of homey. The decor reminded me a lot of the orphanage, that strange kind of aesthetic that was straddling the line between trash, trashy, and grunge. There was an art to making shit look good.

The speakers crackled as we arrived, and Lucy and I got off on a floor with a higher ceiling and more room to walk around in. It looked like Peter was staying on one of the mall floors, where all the stores and clinics and such were stuffed away. Fake tiles lined the floors, broken up in some places, and there were vending machines shoved against every wall that could fit one, little jingles competing to be the most annoying.

The map pointed us around the elevator back, and down a wide road that stretched out through the building, across a bridge, and into the next building over. There were even a few electric carts parked along the road or driving around with people behind the wheel.

"At least it smells better here," Lucy commented.

There were a few street vendors gathered around, some still being operated by people instead of androids. McVendors still like having zit-faced teens behind the counters.

"Thirsty?" I asked.

"Just for you," Lucy said.

I snorted as I bumped shoulders with her. "It should be . . . right there," I said as I compared the map to what I was seeing. Peter, as it turned out, was in an old storefront that had been converted into a tax office of sorts. The old fixtures for whatever sign was there before were still visible over the entrance. The current name was some incomprehensible jumble of letters.

Lucy and I walked in. The entrance had a big conference table, with some mismatched chairs around it; to the side were a few cubicle walls, mostly there to split off the desks in that part of the room from the rest of the area. A huge printer at the back had a "FUCKED" sign taped to it and a smaller printer buzzing atop it.

The only thing that looked less than ten years old was the coffee machine in one corner. Somehow it still shone like it was new and was sitting on what looked like a throne, as if it was revered by the people working here.

"Oh, hey?" a twentysomething girl asked. She looked like she was told to dress in office chic but couldn't be arsed to go the whole way and had stuck to wearing a nice blouse tucked into sweatpants. "What's up?"

"Uh," I said.

"If you're here for help with your taxes, then you need an appointment. If child protection stole your kid, then we can get you in touch with the right people. If you want to rob us, then fuck off, we barely have a grand between the twenty of us, and if you're looking for some other sort of help, well then it depends but we might be able to help."

"I was looking for Peter, Peter Silverbloom," I said.

One of her eyebrows rose and she tugged a pack of gum out of a pocket. "What for? You government? Corpo?"

"I'm a samurai, so neither."

"Uh-huh," she said, entirely dismissing what I'd said.

I frowned while Lucy started to giggle next to me.

CHAPTER FIFTY

SANS BUT LUCRATIF

Nonprofits can be easily split into two broad categories:

Corporate nonprofits are usually run by the PR, propaganda, or public image department of a company, though the nonprofit itself will be its own entity on paper. These exist to make the main company appear more family-friendly or somewhat concerned with the community's welfare.

Community nonprofits are usually run by members of the local community; they exist solely to take care of an issue that a few members of the region have decided to champion in their own time and with their own funds.

More often than not, the community-based nonprofits will fold once they begin to encroach on a corporate nonprofit. They cannot be allowed to steal the good image that a corporation is paying large sums to maintain.

—Quote from A Discourse on Challenges
of the Modern Community, 2039

It took a minute to convince the secretary that yes, I was a samurai, and no, I wasn't at their little nonprofit to murder or otherwise harm Peter. I was beginning to suspect that she had something of a crush on the man we were looking for.

"Peter's office is back here," she said as she gestured to the back, the bangles on her wrists jingling with the motion.

"Lead on," I said.

"So, you two both samurai? Like, for real-real?"

I shook my head. "Just me. Lucy here's my friend."

"Yes, I'm Cat's friend," Lucy said.

I shot her a look, but she was wearing a shit-eating grin that promised future teasing, so I decided that I'd wait a while before explaining myself.

Peter's office at the back wasn't anything special. This wasn't someone who had a fancy setup, either because he didn't have the budget for it or because he didn't want to look like he had the budget. Then again, if Myalis suggested that he was working off a shoestring budget, then I trusted her.

The girl knocked on the office's glass door. "Peter, you have some high-brow guests here."

"Oh, I'm highbrow now," Lucy said.

"You were always high maintenance," I replied offhandedly.

I had to suppress the urge to jump as the door opened and Lucy pinched my rear at exactly the same time. A man stood in the entrance, tall, with a chiseled sort of jaw and bright eyes. His hair was a little untidy, but in that sort of shampoo-commercial way, and he had just a hint of a five o'clock shadow on. "Hello?" he asked.

"Heya," I said. "You got a minute?"

"What's this about?" he asked. "I'm sure I can make some time for you, but I am rather busy right now."

I nodded. "That's all right. Just need a couple of minutes. My name's Catherine, but folk call me Stray Cat. I'm a samurai based out of New Montreal. I had some, uh, stuff that might interest you."

He stared at me for a moment, then turned to the woman next to me. "Can you do me a huge favor and text Martin about my five o'clock, tell him something's come up and that I'll be with him as soon as I can. He knows that I wouldn't put him off for anything that isn't important."

"Hey, sure thing, Peter," she said before backing off. She eyed Lucy and me before leaving.

"Sorry, please, come in," he said as he backed into the office. The table had some trinkets on it and a few random pages stacked off to the side. It wasn't the biggest of offices, but there was room for a pair of mismatched chairs in front of the desk and a bookshelf to the side filled with boring-looking texts. Peter moved behind the desk and clicked his laptop shut. "I'm sorry, this isn't my office, I'm borrowing it for the day. I'm on the move too much to have my own, really."

"You move around a lot?" I asked.

He laughed self-deprecatingly. "All the time. People take you a lot more seriously when you show up in person, which I suppose you know, being here now and all." He gestured to the seats, and I pulled one out for Lucy before taking the other.

"Look, I didn't want to bother you too much, but someone told me you were the guy to talk to, so I figured I'd take my shot, you know?"

"Uh, sure. I get a lot of people who get referred to me. I'm a bit of a problem solver. Or at least I try to be. Never had an actual samurai asking for help, though?"

For all that he carried himself with confidence, there was just a hint in his voice that he wasn't as sure as he would have liked to be. "Hey, it takes all sorts," I said.

"So, what's the issue, and how can I help?" Peter asked.

"Have you heard of the problem with the sewers?" I asked. He shook his head. "All right, well, the long and short of it is that a gang was living down there. They took care of the maintenance, mostly, and in exchange they'd get some stuff. Kind of a weird symbiotic relationship, you know? See, to live in the sewers you need a lot of special augs and a heap of modifications to your body. It's not pretty."

"I can imagine," Peter said.

I nodded along. "So, after that last invasion, these Sewer Dragons, that's the gang's name, started to kidnap normal folk off the streets to make up their numbers. Now, Gomorrah and I—that's another samurai I work with—we took exception to that and may have destroyed the gang."

"That's good?" Peter asked. He was obviously looking for the problem.

"It's all right," I said. "The problem is the people we saved. We have something like two hundred people who were chopped up and given prosthetics against their will. We're talking two hundred pairs of legs, a load of internals, probably a heap of other medical issues, and a whole lot of trauma, I imagine."

"That's more serious than I expected," Peter said. "What do you plan to do with all of them? Are you helping them?"

"We're doing what we can, but right now we're kind of torn. We either try to save these two hundred or so people, and don't get me wrong, we totally can save them. Or we focus on fixing the sewer system before everyone in the entire city has to live without any water and no flushing toilets."

Peter leaned forward, elbows on the table. "That's going to hit the poor hardest," he said. "Everyone in the lower-middle brackets won't be able to afford bottled water if the prices jump, and they're the ones more likely to rely on public utilities for their water."

"It's a pretty big mess," I said. "We're trying to get things fixed before it really goes to shit, but it might be a close call. And no, before you ask, we can't really just . . . samurai the problem away. Or we could, but not well. We just don't have the resources to patch everything."

It was a bit of a sour point, but I'd gone over it with Myalis. Even with drones and automatic systems in place, I wouldn't have the points needed to fix the entire sewer system. Maybe if it were just one issue. Some problem with acidic water, or if we needed new filters. There were plenty of smaller issues I could take care of. The machine back home could make the materials to fix some parts of the system, but not at the speed and not at the quantity needed to fix everything.

Maybe Deus Ex could do it, drop a hundred thousand points into something huge to fix everything, but I wasn't there yet, and the more points I spent on this problem, the fewer I had to use in the next incursion.

"I've basically thrown the issue on some up-and-coming political sort. And if he doesn't fix things . . . I don't know, I guess I'll make him drink sewer water until he changes his mind about fucking with the lives of everyone in the city. We don't need a riot because the water's gone bad."

Peter pursed his lips, then shook his head. "You're overestimating people's ability to be violent."

"Huh?" Lucy asked.

"People that will be violent will be violent in response to something immediate, something happening in front of them or that's making them angry then and there. But for bigger-picture things . . . Do you know how many dirty politicians were killed in their homes by normal people? Corrupt cops? There's a cop who's currently on paid leave living two floors up. He's literally home right now."

"Why's he off?" Lucy asked.

"Got caught touching a suspect inappropriately, after about thirty complaints like that. He also shot and killed some kid a few months back. He was told to do a search of some apartment and he broke into the wrong place."

"And no one's done anything?" I asked.

"People aren't inherently violent," Peter said. "Samurai are the exception. And . . . and I'm going on a tangent, I'm sorry. What did you need help with? This water thing's going to get a lot of good people killed; I'll do whatever you need me to."

CHAPTER FIFTY-ONE

COMMUNITY FEELINGS

There's an essential mistrust of the community. A well-honed fear of your own neighbor.

Who knows, they might be a thief, a murderer, or a rapist? You certainly don't know.

That fear, that's what's keeping us afloat right now. The longer people spend mistrusting their neighbor, the longer it'll take them to realize that the person in the same shit hole as them isn't the one with the boot on their neck.

—Clive Robertson, head of public security for Nimbletainment, 2045

"I, uh, appreciate it," I said. Now I just felt awkward, and I think Lucy caught on, because of course she did.

"Actually, Peter, I think Cat was here to ask about something else."

Peter looked between Lucy and me. "Oh, okay. I jumped to a wrong conclusion, then," he said. "I assumed that you wanted me to help you . . . actually, I don't entirely know. We could collect water and perishables now, before this sewer crisis really takes off. A few days of preparation could save a lot of lives."

"Actually, yeah, that sounds like a fantastic idea," I said.

"We do a lot of community outreach here. Foodbanks, shelter prep, school supplies. They're all different nonprofits, because we need to compartmentalize things, but all of them keep in touch, we have boards online where to share things. If you want, I can get word out that there's going to be a water shortage. It's happened before, we know what to do."

"It wouldn't hurt," I said. "But yeah, Lucy's right. I mostly came here to ask about something entirely different."

Peter leaned his elbows down onto his borrowed desk. "Well, I'm listening. If it's going to save people, then I'm definitely in."

"Those people that the Sewer Dragons kidnapped, the ones I mentioned before, we need to help them; right now Gomorrah and I are focused on saving the city, but I'd feel pretty fucking awful about myself if I left them to rot, and I doubt there's any system in place to help."

"That would require medical assistance for a lot of people," Peter said.

"It is a lot," I said. "Do you think you can help?"

"You won't be too surprised to know that this kind of thing comes up often. Usually it's someone in the community who needs an operation, or some new organ, or who lost a limb in one of the factories. When people can't afford the help they need, they often turn to us, and we in turn look to the rest of the community. I've done more charity runs than I can count."

"Could you do something for the people the Sewer Dragons kidnapped?" Lucy asked.

Peter nodded. "I think we could. Two hundred . . . that's a lot of people who need help, and it sounds like it will be expensive help too, but across the millions of people living in New Montreal, that's only a few dozen credits each. It . . . I don't want to bother you, Miss Stray Cat, but could you pitch in as well?"

I only hesitated a moment before nodding. "Yeah, I can help. I've been thinking . . . I have this neat machine that can build prosthetics for people, at least I think it can. I'll need someone to operate it, though, and I don't think they'll be the fancy self-installing, tailor-made sort of prosthetic."

"If you could provide them, we can find someone to install them," Peter said. "We have a few mechanics, some doctors and ex–medical students. I'm sure they'd be honored to work with samurai tech, or if not we can probably pay them directly; that would be a lot cheaper than buying the things outright."

I nodded. That would help. The blueprints would cost me some points, but fuck it, a few hundred points to help a few hundred people. "I don't know if they'll be the greatest, but I'll make sure they're functional, at least. And I don't see why we should necessarily limit ourselves to the people the Sewer Dragons took. Within reason, of course."

"I can set up a clinic. Give me two days, three at most, and I'll have a place for you to store whatever you make, and some people to run the place."

I glanced at Lucy, and she nodded. I think she was impressed, which to be fair, I was too. "All right. I'll take your word for it. I think I can provide security too."

Peter winced. "We . . . we would like to trust everyone in our community, but some of them come from rough backgrounds, they never got the education they needed, or the care they deserved, and . . . yes, some might think that robbing a samurai's clinic might mean a big payday."

A couple of my mecha-cats would make them reconsider, I figured. It was like having guard dogs, but with railguns. "Yeah, don't worry there," I said. "The folks we're helping, they'll probably need more than just some fancy new limbs, though. Therapy for some of them, I guess, and they might need more hospital time."

Peter leaned back into his seat, a frown squeezing his brows together. "If we can prove that it works, then we'll definitely get a lot of requests from people who need the same sort of help, which will mean a lot of donations. The community helping the community is what we're all about here."

"Cool," I said for a lack of anything less awkward to say. Peter might have been a pretty cool guy, but he struck me as a bit idealistic. Like, I didn't doubt that he'd seen some shit, probably a lot worse than most people did, hidden away between their homes and work all day every day. Hell, I knew that bad shit was going on all over, but I could still tune it out, dive into my media feed and bitch and moan about how someone somewhere else was doing something wrong.

I figured Peter was some sort of masochist, getting off on the suffering that people brought to him, then getting off again on helping them through it.

Or he was just genuinely a nice person, but that didn't feel as likely as my first idea.

I stood up, and Lucy bounced to her feet a second after. "All right, you get that clinic going, and I'll provide the shit we need to help people. Can you handle the, uh, mental stuff?"

"We don't have any proper therapists," Peter said. "But we have a lot of good people, with big hearts. Sometimes that helps enough that people are able to get back on their feet."

"Right," I said. "Look, I know I'm coming out of nowhere with this, so I appreciate that you don't mind helping. I'll try to return the favor, you know? If any corpo-types cause trouble, or if some government jerks try to mess things up too much, you give me a call, okay?"

"Thank you," Peter said. "I think half the time we lose a clinic, or a fundraiser goes wrong, it's because someone outside the community got greedy. It'll be nice to know we can actually fight back."

"Yeah, yeah," I said. "We'll keep in touch too."

Peter stood up and rushed to the door to help us out. We made some meaningless small talk on the way out and finally broke off as soon as we were back out in the main corridor.

"We were out of there fast," Lucy said.

"Yeah, sorry," I said. "Just . . . I don't know. Not a bad feeling, just, I'm feeling jittery?"

"Sexy jittery or annoying jittery?"

"Annoying," I said. "We've done nothing but talk to people all day, that and a bit of moving around. It feels like at any moment things will go tits up, in a bad way."

Lucy looped an arm around mine and pulled me closer. "You worry too much," she said. "Maybe we should head back home, try to relax you a bit?"

I sighed, then leaned back into her. "Yeah, that does sound nice."

"And maybe that pretty dress of mine's arrived, and I can put on a show for you? Or . . . nah, maybe we can just order something from room service, find some PJs, and do some cuddling?"

That did sound nice. "We don't have PJs."

"Well, it'll either have to be nothing but some old T-shirts, or we can order some same-hour-delivery clothes. Whichever you think would be more fun."

I laughed, then turned as Lucy gave me a quick peck on the cheek.

"You're taking on too much again," she said. "Always playing the big damn hero, but never looking out for herself. Don't get me wrong, I think heroes are hot, but I prefer the live ones. So you need to take a break when you can afford to, okay?"

"I guess," I said.

"You're not responsible for everyone's lives, Cat. But I am responsible for yours, so if I tell you that you need a break, I'm being serious."

"Oh, you're responsible for me, huh?"

"Damn right," Lucy said with unflappable certainty. "Now let's get home, my feet are killing me."

CHAPTER FIFTY-TWO

COLLAR AND LEASH

Why? Why can't we just be kind to each other? Is that too damned much to ask for?

Just a shred of decency? A bit of empathy?

Every damned religion is about making themselves look good and everyone else look like madmen. Every country does the same damned thing. We split into parties and degrade each other, always whipped on by some greedy fuck who just wants to make himself a tiny bit more powerful.

Why? It's just hurting people. It's just looking at your fellow man like they're not even worth being considered human anymore?

Can't we just be kind to each other? Fuck! It's not even hard!

Just put yourself in their shoes. A kid could do it! Stop thinking that everyone is an enemy just because they're a little bit different. Stop putting money before the lives of your neighbors. Stop being a cunt even though it's the only thing you know.

I didn't want it to come to this, dammit!

—Final words of the Senate Bomber, 2028

"My arm's asleep," I complained idly.

"I can move," Lucy said, though she didn't actually make any effort to move.

We were both on that fancy bed, sprawled out and enjoying the luxuriant comfort of brand-new PJs. Lucy was tucked into my side, where she fit snugly, and we had thick sheets over us, the fancy self-warming kind that were just shy of uncomfortably warm.

I yawned, but even though I was tired and it was getting late, I wasn't really ready to sleep. I just wanted to cuddle, to recharge because the next day was going to be troublesome.

"Nah, don't," I said. I pulled Lucy a bit closer into my side, numb arm be damned.

Lucy made a content little noise and turned onto her side, one arm wrapping itself around my torso even as she put her head on my shoulder. "Sleepy?"

"Nah," I lied. "Thinking too much."

"About?"

"Tomorrow," I said. "We need to get you some more protection stuff. Just in case."

"I'll be fine," Lucy said. "I'm hardly anyone's priority. My role is to be the pretty eye candy."

"Yeah, but you're my eye candy, and I want you intact."

Lucy chuckled, and I was distracted for a moment by the sensation against my side of her restrained laughter. "You're like a kitten that doesn't want to share."

"Exactly."

"So, do I get crazy armor too? Because I'll be pretty disappointed if I don't get to wear that dress."

I hummed and leaned my head down so that I could press my cheek over her head. "Maybe not something so clunky," I said. "We need . . . something so that you can carry that gun on you."

"That dress doesn't exactly have pockets," Lucy said.

"A thigh strap, maybe?" I said, and then I considered Lucy's thigh with a strap around it. It was a nice mental image to have. "Something so that you can grab your gun in a hurry."

"If I have to wear a thigh strap, you have to wear a leash," Lucy said.

"A leash," I repeated.

"With a little bell," Lucy added.

I huffed. "I'm not going to wear a leash."

"Fine, just a collar, then."

"I'm also not going to wear a collar," I replied. "But . . . maybe you wouldn't look bad with one."

"I wouldn't look bad in anything," Lucy said, which was an entirely fair statement to make. "Well, never mind, I'll order one online later."

"Are you serious?" I asked.

"You only want that thigh holster thing so that you have an excuse to ogle my legs."

"They're very nice legs," I said.

"And I'll get a leash so that I can parade you around the room. And it'll give me something to grab on to. In the absence of any other clothes, I mean."

I shook my head. "Pervert."

"Just a little," Lucy said. She hugged me closer, and I wrapped an arm around her back.

If you don't mind me intruding in this rather intimate moment, then I do have some suggestions.

I closed my eyes but nodded for Myalis to go on.

Disregarding the purchase of a collar and leash for the moment. There are several options that could help keep Lucy safe. Protective screens, security drones, shield emitters, and a host of more offensive options. Many of these are quite obvious, though.

I hummed for her to go on.

Seeing as how you may have other, larger purchases in mind for the near future, I would suggest something a little less expensive. From the general-use Vanguard catalog, there is a single-use personal teleportation device. It is the only such item in that catalog and requires that an arrival location be set, somewhere where the teleported can land regardless of the situation from which they were pulled. The device itself can take many forms. In this case I would suggest a piece of jewelry.

Lucy would like that, and it did sound like a decent idea. If things went crooked, which they might, having an eject button that would immediately pull Lucy out of danger and place her somewhere safe would be awesome. Maybe the drop-off point could be right here, over the bed. A soft landing, and she could check out the kittens and make sure things were safe here while I took care of whatever triggered the teleportation device.

The device can trigger based on vital signs, on a manual trigger from you, or it can be set to trigger at my discretion, for example in the case of an immediate threat that neither you nor Lucy can perceive.

I quirked an eyebrow at that.

The time it takes for you to twitch a muscle can feel like relative years to an AI such as myself. I could trigger a teleportation device, enter all the relevant parameters, and have Lucy be beyond the range of any trouble in the time it takes for the bullet of the average handgun pressed up against her skin to exit the barrel.

I blinked. Sometimes Myalis was a little scary. Then again, she was scary while being protective of Lucy, which I was super-okay with.

I sent her a text. "Thanks. I'll take it. Lucy needs new augs too."

That can be arranged quite easily. Her own are laughably out of date, even by Earth standards. They were also riddled with viruses, spyware, and several backdoors that were either datamining her or using her augs' processing power to mine cryptographic currencies.

"Were?" I sent.

Obviously, I could not risk cross-contamination with your own augmentations and equipment, so I removed any such interference. The children's equipment was likewise cleaned when I had a moment to spare. Though her equipment, even with better software, is still terribly inefficient. Your own is an order of magnitude better but still lags behind compared to what I wish you had.

I nodded before sending another text. "Thanks. <3 I'll spend a few points on my own augs, too. Get you some more breathing room."

Myalis and her help was . . . basically more than half the reason I was a threat as a samurai. Sure, I could shoot some CEO, but Myalis transferring the contents of their bank accounts to some charities was a lot more devastating for a company.

You're very welcome, Catherine. Now, you should consider sleeping. Your day tomorrow is likely going to require a lot of energy to get through.

I shook my head. "Lucy's still awake," I texted.

She is not.

Blinking, I stretched my head to the side. Lucy had a hand balled into a fist next to her mouth and was squeezed into my side in a way that I couldn't imagine being all that comfortable. Still, she was breathing softly, eyes shut against the soft light from above the four-poster.

I glanced over to the smart light above, closed my meat eye because staring at a light was stupid, and flicked over to my Cyberwarfare tools.

Using those to turn off a light without speaking might have been overkill, but it worked, so I was hardly going to complain.

Lucy muttered something in her sleep, so I snuggled around to hug her better, then pulled up the blankets until they were tucked in just under her neck.

It wouldn't last. Lucy moved in her sleep. I'd been woken up by enough kicks to the shin to know that much about her.

I kissed Lucy on the forehead, and she mumbled something before making a kiss noise right back at me. I couldn't help a chuckle. "Good night, Lucy," I said. "And good night, Myalis."

Good night, Catherine. Sleep well.

CHAPTER FIFTY-THREE

THE GEM

A diamond is a woman's best friend.
But a goddess is adorned in painite.

—Pandora ad, 2049

Lucy spun around, then came to a dizzying stop. The long pleats of her dress wrapped around her legs before gently unfolding. "What do you think?" she asked.

"You look gorgeous," I said.

She really did look great. The dress was all dark purples and lighter grays. She wore a sort of jacket-thing with padded shoulders that sank down to a thin waist and wrapped around her hips. The main portion of the dress was a smooth, silky material, with a generous window over her bust and enough support to make things more interesting. It was still functional, though, pretty without getting in the way.

My points were down to 10,644, but that did mean that I had two things to present to Lucy. Unfortunately I didn't have a better box for them than the ones they'd come with. "I have gifts," I said.

"Oh?" Lucy asked. She turned away from the mirror and looked my way. "What sort of gifts?"

I handed her the larger of the two boxes. "That's . . . a meh gift. It's a thigh holster, for your handgun."

Lucy oohed appropriately and opened the little case to reveal the straps within. They were the same gray as part of her dress, even the texture on the surface matching. "Nice. Myalis has an eye for detail, huh?"

"Uh, well, I did ask for something you'd like," I said.

Lucy laughed and pulled me into a hug. "Thanks. It'll look great. Really complete that femme-fatale look."

"Uh-huh," I said. "I have two more gifts," I said.

"Oh, gifts plural. You know, what with the dress and the shoes and now the thigh holster—which is admittedly a bit weird—I'm starting to feel a bit overwhelmed here."

I snorted. "You'll like this one," I said. "Turn around."

Lucy turned, and I walked her sideways so that she was standing in front of the mirror. "All right," she said, meeting my eyes through the reflection.

"The next gift is this," I said, a hand coming to the side. "Myalis, the augs."

Here you go.

New Purchase: Cyberwarfare-Capable Class I Augmentation
Points Reduced from . . . 10,644 to . . . 10,594
The package was fairly large, and I had to use both hands to open it, ruining the moment I wanted to make a little. Inside it was a large tubular syringe, with a pad on one end and a thumb trigger in the middle.

"I need to press this into your eye," I said.

"Oh, yuck," Lucy said. She made a face but then brought a hand up to her left eye. "Should I keep it as wide open as I can?"

"You don't mind?" I asked.

"Well, it's you, so you're hardly going to poke my eye out." She very clearly rolled said eyes.

"Right, well, don't move," I said. The tube expanded when it came closer to her eye, pushed it open, then connected in place with a faint click. A light on the side of the device went green and I pulled it back. "Did that hurt?"

"No, not at all," Lucy said. She blinked a few times. "Uh, my augs are off now, though."

"That's part one," I said. "I also need to jam it against your neck."

I lifted her hair and found the port for her augs right at the base of her skull. A compatible port slid out of the end and jammed itself into place. The lights on the side of the tube went from red to orange to yellow to green in the space of twenty or so seconds, and then it dinged.

"I think it's done," I said. "Myalis said that it's part hardware change, part software. Basically, it's . . . bullshit nano stuff replacing and adding more bits to your old augs. So you don't need to tear them out."

"Oh, nice," Lucy said. She blinked and then grinned. "Well, they're back online. I can't see any difference, though."

"I don't think you should," I said. "Faster, no viruses or anything, and some Cyberwarfare stuff. Oh, and a better connection to Myalis."

"Nice," Lucy said. "I can send her more juicy memes."

"You send my alien space AI memes?" I asked.

"She sends some back. Myalis is a bit of a shitposter, but she has this thing about cat pics."

Cats are fascinating creatures.

"I'm surrounded by weirdos," I said. "Not even my head is safe."

Lucy elbowed me lightly in the ribs. "You're not so normal yourself," she said.

"All right, all right," I said as I reached up and grabbed Lucy's shoulders. I turned her back toward the mirror, then fished my last present out of my pocket. I snapped open the box, then grinned at the necklace within. "Third gift."

"You said two."

"I'm bad at math," I said.

"Oh," Lucy said as I carefully wrapped it around her neck, then laid a kiss in the crook just behind her collar.

The necklace was made of something silverlike, long, Möbius-strip links that clasped together at the back with a screw clasp. The pendant sitting over Lucy's sternum was a bit . . . silly. A small grinning cat head, the eyes replaced by a pair of purple gems.

"It's pretty," Lucy said.

"I, ah, hope you like it," I said.

She leaned back into me. "I love it," she said. "But I love you more, you silly, sentimental kitty Cat."

I hugged her, and for a moment we enjoyed just being close.

But time, as always, intruded on us.

Someone knocked on the door, and I let go of Lucy. "One of the kittens?" I asked. I walked over and opened it. If it was some actual trouble, Myalis would inform me.

Junior was on the other side, no expression on her face, even on seeing me in pawprint PJs. "There's a pair of nuns here to see you."

"A pair of nuns," I repeated. What was my life coming to when that wasn't implausible. "Is one of them Gomorrah?"

"Think so. Looks like the same samurai as in that Two Girls One Flamer meme," she said.

"Please don't look at any meme that I'm part of," I said, knowing full well that it would be easier to ask the sun not to set.

"Whatever," Junior said. "I've done my part. She's in the living room."

"Right. Thanks." I shut the door, then turned and started looking for my clothes. "Where's my under armor, I need to get dressed too."

"I can go play distraction for a while," Lucy said. She pecked me on the cheek on the way out. "Your stuff's all on that chair, by the way."

"Thanks," I said.

I didn't take too long to squeeze into all of my gear. Then I ran into the washroom and jumped into my armor, which had fortunately dried up and didn't stink of anything. After securing my helmet on and making sure that my jacket was on straight, I left the room and stomped—quietly—over to the living room.

Gomorrah was there, in full regalia, though her mask was left on the kitchen counter and she was sipping some soda through a straw. Franny was sitting on one of the stools, an amused smile on as she teased Nose, who seemed to have a lot of questions today. Or a sudden crush on the redheaded nun.

"Hey," I said. I took off my helmet and set it next to Gomorrah's mask. "Didn't know if you'd show up."

"It's an excuse to get away from the church, and to actually get something done. Yesterday was an . . . interesting day."

"Any trouble?" I asked.

"Plenty," Gomorrah said.

Franny laughed. "The sisters were nice to all the refugees the first day. Now, their patience is wearing thin. So much for proper demeanor and candor."

"Figures," I said. "So you wanted to come with?"

Gomorrah nodded. "It'll mean a day away from all the drama. I think the threat of me returning eventually should be enough to keep everyone in line, at least for an afternoon. And it means that I won't have to be there. You know, the sisters used to boss me around? Now, they can't take a bath without asking for permission first."

"Literally?" I asked.

She glared. "I was being figurative, of course."

Lucy giggled. "Of course. It'll be fun to be with others. It can be a double date!"

Gomorrah's face froze for just a moment before she composed herself. "Franny is just coming with me to get out of the church as well," she said.

"Yeah," Franny said a little too quickly. "It's stuffy over there."

Lucy and I glanced at each other and communicated a novel's worth to each other in a few seconds. "Well, whatever you say," I said. "Do you think we can head over in the Fury? It'll be nicer than taking a taxi over."

"Will Gomorrah need an invite?" Lucy asked. "Jeff might be surprised if two samurai show up when he's expecting one. And you're supposed to bring a plus-one, not plus-three. There might not be enough seats or whatever."

"I'll send him a text," I said. It was a decent idea.

"We can use the Fury," Gomorrah agreed. "Should we head out now, or . . ."

"I guess?" I said. It was a bit past noon. The gala was an evening thing, but being early did not hurt. It was that or we stayed here and chatted. "You know what, let's head over now. If we're too early, we can piss off and go do something fun to kill time."

CHAPTER FIFTY-FOUR

MOMENTS

There are between a hundred and fifty and two hundred galas of importance every year. Half of these are directly in service to something. Modeling shows, auctions, art trades, art exhibits, fund-raisers, political plays, and a few other niche events make up the majority of the social events for the well-to-do.

Being invited to all of them is next to impossible. Still, a proper socialite should try to attend at least two such galas a month, not including the more seasonal Christmas and midsummer events.

This, of course, means a certain level of preparedness . . .

—Excerpt from *Socializing for the Nouveau Riche, a Primer*, 2046

Gomorrah drove us around the top of the skyscraper, the car angling to the side just enough that we could really take it in.

I had a certain set of expectations for what the gala would look like. Lots of fancy folk, some champagne, and maybe some dancing?

It looked as though Burringham's gala took up the entire topmost floor of a skyscraper; a whole section had glass walls and a glass ceiling, all that right next to the landing pads where a couple of cars were already idling away.

We weren't the only people snooping around. There were drones with flickering safety lights buzzing around the building like circling vultures, and a pack of paparazzi were stalking by the entrance, only held back by some red velvet and mounted guns.

Gomorrah swooped in and landed us with a faint lurch right next to the end of the red carpet. The Fury probably looked strange next to all the Italian sports cars with its more muscle-car-like aesthetics.

"I'll set the autopilot to fly circles around the area," Gomorrah said. "We'll have close air support if we need it."

"Ah, right, it's always better to have close air support and not need it, than to need it and not have it," I said wisely.

Lucy giggled in the back, and I grinned as I shoved the door open.

A few lights flashed, and I couldn't help but overhear the dozens of paparazzi asking themselves who the hell we were. They sounded like seagulls arguing over fries.

I stepped to the back and opened the door for Lucy. She made a show of stepping out one long leg at a time and of delicately taking my hand to help herself out. Franny opened her own door and stomped out with a glare for anyone who cared to look.

With Lucy hanging off my arm, a huge grin on, we walked across the carpet with Gomorrah and Franny trailing behind us and dutifully ignored the calls and questions and occasional camera flashes.

This is amusing.

"What's amusing?" I asked after making sure my helmet was blocking any sound from exiting.

Some of these people are attempting to break into your equipment's software. Others are purposefully using filters that depict yourself or Lucy in unflattering ways.

I frowned. Trying to hack into a celebrity's shit was fine. I'd probably do the same in their place. But fucking with pictures of Lucy? Why would they do that? To plaster the images on some of those shitty media feeds that got off on making people look like shit? "Can you fuck up those messing with the pictures?"

Oh, certainly.

"Uh, would doing that be like, beyond your mandate or whatever?"

Technically, but it's also amusing.

"Well, as long as you're terrifying while on my side," I said.

The entrance into the—was it a hall? A showroom? A ballroom, maybe?—gala-place was being blocked by a team of guards and combat androids, as well as the same woman that I'd seen with Burringham, his secretary lady. She was armed with a digital clipboard and a scowl, though it relaxed when we came closer.

"Stray Cat," she said. "And your plus-one?"

"This is Lucy," I said.

She nodded. "Can you decrypt this file, please, as proof of your identity?" My augs were pinged, and I received a decently hefty file from her.

Oh, it's a puzzle! And solved! Very ingenious, though.

"Uh," I said. The file transformed, its name changing to "Solved. 🐱" I sent it back, and other than a raised eyebrow, the secretary didn't make a fuss about the new filetype. "The samurai behind me is Gomorrah, and that's her plus-one."

"Two samurai," she said. "We'll take that into account. I'm certain Mr. Burringham will be overjoyed. You are still quite early. The music will be starting in approximately twenty minutes, and the main event isn't for another two hours. Still, you should find some entertainment available."

"Cool, thanks," I said. I nodded to her and, with a hand over Lucy's on my arm, I walked into the entrance lobby.

The room was grand, with big pots on pedestals and oil paintings hanging off the walls in gold-leafed frames. It was all very fancy, and yet it was also obviously a killbox. A long narrow space, with guards at the end and planter boxes placed so that they'd provide cover for the same guards.

My Cyberwarfare augs helpfully pointed out all the hidden weapon emplacements in the ceilings and the explosives hidden in the Ming vases.

Burringham really wasn't fucking around with the security here. Was it because he knew Gomorrah and I were here, or was it just normal paranoia?

It had me a bit on edge as we walked across the room and through a set of double doors that led into a grand ballroom.

"Oooo," Lucy cooed as her head tilted back and she took in the room. It was rather large, with a cleared dance floor in the center illuminated by a crystal chandelier that had to outweigh the average hovercar just in crystal shards. A wedge-shaped stage took up a corner of the hexagonal room, currently empty except for a grand piano.

All around the circumference of the room were tables with holographic QR codes floating above them. They already had ice buckets with wine bottles on them, next to freshly clipped flowers.

A bit of classical music was playing quietly in the background, more than enough to make it hard to overhear the few conversations going on. So far, there didn't seem to be that many people present. A dozen or so in all, mostly grouped up in little bunches across the room and chatting to each other. Sometimes a hearty laugh would echo out across the hall, but otherwise it seemed perfectly quiet.

There was staff, of course, and I saw some discreetly adding a few chairs to some of the tables while others did some last-minute prep work.

"Looks like we're early," I said.

"That's fine," Gomorrah replied. "We can sit down and just do nothing. It'll be a nice change of pace."

"We could dance," Lucy said. "There's music playing." She turned to me, stars in her eyes and an easy smile on her lips.

"Do you know how to dance?" I teased.

She pouted, but that soon faded in favor of a dangerous grin. "No, but you know how enthusiastic I can be about learning new . . . physical activities."

"Urgh," Franny said. I glanced her way only to find her looking away, her cheeks matching her hair.

Jeff Burringham has been notified of your presence and is on his way.

"Ah," I said. "Burringham is coming." I could see the guy walking with one of the serving staff next to one of the discreet doors hidden next to some elaborate statue thing. "Let's say hi to him, you can show off your pretty dress, and then we can see about that dance?"

"That does sound nice," Lucy said.

Our little group idled over to the side, toward a table whose QR code labeled it as the one reserved for us. We were more or less right across from the stage and right next to the table where Burringham himself was sitting. A place of pride? Or just somewhere that Burringham could show us off?

"Stray Cat!" the man in question said as he approached, his arms raised in a happy greeting. "And Miss Gomorrah. I'm afraid we haven't met yet, but I have heard of your exploits. You're one of the city's shining jewels."

"Thank you, Mr. Burringham," Gomorrah said rather coldly. "I'm merely doing what I can to help. I hope that you're someone who takes your responsibilities just as seriously as I do."

"I think you'll find that I am," he said. "I've already begun contacting a few friends to get things moving along in the sewers, since the two of you brought it to the city's attention. We have inspectors down there right now, and a few journalists have started to investigate the entire matter. I'm making it a big part of my campaign. But enough about that, I want to make sure you're all quite comfortable. Is there anything I can bring you?"

"I think we're fine," I said. "Though, maybe bring the volume up a notch? Lucy wants to test out your dance floor."

Burringham looked surprised for a moment before he grinned. "I'll do you one better, just give me two whole minutes. And Miss Lucy, your dress is stunning."

"Thank you!" Lucy chirped.

The guy had his moments.

CHAPTER FIFTY-FIVE

DANCING TO THE MUSIC

Ain't no bitch like a corpo bitch.
—Common corporate idiom; origin dates back to the early 2020s

I had to thank Burringham later. He found a pianist, some older guy with graying hair and a nice suit who sat behind the grand piano on the stage and started to play this nice, slow piece. The sound echoed across the hall: brilliant, upbeat notes that sounded happy.

Lucy loved it.

She was grinning ear to ear as I held her close and guided her around in little circles. We didn't know how to dance, and neither of us gave a shit.

I raised an arm above Lucy's head and she spun around before I pulled her in again. The pianist somehow managed to change the timing on the fly, so that it looked like we were dancing in sync with the music.

I didn't know what Burringham was paying the guy, but it wasn't enough.

For all that the dancing was fun, it didn't last all that long. After five minutes, Lucy was huffing and puffing, face reddening around her cheeks, and our dance turned less energetic as she collapsed against my chest and I held her close so she could catch her breath.

"That was nice," she said. "But, ah, I think I need a minute to breathe, and a drink."

I chuckled. "We can dance more whenever you feel like it, you know. Big fancy gala or no."

Lucy grinned up at me. "I wish you weren't wearing that helmet, you deserve a kiss for that."

"I think I deserve a lot of kisses," I said.

Lucy laughed and pulled back. The pianist seamlessly moved into a piece that sounded a little more neutral, like expensive elevator music, and I found myself being tugged along toward a table next to some large vases that had punch bowls and bottles of wine and a man in a butler's outfit pouring cups for people.

I realized then that I couldn't really eat without taking my helmet off, which was going to be a problem later. For now, it was enough that Lucy could grab a cup of some fruity-looking punch with ice in it that the butler poured for her.

"Okay, so, what kind of political bullshittery are we going to do here today?" Lucy asked.

"Political bullshittery?" I asked. "I'm mostly here to show you off and to eat free rich-people food."

Lucy giggled. "Well, I can't say no to either of those, but I'm sure we can do more than that." She gestured with her head to the rest of the hall, which had been steadily filling up as we danced. The event didn't start for another hour, but it seemed like being early was pretty popular, and maybe a quarter of the seats were already filled.

"I don't know, what more do you want to do?" I asked.

"Well, half the people here are celebrity sorts. I think I even recognize a couple of them. They're not worth talking to. They're probably livestreaming all of this, which is neat, but really I don't see the point in chatting with them. A quarter of the people here are CEO and political types. They should have their fingers on the pulse of the city, you know? We might be able to get them to help with the sewer thing."

"They're the ones who stand to lose from the city going tits up," I said.

"Yeah, exactly. Plus they're easier to impress than the celebrity sorts."

"What about the last quarter?" I asked. Maybe Lucy spending so much time watching soap operas was coming in handy after all.

"The last bit is a toss-up. There's some kids here who are obviously just being dragged along by their parents." She gestured to one such group. A few younger boys and girls, mostly older teens and young adults, all looking like preppy corpo kids who had been forced to clean up and put on fancy clothes. "And then there's our group, of course. Too awesome to fit in any of the other boxes. Some of the people here, though, I bet that they're the sort who just won, and now they go to galas because that's all they really have left to do."

"They won?" I asked.

"The game of life, or whatever. You know, inventors, the people who own some of the bigger corps. The ones who are rich enough that they make the other rich people look poor."

"Is that what you're aiming to become?" I asked.

"Nah. I don't have the right kind of luck to be that kind of person. Besides, I think you need to be a college dropout, and I've never been to one of those."

"So, they're the ones you want to meet?"

Lucy shook her head. "Hell no. If they wanted to fix things, things would be getting fixed. Nah, I'm thinking more about the CEO and political sorts.

Just get Myalis to point them out in the crowd and we can head over and flirt with them."

"Flirt with them?" I repeated.

"Not the sexy way, the political way. All intrigue and stuff," Lucy said with the confidence of someone who was most definitely not an expert.

I shrugged a shoulder. Didn't sound like the worst idea I'd ever had. "Sure, why not. I don't know how you're going to introduce yourself, though."

"I'm just going to walk up to the nearest one and say hi," Lucy said.

I quirked an eyebrow at that, realized she couldn't see the skepticism on my face, then spoke to Myalis. "Think we can get one of those breakdowns like Lucy wants? Most influential dirtbags list. Maybe a hot and cold meter, but for importance?"

I'm certain I can accommodate. Though you really should consider invest-ing in a Social Warfare catalog if you want this kind of thing to work better. All I can do now is simulate a limited and less accurate version of what the software in those catalogs could manage.

"I'm sure you'll do great," I told her. I didn't exactly feel like investing points in something like that, not right then and there. Though I bet it was all sorts of fucked up at higher tiers. If a weapons catalog went from pew-pew handguns to planet-fucker, then I figured a social program went from "learn to be less awkward" to "mind-fuck the population."

I followed Lucy as she guided me over to a small group to one side. Mya-lis gave me names, as well as their careers. We had a bunch of C-something-Os, all of them women in nice dresses, though none were quite as nice as Lucy.

One of them, a supervisory board member (whatever the fuck that meant) from Sunrise Weapons, turned our way and smiled. "Hello," she said. "When Burringham boasted that we'd have a real live samurai at the gala, I thought he was full of himself, I didn't expect there to actually be two. It's a pleasure to meet you. I'm Sarah." She extended a hand right past Lucy and to me.

This is Sarah Mauve, she's the CHRO for a political lobbying company. She's an expert in public-perception manipulation for fringe clients. At least, that's what I've read off her bio.

Lucy grabbed her hand and shook. I had the impression she wasn't grip-ping Sarah's perfectly manicured hand lightly, either. "Hi, Sarah. I'm Lucy. This is Cat."

"Hello," I said. I couldn't—and didn't bother—disguising the humor in my voice. "Sorry to butt in, we were just a bit bored."

"Figured we might as well make some more friends while we were here," Lucy added. "These kinds of things are more fun when you know people, right?"

"Of course," Sarah said, her artificial smile never wavering. My augs suggested that a good chunk of her face was as artificial as the smile. She gestured to the other women one by one, introducing them as she went. I forgot the names nearly instantly. At least I had Myalis's little notes over their faces to help me pretend that I was paying attention.

When Sarah was done presenting everyone, Lucy started to dig into her. I think that Sarah had placed herself as the top of the pack, and that meant that she was the biggest bitch here, at least as far as Lucy was concerned.

"I love your dress, Sarah," Lucy said while reaching over to pinch some of the fabric of one of Sarah's sleeves. They were made of some thicker, shiny material. "Is this plastic? I like it, it matches the plastic of your skin."

"Thank you," Sarah said. "I like your necklace, very thrifty."

"You like it?" I asked. "I just got it for her today. It's worth more than this building." That was probably a lie, but Sarah was a bitch, so I didn't really care.

Lucy touched the necklace with the tips of her fingers, then shrugged. "I find it pretty," she said. "Anyway, is everyone here representing a different company tonight?"

That seemed more familiar ground to the others, who were eager to drop whatever Sarah was on in order to shill their company, especially when Lucy started asking them what those companies did and seemed genuinely curious to hear them all speak.

Lucy could be scary sometimes. It was kind of hot.

CHAPTER FIFTY-SIX

SPEAKING UP

North America is an interesting study in the long-term effects of propaganda. Most countries have a strong media presence that constantly repeats to their citizens that their country is the best.

The U.S. propaganda arm was both subversive and constant, and its citizens ate it up.

That was, until everything fell apart.

—Excerpt from *A History of Patriotism and Propaganda*, 2031

"You've been busy," Gomorrah said as I sat down next to her.

"Yeah, I guess so," I said.

It certainly wasn't wrong. Lucy and I had spent the better part of two hours standing in more or less the same spot and talking to an entire ensemble of people. I think Lucy had planned it, first targeting some social folk who would welcome her questions, and then waiting for their plus-ones to come and join in on the conversation. That eventually led to more and more folk approaching us. I think the plan was to create a space where it was acceptable to just come over and chat.

I'd shaken more hands in those two hours than I had in the last eighteen years.

It was probably for the best, though, that I didn't get more than two or three minutes to chat with each person. Any more than that and Lucy butted in to guide them to some other conversation—in a manner that was disturbingly similar to how she handled the kittens—but I managed to mention that I was here because Burringham agreed to help me fix the sewers a dozen times.

Some of those people were important-looking folk, CEOs and shit, and a lot of them seemed pretty eager to impress.

They reminded me a bit of the younger kids at the orphanage, the way they looked up to Lucy and me and really wanted to make us . . . care or whatever about their little companies and their recent promotions and shit.

And just like the kids at the orphanage, I figured I could get them to do shit for me, just because of that desire to impress.

It was seriously strange, and entirely exhausting.

"I'm more tired now than after that night we spent in those caves," I said.

"Caves?" Franny asked. She was sitting on Gomorrah's other side, nursing a rather fancy (though I imagined nonalcoholic) drink.

"They were mines," Gomorrah said. "This little nowhere town called Black Bear. They had a small offshoot of the last incursion to hit the city."

"Gom and I cleaned it up," I said. "It wasn't all that fun."

Lucy shifted in her seat next to me. "You didn't tell me all that much about it," she said.

I shrugged. "It wasn't all that interesting? I mean, it was scary. We had to scout through these big caves."

"Tunnels. Or, more precisely, mineshafts," Gomorrah corrected. "The Antithesis dug themselves in and started to collect biomass. I think the idea was that they'd be hard to root out after a while and then they would spread out more."

"I mean, to be fair, it kind of almost worked? If it weren't for Deus Ex and her weird Family gang finding them, they might have grown for a while. I guess. They did attack the town, though, so maybe not."

"I'm sure the two of you were very brave," Lucy said.

"Cat kept blowing things up, usually while within the blast radius," Gomorrah said, tossing me under the bus.

"And you almost lit me on fire," I shot back. "Like . . . several times."

"But you both came out of it alive and well, right?" Lucy asked. "So I guess you worked well together."

I turned toward Lucy. "We're not kittens, stop doing the whole 'work together nicely' thing on us."

"Kittens?" Franny asked.

"Cat here has a group of children that she keeps," Gomorrah said.

Franny turned toward me. "Keeps how?"

"We're all from the same orphanage. I'm not about to send them back."

"Is anyone trying to adopt them now?" Franny asked.

"I mean, no, but I figure they're still better off. Hell, I know they are. The orphanage sure as hell didn't match up to our penthouse. You've seen the place, it's nice. Besides, we bought a building and are remodeling it. It's gonna be real nice. The brats will have proper rooms and shit, it's going to be great."

"I feel like I should be worried about the state of those kids," Franny said.

Gomorrah shook her head. "No. Cat might be a little strange, but she does care for her equally strange family, I think."

"I'm a perfectly acceptable parental figure," I said, and then I proceeded to ignore Gomorrah's disbelieving laughter and the way Lucy patted my knee under the table.

"There're a lot of people that still want to talk to you, you know," Lucy said. She twitched her eyes to the side, and a glance in that direction revealed a few little pairs of people not too far from our table. They were mostly talking to each other, but it didn't seem entirely animated, and it didn't take an expert in body language to see that they were all sort of facing our way.

"Why aren't they coming over?" I asked.

"Manners, I'd guess," Lucy said. "There's a sort of . . . social pressure thing that says that you can only approach someone important when they're willing to talk. When we were schmoozing it up early we were open and ready for that. Now we're all closed off."

"That sounded vaguely sexual," I said.

"That's because you're a pervert," Lucy said matter-of-factly. Franny nodded from her end of the table.

"So, what do you suggest we do, oh Lucy, great social expert?"

"We let them chill out. Maybe do more talking after the food's served? It'll make it seem like talking to you is more of a privilege if some people get snubbed."

"You seem honestly good at this kind of thing," Gomorrah said. "Would you advise me on what to do?"

"Whatever you want. Cat's put herself out there as someone who's willing to at least talk to important people, which is probably going to be both good and bad. They'll think she's reachable, so they might ask her for help, or offer things, and both of those could be either good or bad, I guess."

"Great," I said. I think my voice made it clear that I thought it was anything but.

Lucy leaned into my side. "Don't worry, Myalis and I can tell anyone trying to do product placements and stuff like that to piss off."

"Well, at least there's that," I said.

I sat up a little straighter as someone walked out from the crowd surrounding our end of the hall and walked right up to our table. Burringham and his faithful secretary. He grinned as he sat across from me.

"Hey," I said.

"Hey yourself," he replied. "You've made quite the splash tonight, both of you. I'm glad you seem to be enjoying yourselves."

"It's not too bad," I said. "Though I'm starting to wonder when the food will come around."

He nodded to his secretary, whose eyes went blank while she stared at her clipboard-pad-thing. "I'll make sure you only have the best. It'll be worth the wait, promise. I just wanted to say hi and make sure things were going well. I know we agreed that I'd work on the sewer issue—which is important enough that it needs to be addressed anyway—but I was wondering if there was anything else. I'm about to make a small speech, and while it's last minute, I might be able to squeeze in a mention of any passing issues you have."

"That's awfully kind of you," Gomorrah said with more diplomacy than I could probably muster. "I appreciate the gesture, but I think that, like Cat, I'm mostly focused on bettering the city, and myself."

"You really are New Montreal's gems," Burringham said. He tapped the table, then pushed himself up. "I'll be back after my little speech. Don't worry, it won't be too boring. At least, I hope it won't be."

"Break a leg," I said.

Burringham left, his secretary trailing after him again. It didn't take long for the crowds to start to disperse, enough that we could make out Burringham on stage, grinning and laughing with someone before he stepped up to a lectern. "Hello, everyone," he said.

That quieted down the last of those talking, and there was a sudden rush of people going to their seats.

"Don't worry everyone, I won't talk your ears off. I haven't eaten either, and having passed by the kitchens I can think of little else but chowing down," Burringham said. He was smiling, and despite the unfunniness of his joke, it still got a few easy chuckles from the crowd. "Today is a very special day. We're here to meet each other, trade some good gossip, and have a good time, but I'd like to take just a moment to talk about a few important things."

I reached up and wrapped an arm around Lucy's shoulders. I didn't believe that it would be short, not for a moment.

"First, I'd like to thank you all for coming. It would have been quite embarrassing if none of you showed up to my gala."

Catherine. I thought it would be wise to inform you that there's a person with a gun across the room. They seem to be about to fire on Jeff Burringham.

"Fuck," I said.

I *knew* things were going to go pear-shaped.

CHAPTER FIFTY-SEVEN

ASSASSINATION

Assassinations are—of all the black jobs—somewhat expensive.

The price, of course, varies. If the target is the average civilian with a public-facing job with low security, then it can cost as little as 500,000 credits to have them shot by an amateur gunman.

The price tends to rise from there, unfortunately, but we do make sure that those prices are justified, and we also have an industry-wide price-match guarantee on any and all contracts taken out.

It's a very competitive business, after all.

—Interview with Professor Hands, President of Off-Corp LLC, 2048

I glanced up and found the man immediately, the red outline that Myalis was painting on my augs helping to spot him.

He was a normal-looking kind of guy, a bit sweaty in his six-figure three-piece, but otherwise he didn't stand out from the other corpo-likes attending the gala. Just another guy here to chat it up, drink some expensive crap, and listen to Burringham talk about how great he was.

The difference was that most of the other corpos in the building didn't have guns mounted on the inside of their forearms, and if they did, they weren't aiming them at Burringham.

I reached my arm around and shoved Lucy back. Her chair tipped over and she screamed as she flailed. "Sorry," I said, but my attention was elsewhere.

Lucy was safe-ish, at least I hoped she'd be out of the way of any shooting. My augs locked onto the assassin and my Cyberwarfare software cut through his security as if they were little more than cobwebs. I had a lot of options from there, but turning all of his augs off seemed the easiest.

He noticed, it was obvious, the way his eyes widened and his arm went limp. Burringham was safe.

Then the asshole grabbed his prosthetic arm with his meaty one, tugged his wrist down at an angle that looked frankly disgusting, and aimed it toward the lectern.

The bang of the first shot was like . . . well, a gunshot in a crowded room. People screamed, some ducked under tables, and Burringham's speech cut off with a scream.

The railguns in the back of my suit deployed, unfolding with smooth efficiency before both of them fired, leaving twin lines of smoke in the air connecting me to the gunman.

"Shit," Gomorrah said in a very un-nunlike fashion. She stood up, grabbed an indignant Franny, and moved her closer to Lucy. "Go," she said to me.

The implication was clear. She'd keep Lucy and Franny safe while I went out and took care of all the more troublesome shit.

I nodded to her and jumped onto and over our table.

There were two choices here. Either I took care of the gunman, or I tried to see if I could do anything for Burringham. In the suddenness I didn't see if he was injured or not. The gunman might give me answers, but Burringham's health mattered more.

That decided it for me.

I shot off toward the stage and arrived just as the first of Burringham's security detail reached him. I found some beefy guy stepping up ahead of me, but I shoved him to the side and dropped to one knee next to Burringham.

He wasn't shot anywhere nice and romantic like the shoulder or in the leg; instead he had a nice pinprick wound right in his side. His arm was probably raised to gesture when he got hit.

"Take off his jacket," I said.

"Ma'am—" one of the security guys started to say.

"I'm healing him here and now," I said. "But I need to know more about the wound."

"'S fine," Burringham said. He waved the security off with an arm.

"We should at least move him to somewhere more secure," one of the guards said.

I considered it for a second, then nodded. "Get him up. Is there a medical station we can bring him to?"

"There's a nurse's station one floor down," the guard said.

"Is the kitchen closer?" I asked.

"Yes."

"Kitchen, then," I said. "Myalis, can you tell me anything about Burringham, the gunner?"

The gunman's being moved out of the hall by security; he's currently attempting to trigger a suicide device planted in the base of his jaw, but you deactivated it.

I chuckled as I backed up and let one of the guards scoop Burringham up. We ran past his secretary, who was so pale I was afraid she might faint; the trail of blood we left as we ran past didn't help.

"Clear out!" one of the guards said as we burst into the kitchen. The chefs and others working on fancy meals jumped, but they backed up as more guards poured in.

"There!" I said as I pointed to a stainless steel table currently covered in trays with little cake slices on it.

One of the sous chefs had time to grab a tray off the top before we arrived and the guard at the head of the pack swept the rest off and sent what was likely a few thousand credits' worth of dessert crashing down.

"Jacket off," I ordered.

The guards pinned Burringham down, and one of them sliced his coat off with a stupidly sharp knife.

It didn't look good. The hole in his side was pouring blood out with little spurts, and there were dozens of other, smaller holes all over his chest, obviously sliced open from the inside.

The gun the assassin used was chambered with nine-millimeter rounds. The projectile seems to be an explosive fragmentation bullet. The sort used by some Vanguard to kill lower-tier antithesis.

"Okay," I said. "Let's get more blood in him, and let's patch him up. Something quick."

New Purchase: Class II Nano-Regenerative Suite
Points Reduced from . . . 10,594 to . . . 10,494

A familiar box appeared next to me, and I popped it open and jammed the nano-feed-thing needle into Burringham's side. The same thing I'd done with Rac just a couple of days ago. The second tube I tugged out and pressed over his neck. I figured there was a vein or artery or whatever there. "Hey, Burringham, you got any augs that will help you?"

"S-sure," he said. "Best, best money can buy."

"Cool," I said. "You'll be just fine, by the way."

One of the guards moved in close; he had a red cross on his shoulder and a large first-aid kit that he dropped on the table above Burringham's head. "Going to monitor his vitals. What did you administer?" he asked as if making conversation about the weather.

"It's a Class Two Nano-Regenerative suite," I said. "Second-tier samurai medical tech. Lots of little nanorobots that'll reconstruct his insides, and, ah . . ."

We both watched as a spider drone scuttled out of the box, ran over Burringham's chest, then burrowed into the gunshot wound on his side.

"Wh-what was that?" Burringham asked.

"Nothing," I said.

The medic only paused for a moment before applying patches to Burringham's chest and flicking open some things on his big kit. He seemed ready to inject Burringham with a whole host of drugs but was waiting and staring at his displays. "Blood pressure's staying stable," he said.

"Bleeding stopped," I said with a gesture to Burringham's chest.

There are lots of small metallic fragments spread across his insides. Judging by the radiation readings, the bullet was encased in radioactive materials. I retract what I said about the round being purchased by a Vanguard.

"We're going to need a small container for radioactive shit," I said.

The little spider drone squeezed out of Burringham's side with a squelch. It landed on the table, and then little pincers let go of a bloody mess of metallic things before it dug itself back into his wound.

"Uh," I said.

"We'll take care of it, ma'am," the medic said.

"Cool, cool," I said. I backed away, then beelined for a sink where I turned on the tap and washed the hands of my suit.

"Ma'am?" one of the guards asked as he approached me. There were nine of them in the kitchen by then, just milling around and being very suspicious of all the kitchen staff. The only one who seemed genuinely busy was the medic, and even he was waiting and chatting with Burringham in low tones.

"Yeah?" I asked.

"The gunman has been apprehended. He's still alive."

"Oh," I said. "Was anyone else hurt?" Those two railgun shots might have . . .

"No, ma'am. The hall was locked down, and the guests have been told that things will proceed in a moment. Did you wish to be there for the interrogation?"

"You're doing that now?" I asked.

"Before the city's police arrive and try to interrupt things, yes," he said. "We don't want the city police interfering here. The building's own PMC branch is helping us secure the area; they don't seem keen on poking their nose in just yet."

"Well, uh, yeah, count me in," I said.

If our guy was still alive, maybe he could tell me why he wanted to interrupt Lucy's big night and kill Burringham.

CHAPTER FIFTY-EIGHT

INTERROGATION

Gentrification of music and art is a bitch, ya know?

Man, used to be that art meant something. Now some punk kid in some backwater shit-hole neighborhood makes some trash-can hip-hip about how shit life is, gets picked up by a label, and a week later he's ODed off some blow he sniffed from his new corpo wife's rack, and meanwhile everything he's made, everything he stood for has been mined and broken apart and sold to the highest bidder.

—Scoop Doge, from his penthouse suite in Ohio Two, 2051

I figured that with about a dozen heavily armed dudes looking out for him, as well as his nervous secretary, Burringham would be just fine if I left him for a bit. Anyone who could kill that many guards to get to him would probably kill him whether I was there or not.

The healing kit I'd left jabbed into him would take care of his injuries in the meantime. He'd be just fine.

"So, where did you hide the assassin again?" I asked.

The guard gestured ahead, down one of the corridors that I imagine most guests weren't supposed to see. It wasn't nearly as well-decorated and opulent as the rest of the hall. "Security room. We have a medic working to keep him alive."

"Shit," I said. "What's his condition like?"

"Not very good," the guard said. "Your shots didn't kill him immediately, that's all I can say."

I nodded. I'd have to buy a second kit to keep him alive. Great. That was exactly what I wanted to do. Spend some of my hard-earned points on a man who had just tried to shoot someone. A politician, mind, so it was only like shooting half a person, but it still counted.

The security room, as it turned out, wasn't so much a single room as a small area marked off for the guards and the like.

There was a small waiting area, with a few couches and a TV against the far wall, as well as a counter with a microwave and mini-fridge. The other side of the space had a glass door with an armory behind it, and past that a corridor with doors on either side.

There was only one door currently being guarded.

The guard accompanying me guided me over to that door. It opened into a white-walled room with an interrogation table in the middle cast in harsh industrial light. The gunman was on the table, face locked in a grimace, his clothes tossed off and piled up to the side where someone had obviously cut them all apart.

His mechanical arm was missing at the shoulder, and his other hand was handcuffed to the edge of the table.

A guard was wiping his chest around an already bloody bandage. "How is he?" I asked.

The man screamed and twisted on the table, tugging at the handcuff as he did so. He opened his mouth, and it was clear that someone had torn out some of his teeth.

"He'll live," the medic guard said. "The shot didn't do him any favors, but it missed most vital things."

"The shot, singular?" I asked.

The medic nodded. "One hit his mechanical arm. Tore a gash into his back on the exit. Nothing too serious. Second hit him high in the chest. Punctured lung, three broken ribs, some internal bleeding. I have him filled with foam to keep the bleeding down. Haven't sedated him."

"Why's he missing his teeth?" I asked with a gesture to his face.

The guard looked up. "Suicide capsules in his teeth. Aug-linked. They didn't go off."

"Ah, that's my fault," I said.

"They could have been triggered manually if he crushed them enough, so the teeth had to go," he said matter-of-factly.

"Shit, that sucks," I said. "So, he's going to live, huh?"

"He should, assuming we get him to a hospital within the next twelve hours or so. I haven't administered pain medication yet, I don't want him hazy for any interrogations."

"Nasty. We get an ID yet?"

The guard who escorted me into the room was the one to reply. His eyes were glowing, a telltale sign he was deep into his augs. "No ID. He entered the gala under the name John Black, but Mr. Black's actual location was confirmed minutes ago; he was unable to attend because of other matters. We're investigating."

"Is his face real?" I asked. To pass himself off as someone else . . .

"The files on Mr. Black's identity were changed. He's a close match, appearance-wise."

"Huh," I said before I leaned down atop the table, then pressed my hand over the guy's sternum as he tried to push himself up. "Hey, buddy, what's your name?"

He screamed into my face, which was a little rude. His eyes locked onto my helmet, and he spat a gob of blood at me that splattered against my visor and immediately slipped off and splattered on the table.

"Okay," I said.

You might want to consider connecting to his augmentations and use those to identify him.

"Not a bad idea," I said. I noticed the medic looking up at me, but other than checking the bandage, he didn't interfere. I opened my Cyberwarfare software and linked back into the guy's augmentations.

Just about everyone had physical identification of some sort, but a lot of shops and places accepted aug-based ID. Our mystery friend's augs had plenty of ID; those at the top were all linked to Mr. Black, but he had about a dozen more past that.

"That's a lot of IDs there, buddy," I said.

"Probably a professional, then," the medic commented.

"Yeah, I bet. You don't hire a chump to kill someone like Burringham when there's this much security around," I said.

"The arm scanned as a normal prosthetic," the medic added. Was he making excuses for why they'd failed to nab the guy?

"I'll bet," I said. "Myalis, you have any clues here?"

Checking the IDs . . . they're all false except this one.

One of the IDs grew in my augs. Ralph Slim. Nearly the same face as the guy I was holding down, with some slight changes around the eyes and jaw, and a bit more scruff, as if he hadn't shaved in a day or two. He was almost handsome.

"Ralph, huh? Yeah, I'd change IDs too if I were called Ralph Slim," I said.

Ralph glared up at me. "I'm not saying shit," he said.

"You don't need to say anything, Ralphy, I have . . . well, Myalis. She's a friend, currently living in my gray matter rent-free. She's real good at digging into stuff. You wouldn't believe the gossip she can dig up on people in a few seconds."

If I could, I would be blushing.

"Do you want to spill your version of things while she gets to rooting around? Because what you're working for here is sympathy."

"What?" he asked.

"Sympathy. Specifically mine. See, Myalis doesn't care, she's going to come up with the cold hard facts, and those never make anyone look good. Doesn't matter how vanilla your tastes are, they'll still make some people hurl. Now, your continued existence depends entirely on how I feel about you in the next couple of minutes, and she's not going to paint a pretty picture."

"Just, just hand me over to the police!" Ralph said.

"No," I replied. "I don't want to."

He started to twist and fight back, but against the handcuffs holding his arm down, as well as the weight of my suit on his collar, it only made a racket. "You can't do this," he said.

"I . . . I'm literally doing this right now? All I've done so far is hold you down. I haven't even started to ruin your life."

"I've, I've got a wife, and kids!" Ralph said.

He doesn't.

I jabbed him in the ribs. "No lying, Ralph," I said.

"I . . . come on, I'll pay you!"

I shook my head. "I'm richer than you." Which was a weird thing to say.

"Ten million credits. Fifty million!"

He really wanted me to like him. "What do you want for that many credits? For me not to question you?"

"Please!" he begged.

I shrugged, then stepped back while leaving a hand on his collar. "Hey, you want to question him in my place? I'll do the torturing, you do the questions. I really don't know how this stuff goes anyway. Out of my depth here."

"Certainly," the guard said. "We have training for this. Try not to do anything debilitating."

"No problem," I said.

"Wait! Wait!" Ralph said.

"You know, your answers are worth . . . about fifty to me."

"Fifty million?" Ralph asked.

"No, points. That's fifty points' worth of Vanguard-grade torture equipment. I don't know what that'll look like, but I'm sure it'll be pretty fucky. I've got the impression the aliens have seen and done some fucky shit, you know?"

"Hey, hey, I'll tell you what you want to know, please."

"I don't actually have a torture implement catalog," I said. "But I do have one for sex toys, and I'm very sure that they're close together. You know, putting the M in BDSM."

"I'll fucking talk!"

CHAPTER FIFTY-NINE

POPULARITY

This cask behind me contains 37.4 liters of fermented fruit wine. None of the fruits used in the fermenting process are available on Earth. The cask has been aged six thousand years in a sealed vacuum.

This wine, which we are assured is appropriate for human consumption—though we hold no liabilities on such matters—has a provenance which can be traced back to Samurai Blitzo, who purchased it directly from the Protectors. It is Lan Igiro wine, cultivated as an alcoholic beverage by an extraterrestrial species.

A treat for any amateur or professional sommelier, and a unique and daring addition to any collection. Please note that our next item is a remarkable cheese, also of extraterrestrial origin.

We will begin the bidding at 1,000,000,000 credits.

—Excerpt from the 2050 Rarest Goods Auction

"Hey," I said as I approached the table. The main hall was, surprisingly, still full of people. Some waiters were going around and filling people's glasses with champagne. Some people had left, but they'd been replaced by an equal number of additional guards hanging out by the edges of the room.

Lucy was sitting between Gomorrah and Franny, looking rather relaxed with a long champagne flute pinched between her fingers. "Hi, Cat," she said.

"How's Burringham?" Gomorrah asked.

"Alive," I said. "Why're there still people here? They stopping folk from leaving?"

"Oh no," Lucy said. She shook her head. "This event went from a cool event to like, the most talked-about one. Come on, the host almost got assassinated, the assassin was shot by a samurai, and another samurai's sitting here, as if she doesn't care about it all. Not that Gomorrah doesn't care, I'm just saying."

"So . . . what? It's become a sort of bigger event because Burringham almost died?"

Lucy nodded. "You know how we used to run out to the nearest corner store? Which times do you remember best, when nothing went wrong or when we had to run away from some angry muggers?"

"All right, fair," I said. "Still fucky."

"Some people left," Lucy said with a shrug. "I bet a few of the people here are spamming their media feeds with news about what's happening. Drama chasers. Others are just happy they're here. You know they're showing up in a lot of camera shots, that's food for any celeb."

"And I bet the media are swarming this place," I said.

Lucy nodded. "Oh yeah. I bet this will have more airtime than the next ten school shootings combined."

"I don't much care for the media stuff," Gomorrah said. "But having a small amount of renown can help with some things, or so I've been told. So, did the gunman survive?"

"Yeah," I said. "His injuries weren't all that bad. Not good, mind, but he'll live. The mercs keeping this place safe have some medics, they're keeping him healthy. Got him to spill."

Gomorrah raised a hand in a "one moment" gesture. The next thing I knew I was receiving a call from her.

I answered. "Let's keep this quiet," she said.

"Not a bad idea," I said as I sat across from Lucy. I muted the speakers on my helmet, so no one could hear us chatting. "So, want to take a guess at who's responsible for all of this?"

"The mayor?" Gomorrah asked.

I laughed. "Well, all right, so I can't actually confirm it. But our assassin buddy was hired on short notice from some gun-for-hire contractor company. Like Uber, but for hit men, you know? Anyway, he had a lot of details about the place and about who would show up and plans for the building. Myalis was the one who figured it out, actually."

"That it was the mayor?" Gomorrah asked.

"We don't have outright proof," I said. "But the blueprints for the building are city blueprints. They have the city of New Montreal watermark all over them. DRM and everything."

"So, if it's the mayor, he was lazy enough to give his hired killer some information that he had access to," Gomorrah surmised.

I wiggled my hand over the table. "Eh, maybe? It could be someone else being clever, trying to pin it on the mayor, but, well, Dupont's a twat and he has plenty of motive. Far as I can tell Burringham's shaking things up and is a whole lot more charismatic. He might actually have a good chance."

"We'll have to investigate that assassin organization," Gomorrah said.

"I'll pop by for a visit tomorrow morning, see if they feel like telling me anything. Worst case, I drop a few points on better Cyberwarfare stuff and Myalis helps me figure it out. Or I could ask Longbow."

"The samurai? You think he'd know?"

"I think his whole 'big brother' persona is a bit more 1984 than you'd guess at first glance. He has this whole surveillance network thing. Or access to one. Bet he could figure it out in a couple of seconds, if he's not too busy LARPing or something."

"All right," Gomorrah said. "So what do you intend to do about all of this?"

I leaned my elbows down onto the table. "Don't know, actually," I said. "Feels like I should do something about Dupont, but that's straying away from samurai business and closer to just . . . political bullshittery. I don't mind showing up to places like this if it means helping the city, but chasing down assassins feels like a whole different thing, you know?"

Gomorrah nodded. "I know what you mean. We might not have too much of a choice."

"Aren't you supposed to be all nunlike and say that nonviolence is always a choice?" I asked.

She shrugged. "Nonviolence is always a choice. Violence is also always a choice. We could just blackmail Dupont, if you actually learn that he's responsible."

"Think he'd listen to blackmail at all?" I asked.

"I never interacted with him. But the way you spoke of him made him sound mostly reasonable. If in a less than civil way."

"Yeah, that sounds about right. Fine, I'll find out if he really did call out the hit on Burringham, and then if it's Dupont, maybe I'll pay him another visit." I shifted so that I was sitting straighter. "That all?"

"I think so," Gomorrah said. She ended the call before speaking to the others. "Sorry about that."

Lucy grinned. "You know, if you insist on having alone time with Cat so much, I might insist on the same with Franny here."

"Down, girl," I said.

I was about to comment a little more when I heard a shuffling across the room. People were still whispering and talking to each other, but the pitch and tone changed, like a wave across the entire hall.

Glancing around, I saw a lot of heads turning toward the stage, so I followed the collective gaze and found a familiar face walking up onto the stage. Burringham, looking a pinch pale, and in an entirely new suit, hair obviously still wet and freshly brushed.

My augs told me he still had the Nano-Regenerative Suite on him, tucked under his partially open jacket. He walked up to the lectern and cleared his throat. "So, where was I?" he asked.

There were some nervous chuckles and genuine laughs from the people in the room.

"I'm truly sorry about the interruption. I assure you we've heightened security quite substantially. It should prevent anything like that from happening again. At least, I hope so, the last lesson was on the painful side, so I hope it sticks."

He grinned at everyone, as if he were talking about stubbing his toe on stage instead of being shot.

"Ah, I really have forgotten where I left off. I think I was thanking our guests of honor for tonight? The valiant samurai, Gomorrah, and especially Stray Cat, to whom I now owe my life, I suspect." He started clapping, and soon everyone else was clapping along too.

It felt at once hollow—these people, with maybe three exceptions, didn't give a flying shit about me—at the same time, I felt an unfamiliar warmth rising to my cheeks.

The clapping died down soon enough and Burringham took to talking again. "Now, tonight's hero isn't the only one I want to thank. All of you deserve a round of applause for not panicking. I've been informed that you were all quite restrained and empathetic, and I appreciate that. As this city moves forward, especially so soon after a disaster like the incursion that we just survived, it's important that we all try to come together and especially work together to fix our home."

I sat back and half listened to Burringham as he worked the crowd. His miraculous return was working in his favor, I suspected.

You might be interested to know that your ranking in the popularity charts has changed quite substantially. Welcome to the under-thirty-thousand bracket. Though you are still behind Gomorrah.

I blinked. I'd become more popular? For the stunt we pulled?

But that raised the question: How had Gomorrah stayed ahead?

CHAPTER SIXTY

EMOTING

Emoji, in the form that we readily recognize them as, appeared even before the advent of the internet, though they only really became popular with the standardization of communication systems. Things like Unicode made them somewhat reliable across multiple platforms, and eventually they grew to become a standard part of the modern lexicon.

As text-based communication became more popular, and eventually ubiquitous, the humble emote began to replace entire words. It even made sense. A smiley face could convey as much as an entire paragraph, at times.

Today, people have entire catalogs of custom emotes, and emoji artists are some of the most well-paid custom art makers in the modern world. A signature, person-specific emote can mean a lot to its user.

:)

—Professor Besters, lecture on New English, 2025

The evening ended with a much more subdued tone than I was initially expecting it to.

Lucy and I had another turn on the dance floor, this time alongside a few dozen others who were willing to brave Lucy's stumbling dance moves, and supper was served. It was all terribly fancy stuff that made even the fancy stuff back in the hotel look unfancy by comparison.

Once the dancing was over, and a few political sorts who weren't Burringham gave some quick speeches, the evening sort of just . . . wrapped up.

A few of the attendees were drunk enough to need help finding the exit, but other than some raised voices, they didn't make much of a fuss. The crowd basically just thinned out bit by bit until I glanced at my aug overlay and realized that it was so late that it was almost tomorrow.

Lucy, Gomorrah, Franny, and I were heading for the entrance when I heard someone call out to us.

Burringham ran over, a big grin on and his cheeks a healthy rosy color. "Stray Cat, Gomorrah," he said as he came closer. "I just wanted a quick word, before you take off."

"Sure," I said.

His smile, if anything, widened. "I have to thank you both, especially you, Cat."

"Didn't you thank me on stage already?" I asked.

He nodded. "Yes, but there's something impersonal about that kind of message. It's all pageantry and show. I meant every word I said, but I feel like the method of delivery robs some of that credibility." He shook his head. "Sorry. The hour and the day's events are robbing me of what little eloquence I have."

"Oh, don't say that," Lucy said. "You're still perfectly charming, no matter the hour."

Burringham laughed. "Thank you. If you're ever on the lookout for a job, by the way, please avoid politics, for my sake. I prefer it if my competition isn't better than I am at charming people."

Lucy giggled and pressed herself closer to my side. "I'll think about it. Maybe cut you some slack."

"So, " I said. "Are you feeling all right?"

"Yes! Very much so." He rubbed at his side where I knew the gunshot had been. "There isn't even a scratch to show for the trouble, and I genuinely feel splendid, like I've just woken up from a long night's rest midway through a vacation and found myself ten years younger. I could get used to feeling this good."

"It should last a little bit. At least until the nanites die off. But try to avoid getting shot again; I don't know how much they could do for you then."

"How are you mentally?" Gomorrah asked.

Burringham took a moment longer to answer that. "I'm a little worried, I'll be honest. It's my first assassination attempt. I thought, hoped, that New Montreal politics were a little more chivalrous and decent, but I suppose not. I think I might jump at every loud sound for a while. Also, I've developed something of a new appreciation for arachnophobia."

"Huh?" Franny asked.

"One of Miss Stray Cat's healing tools was shaped . . . uncomfortably," he explained. "I'm sure she can show you what I mean."

"Sorry about that, I don't have a say in that kind of thing," I said.

You literally do. Though some things are designed to be maximally efficient. How else do you think I'm managing to sneak so many feline references into your equipment?

I chose to ignore Myalis and her weird form of bullying for the moment. "Anyway, it was good working with you, Burringham."

"Jeff, please," he said before we shook. "By the way, did you intend to, ah, how can I put this delicately? Dig into the matter of the gunman more than you have?"

"I don't know," I said.

Gomorrah shook her head next to me. "It's not one of our priorities, certainly. Of all the things we could be doing, chasing after assassins who are likely working very hard to hide themselves isn't high on our list of priorities. We agreed to work with you because you agreed to help save the city. Keeping you safe and alive is convenient at the moment, but . . . ah, how can I put this delicately?" she mimicked. "You're still just a smooth-talking, charismatic politician."

"I am all of those things," Burringham admitted. "But I hope that I'll be able to help the city, truly."

"We'll see," Gomorrah said. "Come on, Cat."

"Yeah, I'll be right with you," I said. I patted Lucy on the shoulder and nodded toward Gomorrah, and she understood right away, detaching herself from my side to go and chat up Gom and Franny.

"You wanted to talk?" Burringham asked. We were more or less alone next to the exit, the one helmeted guard standing by the doors facing away from us. The only music playing was some prerecorded orchestral-type stuff, low and slow in the background.

"A bit. Look, I have a lot of hope riding on you, Jeff. I don't trust political types. I don't like all of this . . . pageantry and all this richness. Fuck, I've seen enough credits wasted here tonight to get a hundred orphans through college or whatever. I figure that you're not an ass, you're just clueless. At least, that's my more charitable interpretation of shit."

"I see."

I nodded. "So, yeah. You want the keys to the city, and that's fine by me. Just make damned sure you make the place better, all right?"

"I will do my best, I promise," he said.

I turned, then waved him off over my shoulder. "We'll see, Burringham. I'll look into those assassins tomorrow. Got a hunch it might be best to nip that in the bud. Keep in touch, all right?"

Stepping out, I crossed the long entrance corridor, then walked into the open air. I didn't realize it until just then, but the hall had been a little suffocating. The richness of it, I guessed, the way that everything around me felt both fragile and expensive, it was weird, like being stuck in a wall-less closet. The open air of New Montreal felt much better.

"Cat?" Lucy asked. She stepped up to my side and fit in next to me, like a missing piece that was entirely meant to be there. "You okay?"

"Yeah, lots on my mind."

"Want to be distracted, or do you want time to think?"

I chuckled. "A distraction wouldn't hurt," I admitted.

"Awesome! I was just about to convince Gomorrah and Franny to go on a double date."

"Oh?" I asked. "Are they actually, you know, gay-gay?"

Lucy wiggled her hand in the air before her. "Everyone's a little gay; they both have above-average amounts of gayness."

"Ah, yes," I said. "Above-average gayness. How eloquently put. So is there like, a curve here? A ranking?"

"I was thinking of a sliding chart? Like one of those color wheels, but flat. You've got hella gay on one side." She gestured between us. "Then moderately gay in the middle." She gestured to our favorite nuns. "And then you have non-gays at the other end."

"Does the fact that a flattened color wheel looks like a rainbow mean anything?" I asked.

"Happy coincidence."

"I have the impression that your system might not work for everyone," I said.

She shrugged. "I'm sure I could fit a third dimension in there somewhere. So, double date?"

"Did you actually tell them it was a date?" I asked.

Lucy snapped her fingers. "That's it. The third dimension can be usefulness."

"Usefulness?"

"Yeah, they're both very low on that score. So they don't need to know that it's a double date because that would just confuse them even more."

"Uh-huh," I said.

We reached Gomorrah and Franny, who were waiting next to the Fury. "Lucy convinced us to head out and grab something light to eat," Gomorrah said.

"I am easily convinced by ice cream," Franny added. She leaned back against the car, arms crossed and looking cooler than anyone wearing a nun's habit should. "It's my one fault."

"Your one fault?" Gomorrah asked.

"Keeps me humble."

I laughed. "All right, ice cream it is," I said. "I think it'll make for a nice nightcap for us."

"But then we need to go home, we have kids to look after, you know," Lucy said.

Franny turned around. "You two sound so old," she complained.

CHAPTER SIXTY-ONE

INTROSPECTION

Existential crisis?
    Existential crisis deez nuts!

> —Last words of celebrity host John Lewort
> before his on-air suicide, 2048

The next morning, after breakfast with Lucy and the kittens, and after texting Rac to make sure she was okay (apparently she had stayed the night in the museum and had collected "heaps of the good trash" for me) I headed out with all of my gear. Armor, launcher, a couple of guns, and of course my sword hanging by my hip.

I could have just stayed at the hotel, or maybe I could have gone to check on the museum, where the contractors were supposed to have started working already. But that didn't feel quite right.

Sitting back and doing nothing wasn't something I was all that keen on. I would get restless, and start worrying about things. I used to be able to distract myself with my media feeds, but since becoming a samurai, things like sensationalized news just didn't hit the same. I wasn't able to get angry at whatever the feeds told me to get angry about as easily as I once had.

It had taken one glance at my feed and at the top news story of the morning to convince me to get up and go do *something*. That the top news story was still last night's assassination attempt might have had something to do with it.

Where are we going now?

I stepped out of the elevator on the main lobby floor of the hotel and started toward the door. There were more people with camera augs out that morning, following me with their strangely blank gazes as I started out across the room.

"This morning we're going to check in on a couple of things," I said. "First, that assassins-for-hire group. They're bound to know something. Then we'll maybe pay Dupont another visit. Because I've been thinking."

What have you been thinking about?

"I killed Doc Hack. Probably a couple of his stooges too."

Are you feeling guilty about it?

I shook my head. "No. He was a delusional bastard. Maybe someone could have reformed him, but he was actively hurting people. Can't say I'm all that sympathetic. Probably a bit fucked up, but, yeah, that's how it is."

Then what is bothering you?

Myalis was being very pop-therapy-ish that morning. "What's bothering me is that I was willing to kill Doc Hack for being a dangerous freak, but I wasn't willing to do the same to Dupont, who's arguably a worse menace to the city."

Interesting. Your reluctance to rely on violence at the time isn't too strange. Humans generally need to be primed for action before they're willing to resort to aggression. That means that specific environmental factors need to be fulfilled in order for a human to consider violence.

"Like what?" I asked.

For one thing, if an area is considered a peaceful one, one that the subject sees as a safe area, then they are less likely to resort to violence than if they find themselves in an unfamiliar, hostile environment. The actual psychology is a lot more complex than that. A human brain is little more than meat with delusions; it's no wonder that while generalizations can be made, these will not hold to any scrutiny beyond grand statistical conjecture.

In your situation, specifically, Doc Hack's termination was done in a hostile environment, after violence had already occurred. He posed an immediate physical threat to your own safety, and replied to aggression with aggression.

"All right," I said.

Whereas you met Dupont in an office space. Not one you were intimately familiar with, but one that you recognized through cultural osmosis. It was not a violent environment. He also didn't pose an immediate threat to you or those close to you. The threats he could level against you were more social and metaphorical.

"So that's why I didn't sword him?" I asked. I came to a pause in the lobby. I . . . didn't quite know where I was going, so I sat down on one of the little benches to the side and set my elbows on my knees to think. Probably gave the paparazzi sort plenty of great pic material.

No, the reason is significantly more complex, and one that I can only guess at—though my guesses are generally very accurate, of course. The reasons I outlined are those that are simple enough for you to understand them.

"Huh," I said. "Well, thanks for dumbing things down."

It's my pleasure, Catherine.

"You're not worried that your samurai—Vanguard is a bit of a sociopath?" I asked.

You're not.

"I don't feel bad about killing someone. Heck, I never even bothered learning the names of some of the mooks I shot up."

That doesn't make you a sociopath. I'm afraid that a lack of guilt over pain caused to beings seen as unimportant isn't the only requirement to be considered such. You are merely, to put it in terms you'd understand, a stone-cold bitch.

I laughed, rocking back in surprise and scaring off some tabloid-chasers who were getting closer. "Not the answer I was expecting, but all right," I said. I pushed myself to my feet and stretched my back as best I could in my armor. "Let's head out."

Where to?

"First, those assassins-for-hire, like I said. We don't actually know if Dupont is responsible, so before I blow his brains out for something he didn't do, I'd like to confirm that he's the right asshole. And if he isn't the right one, then I guess we'll dive into a whole new rabbit hole until we find out who it is and pay them a visit."

It is possible that Burringham has adversaries beyond the current mayor. I imagine that some of his proposals are unpopular with some corporate entities.

"Yeah," I said. "I'll bet. Anything that makes people's lives better without also enriching some other asshole isn't good in anyone powerful's playbook."

That isn't entirely true. Humans have an interesting ability to lack empathy on a wider scale, which often translates to making choices that benefit themselves in the shorter term while harming others in the longer. The power-first system that most of Earth operates under exacerbates that.

"Then why the hell hasn't someone done anything about it?" I asked.

Why haven't you?

I grumbled at the non-answer while beelining toward the exit. It was only when I was outside that I realized I didn't have a ride to get me over to where I needed to be. "How many points do I have left?"

Current Point Total: 10,494

"I imagine that's enough to purchase a ride?"

You no longer want to use taxi services? In either case, yes, it is more than enough to afford a vehicle. What sort of transportation are you looking for?

"Something small and fast. With, ah, room for two? I don't think it needs to be well-armed or anything."

I see. In that case, I have two options I think you should consider. The first, and more expensive, of the two is an iteration of the mechanized cat robots you have used previously, this one with room in its torso for a pair of people on adjustable racks. It can fly, walk, and run at great speeds, and should be quite intimidating to most. It can even defend itself and be equipped with a few weapons, both concealed and not.

"That sounds super-stupid," I said.

The other option is a much simpler hovercycle. There are a multitude of choices to be made there, but I would steer you toward a lower-cost option. Self-driving, relatively nimble, faster than many of the vehicles on the market. You can even find some models with basic stealth capabilities at relatively low prices.

"A motorcycle might be nice," I said. It would at least be cooler than riding inside a giant cat mecha. "How much are we talking here?"

Two hundred points for the catalog, another two hundred for a relatively inexpensive hovercycle.

"Yeah, all right, I can afford that." And it would get me around a bit faster, which might be important.

New Purchase: Lightweight Single-User Cockpitless Hover Vehicles
Points Reduced from . . . 10,494 to . . . 10,294

New Purchase: Stealthed Mark IV Monocycle Hoverbike
Points Reduced from . . . 10,294 to . . . 10,094

A bike appeared before me. It was a little shorter than the average hovercycle, though that might have been because it only had a single wheel at the back. The front swept forward, sharp and sleek and angular, with thrusting jets poking out of little openings in the frame. The entire middle top was a long seat, leaned so that the person on it would be lying down with their hands tucked into a pair of handle gauntlets.

"Two can sit on this?" I asked.

Not comfortably, but someone Gomorrah's or Lucy's size should be able to huddle in before the pilot.

"Oh, that does sound nice," I said.

I swung a leg over the bike, shifted my rear around until I was comfortable, then placed my feet in the stirrups while the bike kept itself upright.

Leaning forward, I grinned as a transparent panel unfolded from the front of the bike and the handles adjusted to be at just the right distance for me. "All right, let's go for a quick flight."

CHAPTER SIXTY-TWO

ATTEMPTING COMMON SENSE

The average hover vehicle isn't that much more expensive than what you would have paid for a new car in 2025, accounting for inflation.

The difficulty lies in all the fees, taxes, and hidden costs that come after the vehicle has been locked into a payment plan. The driver needs a license, needs to enter the gacha with the Ministry of Transportation for permission to use the air roads, and needs to pay for the three different insurances necessary to use a vehicle. That doesn't include refueling cost, for either fossil-fuel-powered vehicles or the kWh rate for electric vehicles. Nor does it take into account the cost of things such as parking spaces and obligatory maintenance, or the cost of the subscription services that allow the driver to use their mirrors or anti-collision assistance.

—*The True Costs: An Analysis of the Roads of Today*, 2041

My grip on the handles tightened and I gritted my teeth as I narrowly avoided braining myself on the overhang over the hotel's entrance hangar.

I shot out over the city and through a lane of busy traffic. Automatic proximity horns blared in warning as I cut in between two vans, then turned so that I just barely managed to slip in between two skyscrapers.

I threw my weight to the side and slowed down to a hovering stop over the city. "Oh, shit," I breathed.

You might want to consider letting the hovercycle's autopilot take care of any future flying.

"Yeah?" I asked as my heart started to calm down. I glanced down and felt a bit of vertigo tugging at my stomach as I saw the ground far, far below. I was over a few skyscrapers, the lights pouring out of their layered windows acting like an arrow to the street below, only broken up by sky bridges that led from one building to another.

A lane of traffic some fifty meters down created a blurry mess of cars in every shade of monochrome in the foreground.

I swallowed past the wriggling in my chest and took a few more breaths while focusing on the horizon, instead of the drop. It helped a bit. "I didn't think I had a fear of heights, you know," I said.

Perhaps the different circumstances are what's causing your vertigo?

"Yeah, I guess," I said. I'd never seen the city from this high up without being in a hovercar, or atop a nice, stable building. This was different. I was basically straddling a piece of high-tech machinery that was between me and a very long fall. "I think I wanna learn how to fly this thing, a little."

Certainly. I'll turn on the flight-assist mode. It will correct any major mistakes you make and give you some hints. It isn't as capable as actual learning software, but it should assist.

A few images appeared over my vision, especially as I looked down. A superimposed image of the handles being twisted back and forth to tell me how to give the hovercycle fuel, and instructions on how to use the pedals to aim the cycle up and down. "Neat," I said. "We'll go slow, I think. Ah, can you point me toward our destination?"

Do you intend to arrive there the standard way, or did you intend to arrive in a more violent fashion?

"Let's go in through the front door," I said.

Understood. Mapping your trajectory now.

I blinked as a second overlay appeared before me, an opaque line that cut across the city, then down in between the maze of skyscrapers. "Simple enough," I said.

I did start off slow. Even the mom-vans below me were zipping by as I worked to angle the front of my hovercycle along the line I saw, then gave it a bit of gas. I overshot the first turn a little, but there was more than enough room to realign myself, and on the second I turned a little more aggressively, some of the little jets at the front of the cycle burping out little lines of flame that helped the bike turn. There were levers near the handles that controlled those, but for now the bike was controlling them automatically.

The line leading me on veered off and around one of those more artsy skyscrapers, the sort that didn't want to be just another large rectangle covered in neon ads, and instead turned into some modernist mishmash of vague shapes squished together and covered in neon ads.

I hugged the walls of the skyscrapers to slip around a row of hovercars, then leveled off next to an entrance in the bottom quarter of a building.

My bike dipped down, the rear wheel touching the pavement with a lurch just as I came up to an automatic tollbooth.

Do you want to hack into that booth?

"Eh, I guess? Wait, what would set off fewer alarms?" I asked. The parking garage was . . . a parking garage. A lot of lifts designed to hold cars on multiple floors, and tight roads that probably made it a bitch to find a place to stash someone's car.

Are you genuinely concerned about stealth?

"Well, it's my gimmick, isn't it?"

I thought your gimmick was more trying to be stealthy and failing, but I'm always eager to see you try new things.

I grumbled as I rolled my hovercycle closer to the tollbooth, then let the booth scan the bike. I was about to tell Myalis that I'd pay normally, to avoid setting off any anti-hack alarms, when the cost of the parking flashed up on screen. "Oh fuck no, we're not paying that," I said.

You're quick to change your mind.

"It's called common sense," I said as I squinted at the screen, then used my Cyberwarfare augs to break into the system and give myself a free pass. Then I deleted a zero from the price they were charging, because it was nonsense.

There were berths specifically for smaller vehicles, but I rolled right past those and parked my bike on the sidewalk next to the elevator banks. "Does this thing have a way to tell people not to fuck with it?" I asked.

Not in an inconspicuous way, no.

I shrugged. "Can you set it to drive in circles, then? Stay warmed up and close to the exit for when I have to go?"

I swung my leg over the hovercycle, then tugged my coat on straighter while the bike leaned back upright and took off on its own with just a slight whine.

The elevators opened as I approached, and I slid in next to an older lady whose eyes were glazed over while she looked into a pair of those old aug-glasses with the holographic screens that were all the rage for like, a month before I was born.

I switched off the exterior sound on my helmet. "Which floor are we heading to?" I asked.

I'll take care of that. The group you're looking for is called the Hitman Cooperative. They're ostensibly a nonprofit middleman organization that ties hired killers to potential contracts.

I nodded. Made sense. "So I bet their entire gimmick is that they pretend to be all discreet and the like?"

Essentially. We will need to see if they actually do as their advertising suggests.

The elevator stopped, and I walked out right into what was obviously a killbox. It wasn't as fancy as the killbox back at the gala. The explosives on the walls weren't hidden here, and the large turrets at the far end of the passage pointed all the way down the marble floor and right into the elevator.

"Uh," I said.

Perhaps a stealthy entrance would have been preferable after all.

I didn't get shot full of holes, so I stepped up and out of the elevator, the old lady behind me never even noticing that she was downrange of a lot of firepower. The door closed with a whisper.

I started across the corridor while eyeing the guns and cameras, then finally the desk behind that. There was a generic android behind the counter, plastic smile locked in place even as its eyes tracked my progress across the room.

Smooth jazz played in the background, only interrupted by the slight whine of the servos in the guns moving to follow me.

"Greetings, Samurai Stray Cat, and welcome to the Hitman Cooperative. How may we assist you?"

"Hey," I said. "I'm looking for, uh, information on a hit that was taken out?"

"You understand that we keep all information entirely confidential here? It's part of the Hitman Code of Honor!"

I raised an eyebrow. "You have a code of honor?"

"Of course. Do you wish for an e-pamphlet of the code?"

"No thanks," I said while waving the offer off. "Look, I really do need to find out who took out this one, specific hit. The gunman failed already, and I don't feel like causing trouble here."

"I understand your frustration," the android said with canned sincerity. "Do you wish to speak with a manager?"

I felt dirty. "I . . . guess?"

"One moment please. I will fetch the nearest Hitman Cooperative manager now. In the meantime, please take a seat. How do you like your coffee? Or perhaps you would prefer tea, or an energizing soda drink? All free— asterisk—as part of the Hitman Cooperative's Operation Killing the Bad Press."

"I think I'll just wait," I said.

CHAPTER SIXTY-THREE

A VERY NICE AND CIVIL DISCUSSION

The art of writing died in 2023, and it's a machine that killed it.

—GPT-9, 2023

It took ten long minutes for a manager to finally show up.

She was a middle-aged woman, with a swept-back haircut and a suit right off the rack from Corps-R-Us. She walked over and bowed her head, fake smile locked firmly in place. "Hello, Miss Stray Cat. I'm August, one of the on-site managers of the Hitman Cooperative. If I understood correctly, you're looking for some information?"

"Yeah," I said. "One of your employees shot someone, and I shot them in turn. No one died, because . . . well, mostly luck, I think. But I'm not too keen on relying on luck in the long term."

"I'm very sorry," August said with all the genuineness of a pair of brand-name sneakers bought from a guy in a trench coat. "I have reviewed the case in particular, and I assure you that the gunman was not an employee of the Hitman Cooperative."

"He wasn't?" I asked. "He certainly got paid by you."

"It is possible that he was a contractor."

"Possible, or he was?" I asked.

"Such information is—" she began.

I raised a hand, stalling her. "Look, August, I don't give a singular fuck about what you are or aren't allowed to disclose, all right? This is 2057, there's no such thing as private information. That means that what I want to know is something that you know."

"We have a reputation to uphold," she said. "I imagine that our contractors would be very upset to learn that we leaked information about a job to the first person who asks. You understand, I hope? Samurai also rely heavily on their reputation to get things done in a timely manner."

I crossed my arms. She was being an obstruction, which wasn't ideal, not when I needed what she knew.

Then again . . . how much effort was I willing to put into finding out?

"All right," I said. I nodded and started walking toward the door.

"Pardon?" August asked. Her high heels clicked after me. "Miss Stray Cat?"

"Yeah?" I asked over my shoulder.

"You're leaving?" she asked.

"What gave it away? The fact that I'm moving toward the exit?" I asked. Her jaw worked, and I saw her eyes twitch before I reached the elevators.

She jogged to keep up. "If . . . if there's anything the Hitman Cooperative can do to assist you, you only need to ask."

"I told you what you could do to assist me already," I said. This was weird, why wasn't she just letting me go?

Catherine, it seems as though they are purposely delaying the arrival of the elevator. Should I work past their interference?

I shook my head, just a tiny bit. Myalis would catch on. "Look, August, I came here for something, you can't give it to me. I'll figure shit out on my own."

"Of course, of course." She grinned, but judging by the way she was cringing a little, someone was giving her an earful. "We sincerely hope that you, ah, look favorably upon the Hitman Cooperative."

"I mean, you didn't give me what I wanted and made me waste my time after one of your employees—sorry, one of your contractors—shot a buddy of mine in the chest. I'm not gonna insult your little company to your face, but I sure as shit ain't going to compliment y'all either."

"The Hitman Cooperative is merely an organization that aims to provide a service; we aren't responsible, legally, for the actions of any subcontractor, only the actions of our employees."

"Subcons, employees. Same shit, different assholes."

August stared at me for a while before glancing away. "Perhaps the cooperative could assist you in a small way. As an apology for our . . . minor involvement in the incident that led you to coming here."

"Yeah?" I asked. I couldn't believe it was working.

She nodded, then gestured through the air. I received a file. A relatively small packet, encrypted.

August bowed slightly while stepping back. Her smile was back on, relieved now. "We hope you consider the Hitman Cooperative in the future. We're the deadly family you never had."

"Right, thanks," I said. The elevator arrived just then, and I stepped into it, my shoulders only loosening when the door shut. "What's in the packet, Myalis?"

Information, as you might suspect. In particular, the routing information for a payment that, once fees and the Hitman Cooperative's cut are taken into account, match the amount paid out to our gunman.

"Well, well," I said. "So, who paid him off?"

That's the interesting part. The person who paid used a third-party money laundering system. NayPal. It isn't an entirely secure method to make a transaction, though. I was able to dig deeper and track the transaction to a small nonprofit.

"A nonprofit?" I asked.

Yes. The Burringham Gala Planning Committee, LLC. Technically labeled as a nonprofit organization.

"What the fuck," I said. The elevator arrived at the floor with the parking garage, and I stepped out just as my hoverbike came around the corner and slowed to a stop before me. I was still trying to process what Myalis had figured out as I swung a leg over the seat and sat down.

Had Burringham hired someone to shoot him?

That had to be one of the most contrived and stupid suicide attempts I'd ever heard of. The city had a thousand skyscrapers to plunge off. Hell, a few of them were pretty popular jumping-off points for burnt-out suits.

That didn't make sense. So maybe he wasn't planning on dying?

I gave the hovercycle a bit of gas and eased my way out of the building, then upward. Once I reached the skyline I turned over and landed on a rooftop landing space next to some fancy rich-type's car.

"Do you think Burringham planned on me saving him?" I asked.

It is possible. Though it doesn't fit with the psychological profile that Longbow sent you regarding Jeff Burringham. He has used underhanded methods and trickery in the past, but never to aggrandize himself, and never while putting himself or others at risk. Usually it's as a tool to allow an opponent to trap themself.

"Yeah, this doesn't fit," I said.

Where are you heading to now?

I glanced down, then around me, at the wider city. "Well, I guess it wouldn't hurt to go pay Burringham a visit. Can you follow the money trail any deeper?"

One moment. Burringham is currently at a meet-and-greet in T-Man Square. As for the money trail, it isn't as useful as you might hope. Most of the credits deposited in the nonprofit's accounts were placed there from donations coming from various other organizations or corporate entities. Jeff Burringham is the largest contributor. The money there is controlled and spent by a number of people. The purchase leading to the hiring of a hit man was disguised as additional security expenses.

"Great, so the person we're looking for has a sick sense of irony." I noted the opaque line guiding me across the city, then gunned it to follow after it. "We don't have an exact idea of who could have made the payment?"

Not an exact idea, no. A list of suspects can be provided. Jeff Burringham himself isn't directly able to spend the money in the foundation, but it is possible that he, or another, tricked someone else into making the purchase.

"Who signed off on it?" I asked.

His secretary. She also signed off on fourteen other purchases within the same hour.

So someone could have slipped the order, or the payment for the order, in with the rest. We were dealing with someone who was actually clever, which was always a pain in the ass. I liked it when my enemies were brain-dead idiots.

"Think Burringham might be able to help us narrow it down?" I asked.

It's possible. There are other options for discovering the culprit, but they would take either time or a spending of other resources. Which raises the question: How much do you want to invest into all of this?

I frowned as I drove over a sky bridge, then blurred past a hovering police platform, the two cops within not even glancing up from their doughnuts.

"I don't know. Look, let's bother Burringham now, and then we'll see what we see. If we need to spend too much on this, then I'll poke Longbow about it, maybe he can figure it out. I can probably do other, more productive things with my afternoon."

Wonderful. You should also consider spending more time at home with your family. You need a little more rest still.

"I slept for like, ten hours," I said.

You spent that many hours on a bed. The things you did there did include sleep, but not for the entire duration.

I pouted.

CHAPTER SIXTY-FOUR

TRYING OUT THAT STEALTH STUFF

You can't just lie down and expect someone higher up the chain to notice.
You need to make noise. To make yourself heard. To participate in the political machine.
—M. Breaker, political activist during a street interview before the 2027 Minimum Wage Protest bombings

Burringham's meet-and-greet thing was held in a large city square set in the middle of one of those fatter, more squat skyscrapers that had bridges leading to all the other buildings around it. The square was partially open above, with a ring of glass panels over the center of the square.

An entire squad's worth of heavy-looking military trucks were hovering around the square, roof-mounted guns tracking any vehicle that came even a little too close.

It looked like Burringham wasn't cheaping out on his security. Couldn't blame him there.

I moved down below the building with the square, then found a parking garage a few floors over where I left my hovercycle before taking off.

I had to navigate my way up a few floors, then across a couple of bridges. I wasn't the only one heading that way. The majority of the foot traffic I encountered was heading the same way.

When I arrived at the square proper, I had to stop and take it in. There were small stores lining the edges, with ads plastered all over them, but for the most part the square acted like something of an open space. There were real trees in large planters with benches around them, and the ground was covered in large flagstones. It felt almost like we were outside instead of within the topmost floor of a stubby building, larger skyscrapers towering out above.

Some fuckery with holographics painted the sky on the windows above as blue and only a little cloudy, instead of the constant gray and drizzly they were in reality.

The square might have been meant as a peaceful place for upper-middles to walk around in and meet up. I could imagine some older folk doing tai chi or something here, but right then and there the place was packed.

The center of the square had a spot where a campaign bus was parked, and behind that was a light hovertank, barrel pointing high to remind people not to fuck around.

That was where Burringham was, in a little island of peace, surrounded by guards and hovering fence posts. A few armed dog-robots were sitting nearby too.

A line of people stretched out from where Burringham was all the way back to the entrance, snaking around little guiding signs all the way. Just normal-looking folk who passed through some security checkbox, then filed into the line.

At the end they shook Burringham's hand, maybe spoke a word or two to him, and then they were encouraged to move on by one of Burringham's guards. He smiled the entire time.

"Great," I muttered under my breath. If I got into line now, it might only take an hour for me to reach Burringham. The security around him looked pretty tight too. They might give me a pass, and if I poked at Burringham and asked him for help, he'd certainly let me get closer, but that would mean that I had to ask him for help, for permission basically, just to get close to him.

That left a bit of a sour taste in my mouth.

I flicked on my invisibility while shuffling between two others. A kid nearby gasped and started to look around for me, but as far as I could tell no one had really noticed that I'd gone invisible. That was kind of the point of invisibility, though.

Squeezing my way through the crowd, I reached one of the tree planters and jumped up onto the lip of it, then cut through a row of people on the other side of it. It didn't take long to get to the edge of the cordon protecting Burringham himself.

That part would be trickier to move past. There were actual hovering bars in the way, and robots scanning the area next to flesh-and-blood guards.

I circled around the area, then found a crack in the perimeter next to the tank. I guessed that no one wanted to try their luck next to a couple of tons of "fuck off" with a gun longer than most people were tall.

After that, it was just a question of walking around the busy official-sorts that Burringham had toiling behind him. I saw his trusty secretary nearby, on an office chair that looked entirely out of place in the square and with a laptop sitting crooked on her lap.

I moved past her, then over to Burringham's side. It took me a moment to fiddle with the controls on the speakers built into my helmet. I didn't want to talk loud enough to be overheard. Once I had everything set up the way I wanted, I waited.

Burringham was talking to a twentysomething mom of three, who apparently really wanted him to help with the cost of rent. She was teary-eyed when she explained that rent was increasing faster than her pay, and that she had to start making choices that she didn't like. Food or bills or a house where the kids didn't need to share bedrooms.

Burringham gave her some platitudes about trying his best, and then he foisted her off on some intern-looking guy who said he'd see if the increases in her rent were legal.

Not that them being illegal would help any, I figured.

Burringham took a deep breath when she left, his smile resetting from "happy to talk to you but also sad about your situation" to just plain "happy to meet the next schmuck."

"You're good at this," I said.

He jumped, eyes widening as he looked around—and right through me—for whoever had just spoken next to him.

"My specialties are big explosions and stealth," I said. "Admittedly I'm better at the big explosions."

"Stray Cat?" he asked. "Where are you?"

I reached out and grabbed him by the shoulder. "Right here," I said.

"Oh," he replied. He raised his other hand and made a small gesture to one of his goons. They were quick to step up and slow down the next person in the line. Then he touched his ear, the universal sign of someone on a call. "What, ah, can I help you with? You know, you didn't need to sneak all the way here."

"Your guards looked twitchy," I said.

"They'll be twitchier when they learn you snuck past them," he said. "Should I be investing in better guards?"

"I dunno. I'd like to think I'm pretty damned sneaky."

"I'll see what I can do about it," he said with the same tone and friendly smile he'd given to that woman just a minute ago. "Ah, I've sent a text to the guards, they'll stand down if you want to, ah, appear."

"I think I'll stay like this," I said. I didn't need to give him even more good press. "Look, I had some time on my hands, so I poked around at the Hitman Cooperative. One thing led to another, and we know who paid to have you shot. Or at least who greenlit the payment; they might have been tricked or just approved of a payment set up by someone else."

"Who are your suspects?" he asked. "I can have my own security look over them, if you want. It would narrow it down; so far we have nothing."

I nodded. "Myalis, you got that list?"

Sending now!

Burringham blinked as he received the list. His brows drew together, and then he started to turn around, toward his secretary. He stopped mid-turn. "Really?" he asked.

"Surprised?" I asked.

"Obviously," he snapped. "I didn't expect to have paid for my own assassination. Dammit, I invested a few million into that side company, of my own money. It wasn't meant to be used to *shoot* me."

"Well, it worked, as far as I can tell." I gestured to the crowd, then realized he couldn't see it. "You're looking pretty popular this afternoon."

"I'm on the news. We both are. It'll pass in a day, maybe two, but I wanted to capitalize on it while I could. Prove I'm in good health for the constituents."

"Right," I said. "Look, I don't know how much more time I can spend on this investigation thing."

"No, no, you've done a lot already. I have some good security, and you just gave them a great lead. I'll look into it some more. By the way, you'll want to see this." He gestured, and I received a text from his aug-line.

It had a compressed folder that I opened and eyed up. "What is it?" I asked. A few of the files there had familiar names. I saw my own, and Lucy's name too.

"That's from Child Protective Services. Someone's pressuring them to do something about your . . . ah, orphanage-like situation."

I closed my fist. "Oh, yeah?" I asked.

"I wouldn't worry overly much, it's something we can get rid of without too much trouble. Though, to be perfectly honest, you might want to cut out some of their arguments at the knees, if you can."

"Yeah, yeah, I'll see about it," I said. "On that note, I'm off. Good luck, Burringham. Don't get shot again."

"Ah, thank you, Stray Cat," he said.

By the time I found a spot to sneak out of the cordon from, a lot more guards were moving around, and some were tossing flour on the floor, of all things. Cute.

CHAPTER SIXTY-FIVE

RECKLESS

Once a commodity's price has reached the lowest it can possibly go without becoming unprofitable to sell, the focus of the market becomes less the price of the commodity than the methods around the sale of the commodity.

That means shipping cost and speed, packaging, and things like customer support and additional sale incentives.

—Memo to Amazon subsidiary retailers, 2028

I sat on my hoverbike, helmet in hand, and just . . . took a few minutes to breathe.

I was hovering a couple of kilometers above the city, sitting in the sky in a way that would have been a huge waste of kerosene if my bike had been even a little more normal than it was.

"Not too sure what the next step is," I admitted with a yawn.

Something about the thinness of the air was making me tired. Or maybe it was just shortness of breath, from all the smog in the air this high up.

Your itinerary is rather empty at the moment. Perhaps you might consider returning to the floor you purchased? The renovations should be under way as we speak.

"I could check on Rac too," I said. Poor girl; probably thought I'd run off. Though I bet she was still worshipping that machine. "Yeah, not a bad way to waste an afternoon. Let's go pick up Lucy first, though."

I gave you ninety-nine percent odds that you'd want to do that.

"You know, when people call out the odds they gave something, it's not usually so high," I said as I tugged on my helmet.

Most people aren't as certain of things as I am.

"Fair enough," I said. I leaned down, rooted around with my augs to find the controls that took the bike off its hovering mode, then glanced around until I found the glowing path leading all the way back to the hotel.

I gunned it, grinning as I tried to push the hoverbike to its limits and see just how fast the thing could really move. As it turned out, that was pretty damned fast.

"Oh shit, shit!" I said as I steered up and rolled over a line of traffic that I probably would have had more time to react to had I not been moving so fast.

Reckless as ever. Do you want to know the odds I give you of crashing?

"No, I don't think I do," I said. I took her advice and slowed down as I slid into the next curve.

The hotel wasn't all that far, so after a couple of minutes of cruising along at a reasonable and entirely safe speed, we swung around and into the parking level I had gotten used to using when entering the hotel.

I slid my bike close to the entrance, then swung off it while flagging down the nearest valet. "Can you park this thing somewhere close?" I asked.

"Certainly, ma'am," they said. From the smug look they shot back to the other valets, they'd just hit the equivalent of the bragging-rights jackpot.

I waved them off before heading into the lobby.

Almost as soon as I stepped inside, one of the workers behind the counters at the far end of the room went around and jogged over to me. "Miss Stray Cat," She said. She was a cute twentysomething, in a stylish burgundy uniform that hugged her in nice ways. "Forgive me, ma'am, we received an urgent-sent package for you, but it flagged our security."

"Oh?" I asked.

She nodded. "We only just received it. We were going to send a letter to your suite, but seeing as how you're here now, I thought it wise to inform you in person, ma'am." She smiled, all big and proud.

"Oh, well, thanks," I said. "I don't recall ordering anything. What's in the box? How big a gift are we talking here?"

"It's just a small package, ma'am," she said while making some gestures about a foot across. "Our in-house security scans flagged it as potentially dangerous material. Did you want to see it?"

"Sure," I said. "Where's it from?"

"The offices of Mr. Burringham. Sent express, via private courier."

A gift from Burringham?

I opened my augs and sent him a quick text. *Hey, Jeff, did you send me anything?*

I got a reply before the cute lobby worker and I had even reached the nearest side door. *Yes! Hope you enjoy it!*

Reassured, I let the lobby girl step up ahead of me and lead me through a couple of long corridors. They lacked the opulence that the rest of the hotel had, but they were clean and someone had still made an effort to decorate.

"So, what's your name?" I asked.

"I'm Eleanor, Miss Stray Cat," she said.

Using my full name. Or at least my title. She was being all professional. "You work here long?"

"Since I was sixteen. My parents both worked here too. It's becoming something of a generational thing."

"That's cool," I said.

"Here we are," she said with a gesture into a room. There was a label above that read "Security" and on entering I found a long room with packages on a slow moving conveyor at one end, all of them sliding through a large machine with enough radiation warnings on it to give a radiophobe nightmares. That was on the other side of a glass wall.

"That's the package, ma'am," Eleanor said. She gestured to a table on our end of the room. There was a plexiglass box on it, with an airtight hatch and a smaller conveyor leading into it. A way to separate the box from the others?

"Right," I said as I walked over and tugged the hatch up. "I bet it's something stupid. Guy who sent this is a politician."

Eleanor walked over to a wall and tapped it, revealing a screen inlaid into it. Fancy shit. "Ah, says here the box was flagged because . . . residues of something explosive."

What would Burringham send me that could explode? Fireworks? A gun?

Idly, I upped the shielding doohickey on my jacket and shifted in my armor. I probably didn't need to worry, though. "Well, let's see," I said.

I grabbed the box, then shook it a bit.

The box is sending a constant connection signal.

"Weird," I said. I tapped into it with my augs, and all I got was an ID check. I'd received shit from online retailers before that had something similar. Maybe this was the fancier version of that?

I sent in my credentials.

My hearing shut with a pop.

I tried to scream, but I couldn't expand my chest to pull in any air.

I blinked, but for a long, long time, I was blind.

No pain. No pain, but disorientation. I was on my back?

Catherine? It's hardly a good time to be lying on your back. Your vitals read as mostly positive, and your armor's integrity, while damaged, isn't compromised. Can you get to your feet, check yourself for injuries, and take stock?

I coughed, and the pressure around my lungs faded. It was my armor, tightening around me like a sort of vise. I took some strange pleasure in breathing easier, and more when my hearing returned with a pop.

An alarm was blaring, water was pouring down from above, and as the glass on my helmet faded, I could make out a room filled with a thick smoke that was quickly being shredded by an active fire-suppression system.

I half turned, then pushed myself up to my feet.

The table where the package had been sitting was a wreck, the entire thing blown apart, and the wall behind it was smeared in black soot.

A concussion explosive. Look at the walls, those little pinpricks of scarring.

There were little streaks all over, and a few little bits of metal stuck to the wall. "What's that?" I asked.

Shrapnel. The bomb was designed to kill an unarmored person.

But I was armored.

I blinked. "Eleanor?" I asked.

I found her behind me, pressed up against the wall, blood pooling around her. Her mouth was open, one eye wide, the other a gory mess.

"Oh, fuck," I said as I dropped to a knee next to her. "Myalis!"

Catherine, I can't detect a heartbeat. One moment, she has active augs . . . but they're not reading anything from her mind but faults.

"The fuck does that mean?" I asked. I tugged her to the side, laying her flat on the ground.

It means she's dead. I'm sorry, Catherine.

Just like that.

"Fuck."

I wasn't attached to her. She was a greeter or something, just another cog in the hotel's machine, but fuck, she was nice and polite. She'd been helpful, and now she was dead.

"Fuck!" I said, this time with more anger, more confusion in it.

The door burst open and a staff member took one step into the room, stared around with an open mouth, then ran off.

"Myalis, who the fuck sent that box?" I screamed. That thing was going to be sent to my rooms upstairs. It was going to be in the penthouse with the kittens, with Lucy. Hell, with me while I wasn't wearing any armor.

Some fuck had just tried to kill me and my family.

My hands shook.

CHAPTER SIXTY-SIX

RETURN TO FORM

The government ignoring the mental health issues of the average citizen is fine. Except for real nutjobs, it's hard to really tell if a person's depressed or broken inside or whatever.

Basically, as long as it's an invisible problem, it's not a problem that you can really run a platform on.

But the mental health of samurai?

A samurai who loses it? Who sees one too many people get gibbed by aliens? Well now, that's entirely too fucking scary to think about.

—CandidCast podcast interview with political psychologist
Hulo Wells, 2038

A pair of guards stopped me just outside the room, and for some reason, when they gently led me into another part of the floor where there was a sofa to sit on and a few chairs for the guards to occupy, I didn't protest or fight back.

"Miss Stray Cat?"

I leaned forward and clasped my hands together. It stopped them from trembling a little.

Catherine. You're entering a state of shock, mild though it may be. Give yourself some time to process the adrenaline in your system. While that is happening, let's go over the events that just transpired.

"Not the time, Myalis," I muttered.

It is precisely the time. Focus on the cause. A human brain may only have a few simple and animalistic responses to threats, but that doesn't mean that it is entirely useless at deconstructing a threat once it is past.

"Fine," I said.

"Miss Stray Cat?" the guard asked.

I raised my hand in a "one moment" gesture, and the guard backed off for the moment.

First, you entered the room because you received a package, one addressed directly to you, but which set off an alarm.

I nodded.

Second, you inspected the package. It asked for your identification. On giving it, the trap unraveled and an explosive device, likely a concussion-based device with a shell meant to create fragmentation. This caused you very mild harm in the form of a light concussive blow. It also killed the young woman assisting you at the time.

I closed my hands so hard my fingers hurt. "Yeah."

Good. You seem to understand the situation. Your current state is caused by a few factors. First, the surprise of an unexpected attack. Second, the light injury you received. Third, the death of the young woman assisting you.

The first and third causes are the ones I will address now. This location, the hotel, is one that you thought was safe. You lowered your guard. An understandable reaction, though one that has backfired in this case. This can be alleviated in the future by heightening your caution. The death of the young woman is unfortunate, and to some degree you are to blame.

I swallowed.

But the majority of that blame lies not on you, but on the person who attempted to assassinate you. Aim your anger there first.

"Okay," I said. It wasn't very loud. I didn't sound like myself.

I have observed your kittens and Lucy to ensure that they are well.

I jumped to my feet, and one of the guards stumbled back and almost fell off his chair at the sudden motion. "The kittens," I said.

Are safe. I have encouraged Lucy to move them away from the doors and windows and have heightened the level of alert on all the security measures within the suite. They are currently as safe as I can make them.

"Oh," I said. I felt my heart racing again, but it soon started to calm down, at least a little. "Okay, okay," I repeated, mostly to myself.

I've tracked down the most likely suspect, as well as their motive. I don't believe an attack on the kittens or Lucy would be something they'd plan on doing. Still, I would strongly advise that you go observe your found family for some time before taking any other actions.

"You want me to go see Lucy?" I asked.

Yes. A lot of your emotional stability relies on her. A large part of your self-identity revolves around the notion that you're the one who provides for the orphans you care for. Lucy, in turn, has based her self-identity on providing for your emotional and sexual needs while caring for the orphans' own need for a stable figure.

"Uh," I said. The shock was wearing off, probably. Now I was just feeling rather naked in front of Myalis's dissection of me. "What's all that mean?"

It means that you should go hug Lucy because I don't currently have the arms to do so.

I let out a dry chuckle, then switched my helmet speakers on. "All right, sorry about that, I'm going to head out."

"We had questions, miss," one of the guards said.

"I'll have Myalis send you the recording," I said.

Done.

"You'll be able to figure it out from there, I think. Meanwhile, I'm going to go check on me and mine. And . . . and if you two can send me Eleanor's . . . never mind. I'll look into it on my own. The fucker who did this: I'm going to find them."

I stomped out of the room and down a corridor. It was only when I was at the end that I realized I had no idea where I was going.

Myalis helped, highlighting the path to the nearest elevator with some handy floating arrows.

I got in, then rode it up to the penthouse floor, all the while trying to keep the shakes at bay. Myalis was right, it was just shock or some shit like that. Was it too soon for PTSD? Probably. I'd deal with it. I'd make the bitch who scared me deal with some traumatic stress too.

The door opened, and I walked out of there just a little bit faster than might have been necessary.

I arrived at the penthouse's door and opened it without knocking.

One of my mecha-cats was waiting for me on the other side, all weapons deployed and pointing at the doorway. I edged around it and moved into the kitchen and living room space. It was empty. Weirdly empty, even. Dirty dishes left behind, the TV playing one of those almost-porn cartoons, but on mute.

Plenty of signs of recent kitten occupation, but not a kitten in sight.

My ears twitched as I heard something shuffling deeper in. I jogged over to one of the first doors past the kitchen, one of the rooms that some of the kittens had taken over as their own. The twins, maybe?

I knocked, and someone moved within and opened the door.

Daniel stared at me. "Yo," he said.

I sighed. "Hey."

"Figured it was you. If it wasn't then there'd be a lot more shooting. Also, if it was someone that could get past the robo-cat out there, then we'd all be fucked anyway, might as well die first, right?" he asked.

"You're a moron, Daniel," I said.

He grinned, then looked over his shoulder. "Lucy, it's your mentally stunted wife."

The door opened wider a moment later, and Daniel almost tripped without it to hold him up. "Go watch over the kittens," Lucy said before she squeezed past him, then collided with my chest. "Cat."

"Lucy," I said.

I squeezed her close.

"You're . . . squishing me," she complained.

I hesitated, then broke the hug and took a step back. Getting out of the armor took several long seconds, but I was rewarded with another hug the moment I was out of it, this one much warmer and closer.

"Myalis filled me in," Lucy muttered into my neck.

"Yeah?"

"Yeah," she repeated.

"I was just worried about you guys," I said.

She poked me in the ribs. "And we were worried about you. But we're okay, and you're okay. Right? You're not hurt?"

I shook my head. "I'm fine," I said. "Armor took the blast no problem. It . . . kinda scared the crap out of me, but I'm fine otherwise."

Lucy nodded. "Good, good." She leaned back enough to meet my eyes, and for a long moment she just stared at me, inspecting me closely. "Do you want to talk about it?" she asked.

"Not really," I admitted. I was still wired up, still a little nervous. Twitchy, maybe.

Lucy grabbed me by the wrist, then tugged me along after her and toward the living room. "Come on, we should sit," she said.

"I can't stay for long," I said.

"You can stay for long enough that I can reassure myself that you're okay," Lucy said. There was no give there. If I just up and left I'd regret having four ears when Lucy whined all four of them off later.

"Fine," I said. I sat on the bigger couch, then sighed, sat up, and tossed some magazine out from where I'd sat.

Lucy promptly sat herself down on me. "There," she said. "No escape anymore."

"I could lift you off me," I said.

"And risk bruising my delicate skin with your brutish hands?" Lucy asked, faux-demurely.

I rolled my eyes, but the banter helped. I could feel some of the tension bleeding off my back. "Thanks, Lucy."

Lucy laughed and tipped sideways until I had no choice but to hug her. "I love you too," she said.

CHAPTER SIXTY-SEVEN

THINGS GET BETTER

One of the best fields for the able-bodied, regardless of nationality or gender, is security. The training is usually covered by the corporation, and the work pays quite handsomely. Only a fool would underpay the people in charge of keeping them alive and safe.

Men are usually preferred, but women and some younger men prefer female-presenting guards. It's very much an equal-opportunity job.

Also, sometimes you get to beat up reporters and hobos.

—*The Coach's Playbook*, a guide to becoming corporate security, 2032

I stormed through the lobby, a woman on a mission. It was hard not to notice the additional security they'd put up. More guards by the doors, more personnel behind the counters so that clients coming in were treated faster. They even brought out a few of those dog-drones with the spinal-mounted guns. Ugly, but it made the point.

"Ma'am?" one of the hotel employees asked as he jogged to catch up.

"Yeah?" I asked without slowing down.

"We've, ah, heightened security. We're working with some private investigators to track the origin of the package. The hotel apologizes for what happened. That box shouldn't have gotten past security."

"You didn't fuck up," I said. "I did. And now I'm going to go pay the bitch responsible a visit."

The employee's head bobbed up and down. "Thank you. Eleanor didn't deserve that."

"She didn't," I agreed. We stepped out into the parking tunnel, and I saw a pair of valets scurrying to push my hovercycle closer. "I'll be back in a few hours. Do me a favor and keep the security on alert until then?"

"Certainly, ma'am," he said.

I nodded and moved over to my bike, a leg swinging up and over before I fixed my jacket behind me. I leaned forward, turned on the bike with a twitch of my augs, then gave it gas.

Setting destination now. Just follow the lines. I'll keep an eye on the hotel while you're out. Their added security is simple, but it should assist to some degree.

"Going to be expensive for them," I said as I flew up and merged into a high-speed traffic lane filled with nicer corpo rides.

Possibly. But the hotel's PR staff is already disseminating information about the attack.

"They're spreading news about it?" I asked.

Oh yes. A Vanguard was unsuccessfully attacked in their hotel. An employee died, and now their security measures are increasing to such a degree that the entire establishment will be much harder to enter. They're playing up their part of the narrative. I think the idea is to create the impression that the hotel is a place where incredibly dramatic things happen and one where the management are quick to react to such threats.

I sniffed. It sounded stupid to me. But then . . . I could imagine Lucy gleefully telling me about how such-and-such a place had someone try to assassinate a samurai. It would get their name out there a lot more than usual and in channels they couldn't normally advertise in. Sickeningly clever.

I didn't have the energy in me to really give a shit.

The traffic ahead of me slowed down enough to start grating on my nerves, so I dipped under the cars ahead and shot past them in complete disregard to a whole heap of laws. It was a good thing I didn't have a license, or it would have been revoked on account of my driving already.

"Where's this leading to?" I asked.

A restaurant called the Yawning Eve. It's one of the highest-ranked eating places in New Montreal. Rather exclusive.

"Fancy as all hell, I'll bet," I growled.

I caught sight of the place as I curved around a few skyscrapers. A slim tower, with a large doughnut about three quarters of the way up, all glass walls with a few landing pads just below it. I'd probably seen the building a thousand times before in media pics and while taking buses across the city, but I'd never paid it any attention.

Diving down a little, I rode over to one of the cleared landing pads and slowed down. The bike's computer flicked on an auto-assist that helped me come to a smoother landing than I'd ever have been able to manage myself.

I climbed off the bike, then started walking toward the one entrance near the pad.

A valet ran over to me. "Greetings, and welcome to the Yawning Eve, do you have a reservation?"

"No," I said.

"Ah, in that case, do you wish to make one?" he asked.

We reached the doors, and I tried them once before realizing we were locked out. There was a keypad next to the door. It took my augs a split second to unlock them. "I'm going to go visit someone who's here," I said.

"You, ah, can't do that, ma'am," the boy said.

I paused, then stared at him. "Do you really think you can stop me? Save yourself . . . yourself, and run over to someone who can do more than hook himself onto my ankle and get dragged along, all right?"

"Uh," he said.

A car landed on the pad behind us, some sleek luxury thing. "Look, an actual client."

I stepped in while the valet hesitated. The entrance was a little tight, with a spiral staircase leading up to the floor above where the tables for patrons were all laid out with spectacular views of the city.

Stomping up the stairs, I was greeted by a butler-looking guy with a towel over one arm and about six security types. Most of them didn't match. Different armors and gear. I figured I was dealing with the security from a few different clients.

"May we help you, ma'am?" the butler-sort asked.

"Burringham," I growled. "Where is he?"

"We don't disclose who our guests are to—"

He paused as my shoulders slid open and my railguns installed themselves next to my head. The panels over my thighs opened as well, and a few lights in my armor started to glow a rather ominous red. "Burringham. Now."

The butler swallowed, then nodded. "Right this way?"

I followed him into the main part of the doughnut. The floor on the edge was made of rounded glass, though there was a rail around it to stop people from stepping out onto it. The view really was spectacular, even though everything was as gray as it always was over the city.

I found Burringham sitting across from a CEO-looking type. His secretary and some other assistant were standing not too far away, by an entrance into the tower proper.

There was, of course, more security. I recognized most of them as the guys Burringham had hired. They eyed me up and down but didn't seem entirely nervous.

Myalis tapped into their coms, and a quick glance at their texts almost had me smiling. Their boss seemed to think that if I was there for trouble, then they wouldn't see me coming.

"Stray Cat!" Burringham said. He gestured to the table where a few entrées were laid out. "I wasn't expecting you, but I'm sure we can find a chair for you. Maybe even a bigger table if you want to join us. They have these little breadsticks here, I swear they're addictive."

"No thanks," I said. "I'm here for something else."

"What's wrong?" Burringham asked.

"Should I . . ." his guest said.

Burringham shook his head. "It'll be fine, I'm sure. Stray Cat's a friend," he said with one of his winning smiles.

"Just had a few things I needed you to know," I said. "First, I figured out who sent that assassin after you."

"You did?" Burringham asked. "Great. Who is it? I'm sure we can make an example of them."

"Problem is," I continued. "They just tried to kill me too. Sent a bomb to my hotel. They actually did kill someone. Nice girl by the name of Eleanor. Hotel staff."

"Are you okay?" he asked. I could have sworn his question was genuine.

I waved the comment off. "I'm fine. Got to wonder though, why in the fuck is your secretary trying to blow me up?"

I'd been eyeing the secretary from the corner of my vision the entire time. She was tense, but not more than one might expect from having a samurai just show up. The accusation had her squirming, though. "Mister Burringham, I can assure you," she began.

"Shut up," I said over her. "Actually, no, don't shut up. Instead, why don't you tell me what in the fuck you were thinking?" I moved over to her while the other assistant scurried out of the path in a hurry.

"Linda?" Burringham asked.

"You're lying," the secretary said.

"It shouldn't be that hard to prove that you're not the one," I said. "But I've got this itchy feeling that tells me that it really is you. Which makes me want to know, really, why? What'd you get out of it?"

She swallowed, then glared at me. Her silence stretched for a long moment.

She has just sent a message to the security guards around you. I intercepted it. She asked them to apprehend you.

"Did you really just ask the guard here to arrest me?" I asked.

"You . . . you pose a threat to Mr. Burringham and his campaign."

"Linda, what are you on about?" Burringham asked.

I glanced at the guard in charge. He shook his head. "We're paid well, but not well enough to interfere with whatever this is," he said.

I nodded. "Hey, Burringham, could your CEO buddy over there do us a favor and arrest her? Just in case your own security is compromised. I got the feeling they're clean, but just in case."

"I . . ." Burringham turned to his guest, who nodded. "Certainly?"

I nodded in turn. "Cool, cool. Oh, and Linda? This is for Eleanor."

I got to say, that meaty feeling of my fist meeting Linda's cheek was incredibly cathartic.

CHAPTER SIXTY-EIGHT

THINGS GET WORSE

We've had a couple of hard years, we've survived them.

But things are about to get worse.

—Deus Ex, open letter to the Family, 2056

Burringham walked into the kitchen carrying two cans of soda. He extended one to me.

I looked at it for a moment, then took it to set it on the counter next to me.

The staff had cleared out, and when Burringham pulled a few strings, they let his guards use the fridge. A big metal box with only one exit that was uncomfortably cold. A great place to keep someone like Linda while they asked her a few pointed questions and some quickly hired infosec-types ran through everything her augs had picked up.

"We keep meeting in kitchens," Burringham said. "And it's never a pleasant sort of meeting."

"Twice isn't that often," I said.

"You say that, but it feels pretty frequent to me," he said with a smile.

I stared at him, and even if he couldn't see my face . . . his smile dropped.

"Sorry," he said. "It's . . . a habit to try to comfort the people I'm talking to. Get on their side, make them feel . . . like people, I guess. It ought to be common courtesy, but it's a skill I literally had to learn."

"Hmm" was all I could say to that.

Burringham popped the tab on his can, then took a long swallow. "Not supposed to be drinking this shit," he muttered before taking another. "You were right. About Linda."

"Myalis did most of the work," I said.

He shrugged. "Then it was right. Everything was covered up, but . . . Linda's not some expert hacker. She knows enough to get by, more than most even, but now that the people with the right skills are actively looking, it's all there. She hired some thug to shoot me."

"You could have died."

"She paid extra for him not to lethally shoot me, you know." He made an explodey gesture with his free hand. "He was supposed to shoot me with some specialized gun. Fancy, sure, but not as lethal as some other guns. He was paid a lot more to aim low. Guts, legs, my balls."

"That would have been interesting," I said.

Burringham chuckled. "The memes would have been . . . oh, awful. Burringham, a politician with no balls. They make themselves."

"Was it all for the press?" I asked.

"All for publicity," he agreed. "Linda . . . fuck me. I knew she'd go far, but not . . . not that."

I shook my head. "You knew she'd be willing to hire an assassin?" I asked.

"For someone else, maybe. Not for me. Not as part of some fucked-up publicity stunt. I swear, I've heard about this kind of thing in movies and soap media, not in active politics."

"She tried to kill me," I said.

"It didn't take," he replied.

I turned toward him. "Eleanor . . . don't know her family name. Cute girl. Real polite. Had small dreams, but seemed set on reaching them. She's dead now. Don't cover this shit up for publicity, Burringham, don't play games. Do the right thing."

"That'll make it harder to win any election."

I shoved the can he'd given me into his chest. He almost fell on his ass. "If you can't win while doing the right thing, then the entire system's fucked. At that point, you might as well get out the guillotines. And if that happens, you've got a real bougie look to you, Burringham."

He swallowed. "I understand. I'll do what I can. To make sure things are set right, and, and for Eleanor."

"Good," I said before walking out. I didn't even know what I was waiting for in there. I probably just didn't have anything better to do.

You have a guest coming to meet you.

"Oh?" I asked, not really interested.

Deus Ex is heading toward the hotel. She sent a low-priority message for you just before you started speaking with Burringham.

"That's weird," I said. Now my interest was piqued. Just a little. "I bet some shit's going down and she needs me to pick up a shovel. I swear, I don't get a break."

You are a Vanguard. Being at the front means that while you have many behind you, there's nothing ahead of you. It's all too easy to find yourself pulled in many directions at once.

"Fucking tell me about it," I said.

The restaurant was mostly cleared out as I made my way through it. The staff were sitting around the tables usually used by their clients, chefs and sous chefs and all the others just . . . lounging around, chitchatting or staring off into their augs.

I hoped they were getting paid for their sudden time off.

No one had touched my hoverbike, but the thing was now covered in a wet sheen. At some point the gray clouds had given up on holding back the rain, and a light shower came pouring down on the city.

All that meant was that more power was diverted to the neon signs so that their glow could pierce the gloom. There was no washing away the shittiness of the city. Not with something as mundane as an afternoon shower.

I got on my bike, set the GPS onboard to lead me back to the hotel, then took off. "Can you tell Deus Ex that I'll be there in ten," I said.

Message sent. She will be waiting for you in the bar two levels below your penthouse.

I didn't even know there was a bar at the hotel. Though really, it shouldn't have surprised me any.

I flew through densely packed traffic, avoiding cars and trucks and generally disregarding any traffic laws that I found inconvenient or that slowed me down. When I arrived at the hotel, someone ran up to take care of my bike. There was still a lot more security, but they let me in without comment.

And then it was up to the bar.

The place was nice. TV screens on the walls gave the illusion that we were far, far above the clouds. All the seats and tables were white, with golden trim that complemented the marble statues in little alcoves along the walls. There was definitely a theme going on. Greco-Roman, maybe? Angelic? Some weird mix of the two?

Deus Ex seemed to care as much as I did about it all. She was at the bar, sitting down with her elbows on the table and a fruity cocktail sitting before her.

"You old enough to drink?" I asked as I sat next to her. I pointed to her drink while glancing at the bartender. "One of whatever that is."

"It's virgin," Deus Ex said. "And you probably wouldn't like it. It's very sweet." She glanced up to me. "How are you doing?"

"Meh," I said honestly. "Long-ass day. Sorta-betrayals, explosions going off in my face, some . . . bullshit AI therapy sessions that shouldn't have worked but did, a little."

Deus Ex chuckled. "That sounds like a normal Tuesday to me," she said. She moved her drink closer, twisted the straw around, then took a long sip from it. "Oh, this is good," she said.

The bartender set an identical glass in front of me, nodded, then walked off.

I hesitated. I didn't want to take my helmet off. It was safe, it was—

"No one's going to blow your head off," Deus Ex said. "And if they do, I'll avenge you, or whatever."

"Wouldn't you be dead too?" I asked.

She shook her head. "This isn't my main body."

I turned toward her. She looked plenty real to me. A pipsqueak in form-fitting armor that looked real high-tech, glowy bits and all. "What's that mean?" I asked.

"It means that I'm at home right now, and that this body's remote controlled. You don't think I'd go out in the field wearing this little armor, right?"

"Shit," I said. "How many samurai are like that?"

"A few," Deus Ex said. "Most are who they seem. It's not a big deal. Really, it depends on the catalogs they've invested in. A lot of them have some way of keeping you alive. Those that don't invest in something like that tend to . . . not stay alive, I guess. Or they become really good at ensuring that all the threats around them are taken care of before they might get hurt."

"Scary," I said. I took off the helmet and breathed in for a moment as I set it next to the drink. I took a sip, then recoiled while a shiver ran down my spine. "Oh, shit, that is sweet," I said.

"I did tell you."

I shook my head to ward off the sensation. "Did you call me over just to prove that you like sweet things that much? Or was there, like, business?"

"It's business," Deus Ex said. "That's all everything is, really. Even the fun parts."

"Fine. What's this business, then? You going to help with my sewer problem?"

Deus Ex looked up to me, blank and confused for a moment before understanding flashed in her eyes. "Oh, that. No, I'm here for something more important."

"And what's that?"

"We're going to get another incursion soon. A lot of them, actually. And they're going to be the worse sort. We're going to need every samurai we can get working as hard as they can to weather this one."

"Another incursion? We had one days ago."

Deus Ex licked her lips. "Things are . . . complicated. I'll invite you and Gomorrah over to my place. We can go over things there, where it's more private. Suffice to say, there's going to be another."

"Aren't they supposed to be once every three months?" I asked.

"No, that's what people who don't understand statistics say. On average, in a year, yes, there will be about one every three months. But if you look at the actual dates, they tend to be grouped up. Three months is the average time between them, but only because there might be a long time between two sets of incursions."

"Right," I said. I could do that much figuring out in my head. "So, another fun romp, killing aliens and getting points and all that?"

"Something like that," Deus Ex said. "It's going to be a serious one. Not a deep incursion, but a wide one."

"I don't know the difference," I admitted.

"I'll show you, but not here. Clear your schedule for tomorrow afternoon." She grinned, and whatever seriousness she cultivated disappeared with that cocky smile. "You've never been to space, right?"

CHAPTER SIXTY-NINE

NICE

Limits? Why would anyone bother with those?
—Longbow, to the government of New New Mexico, 2054

I met Gomorrah on the roof of the hotel the next morning. She had her Fury parked right on the edge of the roof between two of those big vent things and what I suspected was a folded gun emplacement.

"Hey," I said.

"Hi," she replied as she looked me up and down. "You look strange," she said.

"Wow, thanks," I said. "What's that even mean?"

Gomorrah shrugged. "You're holding yourself differently than usual. Less cocky. You look less self-assured, I suppose."

"I'm wearing my armor, you can't actually tell how I look," I said. I gestured at her. "You've changed a little yourself. New gear?"

"All new, actually. It's a similar design to my last, but up-armored a little. Better environmental protections too. I have a catalog for that kind of thing."

"That's neat," I said. "I still have . . . honestly, a lot of points to spend. I should look into that."

"They don't help you." I glanced at her, no idea what she meant by that. "The points. If they're just sitting there, not doing anything, then they're not helping you."

"Oh," I said. "Yeah. I know. It's just hard to spend them, you know? What if I need something big soon?"

"What if you need it and you don't have it? Infinite options are nice, but a concrete item in hand is nicer. This is that whole bird-in-the-hand parable. I suppose there's no harm in saving the points up for a while, as long as there's a goal behind the saving."

I shifted my shoulders uncomfortably. "Fine, fine, I'll make a point to spend my points. Hah."

Gomorrah chuckled, then jumped backward onto an air duct. She started to swing her legs back and forth, a slow *thunk-thunk* beating against the bare metal duct. We both looked up to the gray skies, then back down. At least it wasn't raining yet.

"So, you and Franny get it on yet?" I asked.

"Cat," Gomorrah said. "Stop speculating about my love life."

"Oh? You have a love life to speculate on, then?" I asked.

She glanced my way, then back down. "No, no I don't."

"Ah, that's rough. Lucy's plotting some double-date kind of thing."

"Please don't get Lucy of all people involved," Gomorrah said.

"You don't like Lucy?" I asked. That . . . genuinely hurt. Gomorrah was probably my best friend, even if we'd only known each other for a couple of days. They'd been long, eventful days.

"Oh, I like her fine. Better than I like you, certainly. She doesn't explode things in close proximity to me. Or invite me to galas that end in shoot-outs." I laughed, and Gomorrah chuckled. "No, I don't want you to tell Lucy because she is entirely too convincing."

"Oh!" I stood a bit straighter. "That means that with the right sort of convincing, we could get somewhere," I said.

Gomorrah sighed and leaned back. "You're, as the old nuns would say, a bit of a bitch."

I snorted as I walked over, then sat down with my back against the duct she was using. "A bit, yeah," I admitted. "Sometimes I try not to be, but then life happens, you know? Still, I'm a bitch with some great friends, so I can't be doing everything wrong."

"Oh, Christ," Gomorrah gasped. "We're friends, aren't we? Where did I go wrong?"

"Oh, ha-ha," I intoned.

We both twitched as a high-pitched keening came from above. Something fast was dropping through the clouds, a gray streak shooting right toward us. That was either our ride, or someone had decided to take us out cruise-missile style.

The vehicle slowed down and came to a hover a few meters above before it dropped down at a more reasonable pace. It was a big sucker, maybe fifty meters long, with a sloped front and two long, curved nacelles on its side. It reminded me distinctly of the two big guns that Deus Ex tended to have hovering next to her.

The ship came to a gentle stop even with the edge of the roof, and then with a hiss of releasing pressure, a door opened up on its side and slid back into the armor of the hull. The entrance was a good long step past the edge of the building, and no one seemed inclined to lower a gangplank for us.

"Welp," I said as I climbed to my feet. "That's our ride, I'll bet."

"I would hope so," Gomorrah said. "I don't think I've ever seen anything that advanced. God, the number of points that thing must cost. All of my scans are just bouncing off it."

"Nice," I said. I walked over to the edge closest to the door, then glanced down. There was a whole lot of nothing below before the pavement started. There was nothing for it, though, so I took a step back, then jumped up and into the ship.

Gomorrah followed after me, bumping into my back in what was clearly a tiny airlock of sorts.

The door slid shut, and then another opened, and we moved out into a long corridor. The back had a lounge area, with sofas all around a little table and a door at the rear that led . . . somewhere. The front had direct access into what looked like a very complicated cockpit, one that was entirely uncrewed.

"Nice," I said again.

My phone app went off, and I blinked to reply. "You're onboard?" Deus Ex's voice asked. "Good. Sit down, and hang on. *Three Vs* is fast."

"*Three Vs?*" I asked.

"*Veni Vidi Vici.* It's the name of the ship," she said. "Come on, you're burning power."

Gomorrah and I moved over to the couches, which immediately shifted to accommodate our forms better. I kind of wished that I weren't wearing so much armor so that I could actually feel the couch as it conformed to my body. I bet that it was damned comfortable.

The ship shifted to the side, rose, then tilted back. And then with a lurch so hard it felt like someone had just shot a pillow against my entire body from a cannon, the ship took off. The screens on the sides of the room showed first New Montreal, then the gray clouds above, and in short order, a thinning atmosphere as we rose and rose. The constant pressure had to mean constant acceleration, which was impressive all on its own.

"The ship will auto-dock in two minutes. Just . . . ignore the mess, I haven't cleaned up in a day or two," Deus Ex said.

I wanted to chuckle, but I was busy being crushed into the padded seat.

Then the acceleration stopped, and I felt myself growing nice and floaty.

We were in space. I saw the gentle curvature of the planet next to us, and below I could see the line where day became night, crawling across the surface.

"Whoa," I said.

"Yeah," Gomorrah agreed.

We only stared for what felt like a couple of seconds before gravity reasserted itself. It was wrong, though.

I stood up, and it felt as if I was sticking to the ground. The more I raised a limb, the stronger the pull, like playing with two strange magnets close to each other. "Weird," I said.

Artificial gravity. The ship is from a Class III catalog; it comes standard with a basic artificial gravity system. It's nothing too impressive.

"Uh-huh," I said.

We coasted along for a little bit, and then the ship started to maneuver. If it hadn't been for the sight of Earth moving on the screens, I might not have noticed.

The ship slid forward, then stopped with just the smallest of lurches. "Welcome to Delenda Est," Deus's voice came over hidden coms. "My home away from all the bullshit below."

The door of the ship hissed open, and Gomorrah and I glanced at each other before heading for the airlock. That had all been . . . so easy. I had taken train rides that were more complicated than that one hop in a shuttle.

We squeezed into the airlock, waited for it to cycle, then stepped into another airlock that did the same, though this one had a faint mist filling it. "Just disinfectant," Deus Ex said.

The door opened, and we found ourselves in a corridor, long and painted a matte black and gray, with a few recessed lights along the edges of the ceilings and floors. Deus Ex was standing in the middle of it, unarmored except for a jumpsuit.

"Hey," I said.

"Hey," she replied. "Come on, this way."

"Did we really have to come all the way here for a talk?" I asked. "It seems like a bit much."

"It's a talk about important, secretive things. Trust me, I'd really rather not have you in my home," Deus Ex said. We took a bend in the corridor, past a bulkhead. The room past that had a wall filled with planters and hanging vines, and across from it a long window that overlooked the planet below, and part of the station. It was far bigger than I imagined, a sort of tube with growths sticking out of it. The *Veni Vidi Vici* was anchored onto the side, only about a third as long as the rest of the station.

"Do you live up here alone?" I asked.

"Not quite," Deus Ex said.

She opened another door with a gesture, and we stepped into a wide, circular room. There was another floor above, with rails all around it, and a bridge spanning the gap. In the center was a large bank of screens and computer-looking things that ran from the floor to the ceiling above.

There were also about four more Deus Exes in the room.

"Yo!" one of them said. She was just a pinch different than . . . herself. A bit chubbier around the cheeks, and a good two inches shorter. She was also wearing flannel PJs, unlike all the others in jumpsuits. "Yeah, I'm the meat-me," she said. "Be amazed on your own time, Stray Cat. We have business to do."

Deus Ex, presumably the real one at that, led Gomorrah and me to a long sofa that wrapped around an awkward corner of the room.

"I'll get refreshments," one of the Deus Ex . . . clones said. Were they clones? They certainly looked the part.

"Sit, sit! I have a lot of stuff to explain to you two, but I also have better things to do," Deus Ex, the one in the flannel PJs, said. She spun around and fell back onto the couch, where she slumped there like someone who had never had back problems before.

"Right," I said as I took a seat at the end facing her. Gomorrah sat next to me, legs together and rather demure. "So, you going to explain why there's a bunch of you going around?"

"They're meat puppets," Deus Ex said. "It's complicated, but basically they're cloned bodies with part of a brain, but all the bits that make a person a person are just never grown. Instead there's a computer that's linked to one in my head. The clones only think thoughts that I'm thinking, basically."

"That's really fucked," I said.

"It means I can be in many places at the same time, and I can do actions that might result in my demise without worrying about losing my actual body."

"What if one of them wakes up?" Gomorrah asked. "Or develops a personality?"

"They're vat-grown without that part of the brain. It's empty. So they can't have anything like that," Deus Ex said.

"But they are human, right?" Gomorrah asked.

The girl shrugged. "As human as anyone else, yeah."

"Then what about their souls, their personhood?" Gomorrah asked.

"I can't be bothered to care about something that doesn't exist," Deus Ex said. "But hey, if you bring me a jar-full of soul, or a cup of spirit, maybe I'll change my tune. If the clones did develop a personality, which they can't do because they don't have the parts of the brain where that kind of thing is processed, then that would be interesting. I always wanted a little sister."

"Really fucked," I muttered.

"Give yourself a year or two," she said. "Or visit some other Vanguard. You'll find that this is pretty tame. But all that's besides the point."

A hologram appeared, floating between us. At least, I figured it was a hologram from the way it appeared and just floated there. It didn't have any of that fuzziness that I associated with advertising holograms, and it was fully solid-looking. A brownish-red ball, part of it obscured in shadows. The surface was pitted, and there seemed to be something like clouds hovering over it.

"Mars," Gomorrah said.

"Is it the color that gave it away?" Deus Ex asked. "Yeah, that's Mars. Real-time too. We have a lot of satellites around the planet right now."

"Why?" I asked.

"Because we were careless and stupid. There was this lull in the number of incursions about five and a half years ago. Maybe a bit more than that. Turns out there was an incursion in that time, a stealthier one. But it wasn't aiming for Earth."

"There are Antithesis on Mars?" I asked.

"And they had a few years to settle in. Good news is, Mars isn't exactly a jungle. The aliens had to make their own biomass from scratch. Bad news is, the Antithesis are good at doing just that."

"How do you make biomass from scratch?" I asked.

Deus Ex gave me a look. "You need an education. Basically, on Earth, little creatures eat dirt and rocks and whatever, then bigger creatures eat them, then bigger ones eat those, and so on. Plants can pull nutrition out of the ground from base elements too. It's all part of the very bottom of the food chain."

"And the Antithesis replicated that?" Gomorrah asked.

"With better efficiency than any creature on Earth could manage. Mars has changed in these last two or so years. At this rate, given fifty or sixty years, it'll have its own proper atmosphere and will be somewhat livable," Deus Ex said. "If that were all the Antithesis were doing, we might even consider leaving them be for a little bit before wiping them out."

"But that's not all they're doing," I said.

"Of course not. We've been preparing an all-out offensive against the planet for nearly a year now. We have forward bases on the ground, the beginnings of a space elevator, orbital facilities, the works. But the Antithesis on Mars are on a whole other level. You won't see anything below twenty running on the surface. Higher numbers are frequent. And about three months ago, they launched an assault on Earth. That was when the planet was a hundred and twenty million kilometers away. It'll be hitting Earth . . . tomorrow?"

"Fuck."

"You didn't try to intercept?" Gomorrah asked.

"Oh, we did, and we probably knocked out ninety-nine percent of what they launched. It's that last percent that we're worried about. That, and there's another problem," Deus Ex said.

"Oh, because that's not enough?"

The girl chuckled in a way that sounded far too cynical for someone so young. "If you think that the universe has some sort of sense of fairness, then you haven't been around long enough."

"You're like, three years younger than me, minimum," I said.

She shrugged. "Experience counts for more than age when it comes to being a samurai. Anyway, if you're done insulting me in my own space station, then there's the bad news. We're wildly understaffed. Nearly every top-tier samurai's been leaving for Mars. The fighting there is ramping up in intensity. Some have begun to explore around Venus, we think there might be an incursion there too, but no one can find anything. And that leaves Earth underprotected."

"So you need Gomorrah and me to pick up the slack?" I asked.

"Not just that," Deus Ex said. "That incursion I sent you after: the offshoot."

It took me a moment to recall the incursion in Black Bear. "Yeah."

"The more we search, the more miniature hives we're finding. They're all over the world, and for the most part they're nearly inactive."

"Inactive how?" Gomorrah asked.

"Hibernating, subjugating existing natural systems to feed themselves. We found one where every tree in a forest was linked together by a second-ary root system. We wouldn't have noticed it if it hadn't been for a forest fire in the region that didn't affect those trees alone."

"The Antithesis are staying hidden?" I asked.

"For now," Deus Ex said. "We have some theories. The Mars-Earth incursion had a lot of biological pods designed to release pheromones into the air. Marker pheromones. Nonlethal, plain biological stuff that wouldn't hurt anyone unless they sniffed the stuff straight from the source, and even then it wouldn't be lethal. But some samurai have a theory. That it's meant to spread in the atmosphere, then tell all of those hidden hives to activate at a set time."

"Across the entire planet?" Gomorrah asked.

Deus Ex nodded. "Pretty much. Earth's first global incursion. We're pre-paring to activate everyone everywhere. And that means you two as well."

"Why isn't this on the news?" I asked.

"Because people are stupid but predictable, until you make them panic, and then they become stupid *and* unpredictable, and we don't need that,"

Deus Ex said. "The various PMCs and armies and governments have all been informed. You're probably some of the last ones to learn on the long list of people that need to know."

"How long do we have?" I asked.

Deus Ex blinked, and the floating Mars between us was replaced by a countdown timer. It read thirty-two hours, a few minutes and change. "That long," she said. "I really hope you're up for it, because it's going to be a tough one."

ABOUT THE AUTHOR

RavensDagger is a Canadian writer who wants to make people smile. The best way to do that, he has found, is by pecking away at the keyboard and hoping for the best.

Podium
DISCOVER
STORIES UNBOUND
PodiumAudio.com